MENOKA HAS HANGED HERSELF

SHARMISTHA GOOPTU

MENOKA HAS HANGED HERSELF

SIMON &
SCHUSTER

London · New York · Sydney · Toronto · New Delhi

A CBS COMPANY

First published in India by Simon & Schuster India, 2019
A CBS company

1 3 5 7 9 10 8 6 4 2

Simon & Schuster India
818, Indraprakash Building,
21, Barakhamba Road,
New Delhi 110001

www.simonandschuster.co.in

PB ISBN: 978-93-86797-66-7
eBook ISBN: 978-93-86797-67-4

Typeset in India by SÜRYA, New Delhi

Printed and bound in India by Replika Press Pvt. Ltd.

FSC www.fsc.org MIX Paper from responsible sources FSC® C016779

For
Aisha Gooptu Majumdar…my Rajbala

And

Rochona Majumdar
who fought off cancer and made our everyday battles seem so very small

ACKNOWLEDGEMENTS

This book has been a long time in the making. I always knew how the story would end, but it fleshed out slowly, sometimes in moments of inspiration, at other times uneasily. And a lot changed around me in those years. Aisha arrived in 2014, and motherhood went on to give me an entirely new and different perspective on everything. In this time, I also found new people, and tried to understand them. Their simplicity and their greyness became infused with my characters.

I must thank my commissioning editor Dharini Bhaskar, who patiently read and reread earlier drafts. My editor Himanjali Shankar has been supportive and appreciative, and my thanks are to her and Sayantan Ghosh for their editorial work on the book. Many moons ago, Rochona Majumdar had read the earliest drafts of the first chapters and had egged me on. My friends, Madhuja Mukherjee and Avantika Gupta sounded out some ideas, and gave useful pointers. Annesha Ghosh and Umakanta Roy were able and enthusiastic research associates.

But more than anyone, it is my husband, Boria Majumdar, who, as always, has driven me to find the best in myself, never asking questions of me, but always being there for whenever I need him. My overwhelming gratitude is to him, and my mother-in-law Roopa Majumdar, for keeping their patience with me and holding my hands through the trials and joys of little Aisha's growing up. Sulekha Gooptu, my mother, may well have held her own in the cruel world of bioscope pictures, with her own undying spirit to always fight the odds. This book also remembers Menoka Devi (though it in no way draws on her life), lead actress of the 1930s, who died in penury in her old age. There are many like her, who are unknown and unsung, and who had their moments of glory, in what was, ironically, the disreputable profession of the bioscope. I also remember here Jamuna Devi, who became famous overnight as Parvati of *Devdas* (1935), and whom I had interviewed shortly before her death, along with Bharati Devi, who had a long career as an actress. Both ladies had provided me with rare insights into their world of the pictures.

And finally, Aisha, whose feistiness is what makes the Rajbala of this book. Being a mother made me want, more than ever, to tell this story.

PART 1

Ramola

I

'What a perfectly horrible start to the year...' thought Ramola as she looked up at the clock one more time. Its hands were perfectly poised, one covering the other.

It was five minutes past one in the morning, the first day of 1937. Ramola Devi, star of Indian films, sat at the Victorian desk in her tastefully furnished bedroom, staring out of the window at a deserted Elgin Road. The lamp at her bedside illuminated her fair complexion and delicate features, her silky tresses hanging around her face, reaching almost to her slender waist. Without any make-up she looked almost unreal, her slight frame resting on the velvet cushion of a mahogany chair. Her window overlooked a street lamp and she watched it flicker slowly, as she caught snatches of a telephone conversation in the next room.

'Bad lot, Sir, these ones, but we have to make do with them, that's how the business is...very true, Sir, gives us a bad name, though we do try our best to better their lot, these girls...educate them...I'm sure you will understand...quite, quite...'

Then a minute or two of silence, the person at the other end was having his say.

Then once again, the voice in the next room broke in, 'He should never have opened the gate at that hour, I was very angry myself. We have imported machinery, cameras, all very expensive...but possibly because he knows the studio girls...[laughing], he might have thought he stood a chance with her, if he let her in. You know these classes Sir...though it should never have happened...and I can assure you, we will not deal with it lightly...'

Then the other person spoke briefly before the voice at this end was heard again, this time a markedly relieved tone, 'Absolutely, Sir...this is much appreciated...we have good relations with all the papers...that should be no worry at all...'

The clock in the next room had fallen behind again. It struck one, and Ramola lost Shankar's words in the loud chime.

'Tea, then, any day that suits you, Ramola and I would be delighted to see you again...'

The conversation had ended, and Ramola heard the receiver touch down on the cradle with its familiar tinkle-clang. But almost at once the instrument whirred back to life as more numbers were dialled in.

She had told her maid to make a cup of her favourite Darjeeling tea and as she waited, nursing the hot cup in her cold hands, she shivered a little bit in the morning chill. Her husband Shankar Chattopadhyay, head of Bharat Talkies, was in the next room, making these untimely calls, the last one to the city's police chief, whom he happened to know well, and who had been located at his favourite haunt at the Bengal Club. Luckily for Shankar, if at all one could say that under the circumstances, it was the early hour of New Year's Day, and several among the city's notables were still up and about, ringing in the New Year, and he hadn't needed to rouse people from their beds.

That moment, as Ramola was finishing her tea, he was trying to place a call to the police *thana*. And Anil, his deputy would be on his way there by now. Anil was good in any predicament. He had a way of talking things through with people. He would know how to handle the police. Subol, the accountant at Bharat Talkies who lived inside the premises, had telephoned from Shankar's office at the studio, about an hour and quarter minutes back. Menoka had hanged herself in the bathroom of the women's dressing room, wearing one of the costumes from her new picture. The very thought of it made Ramola feel sick in the stomach. She couldn't, simply couldn't for all her life, fathom the kind of despair that made people take their own lives, leaving behind everything that they had lived for.

'I couldn't do it, if even I wanted to die,' she mused. 'Maybe...it is a thing with these classes, not able to think through a difficulty...excessive in everything, uncouth... drama*baazi*, dramatics in death even...'

She couldn't but think harshly of Menoka's breed, though of course she was horrified at the girl's fate.

Menoka was Ambarish Dev Burma's newest find, and had moved very fast from being chorus girl in one of the theatre companies to one of Bharat Talkies' best new faces. She was a fast learner, and had delighted in being in front of the camera. Menoka had quickly picked up the ways of the studio *para*, the studio environs of

Tollygunge in Calcutta, and even some social graces in the time that she had been at Bharat Talkies. Under Ambarish Dev Burma's direction, she had appeared in two of last year's hits, and had become rather a favourite of the variety papers. Though, of course, Ramola herself had never acknowledged Menoka in any way. Menoka, not too long ago, had inhabited a house of disrepute in Bowbazar, a *beshyabari*, and all respectable ladies kept their distance from such girls even if they had made a name for themselves.

Even that night, Ramola, in her mind, rehearsed what would be her declared indifference to the whole thing. 'So many of these unfortunate women come to us for a better life,' she would say if asked about Menoka. 'We do try our best to uplift them from their fallen lives, but alas, their past often returns to haunt them...' It was a line that one mouthed, keeping up the façade...one that was so carefully crafted and maintained in this 'line' of theirs. But really, how inopportune that this should happen on the first day of the New Year, a time she always looked forward to, when everything seemed so nice somehow. What a very horrible start to the new year.

It had been the night of 31st December, and the city's elite were raising their toasts in the hotels and clubs around Park Street and Chowringhee. Ramola and Shankar had been invited to the year-ending ball at the Grand Hotel, a magnificent affair attended by England-returned Bengalis and nouveau riche Marwaris. Her Excellency, the Lieutenant Governor's wife, the evening's distinguished patron, had taken a great liking to Ramola and they had spoken about making pictures for public instruction. Ramola had worn a shimmering chiffon sari with a short-sleeved blouse, and diamond chandelier earrings and slender diamond bracelets. By far she had been the most beautiful woman in the ballroom, and she had acknowledged it with quiet grace.

Menoka had been out that night, with whom no one knew. She had arrived at the studio sometime after half past ten, woken the night guard and forced him to open the gates. She had been drinking, the guard had said, but seemed in her senses. She had made her way towards the women's dressing room, where costumes were laid out for the rehearsals. A half hour later the guard had found her in the bathroom, hanging by the sari she had worn that evening. Ramola and Shankar had just gotten home from the ball, when the telephone rang, and Shankar had rushed into action so the matter did not get into the papers and no names from the studio were dragged in.

It was a scandal, and the other studios would try to make some gossip out of it.

"Young Actress Kills Herself: Does Bharat Talkies Have an Answer?"

or

"Is Our Cinema Industry a Safe Place for Women? Was it Suicide or Murder at Bharat Talkies?"

Ramola could well picture the headlines in the grubby little mouthpieces that some of the studios brought out in the name of house magazines. Not that it would matter very much, by and by. All the studios used girls like Menoka and they all had things to hush up every now and then. Still, respectability was the motto these days, what with the big studios claiming they made 'serious' films, or that 'so and so is from an educated and cultured family and is trained in the classical arts' when they launched some *kothawali* or other. High class ladies like herself were still a rarity in the studio precincts, and girls like Menoka played those '*devi*s' on the screen that they never could be in real life.

Ramola quite easily predicted the mood at the studio when they opened for work again the day after. '*Ki re, ghatona shunechish?* Did you hear what happened?' Not just the hushed whispers and rabid rumours, but also the smirks and gratification. A *beshya* had died the death that befitted her kind—though Menoka's every endeavour had been to pull away from that past—and any iota of pity was quite evidently unfitting. Menoka had risen to stardom too fast and too soon, and there were many who would have liked to see her dragged in the dust. Not least, some of the other studio girls, who vied with each other to bestow their favours on the likes of Ambarish Dev Burma. Ambarish was Bharat Talkies' top director, who made and unmade the fortunes of the likes of Menoka. By all counts, he was a genius, and he had crafted some of the silver screen's most unforgettable female portrayals.

Ambarish…or 'Saheb'…as everyone in the studio para called him…had a penchant for those women that survived on the margins of society. He almost hunted for them. He picked them up from the city's darkest *galli*s, or like Menoka from among the studio's chorus girls, loved them, and turned them into screen goddesses. Then, without reason he would let go of them, and Ramola believed that he sometimes would go that extra way to drive them to the brink of their senses.

For him, it was almost a game, one that he had to keep on playing, though what she never could fathom was, why did each of these girls fall prey to it? All of them. Again and again. Why did they not see through him? Why in god's name did they not step back, before it got too late? Go away. After all, there were all the other studios. Surely they had known that something was not right? Surely. And still...they had kept on. Was it because of the fame and fortune he promised them? Or did they really think it was love? That he loved them, like he had loved none before? It made her angry again, just thinking of it, stupid wretches, all of them. Before Menoka there was Tara, who had taken to the bottle and one day had just disappeared, where she went nobody knew. And Radha, who begged on the streets before they had found her dead. Ambarish had taken up with Radha's younger sister, and it was whispered that he had kept them both together in the same house, purposefully setting one girl against the other. They were all so very young and he had made them stars of their day, then seen to it that they never worked with another director. Menoka was his muse, and as if from the start of it her fate was sealed.

Two months ago, Ambarish had announced his new picture, with Menoka as the heroine. Her role, that of a dancing-girl who would return the hero's love with deceit and unfaithfulness. It was said that Menoka had resisted this particular portrayal. Ambarish had almost fashioned this character after the real Menoka, even naming her the same. It was one which he had promised would bring her untold fame. Yet, Menoka had not wanted it. It was too close to life for her, a life which she thought she had left behind. Almost like somebody had pulled her clothes off her, made her naked, Ramola reflected.

Menoka had wanted to play the other woman—the suffering and tormented wife, who still got her man in the end. Hadn't she played Sita and Rukmini—those women that people worshipped? And hadn't the public loved her in those pictures? 'But that's the second lead, my dear,' Ambarish had laughed at her. He had insisted that nobody could play the fallen woman the way that she could. They had started work two weeks before Christmas, and in the ten days that this picture had been on the floors, Ramola and Shankar had heard reports of Menoka's misbehaviour on the sets, her frequent arguments with Ambarish, and his relentless pressuring of her to get into the skin of the character. Still, as producer, it had been Shankar's rule to not interfere with the director.

'Remember, Ambarish is good at what he does and how he goes about making his picture is his matter entirely...it's how things work in this place...' he had said to Ramola. What the studio wanted was a good picture, and a hit picture, and there Ambarish Dev Burma had a reputation that few could match. On some matters, Shankar did not brook an argument, and the studio's running was one of those things.

Ramola herself was uncertain in her feelings about Ambarish. She admired him for the work that he did, but often, she had felt discomforted in his presence. Like he was laughing knowingly, 'like a hyena', she screwed up her nose at the thought. Almost like he was waiting, for when she no longer could work her magic on the screen. Of course, he had always seemed to hold her in high esteem, forever displaying the courtesies typical of the high society to which they both belonged. Ambarish Dev Burma was the scion of one of Bengal's oldest landed families, had been to school in England, and was as much at home at a high class tea party as he was in his nights spent at a Kalighat brothel.

Though publicly he had always shown the greatest admiration for Ramola, he had never asked for her to work in any of the pictures that he had made at Bharat Talkies. Ambarish was driven by women in an almost perverse way, and only those that he could push to the ends of hope and despair interested him. Sex itself was only a small part of it. Rather, it was the sense of power that came from being able to lift someone out of the depths of their darkness, to give them a name, and then to show them that in fact they were nothing, or rather no different from what they had been.

'He's going to do it again, what with no dearth of these wretched girls,' Ramola thought wearily. But it really was no good telling Shankar that. As producer and proprietor of Bharat Talkies, Shankar had a very matter-of-fact view of things. Even when he had worked as director, he seemed to have been perfectly oblivious to the bickering that brew behind the making of every picture. Shankar Chattopadhyay was a powerful figure, and few in the business of bioscope pictures, in Calcutta, Lahore or Bombay, could hold their own against him. He had created one of the country's top studios, Bharat

Talkies, and together Shankar and Ramola made the industry's first couple.

It was Shankar who had brought Ambarish to Bharat Talkies in its very first year, and given him every freedom to make the kind of pictures that he wanted. Ambarish, on his part, had given the studio some of its biggest hits. When Ambarish had gotten a new heroine, Shankar had asked no questions. If he had shunted her out in the next picture, there too he had gotten his way. With Menoka too, Shankar had let him have his way, and so far as this whole business went he would do all he could to keep Ambarish's name out of it. Ramola knew that.

'How hard it is to tell right from wrong?', she thought. Bharat Talkies was what it was because of Shankar's untiring efforts, his days and nights spent in building something from nothing. He had given leeway to Ambarish and some others because what mattered was only the name of Bharat Talkies, and they in turn had helped him to create that name. Ambarish was wooed by the other studios, but he had not looked beyond Bharat Talkies. Was it his loyalty to Shankar, or was it because he knew that the name of 'BT' was now bigger than any one of them could ever hope to be? She had often pondered these things and she still did not know.

What was certain, of course, was that the likes of a Menoka were easy sacrifices on the altar of a Bharat Talkies. They came out of nowhere and where they went at the end of the day was nobody's worry. True, they were what they happened to be through no fault of their own, yet, her own upbringing had taught her to loathe such women. Her family had been frontrunners in education and culture, and she herself had been to finishing school in Europe and studied art before she had met Shankar and gone on to work in the movies. Being in the pictures had made her a sensation in her own society, but her background had shielded her from disrepute. She was different in every way from the other kind of woman that went about in the studios—and she herself had always impressed that home truth on studio girls like Menoka.

Still, Menoka's death worried her. Somewhere, was it more than just another of those girls? Was it really more about this world of theirs, this world of bioscope pictures, and its twists and turns? Was it the precariousness of stardom that made her unhappy? Menoka was a star the studio had created. Yet, she did not belong to Bharat Talkies. In truth, she did not belong anywhere. What was it in what had happened to Menoka that made her think of herself? No, nothing, really...the Menokas of this world were meant to come and go, and not be remembered, but she...she was Ramola Devi and she stood for class and culture. Ramola drew herself up from her chair and pulled the silk dressing gown around her as Shankar walked in. He looked worn out but in command, as always, and she knew that he had come in only to cheer her. She smiled and felt calm at the very sight of him, and for that one moment was sorry that Menoka had loved but was not loved back.

II

It was the day after. The police had taken away Menoka's body. There would be a coroner's inquest and autopsy. No one had come for her, and no one at the studio knew if she had anyone to claim her mortal remains. She had come into Bharat Talkies with Ambarish Dev Burma and that was all anyone knew about her. Shankar had done his part. New Year's presents had gone out to the newspaper offices, and full page announcements of the studio were to appear in the papers through that week. It was going to be an important year, and Bharat Talkies would be bigger than ever before.

Shankar walked into the drawing room as Ramola was working though the piles of New Year greetings and fan letters. She always liked to open all her own mail, though most of it went unanswered. One or two she liked to keep, like the poem that a young man had written for her, and which she had acknowledged with 'Thank you, you should keep up your writing.' Shankar had teased her about it. 'So should we get him on contract now, scriptwriter-lyricist?'

That morning he strode in, almost bumping into a chair, then sat himself down on the sofa beside her. 'Meeting this afternoon,' he said, though it was the last thing they had talked over the night before. That was him, forever trying to mind her. Sometimes she would turn to him scornfully, even crossly, saying, 'I quite forgot, thank you for reminding' or 'I'm old enough, thank you Shankar', to which he would grin back sheepishly. But, today she smiled and nodded. Poor Shankar, he had had a hard time the last two days, what with the police coming to the house and all the explaining that he had had to do. That too when he already had his hands so very full.

They were meeting at the studio in the afternoon,

with the heads of all departments who would be working on the forthcoming collaboration with Miracle—to take stock of things. It had been Shankar's coup of sorts. Hollywood's famous Miracle Pictures was going to be collaborator of Bharat Talkies in their forthcoming production of a big-budget historical. It would be the first ever such partnership between an Indian studio and Hollywood and Shankar was keeping everything hush-hush until after his trip to America where he would sign the contract.

The talks had carried on for close to a year, with many meetings with Miracle's India office, and a visit by a team from Hollywood. Bharat Talkies was producing its grandest historical and Miracle Pictures would partner it in this picture's production and distribution worldwide. Shankar himself was directing, with Ramola in the lead role of Mira in this grand production of the story of Mirabai, the princess-devotee who had renounced the world for her love of Krishna. Already, they had taken the sequences with Ramola and Devdutt Chowdhury as Bhojraj, Mirabai's husband. Shankar had created the magnificent studio set of the Rana of Mewar's palace and another one was going to be built for a song set in Mewar's pleasure gardens.

'We have to put our best foot forward with these Americans,' Shankar had said. He was going to carry with him the reels of what they had taken. His friendship with Richard Banter, one of Miracle's top directors, had him on very good ground. 'And it's going to be our stepping stone for bigger things...much bigger...' he would tell Ramola. 'Why can't we be like Miracle someday...or one of the British companies?' The signing was only a formality now. 'The Americans want to get into our markets in a much bigger way, and they want this collaboration to happen as much as us.'

Work on the picture would resume after Shankar got back from America. He would set off on the ship from Calcutta in another eight days to get to Los Angeles, in a journey that would take between six to seven weeks, stopping at Colombo, Singapore and Tokyo. He would return only by late April. With luck, the production would be back on the floors by that month's end, and they would have an all-India and world release that year itself. After the signing, Miracle Pictures would send across its own team of technicians, to stay in Calcutta and work with Shankar at Bharat Talkies until the picture's completion.

Shankar would have liked to stay on in America some more days. He was going back after an interval of nearly six years. But with *Mirabai* already on the floor, he had to make the journey back soon enough. Ramola was not going, much as they both wanted it. Costumes needed to be finalized, song sittings and rehearsals were pending, and she would have to stay behind and oversee everything at the studio.

'I'm going to miss you, darling,' she told him as she got ready for bed that night. He was in his dressing gown at the table by the window browsing through the day's papers. His eyebrows went up, 'But you've got enough on your hands haven't you?'

Ramola sighed, 'How nice it would be to dine again at Milano's.'

As new lovers they would frequently meet for dinner at the newly opened restaurant on Adams Boulevard where Ramola had loved the seafood specials. On weekends, they had champagne buffets and ice-cream at James and Damian, a little dairy tucked away in a back street.

The very thought of those places brought back the fondest of memories. It was where they had met, on her first trip to America, with her uncle, the physician Debiprasad Banerjea. It was 1926 and she had been a twenty-four-year-old studying art. She had met Shankar at a gathering in Los Angeles two days after they had arrived there. He had been there with his American wife, Amy. Shankar had gone from India to work in the movies. He had assisted the famous producer and screenwriter John Seltzer. Amy had been assistant to Seltzer's brother Patrick, and they had met frequently, fallen in love and married.

Ramola and Shankar had gotten on well, and she had been drawn into his world of motion pictures and their making. With her training in art, she could picture the screen like a canvas, and surprised him with her ideas about framing and camera angles. He had made up his mind to return home to set up his own studio, he told her. His marriage with Amy would not have lasted anyways, he said later, because Amy could not have left behind her own world and come to live with him in India. Meeting Ramola had only made him decide sooner. Ramola had never really known how he had handled the whole thing, but she had always had feelings of remorse when she thought of Amy. Amy herself had been civil the only other time they had met, and by then she had known about her and Shankar.

Her own family had been unhappy about her marriage, but she had been too much in love to care. They were in love and they had one dream. To have their own studio, to create something that would be truly world-class. It was not going to be easy. Making bioscope pictures was not what respectable people in this country did for a living, and the studios were the last place for women from good families. But then, she had not always been the very good girl that people thought she was. She smiled as she remembered their first clumsy lip-lock, after one of their afternoons out, when she had drunk too much champagne and he had not resisted her overtures. He had asked her to marry him that same evening.

Shankar might have read her mind.

'You can still come along, you know,' he said gently, eyes fixed on her face, with a look he had on when he was quite plainly adoring her. 'I can check first thing tomorrow with the steamship company?'

She laughed, 'Mmmhm no, not this time. I'll come when we release *Mira*. Let's spend two months there then…but really, this picture is almost making me as nervous as the first time,' she was serious now.

With the hint of a smile, Shankar lifted himself off his chair, walked to the bed and sat on its edge next to her.

'Ramola Devi, nervous? That can't be true…'

Ramola giggled, 'Of course, I'm nervous, aren't you Shankar Chattopadhyay?'

It was a mating call, their rehearsed reiterating of their first lovemaking, when she had teased him unabatedly for being shy until he had grabbed and smothered her.

'Not really nervous, are you,' he whispered in her

ear that night as their bodies moved to a practiced rhythm, both hungry and satisfied at the same time as they sought and pleased one another. When they lay together that night, she hugging him against her breasts and he caressing her bare back, it all didn't matter so much—Miracle Pictures, the grand historical that they were making, or the deceits and brittleness of the world that they had built around themselves.

As she lay awake that night Ramola's thoughts wandered back to her first picture, when they had launched Bharat Talkies. Shankar had directed and also played the hero. It had been the early days of sound in the movies, and they had adapted the story of Queen Padmini of Chittor. In those days she learnt what she would never unlearn. To emote before the camera and make people cry and smile with her. She was the first educated woman to have taken up the movies as a profession, and critics and moviegoers alike had fallen in love with her. After their first picture together Shankar had put in his days and nights into building the studio, and she became a bigger star with each picture. Not all were hits, but they said a star of her stature lived beyond hits and flops. Still, even she was not bigger than Bharat Talkies, though Shankar said *Mirabai* would make her immortal.

Mirabai had already created enough flutter in studio circles. Though the partnership with Miracle Pictures was not public yet, the rumour was that Shankar Chattopadhyay was making his biggest picture. Shankar had not directed in the last three years. He had gotten sucked into business matters and the studio's working, and there were whispers that he had lost his touch. Shankar had shrugged off the insinuation but Ramola knew that it hurt him. He was one of the best directors of their time, only, he had looked beyond himself and worked to build a whole set-up. Only she understood how much he had given up so that Bharat Talkies could become the name that it was today. But he now wanted to return. They had hit upon the idea of making a grand historical, on a never-before scale. And a woman-centric script, like Garbo's *Queen Christina*.

Mirabai was a logical choice. The script would allow them lots of scope for songs, and everyone went to the talkies these days because they wanted to hear their favourite stars sing. She herself was blessed with a good voice, though she had never had any training as a young girl. Some of the other actresses were better singers than her, but hers was the angelic face that people adored. They somehow imagined that Ramola Devi could do no wrong.

Shankar tossed about in his sleep next to her, sucking in his breath like his mouth was dry. On some days, he would complain of tiredness, and she had been worried. Perhaps it was his digestion, she always had to tell him not to gobble his meals. But it really had been impossible, even for her, to get him to see Sailen Kaka, their family doctor. He got headaches and back pains, and she had woken up in the middle of the night to see that he was not in bed. He would go back to his study to work on the script or look over his notes for the Miracle deal. And then still be up on time, fully dressed for breakfast.

The Menoka business had added to his worries. Still,

things should be easier after the America trip was over, after this deal was finally signed and sealed. She would get him to take a holiday then. Perhaps they could go away to the hills for just a few days...her aunt's villa near the tea gardens. It had always been so lovely and peaceful to spend a weekend there, almost away from civilization. Shankar had liked it there. They would have breakfast in bed, play tennis and go for long walks, just the two of them, away from the studio and away from all of the people in their lives.

Rajbala

'*Sunechish?*' Kamala Masi bubbled breathlessly. 'Did you hear? That girl that hanged herself? Menoka *re*. Remember her? She was at Popular, then one or two months at Unique, at the beginning...sweet face but little peanuts for breasts. As if she had nothing there. Remember? Flying too high she was, trying to be a memsahib, now see...'

Raju sipped her sweet tea, not replying. She knew, she had been one of the first people outside of Bharat Talkies to know. Why couldn't Masi shut her mouth when she was getting a headache. Those stunts made her tired. She was good at them, and the better she got, the more difficult they made them for her. And she had to sing, and she had to get carried off...and keep that monkey of a hero's paws off her backside every time he took her in his arms. Now they even wanted her to play with live snakes in the new song.

She could hear Kamala bustling about the kitchen. 'Masiiiii,' she yelled for more tea.

Being Raju Darling was no easy job. A Raju Darling picture was action and romance and adventure all rolled into one, and it meant the cash would come in fast and keep coming in, because her fans came back twice, thrice, even ten and twelve times to watch the same picture. The tickets were low-priced, and the shows were full, and kept going for days on end. That was something that even the biggest stars could not manage.

Stars my foot, Raju snorted. Just big names. Did they have to carry a picture all on their own? She could give any big studio a run for its money. How much money the four-anna, eight-anna *wala*s spent on her, to be with her those two hours in the darkness, over and over again, it made her laugh sometimes. And in a room somewhere, would be a hungry child and a wife, like she and her mother, who could do with those four-*anna*s. She didn't often think of her mother though. She was working too hard, and then, she had moved far, from those days of hunger and fear and despair. She had worked in the bioscope for six or seven years, and her mother was dead and gone. She had kept Kamala Masi with her, though. Not because she had felt anything for her, but because she needed a servant. Kamala knew the 'line' from her theatre days. Some of the stars of the old theatre companies had moved on to the bioscope studios, and Kamala had been at home in the studio *para* when she first took Raju from one bioscope company to another. Though now she kept house, fetched and carried, and cleaned up after Raju.

Kamala came in from the kitchen, tea in hand. She was mulling over Menoka.

'Saheb kept her, everyone knows...otherwise...

Menoka and Bharat Talkies...' Kamala scoffed, 'she was only good for thooose pictures...full-showing, all naked, not a stitch on her...some whore she was, that one...'

She shouldn't have said it, she realized that very same instant, as Raju's head jerked and she turned to glare at Kamala.

'*Bhalo to bhalo*, when she's fine she's fine, then god alone knows what ghost gets her,' Kamala grumbled to herself as she escaped back into the kitchen. Raju could scare her when she looked like that.

'*Arre baba*' she thought as she busied herself neatly slicing pieces of an oversized brinjal to make *begun bhaja*. 'Who remembers now those pictures of yours, mad girl...who knew your name then...I was talking about that *magi* Menoka...'

It was true, her first bioscope pictures, silent ones, never carried Raju's name. Often, there were no title cards even, except the picture's name, *Jawan Taruni* aka Young Girl or simply *Dress Changing Beauty*. Raju, then thirteen or fourteen, opened her sari in front of a running camera, flailed her arms about, walked up and down then disappeared off screen. Or she might go through the motions of taking a bath from an empty bucket, tenderly rubbing her thighs and back, and in between her legs, like she would do at home, then throw a *gamcha* over her still sprouting breasts before slowly walking away. They were short pictures, with no cuts and no background music, and no pretense of any acting. But they had their audience, those that went to the night shows and travelling cinemas, which were cheaper than even the *char* anna seats. The travelling cinemas went to places where they had no picture halls and showed their wares in tents on torn screens.

Sometimes, they would take her photographs, calling out to her to hold some pose or other. To not move or keep her hand too close, so it did not come in the way of her open breasts. One or two even made their way into the drawing rooms of the rich, pored over by the gents after the ladies had retired for the evening. None of these gentlemen had ever asked for the girl in person, and had they done so, Kamala would have made an earnest endeavour to get Raju to rise to the occasion. Kamala sighed, now chopping potatoes for *alu bhaja*... these were bad times, that Menoka hanging herself and then that other girl's body in that producer's garden house, everyone knew what was what, making her drink then choking her throat.

'But the likes of us, *meye manush*, womenfolk, can we stand against men with money? Better be meek, that's what I say, don't fly too high. But no, who listens to Kamala Masi anymore. Who got you into this line, tell me...girl was a lamb then, she and her mother, did what Kamala Masi said...and now...she's her own master...I am nobody, just a *jhi*, a maid...'

'Even a *jhi* would have had more than me...' Raju gritted her teeth as she drank her tea, remembering the scraps that Kamala would throw at them. Then, when she became a star, Masi had tried to get her to see men, rich men, who hung about the studios, and who had quite suddenly become smitten by her. She smiled, remembering how one day she had turned around on a coaxing and honey-voiced Kamala and hit her hard across the face, causing some half-chewed *paan* to jerk out from Kamala's mouth, and then kicked her hard on the leg. She was wearing her *kangan*s, the curved and spiked bangles that she had bought with her own money, and it had made a gash on Kamala's left cheek. Kamala had fallen to her knees with a thud and Raju had walked out of the room, shouting to her to make *macher jhal*, her favourite spicy fish curry and rice for when she returned. Kamala never talked about what happened that day, but she had turned over a new leaf. She stopped telling Raju where to go and what to do, like she had done before.

Most studio girls came into their 'line' holding the hand of some *masi* or other, or even with their own mothers, but how many became stars, like her, thought Raju proudly. Or that Menoka! But was it Menoka that she remembered from back then, or was it that other girl Molina? She couldn't be sure...the one that she first saw doing the naked 'acto', before she got into it herself. Still, after getting over it the first two or three times those ones were easier done than the stunts...hanging from ropes... fights...then getting thrown about by those men double her size...

She lifted her sari to feel her right hip, still sore from where she had fallen.

'And I only got to do one day *chutti*, anyone else would have taken three days. But no. No shooting, but come and do rehearsal...as if that is not work...'

Kamala came in with a plate full of hot *luchi*s, *begun* and *alu bhaja*.

'There's kheer for after,' she had honey in her voice. 'Or, you want it now, with your *luchi*?'

Raju nodded, she wanted everything together. That was one thing about Kamala Masi, she knew how to cook. Raju ate her evening meal with great relish, when she could have *maach-bhat*, fish and rice, or *luchi* like today, or sometimes Kamala's *dalpuri*s and *kochuri*s. She had to eat lightly during the day, but she made up for it after she got back home from the studio. She would eat in silence, shutting her ears to Kamala's chatter as she served her.

As a little girl Raju had inhaled the perfumes of curries and gravies being prepared in the neighbourhood, but her own mother's cooking had been bland and without character. Her early fondness for Kamala had grown out of her cravings and weakness for food, as Kamala Masi had come bearing packets of *jhal chanachur*, hot grams, or small earthen pots of *ghugni* from roadside vendors. Kamala knew Raju well, the way to her head lay through her stomach. She herself was a small eater, but she cooked well for Raju. Kamala knew now that she had to earn her keep.

'You're becoming so thin, day by day,' she groaned as she watched Raju work through the *luchi*s. 'Starving you whole day, that *memsahib* of yours. Look at other girls your age, front side-backside all so nice...so full...'

Kamala believed Raju's going out of hand was all Lily Madam's doing. That Anglo *magi*, that slut, had done some *tuk-tak*, black magic on the poor girl.

'*Tui bol*, if you say, I can get *maach-bhat* to the studio at lunchtime from tomorrow? Should I?' she leant forward eagerly.

'And who the hell is going to do the stunts and dances

after that lunch, *tomar baap*, your father?' Raju's yell almost made Kamala drop the rest of the *kheer*. 'Haven't I told you not to do *bak-bak* in my ear when I'm eating?'

Kamala had a tear rolling down her face, as was often her fate. Raju was eating peacefully again. She had her count. Five of Kamala Masi's *luchi*s, four pieces of *begun bhaja* and seven pieces of the thick round *alu bhaja*s. Kamala always served her more, and she would leave the rest on her plate. It was a matter of practice, as Lily Madam always said.

'You can eat anything you like, as long as you don't stuff yourself up. Remember, what is *thik* for me might be more for you. Don't talk when you're eating. Chew it well...'

It had taken Raju months to master it, and now in her mind she knew the counts and amounts for everything she ate.

'No *bhat* for lunch,' was Lily's diktat. So Raju made her mid-day meal of ripe bananas, for which Lily had nicknamed her '*bandar*'. And while other studio girls her age were often buxom and well-rounded, Raju looked slender but filled out in the right places.

What a pity that Madam had become a little bit like Kamala Masi, she mused as she opened out her long plait and parted her hair, a signal that she wanted her head massaged. Kamala had cleared her plates and now started to rub coconut oil on her head. Raju shut her eyes as Kamala pressed her temples, and made gentle circles with her fingers, messing her hair. How good this felt... whatever would she do without Masi. If only she didn't talk so much...if only Lily Madam didn't do so much

'*Yeh karo, yeh mat karo*' these days...always ordering her around. Why they all wanted to tell her what to do... didn't they all get what they wanted out of her?

Even when it had come to that one picture she was now going to do with another studio, Madam had created so much *jhamela*.

'Why you want to work outside, *idhar kya nahi milta hai*, what don't you get here? *Humko bolo*...you tell me.' As if telling her would do any good. As if she would even understand. That she wanted to get away. From Unique Pictures, Lily Madam and Mishtu Da who thought they had made her...*Made her*—that was what they thought! Could they pick another girl and make another Rajbala?

We all live by our own fates...Kamala Masi was used to saying. 'And it was *my* fate to be a star,' Raju smirked silently as Kamala rolled her hair into a loose knot. Mishtu Da said her contract was for two more years... *two more years*...but they had allowed her one outside picture, that too after so much *jhagra*. She hadn't given in...hmm, now even she knew how to get her way in this line. What did they think that she would never learn the tricks? That they would have their say, always?

But which studio, she had to make up her mind quickly now. New Talkies wanted her for their new adventure romance...Bharatmata...they would enter action if she went with them. She had to wait until she saw him again...she didn't want to go wrong. But that was still another two days.

Ramola

'Take those old ones out of the trunk,' Ramola scolded Bibhu, Shankar's attendant. 'I told you not to pack *saab*'s old gloves, get them out.'

His old ones were a bit worn, they had been laid away for too long. She had ordered him a pair from Hogg Sahib's market. They still had four, no five days, if she counted the day that he was to leave. She had stayed home that morning to look through Shankar's trunks which Bibhu had packed on her instructions.

She was wearing a costume from *Mirabai*, a pale yellow sari, with her head covered and her hair left loose. The blouse had long sleeves, not the short ones that were her favourite. She had started the fashion of wearing short sari blouses and women everywhere wore them now. Would the Mira style sari blouse also become a fad, she wondered, as she leisurely walked across the hallway from Shankar's dressing room where the trunks lay opened out.

She sat down at her own dressing table in the bedroom and studied herself. It was something she did once in a while—go about the house in the costumes from the pictures. 'Helps me be the character,' she would say.

The servants were accustomed to it, and Bibhu had not batted an eyelid when madam had emerged dressed like a *sanyasin*.

'They must sometimes think I'm quite mad,' Ramola thought as she adjusted the pleats of her sari which had got tousled. She had planned to not use safety-pins, to just let it be. The Mira costumes were simple, almost austere. Even the scenes that were set in the royal palace were going to be muted performances. Ramola felt a certain graveness, at times even removed from the things around her when she was thinking her way through Mira.

'This one is so unlike my other characters,' she pondered as she hummed one of Mira's songs. Those had all been a mix of serious and playful—like the good wife who could also sing a song and match it with a few nimble steps, but not this one. It was going to be difficult, no frills of love and romance here.

She felt in the skin of the character. After several years of her practiced playing of the model woman, she had wanted it to be a little bit more. And even as it got closer to Shankar's departure, she wanted to almost embrace this new role of hers—this character of a lovelorn woman. She had times of feeling restless and then settling down again, but today she simply couldn't stay calm, no matter how hard she tried. She wished again that they were going away together, that work was not quite so pressing and that she could be less worried about Shankar.

She looked at the watch on her dressing table, almost eleven. Shankar was going to be seeing Miracle Pictures' India head in their Chowringhee office. Avinash Mukherjee, who ran Miracle's business in India was a reserved, almost shy man, who seemed to her to be of an altogether different stock from those in their line. Shankar had gotten along very well with him, but then he got along with most people. The two men had met frequently over the past months to plan the collaboration on *Mirabai*.

Avinash had met Shankar at a luncheon in one of the Chowringhee hotels. They were remarkably different people, Shankar assertive and outgoing, Avinash careful and observant, but they had the same ideas about movies and movie-making. Avinash admired the way Shankar had given up a Hollywood career and had returned to the country to set up Bharat Talkies. He had taken to visiting the Bharat Talkies studio, and was awed by Shankar's leadership and his untiring energies.

Ramola herself was not part of this friendship between the two men, though she had frequently met Avinash at the studio. With her he was awkward and aloof, mumbling 'Good morning, ma'am' or 'Thank you, ma'am', and she had not given him very much thought, before Shankar had considered collaborating with him on their big-budget production.

Avinash had confided in Shankar, 'Shankar Da, I want to do more...something creative...something that is not only about making money. The bosses will allow it now, I think...'

His bosses in America had learnt to trust him, and he now had more leverage than before. And Shankar had wanted to come back with his own picture, but not just any picture. It had to be something big, something that would make their world sit up and take notice. Shankar wasn't thinking about a single hit picture. He wanted his new picture to be remembered.

Avinash had urged him on, 'It has to be an international collaboration, Shankar Da,' and they had worked overtime to lobby the studio bosses in America.

The all-India market was growing every day and

the talkies were a rage. 'But we lack a world audience,' Shankar would often say. A partnership like Miracle could change that. Still, a lot of groundwork had to be done. Miracle had their doubts about the way things worked in India, more informally and less by the books. Shankar's Hollywood background had helped, and Avinash had done everything in his power to push for the collaboration.

'How can I explain, dada...' he had been almost overcome when they had finally gotten the go-ahead, and as the two men had sat together late in the evening.

'This is my chance to get involved in movie-making... perhaps we can make history together...'

It was going to be a big picture. If only they could make it a success. Miracle Pictures wanted him to steer it for them. A team of technicians would come in from America to work with Shankar, but he would be their man on the ground.

Like Ramola, Avinash too was restless. He sat in his office idly flipping through some magazines, after what had been their last meeting before Shankar would leave for America. He had not been asked to accompany Shankar, as he had very much hoped. His bosses had not thought it necessary, and he had not liked to press the point. *Mirabai* was on his mind now, but even as he looked at his notes and thought back to his morning's conversation, he knew that he would have to take his mind off it, until Shankar's return, when they could get back to work. But that meant he would stray back to Ramola.

Avinash

Avinash loathed admitting, even to himself, his almost obsessive love for Ramola. When he first met her he was intrigued. She was modern and accomplished no doubt, and decorous, yet sometimes almost uncharacteristically child-like. And eager and sincere in her work, as if she was a school girl and not the great star that she was. She had none of the typical airs of stars, and she carried her stardom with an ease that he found quite remarkable. She was older than he was, he had gathered, but the years had been kind on her. On days that she was not going before the camera, she wore no make-up, often no other jewellery except her diamond earrings, and she looked so youthful and untouched that he had had to struggle to keep himself from staring at her. She was such a curious mix of opposites, often quiet yet impatient, high-class but down-to-earth, alive yet somehow solitary.

That she was a big star was the least of her charms, in Avinash's eyes. Rather he tried to imagine her bereft of her stardom, what if she had not been so unattainable in every way. Funnily enough, that same distance between them had drawn him more to her, even as he had fumbled and become overly formal in her presence. A few times, she had caught him staring, but then, she was used to people looking like that. She had gently smiled back, as if trying to make him feel at ease, and he had looked the other way swallowing back a swell of emotions, infuriated at himself for staring.

At thirty-one, the only reason Avinash was still unmarried was that being a hopeless romantic he had not countenanced the thought of an arranged marriage, though proposals had not been few. Secretly vain about his good looks, he was youthful like a boy, with a lithe body and a sensitive face. In love with the idea of being in love, he had in his mind set such exacting standards for a possible mate that the years had gone by and he had stayed unattached. He had never spoken even in his most intimate circles about his closeness with Shankar or about Ramola, fearing he might give away his most secret thoughts, and how he felt about her.

Nor indeed were his desires mystical and psychic as he would have liked to tell himself. She was a small woman, with small breasts, slender arms, a tiny waist, delicate hips and firm buttocks, not really what was the liking in 'the line' for women with more meat on their bodies. But for Avinash, that same fragility created a longing for closeness and belonging. In his most unguarded moments he had imagined Ramola with Shankar, man and wife, feeling the bile rise in him, and feelings of rivalry that had shamed him almost the next minute. At such times, he would force his thoughts back to the new picture, to his newly formed alliance with Shankar and their grand plans together.

Today, he pretended to not notice as Shankho brought a hand to rest on his knee. Shankho was a mild distraction, from the seething in his mind. Shankho loved him, like he loved Ramola, a kind of impossible love, where the lover knew that he would never attain the object of his desire. That perhaps was also the thrill of this kind of love. Shankho acted in bioscope films, and sometimes in plays. His pictures, where he had been cast as the hero had passed unnoticed, but he made a dependable character actor.

'You should have been the hero in those pictures, not me,' he would tell Avinash, eyes locked on him. On days like this one, when he had no rehearsals, shows or shooting, he would arrive at Avinash's office or even his home near Jadu Babu's Bazar.

'*Cholo na*, come on, let's get out a little bit early and go to Europa for drinks,' he had coaxed that afternoon.

His head buried in some papers, Avinash hadn't replied. He liked to keep Shankho guessing.

'*Ki?* Won't you come?' Shankho had asked again, his pleasant face dimming.

'Hmmm, *bhabchi*, thinking...' Avinash had paused for a few seconds to remove his glasses, blow into them and wipe them with his fingers, then had promptly busied himself in a flurry of activity, opening drawers, pulling out some papers, then darting out of his chair and into the inner office, apparently with some significant objective.

All the while Shankho's eyes had followed him. Avinash had plucked a dusting cloth hanging on a hook and started to wipe the wooden cabinet, letting the minutes pass as Shankho waited in the next room. No dust here, Keshta the office boy was doing his job. After a suitable passing of time, he had called out to Shankho, as if he had suddenly remembered.

'I...was thinking...maybe the six o'clock show... Lighthouse? What are they showing? Today's paper...'

Shankho had jumped, grabbed the newspaper lying on Avinash's marble-topped wooden desk and rushed into the room.

'Here, here...let me check the shows...*Ei to*, here it is...Lighthouse six o'clock...*Prince and the Pauper*. And Ruby has...Hindi *boi*...with Ranibala...which one, you decide.'

He had looked up from the page that he was scouring so intently to find that Avinash had slipped away. He was at his desk again, in the next room, feet up now on the marble top of the table. 'I think,' he had declared as Shankho reappeared, 'that we'll go to Europa after all...'

Avinash paid for their drinks at Europa Bar.

'He deserves it,' he thought looking at Shankho. Shankho had ordered a gin and tonic, Avinash coffee as always. Shankho was looking jubilant, Avinash was laughing loudly at his jokes. The truth was he sometimes laughed so loudly to mask tedium. Or, as at this time, his exasperation, at the insubordination of his own body and mind.

A Bharat Talkies poster had captured his view from his seat by the window on the second floor of Europa. And there she was, smiling ever so sweetly. Wasn't there the last time that he had come. Why ever does she appear in every which place. He felt irritable. Yet he had seated himself in that rather odd angle, turned half away from Shankho, and towards the open window. His back upright, legs a little bit parted, his breaths quick.

Seated next to him, Shankho did not notice. He was chatting, he could be speaking to himself. He didn't care really if he did not elicit many responses from Avinash. And then, Avinash was laughing mirthfully... couldn't really have found it so very amusing, what he was saying. Maybe just how he had said it...though he shouldn't think it too funny himself, just his report of some backstage mishaps, regular stuff, really.

Shankho laughed along, his gladness was real, like when he would be drunk. Though really, on such days he would manage to not drink too much, like he would if left to himself. He was used to Avinash's silences and elusiveness. Avinash rarely laughed like today, though he sometimes would make a joke at his expense, which fairly delighted Shankho.

Avinash smirked quietly. Shankho looked like he was ready to fly. It was why he would bear with Shankho, more so of late, when had he needed to fight his feelings of inadequacy, and Shankho's naivety had restored his sense of superiority. He smiled indulgently, even as Shankho did something that he had never dared before. He laid his hand on Avinash's leg, as if to touch him was nothing. Avinash looked out of the window again at Ramola's face etched against the sky. 'I'm going to have to put him back in his place next time,' he thought as he drained his cup.

Avinash knew he could charm people with his quiet, persuasive ways. He knew how to lay bare their neediness, in the face of his own studied aloofness. It had given him a kind of power—over others, and over himself and his bodily desires. Years of physical practice in an *akhara* had taught him to conserve energies and command his mind and body, and he took pride in his capacity for self-control.

For that same reason, he had not found it hard to resist the allures of the studio *para*, whether the women, the drunken parties or the money that flowed. With

Ramola he found that same resolve crumbling. He had wanted her, and he also wanted to see her hurt…and break. She was almost too secure, too sure of herself. And it angered him for his own weakness.

He felt the now familiar sharpness in his head and drew himself back to Shankho.

'…you say, what *jhamela*, what utter nuisance,' Shankho was grumbling.

Avinash smiled, 'What is it?'

'You never listen…' Shankho faked a pout. 'That's what I'm telling you…our Bharatmata studio is trying to get Rajbala…Raju Darling. The boss has got it into his head to enter action…if he can get her. But what of me? What if they try to make me do action…can you imagine?'

'But,' Avinash broke in. 'Isn't she with Unique? Have they released her?'

'*Arre na na*, that girl is *chalu*, very clever. Managed to wiggle one outside picture from Unique. I know their owner, Mishtu Modak…lives under the spell of that Anglo mistress of his, Lily Madam they call her. She made Rajbala…training her and everything…one day no one knew of her, then there she was…Miss Raju Darling…fate, what else…'

Avinash laughed, picturing Shankho in action costume. 'You will have to quit Bharatmata, then, won't you?' he teased.

Poor Shankho, from his tame socials to action, and that too pitted against *the* Raju Darling. He would be like a fish out of water.

'Hmmmm, laugh all you like…Raju Darling my foot…'

Shankho lowered his voice, 'You know what someone from inside was telling me? That she was doing *thoose* types of pictures before...darling of night-shows she was then, show it all...wouldn't be a thread left to cover her body.'

He cocked his head and raised his eyebrows, '...quite young she was that time...and now a star...fate what else,' he rued again.

'Good for her then...' Avinash was feeling empty again. 'At least she's not some high up *devi*, thinking she's too good for everybody...'

Raju

Raju was furious. Another argument with Lily Madam and Mishtu Da. All over again about doing that outside picture.

'You cannot do action with a *bahar ka* studio. Action is the second name of Unique, we cannot allow it,' was Lily's diktat.

All ways to try and stop her. A Raju Darling picture was always all-in-one—action, romance, song and dance, everything. Any studio hiring her would want it all. But Lily Madam was more than clear, 'No kicks, no *ghusaa*s, no fights, *kuch* action *nahi*, no action...' she had said. Now she would have to say no to Bharatmata studio. They wanted her to do action, they too were quite clear.

'What if I don't listen?' Raju mused. 'What if I just sign with Bharatmata? What can they do?'

She wasn't sure really, that was the thing. She didn't even remember now what the contract had looked like. She remembered writing her name on some papers in her halting hand, but that was two years now, after her first hit *Captive Princess*. Mishtu Da had called her to his office one morning. Lily Madam had been there. They had told her to put her name on some papers and she had done it. And now they were using it to hold her back, the two of them. As if she didn't know what happened in the afternoons...inside Mishtu Da's office. That's why he listened to everything she said. What was Unique, before they got her? When Lily Madam was heroine, dancing about in those tight blouses and small skirts? Who knew about Unique then? She had made them, not them her.

It was true. Mishtu Modak, proprietor of Unique Pictures, had almost closed shop when silent movies had started becoming the talkies. The company had made a few passable mythologicals but really stayed afloat with the jungle adventure romances which were meant to showcase its heroine, Miss Lily. Lily did what she called 'the wiggling and jiggling at the studio'. She would swing from the studio's overhead props and false foliage, front and then back to the camera, climb from tree trunk onto the painted branches, her bare legs dangling from where she would perch herself, do somersaults and hip-swinging dances. The company hired girls like Raju from one picture to another. Lily had seen promise in Raju, and on her urging Mishtu had taken the gamble and produced his first sound picture, and launched Raju as Raju Darling.

'So what?' scowled Raju as she strode out of the studio, then crossed the *chowrasta*, the nearby crossing of four busy streets.

It was after five in the evening and her empty insides

growled. She had her head covered with her sari, pulling it over her face on one side, in case she was spotted and followed. In a few minutes she was at Nawab's, a Muslim eatery. The waiter in his uniform knew her and showed her into a tiny cabin, pulling the red curtain to hide her from view. Raju ordered beef *kasa*, a spicy curry made with beef.

'Surely you don't want this, it's cow, *goru*,' Lily had asked, when she had first brought her there. 'You can have egg curry.'

But Raju had nodded her preference for the beef, to Lily's amazement. Even the most hardened of the Hindu girls in the 'line' who smoked and drank did not touch the forbidden meat. Today, as she dipped her bread in the red curry, Raju almost didn't taste the food in her mouth. She had to get one picture, just one outside picture with a top studio to throw off that Unique *chappa*. Being Unique's Raju Darling, how she hated it now. She couldn't, she just couldn't wait another two years. They had said she could work outside...morning eleven till five in the evening, six hours for twelve days a month until before the time of Durga Pujo. That she had managed. But who would take her if she didn't do action.

'If I was with a big studio, like that Menoka, I would get some respect,' thought Raju bitterly. What is Unique? One heroine studio, selling the skin off my back. Making me work to death. As if I'm their slave, not a star... won't even let me try any new thing. Why can't we do one comedy picture? *Nahi chalega*, won't run. Why? Because Lily Madam says so. Won't even give me the chance. Even that gone-to-hell Menoka got to do some good acting. And why not? She was at Bharat Talkies, not some *phaltu* Unique Pictures.

Still, she was not without friends. A sudden smile played on Raju's lips, cutting the sullenness of her face. Anil Babu was there. And that evening she would see him. She could make him do anything.

It had been him that had put it in her head, the outside picture deal with Unique. He had known how to get one over Lily Madam and Mishtu Da.

'As if I have so much brains,' she smirked. No brains, and no mother or father, no English. Nothing...except for these breasts and legs and hands and fingers. Raju licked her fingertips, then took out the mirror from her handbag and studied herself. She had to make the best use of herself.

Anil

I

Anil wanted to be a horse. Or a dog. Or even a donkey, if Raju would mount him. He had got shivers up and down his spine when he had watched and watched again the Raju Darling pictures where Raju whacked and walloped the villains, then mounted a horse, whip in hand and triumphantly trotted off. Or when she danced flaunting her bare waist, her skirt twirling up to show her ankles and calves. What a girl! And she was his, temper and tantrums and all. One instant she would flare up, and then be prancing again, like nothing had happened. Kept him on his toes! And she could cuss! The last hour she'd sulked, spewing abuses at that Madam of hers and Unique studio, and here she was now, her sweet self again.

'Mine, mine, mine...' she was singing, as she hugged the baby doll in her arms. It had arrived by order from London dressed in pink woollens, in its crib of pink silk, and felt like a real baby, soft and cuddly. And it cried and said 'mamma' if you pressed its stomach.

He laughed, and lunged, pulling her close. He had known she would love it. Poor girl, never anyone to look after her, never any nice things. He had seen it in the window at Francis, Harrison, Hathaway and Company on Free School Street but they had had only one, the one that was in the window. He had waited for close to an hour for them to find the old catalogue and placed an order there and then. It was expensive; you could buy two or three bottles of good cologne for that price. The advertisement in the catalogue had said it was a doll loved by the children of the royal household in England. Nothing but the best for his pet! She just needed somebody to calm her down.

He sat her on his knees and cuddled her, a hand around her waist.

'Put the baby...here,' he whispered in her ear and pressed the doll against her stomach. It felt real, the three of them.

'*Ooff maaa*,' she squealed.

He had squeezed the breath out of her. He laughed again. He liked worrying her, just a little bit. He would get the best imported creams and lotions for her, and perfumes and powders. For when he would make her lie down and press her legs and back, and knead the soles of her feet. Then he would spray her with perfumes and dust her with powder. And watch her fall asleep.

No hurry, he always told himself, there was no rush, she was his. Sometimes he would open out her long plait, clucking in distaste at Kamala's handiwork, and lovingly smooth out the tresses to do them up again, neatly and carefully. Raju hated it. Having to sit so still and him take so much time with it. Still, she needed him. He knew their world, the big people...

'We'll show them...' he said to her another time, though he knew Unique would not let go of her without a fight.

They would do everything in their power to keep her. Like that Lily woman telling her she couldn't do action... as if they had a patent on it. He knew how the studios worked, creating their own stars and then tying them down. By hook or by crook. He himself fairly ran the biggest of them.

And it was a saving grace that these girls were all uneducated, and all so young. It didn't take much for the studios to nail them. He needed to see that contract. But he could hardly march to Modak and demand to see it without revealing everything. About him and Rajbala. It would cause a scandal. If really her contract was for another two years they would ask unheard of monies to release her, and he himself did not have that kind of money. And even if he did, Raju did not want to leave her life of a star. He would have to let her carry on, for now, with Unique or another studio, before she was ready for him...their life together.

She had freed herself from his embrace, and was

opening out the bottles of pickles and candies he kept for her. She gestured to him, '*Khaben?* Want some?' She never used the more informal '*tumi*' for him, always '*apni*'. Was it her respect for him? Or...did she still not think him close enough? Why he so often imagined the worst when it came to her, he didn't know. She always seemed happy enough with him.

How he envied Shankar Chattopadhyay. To make a star of Ramola Devi and keep her too! Shankar was a winner. He had made his life out of nothing. But Ramola? Born with a silver spoon in her mouth, acting like she was the Queen herself! Did she know what it was to want and not have? Life was kind to the likes of Ramola Devi, they had had everything, and all too easy. Shankar sheltered her from all worries, like she was a child. He himself had disliked her from the start, when he first joined Bharat Talkies, that was six years ago, though he admired Shankar Da. Still, he had made sure that she liked him, always jumping up to open doors and pull up chairs for her. She liked that, when people danced attendance on her, looked small in her presence.

He lit a cigarette, puffed out a ring of smoke and watched it rise and disappear. Thanks to Ramola Devi, smoking was now prohibited inside the studio buildings. She said it choked her!

He could see Raju pottering in the next room. He smiled as he watched her. How different Raju was from the likes of Ramola. She had spirit. Always wanting to try new things, good and bad. She had smelled his cigarette. 'You didn't give me the first pull,' she scolded, then ran to him, 'give it to me'.

He allowed her one puff then pushed her away, '*Naaaaa*, no more'.

But he secretly loved the way she would run up to him for a puff. Her way of always wanting to do things she wasn't supposed to. That's why she came with him the first time, he suspected, and then every time thereafter. For the thrill of having a secret. And of plotting, and planning together. Like they had planned to trump Mishtu Modak and that Lily Madam of hers.

Raju wasn't the first to wring an outside studio deal. Only, she had had no sense really, of her own worth. *He* had told her. She hadn't even known what was happening inside most of the other studios. He knew, of course, it was part of his job. Some actresses and actors in Bombay were doing it, blackmailing the studios to let them work on their terms.

Bombay had more money floating about, new companies making unheard-of one picture offers to the stars. They were safer here in Calcutta, less money flying here and more control for the big studios. Though, with the smaller studios the star always had more power, to swing things his or her way. And Unique Pictures was no Bharat Talkies. With Bharat Talkies it was different—there even the biggest stars knew their place.

Still, they had their share of troubles, god knew. He had been at his wits end the night that that Menoka went and hanged herself. That rascal officer at the *thana* had fancied he would set him up with one of the studio girls!

'You're a lucky man, Anil Babu, sitting in heaven, with these beautiful *apsara*s...not like us, criminals and thugs, that's our life...what I would give to change places with you for a night…' As if his nights were spent in the company of those whores.

Raju, she was different. And anyway, they had not spent any nights together. Only afternoons and evenings. It was seven or eight months now, and nobody the wiser. But how long could they carry on like this? Somebody was sure to get to know, some time, no matter how careful he was. And Raju, never as careful as she should be. Always too sure of herself, not thinking what could happen.

But then she had not seen enough of the world, and he had everything to lose if anyone at Bharat Talkies knew. He could not have that, not at this time when everything was going his way.

He had been like a right hand to Shankar Da, and Shankar Chattopadhyay now trusted him more than even his wife might know, or even like, for that matter. He knew that his boss watched him closely, and that he liked his quick thinking. And the fact that he could keep a calm head and a smile on his face, no matter what. He'd even had him attend some of the board meetings, telling him to take notes, but Anil had had a feeling that Shankar Da had greater things in store for him. On the Bharat Talkies board sat those that were the toast of Calcutta's high society. A banker, a nationalist leader, a judge, a famous professor, two top directors. In their midst, he was a nobody. But Anil understood his boss well enough. He was forceful and could get his way, but also gave in to people…those on whom he depended. He had already given him charge of the studio's daily business, so he could work fully on the new picture. Not the expenses, though, Shankar Da still approved those. But the boss would open up to him more...in the days ahead, he knew that.

Ramola Devi, now she was a harder nut, for all that porcelain beauty of hers. She did not allow many informalities, and she wasn't the kind that trusted easily. She could also have a sharp tongue, and sometimes Shankar would gently scold her for it. Many of those at Bharat Talkies were there because of Shankar Da. He had a knack for drawing people towards him, and he knew how to keep a balance between all of them. If Bharat Talkies had grown into what it was, one reason was that Shankar Da had kept Ramola away from the day-to-day business of it.

II

Raju smirked, as she looked across the room at Anil.

'He'd be good,' she thought, as he lit another cigarette, '...comic hero...running into things, hitting his head...' Him with his round head, cherubic face, and round popping eyes. How she wanted to do a comedy, what fun it would be. They could do it together, her and him, when they had their new company. Should she tell him? He might not like it. He really was so very serious about everything, so affected by anything she said or did... it wasn't always fun anymore. She frowned. She just needed to grumble about this or that or the other, and watch him start to fret. He wanted her to be happy...all of the time. As if she was a child! As if anyone could be happy all the time.

He put out his cigarette then strolled back to her.

'*Ki*, what's worrying you?' he placed a hand on her head.

'I don't like this place, it's smelly, stuffy...' Raju screwed her nose and tossed her head. 'The first one was so nice, all *sahib*s and *mem*s living that side...even the last one...'

'But this one is closer, easier for you, isn't it?'

True, it was closer to Unique studio than the earlier place, she had had the *durwan* get her a *tanga*.

'But I liked that last place,' she pretended to sulk, watching his face.

'Now, don't you start again,' he put an arm around her. 'You know we have to be careful...that *masima* of yours...at that last place...kept asking...seen your wife somewhere. Very modern girl, I'm very fond of *gaan* myself, I'm sure she won't mind singing for me sometime. Anyhow, that story about me renting a place so you can practice your music which my parents don't approve of, it just didn't hold water. Just that I was paying her so much that she kept quiet. But she would have placed you sooner or later, that gossip*baaz*...then gone to town with a trumpet. And what's wrong with this place? I got all your things here. You said it was nice, now what's happened? I only latched the windows so the neighbours don't pry, haven't you seen how close the houses are?'

'Yes, yes, I know, I have to hide myself, as if I'm a *chor* or dacoit or something...' now she was really sulking. 'If you're so scared, then...why all this...leave me...I still have Unique studio, if nothing else...'

She would issue this threat often enough but it never failed in its impact.

'Why do you have to say that, you know you're meant for bigger things...I told you, you're going to be out of Unique...' Anil was disquieted.

'And how? How Anil Babu?' Raju was in no mind to relent. 'Will you get me into Bharat Talkies? Can you? If you're so close to the *malik* there, why can't you tell them to get me out? Throw the money on Unique's face...whatever they ask...no, you won't, because you're afraid. Look at Mishtu Da, everybody knows what he and Lily Madam are up to inside that office, in the afternoons. Does he care? He doesn't care...he isn't afraid of anyone...'

Anil pursed his lips. What could he say? How could he make her understand? Mishtu Modak had nothing to lose in his own backyard, he had. Modak had no character, everyone knew him to be in the clutches of his mistress. Anyhow, he didn't ever plan to take that Lily woman home, she was his paid keep, like so many such doings in the studio para. Raju, she was different. He might have married her there and then, only he knew she wouldn't... not yet. He had to wait for his time. Not that he had not thought of getting her into Bharat Talkies, somehow. But then, how could he without raising eyebrows? What was he to tell Shankar Da? He was no Ambarish Dev Burma. For the likes of Ambarish, people looked the other way. But people like him had to guard their backs. The studio *para* was always gossiping, people there always looking for something to pin on you, sully your character.

His silence made Raju angrier still.

'Yes, now you have nothing to say...' her voice had risen. 'Why should your great Bharat Talkies have a girl like me? Rajubala only gives *maja,*' she snorted, 'to the *chotolok*, no? Those *char* anna *wala*s, those loafers... how can they put me in a *bhadralok*'s picture? Up the *bhadralok*'s backside, that's what I say...'

It was true, everything about Raju went against Bharat Talkies...its brand of high class entertainment. That Lily woman had hit the nail on the head, when she had said no outside action. No one really could think of Raju as anything but a *masaladar* heroine, '*maal*', as her *char* anna *wala* admirers loved to call her. Action, dances, her body, that was it. But who knew if she couldn't rise above it. That she couldn't be a great actress. He had put it into her head. Now it was his nemesis.

These spats saddened him, though Raju would be herself soon enough. She never dragged it long. Rather, she would be amiable sooner than him. That was her—nothing ever affected her too deeply. She didn't even seem to think things through too much...like...how much he cared for her, or even, why she would come with him... did she really love him? And he...had thought of nothing but her. From when he had first seen her in a Raju Darling picture. He had furtively hung about the Unique studio, one day accosting her outside the gates...he'd been prepared for a sneer or a scolding, even worse. But she had heard him.

He'd been reckless then, he wanted to start a bioscope company he had told her, she and him, equal partners...he might have said anything, to get her. Not that he had not meant it. He had imagined it, she and him, like Ramola and Shankar...only he was no Shankar Chattopadhyay. He was afraid...Raju was right. Afraid of taking a risk. Afraid of spoiling his chances...Shankar's trust in him, his hopes that if he kept going Shankar Da would help him start his own company. And he had Raju. For now. What if he took a chance and failed? What if Bharat Talkies had failed Shankar? Would he still have had Ramola?

Raju was grumbling softly.

'You didn't say what to do...about that outside picture? What do I say to Bharatmata now? Their Sen Babu said, by month's end you will have your advance... you only have to say yes. The boss himself will come to your house with the money. Now if I tell them I can't do action...what? As if I know what to tell these people?'

She nudged him. '*Bolun na*, tell me, what do I tell them?'

He didn't look at her. He didn't know, he just didn't know. Anything he would tell her might then come back to bite him. What indeed was the worth of these so-called agreements that studio people like him would press on these girls, who sometimes couldn't write even their own names? What if she just went ahead with Bharatmata, action and all? And what if she then had a showdown with Unique? If he knew her, Raju would drag him right into it.

Ramola

'This won't do Ramola, and it's no good sulking...'

Shankar was exasperated. Why couldn't she see sense? She simply couldn't afford to lose control, no matter what. And he had told her that a hundred times before. She had her back to him now, standing stiffly by the window, angry. But it was no use, really.

'You're going to have to keep a lid on yourself...this just won't do...' he said again.

Another two days this time he would be on board the ship. If only he could leave behind a part of himself with her! There would be others, like Nishith Babu, who would try her patience. When he wasn't there. When she was running the studio. And she would have to deal with them like he did. Not let it get the better of her, like with Nishith Babu that morning. Anyhow, the likes of Nishith Roy had age on their side and they had to be humoured, no matter how tiresome they got. Bharat Talkies' reputation was built on it, on him having brought them all together, Nishith Roy to Ambarish Dev Burma, even Ramola herself...the best of the old and new.

Nishith Babu had gotten it into his head that Ramola needed tutoring to better get into the skin of Mira. After all, devotionals were his forte.

'*Hocche na, ma, thik hochhe na,* you're not getting it right, my dear,' he'd nodded earnestly, having seen the shot sequences.

'I dislike his all-knowing manner, and I won't have it,' Ramola had declared once they were alone. 'Why on earth did you have to show them to him?'

'Because he kept asking, and I couldn't very well keep putting him off. It's not even a full half hour, what we have now. We mightn't even keep half of it in the end, you know that,' Shankar had retorted.

'And he judges me from that? Is this my first picture? Am I a nobody? To be lectured like a school girl?'

She had not hidden her displeasure and Nishith Babu

had left injured. But not before a bout of histrionics, to which he was given, and which Shankar would have liked to avoid at all cost.

'No matter, *ma*,' he'd nodded tearfully. 'I am just an old man, a Vaishnava *bhakt*. It had been my longest desire to make a picture on Mirabai and her Krishnaprem. But I did not mean to interfere. I have had a long career, and shaped many others, I now want only to be with God... no matter, *ma*, you have my blessings...'

Nishith Babu was getting on in years, but in all fairness, he had contributed in fashioning her screen persona. He had been around since the very early days, when the first silent features were being made, had joined Bharat Talkies soon after her first picture had released and he had directed her in her best pictures. He was a good many years older than she, and she had been an obedient pupil, and he, though affectionate, had often claimed credit for her successes. It was something she had come to resent.

'Why couldn't you just play along? It's not as if he's going to have anything to do with this picture?' Shankar was feeling drained. They'd argued the last half hour, and it really was not worth it. He still had things to get done before Thursday, when he left...just two and a half days.

'Now he's going to play the injured party to one and all, saying we belittled him, that we have no need for him anymore...getting the *oho*s and *aha*s out of everyone under this roof. It doesn't go in your favour, Ramola...our favour, you should know that. Now I'm going to have to go around and speak to him sometime today, hear him out. He's still highly regarded, by one and all, you know that. Why do I have to do this every time, Ramola? *Why don't you learn*?' He found his voice raising and stopped himself.

She turned to him. 'I still don't know what you mean, Shankar...just play along with him. Why do we have to humour people that don't matter? Why do you always say that? It was no business of his, it's not his picture. It's our studio and our picture...you're going to make it how you have thought of it. And I know what I want to bring to Mira...'

'Look, Ramola,' Shankar lowered his voice.

'This is the last time I will say this. There are two ways of doing it. Or anything for that matter when it comes to the studio. You can either tell people on their faces, "I'm the boss", or you can smile your way through things and still get them done how you would like it, like how I do it. You know only too well that I do everything my own way. Only sometimes...' he paused, it seemed an effort to put it all into words. 'It helps to let people think they got their way with you, even if just a little bit. I've found that people take their orders more easily that way...' He paused again, catching his breath.

'Do you think it's been easy with me, with the likes of Nishith Babu or any of the others that think I'm good only for managing the studio...that there's no art left in me? That I'm only the producer, though they will not ever say it. Do you even know what superiority Nishith Babu would direct at me, when he first joined the studio, no matter that I was the boss here? When we were still new, and him joining us made a difference to Bharat Talkies. When you had done only one picture, and I was struggling to get it all together...'

'And…why didn't you ever tell me this before,' Ramola was angrier now at the thought of Nishith Babu making things difficult for poor Shankar.

'Because I saw that he could shape you, that he and you worked well together…in those days. I didn't want you to be affected by any of it. Anyhow, Nishith Babu wasn't the only one. I realized that they had age on their side, they had been around for longer. I was much younger, back from America with big things in my head. People laughed at the idea of a Hollywood kind of studio here—when things around here were random at best… anything could happen in the name of making a bioscope picture. They would call me foolhardy, you know that… some of them who've been with us all of this time would have been happier, Ramola…had we failed…'

'I know that Shankar…but you still kept them…'

'Yes, I did, and that's because just you and I cannot make a world-class studio. We need these people, who are all good at what they do. And for that we will need to play along with them. Keep them in good humour…and, more importantly, Ramola, because it is only too easy for us to be called impudent…that success went to our heads. It is something that makes people band up against you, if only to bring you down. It is something that you have to guard against, more especially when I am going to be away, darling.'

Ramola had a tear rolling down her face. 'Tell me,' she whispered, 'do you sometimes also play along with me, just to keep me in good spirits…like with everyone else here…?'

'Really, Ramola…how did you even,' he started, then

the glint was in his eyes. 'Well yes, darling, you know, given how difficult you can be sometimes, and so angry, one does have to be careful with you, doesn't one?'

'You're horrible Shankar Chattopadhyay,' Ramola smirked through her sniffle. 'Always lecturing me, like I was the last person left on earth.'

He was grinning now, 'You are, for me...'

***

A smile appeared on his face as he looked up from his desk and out of the window. There she was, in her pink cardigan, clutching the folds of her sari, daintily treading her way through the grass, Nishith Roy plodding by her side. Nishith Babu was absorbed in the speech that he was delivering to her, and she nodding demurely, though he could tell from her smile that possibly she was not even hearing all of it. It didn't matter, so long as Nishith Babu was kept happy. People seldom realized, not if one smiled and nodded from time to time.

After lunch Ramola had announced that she was going to see Nishith Babu.

'You don't have to, you know,' he had said. 'He'd wanted to speak with me anyways, he'd said, remember? Some ideas in his head possibly, about how this picture can best be made...' he'd grimaced. 'I'll speak with him, he'll be fine, leave it to me...I do this every day'.

'No, I'll speak with him' she had said quietly.

Anyhow, she'd always been more intimate with Nishith Babu than he, being his protégé, though of late she had distanced herself from him. But Ramola could be as charming as she could be cold, and he watched amused as they walked in the studio grounds, she lessening her pace now and then to keep with him, and he touching her arm or patting her shoulder as she laughed with him.

He'll be in good spirits, the old boy, when I find him later today, Shankar grinned to himself. In all truth, Nishith Babu was fond of Ramola. While he had never really hit it off with the old man. Nishith Babu thought him to be a *sob-janta*, a brash know-it-all, though why he couldn't say. He'd always been respectful enough. He sighed. It was something that he had to live with, people sometimes imagining him to be overbearing no matter how amiable he made himself. But then, he had a studio to helm, he couldn't not be in control. Still, he always did go that extra mile to have people on his side...Ramola didn't.

It would be good practice for her, not having him around these coming weeks...getting people to do her bidding, her way. Anyhow, anything really important could wait until he was back. It would be the day-to-day while he was away, and she only needed to be more patient.

Anil would help, and she thought well of him, thank heavens for that! Anil never lost his composure. That boy will go far in life, thought Shankar.

Anil

Head in his hands, Anil stared at the blotter and ink bottle on the desk by his bed.

No one had any inkling in his lodgings that he worked in the bioscope line. His landlady knew him to be a modest office-goer who paid his rent on time, never complained about the quality of meals and hardly ever had visitors. Had she known, she'd have sent him packing. No matter that she was a bioscope fan. He had himself gotten her tickets for the afternoon shows sometimes.

That was it, with most people. They loved bioscope pictures, but treated bioscope people like they were lepers. Not that he actually acted in the pictures, nor had he any such desire, still, he was of that ilk. What would she say...if she knew of his doings? That he had rented rooms over a Muslim *basti*, near the office *para*, where he took Raju. Before that in a gully off Free School Street. He'd moved two places now, the first one because he couldn't afford it after the first two months, it being right in the heart of the *sahib para*. And the last one because that *bariwali* was getting close to placing Raju, she'd been another one for the bioscope. Though Raju looked very different in her costumes and make-up...but she was sharp that one, even with her glasses. And then Raju, stopping to chat with her, bursting into laughter when she had wondered '*Tomake kothay jeno dekhechi*...haven't I seen you somewhere...?'

Now she didn't like the place he'd gotten. As if he had people waiting to give out their rooms to a fellow that came there on some days with a girl he called his wife. People smelled a rat the minute he got talking. He'd only gotten this last one because it had lain empty the past year, after the Hindu–Muslim trouble in the neighbourhood. He hadn't told Raju that. Not that she would have batted an eyelid, that girl didn't seem to have fear in her.

He'd been at his wits end since that evening. She'd thrown another fit. She had had a fresh row with that Lily woman the day before, and she had gone and said no to the Bharatmata people.

'*Khushi toh*, happy? Now my chance is gone...' she'd sobbed, as he had tried to calm her. She was not going to see him again, she'd said.

'If you want to see me come to Unique studio and get me out of there, else find someone else.'

He'd walked half the way home in despair before he had remembered to catch a bus...it was too long a way to walk.

His cold dinner lay uneaten on the *jal-chowki*, where the manservant Sibhu had left it. Sibhu had already made two rounds, '*Ki go dadababu*, won't you eat?'

His insides were churning. What if she had meant it, that she wouldn't see him again? If even she did come around, it couldn't go on like this. She felt caged, them making her do those very same antics in the same Raju Darling pictures, over and over again...that woman telling her she'd be no good at anything else...the poor girl didn't want even to look at the handbills of her own pictures.

He decided that same instant. He would have to speak to Shankar Da, tomorrow. It was just one day before he left. If Shankar Da trusted him enough he would hear him out. He had to get Raju into Bharat Talkies, somehow, from Unique Studio, even if it was the last thing that he would ever ask of Shankar Da.

'I've given six years to Bharat Talkies...no, to Shankar Da...' he thought as he lay back in bed and stretched out his aching body. He will do it...for me. But what if he says no? His head throbbed.

What indeed would he tell Shankar Da? Could he even put words to it...him and Raju...what he felt for her. That he had to have her...somehow...anyhow...that he couldn't bear it anymore. But then, wouldn't Shankar Da know it anyway? If that was how he felt...about Ramola.

Ramola

It was nearing mid-day. Shankar Chattopadhyay was in his office at the studio gathering up the papers he would need to take back home. This time tomorrow he would be on the ship, on his way to America. It was a mild winter's day but he'd felt warm enough to turn on the fan over his head. Sipping on a tepid cup of tea, he was running through things in his mind, making sure nothing was left behind.

He felt worn out. 'I must be getting old...I'm going to take half the year off after this one gets done and dusted,' he groaned to himself.

His trunks were all ready. Suits, sweaters, silk shirts, had all been ironed, neatly folded and packed and then the shoes and hats and gloves. He'd been unable to sleep the night before, lying awake, a hundred thoughts racing through his mind.

'I'll rest easy only after I've boarded that ship...I'm going to have a glass of champagne...then sleep...'

He was looking forward to it, the luxury of lounging about...reading...watching the waters, lunches and dinners, hearing the band play in the evenings...he'd soon get restless, though, with all that rest, and be rearing to get to work again. Now, if Ramola was with him, the hours would fly, even the long days on board.

He'd not been much of a husband these last months, seeing her mostly at work in the studio, and getting home often after she'd eaten dinner by herself and was getting ready for bed. When did they last dine out, just the two of them, he wondered? Was it at the Great Eastern, the day they had had the Swadeshi strike and had to stop work? Ramola had always protested when he got too preoccupied with work, but this time around she hadn't complained.

He was almost ashamed, thinking of it. He'd get her a present to make up for it. Perhaps that brooch that she had admired. He could stop by the shop on Park Street, on his way back. She had stayed home that morning. He too would be on his way by lunchtime. Anil had stopped by the house early, as he was finishing his tea in the drawing room. 'Some last things, Shankar Da…at the studio…' he'd said. Though what more he couldn't imagine. He'd gone over everything with Anil, in the minutest of details. A little bit tense, he imagined, hadn't sat down even. Well, he had Ramola to go to…while he was gone.

Mirabai was coming along nicely. And for that he had Ramola to thank. While he had spent his days working on the Miracle deal, she'd supervised costumes, coordinated the rehearsals and eased the director's job for him.

Would she turn director someday, he wondered. Direction was still a man's job, but then Ramola was a torchbearer. She had entered the pictures when only the lowest class of women went about in the studios and dignified film acting.

'I'll have to plant it in her head...' he smiled to himself. He had shielded her from the business side of things and she had been glad for it. 'You be the big star,' he would tell her lovingly. She was a determined woman, but in their business there were all kinds, and not all of them gentlemen, or women, for that matter.

'Don't work up any trouble for yourself while I'm gone. Think it all over, speak to Anil...think of me...' he had whispered as he had hugged her under the sheets that morning.

He took another sip of his tea but it tasted bitter. Why was Anil taking so long? Didn't he say half past eleven... or was it twelve? He wanted something cold to drink. He felt the sweat on his brow and loosened his tie. His palms were moist and the tea cup nearly slipped from his hand as he placed it back on the saucer.

He raised himself to increase the speed of the fan but felt a tautness on one side and sat down again. Had to be the late breakfast of *luchi-aludam* he had ordered at the studio. He needed a lemonade to ease it. He picked up the phone on his desk to ring the canteen, but found himself trying to call the house.

***

Almost as if it was destined, Ramola thought. 'You live for Bharat Talkies, and you're going to die there someday,' she had told him angrily when he had missed meals and worked late. How was she to tell that he would take her at her words?

By the time Sailen Kaka had arrived it was only the matter of getting the death certificate. The studio's staff was gathered outside his office, everyone struck into a state of mute disbelief.

It was all so very strange. Why would Shankar suffer a heart attack? There had never been anything wrong with his heart. She had decided to come to the studio after Shankar left home that morning, though she'd said she would be home that day. Lunch at the Grand, she had planned on the spur of the moment. She was going to surprise him. They were having his favourite lobster buffet, she'd seen in it the morning papers and booked two places. She was already out when they had called the house...on her way to the studio. Anil had found him... slumped at his desk next to the telephone, the receiver laid down beside him. He'd stayed at the door for some moments calling out to Shankar before moving up to the desk to touch his arm. He had died so silently...even the bearer who sat on duty outside the office had not known.

'Shouldn't we keep the body another day, madam, for people to pay their respects,' Anil had said.

'No. No waiting, I don't want a *tamasha*,' had been her retort.

She had sat in Shankar's chair till very late, until Anil and the other men returned from the *ghat*. In her first state of denial and defiance she had wanted to accompany them. But as the minutes had ticked by and disbelief had dissolved into a thudding ache, she had let Anil and the others at the studio take over.

There had been so much happening so suddenly, as they had started to take the body outside. '*Ei*, be careful, hold under the head, Subol, take the legs,' someone had shouted to those carrying him out. Like on a busy film set, Ramola thought, with someone or the other always calling instructions, managing things.

As a girl she had been taught that decent women did not show their grief in public. In any case, she did not want to cry or even look at the body very much in the few hours before they took him away. Why do women cling to their dead husbands, she had pondered, as she sat alone after they'd left...as if desperately living their last moments together. She only found it unbearable to look at him that way, like he had fallen asleep in tiredness.

She looked at the bedroom clock through bleary eyes. It was almost two in the morning, already the day after Shankar's death. She was still wearing her sari from that morning.

Was there anyone that she should send word to, she wondered. Her father had died some years before and her mother was a sick invalid confined to her bed in their family home. She did not have any brothers or sisters. The rest of her family she had almost broken with after she had married Shankar and entered the pictures.

Shankar's own father was long dead. His elder brother had taken to petty fraud and Shankar had looked after his younger brother and sister till he left home at twenty-four and his world had been the studio and the people there. Still, perhaps it was better not having a family around her. It meant she had to say less...hear less... the sympathies and commiserations were unbearable, somehow.

Her thoughts went back to that afternoon...to Shankar

in his very last moments. Who was he telephoning? Before he had fallen on his desk? What if she had been with him then? Could she have done something, called a doctor? Saved him? Why had she not heeded those tell-tale signs of sickness? He had died so very helpless, not even able to call out. She struggled to fight back her tears as she went through the motions of changing, washing and getting into bed, staring at the wall in front of her. Not looking at his side of the bed.

She remembered...there were observances. The duties of a widow, duties which people would expect even of the very modern Ramola Devi...the Hindu *shradh* ceremony. Would she wear white now...no jewellery...or hairstyles? She knew so little about what to do and what not. Should she be at home for some days? Should she go to the studio? Or, would that not be right?

It was funny, she thought later, how hunger and thirst and the bodily needs did not die completely even in moments of grief and anguish. Or, at least, she had felt the pangs of hunger as she watched the first rays of light filter in through the early morning mist.

'What should I wear,' she mused as she got out of bed. Like she did every morning. She bathed and chose a white and blue chiffon. She did not wear much of cotton, and her wardrobe really had nothing that was right for a widow.

She decided to go down for breakfast, instead of calling for it in her bedroom, like she did on most days. She needed to see the household staff. 'I'm the master of the house now,' she told herself. They'd been huddled together under the stairs when she had come in the night before and she had walked up to her room without a word to any of them. Perhaps Anil or one of the others from the studio had said a few words to them...explained things. Still, they shouldn't think she was broken, it just wouldn't do.

She ate her toast sitting in the dining room, at one end of the well-polished dining table. Shankar always came down for his breakfast, fully dressed, at the same time every day. He never ate in bed. As she drank her tea, the expensive mahogany table stretched for miles in front of her. Why ever had they bought such a long table? It was too big, and now it seemed about to swallow her. What am I to do with myself the whole day, she thought as she ate. She dreaded sitting about. She would have to find something to do, something useful. To keep her mind from going to the day before, over and over again. From remorse overpowering her into a state of immobility. She ate slowly, dragging that meal, only because it made the minutes go by.

She had drained her teacup when the maid put her head in through the door. Anil Babu had come and was waiting in the drawing room. It was only half past seven. He's not slept, Ramola sighed, as she pulled herself up. As she walked into the large sitting room, Anil looked almost surprised to see her. He had his legs stretched out before him, nearly reclining on the sofa, as if prepared for a long wait. Perhaps he did not expect her to see him so soon. Possibly, he was relieved to see her collected. He stood up, and they sat silently. Then he came to the business.

She would need to call a board meeting. And think

about the future of Bharat Talkies. He was there, of course, she could depend on him, at all times. He had arranged to stay at night in the studio, till things were settled. So she needn't worry too much. She had to rest, get well. He had instructed those at the studio, nobody was to bother her. Also better, he thought, to not receive too many people in the house at this time, not knowing who had what in mind. Shankar Da had explained everything to him, how he wanted things done when he was gone...should they close the studio for two or three days now, before they decided what they would do?

Ramola was thinking of *Mirabai*. What would happen to it now? Who would direct it? So much of their efforts had gone into it. Should she now give up the whole thing? It was not just any picture, and it had stood on Shankar's shoulders.

Her thoughts wandered back to Anil. He was going to see Avinash Mukherjee in a day or two, he was saying. Perhaps he had not heard yet. They needed to know what Miracle Pictures would do...now that Shankar Chattopadhyay was no longer making *Mirabai*.

PART 2

I

Ambarish Dev Burma studied himself in the long ornate mirror in his cluttered bedroom. He had draped his mother's old pink Benarasi, his favourite, the one that she had worn at his rice ceremony. It was fading now, the threads bare in places, the *zari* had lost its sheen. What to do, he thought, fingering the elaborate *karigari*. He didn't trust any of the servants with Ma's things, and he couldn't very well put it out to air himself, girl's job that was. That imbecile sister of his had left with the best things, the rest had stayed in Ma's cupboards, supposedly for the girl he would marry. Ma would do it all herself, putting the saris out to air on the sprawling *chhat*, her trusted Dinu scouring the folds for any *poka*, then lining the folds with neem leaves and little pouches of *kalo jeera* made with Ma's old saris. Ma didn't like the mothballs from the big shops, the smell choked her, she would say. And poisoned the fabrics. Destroyed them.

He was sad when she died. But it had been for the best. He grinned. What if she knew of the girls he then started bringing to the house? He had moved into her room, where she had spent her last days, moved in his things with hers, cluttering it up. But he liked it that way. She'd kept her saris in the big wooden *almari*, all neatly stacked, her jewellery in the hidden safe underneath the saris. What was left of it, anyhow, after she had dispatched the best pieces with that snotty girl. Her diamond necklace that his father had gifted her on the birth of a son, it rightfully belonged to him. But she'd given it to her. And the *pakhi* pendant that he had his heart set on, for as long as he could remember, that exquisite piece from Ma's wedding...of rubies and emeralds and pearls, given by her *dadu*, her mother's father.

Ma had always loved her better...comforted her... shielded that girl...from him. Didn't she herself tell him to take care of her? Now you have a sister, she'd whispered through her tears as she had nursed her newborn girl staring up at Baba's garlanded photograph. He'd tried, but Putu's coming had spoilt things between them, him and Ma. And he had made that girl pay for it. Ma didn't realize, until after Putu was two and her sobs poured out in words. What a pity Putu had not turned out deaf and dumb, like the *mali*'s little boy. He could have carried on then, and nobody the wiser. Her squeals had delighted him, as he dug his nails harder into her sides. He would pull her by her thin hair as she crawled along the marble floors, standing her up on those plump wobbly legs. Then let go and watch her fall, sometimes face down on the stone. And run to find his mother to the kitchen or *kal-ghar*, calling out that Putu had hurt herself again.

Still, it didn't go out of hand until the day she really saw him, his mistake, not closing the door, thinking she would be longer taking her bath. Putu was on the mat by Ma's four-poster bed, face down. He'd said he would take her eyes out if she moved or looked up. The landing had to be perfect, right in the middle of her, his feet straight on those round plump bottoms when he leaped from the bed. Putu yelled, but somehow he didn't hear it. Ma was at the door, her long hair dripping water, wetting the front of her quickly wrapped sari, trickling down her breasts in snake-like patches.

Putu was packed off at fifteen with that donkey Ma chose for her. He had hoped she wouldn't land a match, that burn on her right hand had discoloured and crumpled the flesh and it always showed, no matter what frills Ma stitched on to the ends of her long sleeved blouses. Ma had guarded Putu night and day, sometimes even taking her into the *kal-ghar* with her when she bathed. But even she was not good enough, he had found ways to get at Putu. One time he had gotten half her oily plait, smoothly chopping it off as she cowered against the wall. The other time, when Ma had gotten that dreadful pneumonia fever and had a coal fire in her room, and Putu would nurse her in the nights…it was the only time she'd fought back, even tried to hit him with those iron tongs she would use for the hot water as he had pulled her hand down on the coals. Ma had stirred at the sound of the scuffle and called her out frantically as Putu had screamed, but the room was dark except for the red of the burning coals, and she was too weak to stop it. And by then he had wanted Ma to know.

All those girls…when he got to them he knew he had to be more careful. That was a lesson he learnt once Putu left. Ma might have let Putu stay on for a bit more if not for that night, and once she got better she marshalled all her resources to get her married off, like it was her war against him. Within a year Putu was gone. And Ma was not the same after she went. She talked less, moved less about the house. Like her life had ended. Like he was nothing, nobody. And he knew that she told Putu never to come back, after the one time that she'd come to visit with that imbecile boy, her head glowing with that awful red *sindoor*. Uglier than she'd ever been, with her blunt nose and placid stupid face. She looked like Baba...while he...he was a picture of Ma, him with his slender frame, high forehead and straight nose, his fair skin, and hair that would fall across his face. He looked gentle. It had been useful...with those other girls, one had to be tender with them at first...loving...love was like a drug for that lot, a *nesha*...they couldn't ever get enough of it. You could get anything out of them, if they thought you loved them.

His thin lips spread in a smile as he folded up the Benarasi. Dirty, worm-eaten, puerile little things... one had had a rotten sore on the side of her stomach, scratched it with her dirty finger nails till it oozed pus and blood. What was her name, now...he couldn't remember...but he remembered her face, those hungry eyes as she had waited in the audition room with some pimp. He'd picked her on the spot, to play the second lead he had said, and kept her. He'd changed his mind, he said afterwards...girl didn't have the right expressions... who would dare to question him on that.

Though quite a stir there'd been, all that murmuring turning to silence in front of him...he did rather enjoy it. That was one thing about the boss, now dead and gone. He had never interfered, never questioned. Not even when that Menoka did herself in. She'd gotten him there, sure as hell, he'd hardly have thought it…though…to be fair to him, he did put the angle in her head, sacrifice in the name of love. She had been drinking, crying. She wanted marriage. To give it all up. Like that wife in his *Pativrata: The Good Wife*. What was going to happen to that one, he wondered? With the boss gone, what would the great and good Ramola Devi do now? Stop his picture?

Widows in white…not always as hapless as one wanted them to be. Ma now, she should have let him take charge of things, after Baba. But no, she wanted it all her way. That did it in for that wretched Putu of hers. Ramola made him think of Ma…all that pride. When really they were no better than those little worms that would dance to his tunes. He hadn't ever been able to get even with Ma. Only Putu. Ma had held her own, till the end. He'd again started having his nightly visions. Of strewn limbs and bloody faces. As he lay in bed at night thinking of Ma, he would feel a stirring in his bowels, which kept growing. He could see Putu and those other girls, their limbs severed from their bodies, battered faces and clumps of hair pulled out by the roots. He would turn over to bury his face in the pillow, for he could sometimes sense his mother watching him in the dark, from wherever she was, as more of the girls were battered unconscious by an invisible hand and he saw the blood stream from their noses and mouths.

Often he wanted to feel the broken bodies…made slippery by the blood on them. Ma hadn't deserved him. She'd let him down. The likes of her, and Ramola

Devi, they judged him. What for? For only having his way with the rotten likes of Menoka? Didn't everyone around want the same out of those little tarts? Didn't they all secretly envy him, for getting it all? All of them at the studio that went whispering behind his back. What about Baba? He'd had his way with Ma. She would plead with him saying their little boy would hear...and he had pretended to sleep as Ma had wept in pain. Still, she had cried for Baba, him that jumped from the roof of their Chowringhee estate house one fine morning, just like that, but not before he had planted that horror of a Putu in her.

Just thinking about it outraged him. The injustice of it all. Maybe...maybe...she'd secretly prayed for him to die. That's why she cried. To hide it, that she had wanted him dead. So easy then to put those flowers on his picture, light that foul incense, and be done with it. She had gotten hold of everything after him, zamindari estate, the houses...everything. Maybe Ramola too had wanted the boss dead. So she could have it all. Be boss of Bharat Talkies. Surely she didn't take it kindly that the boss had bullied his way around the place, a woman like her. But, did she *really* think it would all be so easy now, for her? He smiled, it was going to be fun seeing how she did things...her way...

What do you long for, Ramola Devi? He pondered trying to choose a jacket for the evening. Was he good for anything at all, that clumsy bully of an ox you just got off your back? Or, do you still have it all waiting, to be done to you...all of those things you only dreamt of, like they had all wanted it done to them. That's what keeps you all on your toes, doesn't it now? Keeps you from getting too big for your little slippers and high heeled shoes...

II

'*Saala, shuar,* son of a pig. Didn't I say not more than two?' Raju spat at Jhantu from the bed.

Jhantu was wiping the mess on the floor, sulking. 'How do I know...that they had a third one in there?' he nodded towards the bathroom.

'*How do I know?*' Raju mimicked him, gritting her teeth. She grabbed the wooden ashtray from its resting place by the bed and raised her arm, then thought better of it. 'Now make sure they don't go shooting their mouths off on this, or else...you'll have it, I'll put one up your backside.'

Jhantu pulled a glass shard from under his toes and made a face, 'At least you got the money. They gave more, that's something, *na*?'

'Gave? That's something, *na*? Who got it out of them? You, you son of a donkey, you pig? *Ja bhag.*' Raju spat again.

Jhantu pulled up his hunched body and ran to Raju, throwing his arms around her. Raju pushed him away, '*Ja*, get away.'

'*Maap didi*, I'll wash your feet with *gangajal* and drink, don't be angry. I swear on Ma Kali.'

'Na, leave me, move...*saaala*,' she didn't push quite so hard this time.

Jhantu knew the signs of mellowing. He hugged her around the knees laying his head on her legs. 'You'll give me a share, *na*? Of the extra?' he asked eagerly. She pinched his arm, making him wince. 'Hmmm...but you be careful, any rubbish *bhundal* you do again and I'll skin you alive,' she laughed.

Jhantu heaved relief, what a night! The 'party' had a room at Lula Lodge, next to Mangoe Lane. Two of them, *jamai* and *shala babu*, brothers-in-law, they'd said. Jhantu had stayed at the door, as always, dusting the floor and settling down to nod. He'd jumped at the crash inside, then a thud, and a yell. Only it wasn't Raju. Someone on the other side had pulled open the door and he had flown inside to find a third one there, clearly belonging to the party of two. Another brother, did they say? This one was holding his head where Raju had hit him. The crash had been a half drunk glass of some foreign stuff aimed at the party. Raju was frothing at the mouth, and about to go again for number three. She seemed to have forgotten One and Two. Two, then closest to the door had thrown it open, possibly imagining he could fly. But not with him there, *na babu*, Jhantu thought back grimly...they had had to pay for three. It wasn't easy, holding Raju at bay and getting that extra out of them. The party had exited but not before they'd issued some *gaali*s and threats which got Three the other ashtray in his back.

He'd have to go see One in a day or two, with commiserations. Perhaps Raju would agree to another outing with the party (assuredly One and Two this time) after things had cooled. Tempers, they were not good for their business. He had been in the line long enough now, the likes of them just couldn't afford to make enemies. Only, Raju didn't seem to care. And it worried him.

Jhantu went by the screen name Kusumkumar. He was nearing thirty but looked ten years younger and played boyish heroes, and beautiful celestial beings like *yaksha*s and *gandharva*s. He had a pencil thin line for a moustache, smooth arms and legs, and his hair was always well-oiled and neatly combed. Having a widowed mother and two brothers to provide for, he had put his sweet good looks to other uses. He had discovered that some among the *sahib*s preferred the company of men like him to their own *memsahib*s. And had quickly become a favourite at some men's haunts, but after a couple of unpleasant incidents, in one escaping three drunken *sahib*s abducting him in their motor car, he had become wary.

In the studio para, though, Jhantu still offered his services. Disparaged by some as '*nyaka*', unmanly, he was still good enough to handle new girls in their line. He would be gentle, coaxing them with his persuasions. Some others might lose control in a weak moment, thereby risking the job at hand, but never Jhantu. He would go about it steadily, to almost a pattern, of which he was secretly rather pleased. Until he tried it on Raju.

In those early days, before Raju had entered Unique studio, Kamala had set herself the task of finding Raju a paramour, someone she could set up to induce the girl into the ways of men. To teach her what to do and what not with the *babu*s, before Kamala could put her properly in the line. Raju had had her monthlies almost a year, so she was old enough, and if married she would be on her way to becoming a mother, Kamala had reasoned. It was time that she got her bearings or she would come to no good. But Raju had made Jhantu jittery. The girl seemed an imbecile of sorts, a nitwit. As it was, she had a ready smile that made him want to shake her, and the only times she had opened her mouth had been to intake the chops, cutlets and other treats he had bought her. He had not gotten a word out of her and every time he tried to come close she had pulled away, still the smile on her face. Determining Jhantu to exert his full charms.

He'd taken her in a tram to the *maidan*, and though recovering from a spell of indigestion had patiently waited, as Raju had savoured the roadside vendor's spicy *ghugni* and *aludam*. She ate silently as always, scraping up every drop, then raising the plate to her lips and licking it clean, before they had walked again, towards a thick clump of trees. He would do it like in the American films, he had thought. And after he'd made sure they were hidden from the road, seated on the raised ledge around a giant banyan, he had unbuttoned his shirt to reveal his bare chest, while starting to whisper the sweet nothings. He was deciding whether to fall on his knees or put his arms around her when he had felt the first rumblings. Not paying heed, he had dropped down on his knees and placed his head on her lap, face nestling against her stomach. Even as the rumbling had built into a roar. Abandoning stratagem, Jhantu had leaped up frantically looking about, even as Raju had looked on unperturbed. He had tugged off his shirt and trousers leaving them as he had retreated further into the thicket, plonking himself in the midst of some undergrowth.

He was furious. Just as he was making headway. He hoped his predicament wouldn't affect his success.

He had snatched at some large leaves hanging overhead and quickly mopped up, but on emerging from the thicket found Raju missing. Gone also were his shirt and trousers. In their place, to his bewilderment was neatly folded the sari Raju had worn, red and yellow stripes.

He'd retreated into the thicket, then emerged again in the hope that Raju too had surfaced. But almost an hour had gone by and he had lost hope. He should have known, the girl was crazed. *Bajjat*, rotten idiot, he bit back the curses that he wanted to hurl at her. He would extract each and every penny that he had spent from Kamala, that rotting old *magi*, for thrusting her on him. Emerging in his worn out *jangia*s he had tied the sari around himself like a *musalman*'s lungi, cursing, then crept his way back to the tram stop at the *maidan*'s edge, only to find Raju on the spot, robed in his shirt and trousers, wearing her smile.

He had seethed all the way in the tram while Raju had giggled on, unaffected by the looks of other travelers. Two men had thrown them coins, even as they had looked Raju up and down. As he lay that night, reliving the day's disaster, it had dawned on Jhantu that the girl was no imbecile, rather she had something unbeatable about her. And knowing the ways of men, he had remembered the *char* annas thrown at her. Months later, he'd smiled, perched on a broken seat in a musty cinema hall watching Raju Darling as she whirled in gay abandon thrusting her breasts on the one-eyed villain, eyes flashing, her lips smiling. He had known a winner. He also knew why men found Raju so very alluring. Them that liked to have their own women under their thumbs also dreamt of the one that didn't care for them or the world. The one that could hold them by the reins. Be master to them. Play games. When she danced she ruled the hearts of those that watched her, their mouths open and hearts pounding. As they had devoured her every part, she consumed and spent them. Raju was worth her weight in gold. She was the queen the likes of him dreamt of...the one they were always searching for. The one that would get whatever she set her sights on.

But that *buri magi*, that hag Kamala, she was with her always. Raju would greet him with a teasing '*Ki go*, Jhantu Da, how goes?' when they chanced to meet in the studio *para*, but Kamala had given him the cold shoulder. Still, the studio *para* had its alliances and dalliances. Jhantu fielded an envoy, the one and only *nyaka* Natabar, the thin bespectacled dance master who had as much a way with words as he did with his swaying arms, tilted hips, heaving chest and poses and postures. Natabar could be in and out of the studios, even the ones where he had no work, and nobody had ever stopped him. He would step into dance rehearsals and put up impromptu performances, at times he had crafted the steps to a new song. Natabar sometimes slept on the steps of this studio or that, in the cold they even laid out a blanket or two, in case he did come by. When Rukhsar, the Bowbazar girl who was 'second wife' to a certain studio boss died and her body was thrown into a *nulla* in the studio *para*, everybody had known what was what. Only Natabar had danced non-stop in the sun from morning till late noon right before the very same studio's gates, even threatening to tread glass shards, bringing the said studio to a standstill, and the wad of notes to arrange a burial. When Natabar had started to stop by Unique studio nobody had thought much of it. 'It's an art, *didi*,' Natabar had told Raju, 'to keep men under your thumb and also get their money out of them. You are made for it, my *rani didi*...not everyone's job that. It's our *dal-bhat*, the likes of us, our bread and butter, but these bioscope girls...they fall in love. It does them in, *didi*...'

Raju knew it well. Her mother Puti Dasi had pined away for her father, one Ramesh Babu, who had brought her to a small rented room on the ground floor of a tenement in north Calcutta, from where the only view was the mossy walls of another crumbling house. Puti had been a theatre girl at one of the city's old playhouses. He was a widower, and came to her after work and on Sunday afternoons. In a year and a half Raju was born and Puti saw the last of her *babu*. The landlord let her stay on, but she became a bonded servant to him and his wife, who lived on the floor above. She drew buckets of water, washed, scrubbed floors and cooked and by the time Raju was five or six, she was with her mother, running up and down the stairs, fetching this and that and trying to make herself useful, as if trying to earn the two square meals that she and her mother would get. Puti aged before her time, and living in the dingy dampness of the ground floor room she often had fever and a cough that made her breathless. The only person who ever came to see them was Kamala Masi, peeping in through the window of their room with her '*Ki go*?' Kamala was employed by one of the theatre companies on Cornwallis Street, and her day job was to go from house to house with the handbills for the evening shows. In the evenings, she could be serving tea, helping with the costumes, or ushering the respectable ladies to their seats on the upper tier. Raju remembered her first coming by their window in the afternoons when she was six or seven and pushing through the printed handbills. Kamala had tried to coax Puti to return to the theatre, but Puti had not agreed. She clung to the roof over her head, and Raju knew very early in her life that her mother feared everything that lay beyond their little dingy room.

It hadn't kept Raju though. Once she had gotten over the amazement of it all. Nidhu Babu the landlord, who had hair greying at the temples, would watch her from behind as she squatted in her half-wet sari at the slippery *kol-tola*, washing a heap of dirty utensils and filling water to be used in the kitchen. He would drop one or two annas in her utensils as he accosted her in the dark alleyway between the *kol-tola* and kitchen, hastily running his hands over her chest or back, or rubbing himself against her as she steadied herself to stop the wet utensils crashing to the floor. She hadn't thought of being afraid, after all, she knew 'Nidhu Jethu' for as long as she remembered. Only she wondered at first why he would want to put his hand in there, that dirty place from where she let out the turds. Him being so fussy about his puja things being spotless, sprinkling *gangajal* all over the place.

But she hadn't worried too much. She'd seen funnier things, like the time she had peeked into one of the upstairs rooms where Nidhu Jethu housed his boarders, the three office-going *babu*s. She had crept up the stairs that Sunday afternoon to see if she could reach the roof unnoticed, where *jethima*, the landlady, sunned her pickles. A groan and soft '*Baba go*, my god' had made her look in, and there they were, all three of them *babu*s, on the one *takhtposh* bed, two of them with their *gamcha*s around their waists, and *babu* number three pinned down, in nothing at all, hands tied behind his back, rope around his neck, while the other two rode on him, like he was a horse. Raju had watched in bewilderment as *babu* number one had pulled the rope around *babu* three's neck bringing the tears rolling down his face, though *babu* two had soon abandoned his riding position and had stood himself up on three's bottom, laughing as he had struggled to balance himself. Raju too had laughed from her hiding place, she had forgotten the pickles in the fun of it all.

Then there was the attorney Ukil Babu's boy, on the next roof. He had climbed across in the evenings and she had let him put her on his knees and kiss her on the mouth. He had gotten her things. The *chop*s and *singara*s that his mother sent up to him on the roof, where he studied to prepare for his examinations. He was going to be a barrister, he said, like his father. And then he would marry her. One day he had gotten a friend. And sat Raju on that other boy's knees and had him kiss her like he did. 'My wife, *re*' he had said laughingly. His wife, when she came later that summer, was draped in red, her face hidden, a girl not much older than her. Raju had gorged on the sweets they had sent out in the *para*. She had waited for when he would leave for his *sashurbari* with his new wife. That evening she had climbed across to the next roof, and emptied the two ink bottles he had had on his desk, red and blue, on the pages of notes that he had so painstakingly written out in his neat hand. For good measure she had soaked the ink sodden sheaf in a water bucket.

Jhantu Da, he was different. There just wasn't that glint in his eyes, nor ever did his hands shake, even a little bit, like Nidhu Jethu's did when he would lay them on her. And then, Molina and Saraswati, those two studio girls from the day that they took her first naked pictures, them with their hate-filled glinting eyes, and twisting *pan*-stained mouths...leering as she had twirled around, the sari starting to come off where Molina had knotted it loosely for her at the waist. The sari, tangled and messy, lying in a heap at her feet. She had swirled and swayed her naked body, posed and postured until she had felt herself grow giddy, the food in her stomach pushing upwards, towards her mouth again.

Kamala Masi, her eyes too had glinted when she had gone on and on about some golden-hearted rich boy that wanted to see her, marry her and take her home to his mother. What for? To wash his mother's feet, and dance attendance on her, like that Ukil boy's goat of a new wife.

Natabar Da...he had danced round and round her like she was a queen.

'We have no *roop*, *didi*, no beauty, but you...you have everything...something more than *roop*...something that makes them want you. Use it, *didi*, while you have it...it won't be forever.' His anger was like her own, and those like them that were dirt and dust. When she took them she played with them, every time she would turn the game around, leaving them just as they thought they had gotten what they wanted. It was fun, that bewilderment in their eyes, so much hunger. When she came to them she made sure they remembered.

III

Seth Makhandas Khemka wiped another tear off his round face, shook his head despairingly, then gulped down the rest of his tea. His ordinarily rosy visage looked about to burst from its increased ruddiness and he was perspiring from the strain of his exertions. Sethji had been one of Shankar Chattopadhyay's first backers, land magnate who had made his fortunes in the last war when he became a supplier to the *sahib*s. Ordinarily, Sethji would not drink water even at a meat-fish eating place, but he simply couldn't say no to Ramola Beti, not at this time. He had rushed to see her as soon as he had heard, he'd gone to his *des*, his village, for Devi Maa's yearly puja. Never in his life could he have imagined so tragic a *ghatna*, and poor Shankar Babu, always so *hasmukh*, always laughing.

'All *mata*'s will, *beti*' he had wept as Ramola sat quietly, wondering if it did really help, to cry it out like that. Sethji had never seen a bioscope picture, he had a repugnance mixed with fear of it, though in fact he had put his money into films when even the most forward looking among his *bhai*s would not have done it. Shankar had won him over, a Bengali boy who knew business like a *bania*, and 'so educated, brainy, what *buddhi*...' he reminisced through his tears. Makhandas Khemka had prided himself on backing such a highly educated, America-returned man of the future. Though why Shankar Babu had allowed Ramola Beti into films, he never quite understood. Such a beautiful pure girl, her face would remind him of his Devi Maa. These Bengali boys sometimes did go too far in their craze for being modern. Still, it was alright while he was there. 'But, no more, *beti*,' he had implored. 'Bioscope is no place for any *widhwa*...you know it, don't you *beti*...a widow has her honor to guard, *na beti*?' He had shaken his head, 'Not the place for a good girl like you.'

'What Sethji means is Madam needs to rest, she can give her instructions on the phone, and it will be done. That is why I am here, *na* Sethji?' Anil had intervened. But then, Anil had not been himself in the last days, the more since she had returned to the studio, Ramola mused as she sat alone. Perhaps it was the shock of it all. He was trying to shield her, she could see that, taking the responsibilities on himself. After all, he had fairly worshipped Shankar. Though some of his changed manners were plain discourteous...presenting himself unasked in Shankar's office that morning, despite her signals for privacy. It had never happened before while Shankar was there. Surely he had known enough of her to tell that she would not like it. He seemed to be always around her now, arriving at the house as she was leaving for the studio, shepherding her around, insisting she needed to rest more. Jumping to her defense at some imagined affront, even scolding poor Nishith Babu for bothering Madam. He had gone so far as to seek a private appointment at Sethji's *daftar*—'On some important matters of the studio,' he had said, without so much as looking her way. Did he imagine she had taken leave of her senses, in her grief? That now Bharat Talkies was rudderless? That she was now so weakened that she needed to be looked after...like she was only Shankar's widow...like Ramola Devi—the star—was a nobody?

Who anyway had assigned him this task? Shankar would never have wanted it. He would call her his Bengal tigress. She was already so tired of all the kindness around her. A hundred thoughts roamed her mind as she played with the pens on Shankar's desk. What should she do with *Mirabai* now? She had not spoken of it in the three days that she had been back at the studio. Everyone had seemed so uncertain around her, so afraid that they would distress her, though she had been her own self... or at least she thought so. But it had to be taken up, they had a decision to make. Who could have Shankar's imagination? Give shape and form to it. What they had imagined together. Should she speak with Nishith Babu? He might be the only one now, though he was rather fixed in his ways about things.

She had heard every kind of rumour in the last days, most of it through Anil who had dutifully visited her every day. That Ramola Devi was about to retire from the screen. That Shankar Chattopadhyay had debts, and Bharat Talkies might now be sold to an American corporation. That they were looking for somebody able enough to take over the studio's management... somebody that Ramola Devi could trust...she herself being lost to the world in her grief. And then that piece of malice in the two penny paper about her being the home-breaker that had gotten her dues, and that she now wanted to give it all up, do penance. 'Who knew...' she wondered. Amy had never been to the country, and she was already married to Shankar when they had started Bharat Talkies. No one except perhaps Shankar's closest friends had known about his first marriage. How did it get out now? The paper had said 'A source very close to Ramola Devi...' It was so odd. Only days before Shankar had brought it up, the first time since they were married. He had wanted to see his daughter Amelia on this trip abroad, and had written to Amy. Amelia was not yet two when he and Amy had parted. He had never spoken of her, and she hadn't asked. Though he did keep a photograph of her in a drawer in his study at home. A little girl with eyes like his...had he mentioned it to someone else? About wanting to see little Amelia. Perhaps he had, to someone that he had trusted. She had faulted him for it sometimes, for being more trusting than he should.

She had understood him though, when he had brought up Amy and Amelia. They had never thought of having children, it was almost a given. Of course some of the *kothawali*s who became heroines had children from their different marriages but they came and went with one picture or the next. She herself could not have taken time away from her work, nor had she ever wanted it. Shankar neither. They had needed each other to make Bharat Talkies grow, like it was their own child. Though now she wondered if they should have had a little boy or a girl. It gave her a sudden pang. How would it be to have someone to call her own, her very own flesh and blood, theirs? Amy must have found her world in her little daughter when Shankar had left them. A little warm bundle to hold close to herself when she found herself breaking. Perhaps Shankar had missed having a child around him. He could be so adoring, ever so gentle, so much of it was lost on her, when she would tell him to not fuss. She had never been one for too many shows of affection, Shankar just the other way. Perhaps a child would have changed that in her. Why did such things come to mind when it was so late...

She forced her thoughts back to the things at hand. Three new pictures...Ambarish Dev Burma's *Pativrata,* the new director's comedy, and *Mira*. And two of them struck by death. First Menoka, then Shankar, the two so separate, yet somewhere, her mind had not been easy since Menoka's death. What if she had died so suddenly, and Shankar left behind? Would he give it all up? Like how people thought she now should? It would be so easy...to just stop there and then, to not have to think about so many things. To get back home and try to sleep. People would understand, anyhow, they really did think that she should not carry on, without Shankar, her life in the pictures at the very least. That it was her time for bowing out.

Ramola sighed, got up and walked to the window overlooking the garden where she would so inevitably station herself in her moments of disagreement with her husband. If only she could be Ramola and Shankar both...take another life from him, wherever he was. Like in the stories from her childhood, where gods and demons drew strength from different founts...when they had more than one life...and lived so many lives beyond life and death. They became new people, took avatars so they could do new things, rise and not fail, changing themselves from one life to another. Perhaps they had had too great a love of life to ever give up. Shankar had loved his world in the very same way. And he had loved her more than that whole world and everything that was in it. Still, he would have carried on, somehow. And wasn't that what he had taught her, every time that he had succeeded, or even lost? To rise back, to never go wasted. Often he had pushed her to exceed herself. Sometimes it had angered her, that a star like her should not rest on her laurels. But she knew it again now. To forever strive...like the gods...fight new battles, be born anew, for new things.

IV

Avinash Mukherjee waited at the traffic lights on Park Street, one hand on the wheel of his Hillman '14', nibbling the nails of his other hand, which he did when he was nervous. It was lunchtime and he wished he could disappear into one of the busy restaurants or bars in the area, and forget about the task at hand. Pretend it didn't have to be done, put it off one more time.

He was going to see Ramola Devi in the Bharat Talkies studio. Eight days had gone by since Shankar's death and he had still not mustered the courage. He had heard when Ramola got back to the studio, four days now, and he knew that he would have to see her... about *Mirabai*. He was awaiting a reply to his cable to the bosses, but he shouldn't wait another day, he knew that, to tell her that the collaboration was now not likely.

If only she would have the good sense to see things in the light of the changed circumstances. If he was her, he thought, he would simply give it up...the whole *Mira* thing...write off those expenses. Resign to her fate, what they called *kismet*. Bharat Talkies had other directors, but without Shankar Chattopadhyay this picture could not be made, it would not ever be the same. Shankar had put his heart and soul into it. Could it ever be how Shankar had thought it...them together...all those hours spent talking and planning, and dreaming. He had not taken Anil's calls. The boy Keshta had answered the office phone with his rehearsed '*Babu* just went out', dutifully noting the callers. At other times he had put the phone off its hook. He simply couldn't bear its ringing. He hadn't spoken much, these last days, even Shankho had not been able to coax him to go out.

The news had been like a high voltage electric shock to him. Just his luck, he thought glumly. It went bust every time he tried to do something worthwhile. What would happen to *Mirabai*? Would Bharat Talkies still go ahead and make it with a new director? Or would Ramola Devi leave it, as it was, just those few reels that Shankar had taken? Her husband's last, unfinished work. She was the new boss of Bharat Talkies. Her fragile, delicate self, forever sheltered from life's realities, she would buckle under the strain of it all. She was a good actress, no doubt, and beautiful, and could become the talk of town with a new sari-blouse or a new style of the *khopa*, but he doubted that she was capable enough to run the film business. Shankar Chattopadhyay had run Bharat Talkies almost single-handedly, and it was no easy task to match his caliber or energy. The different people there, each looking out for himself…those that so long had been tame only because of Shankar's presence. They would try to get the better of her, and who knew how long Bharat Talkies itself would survive. The widow would probably be given to fits of nervousness. Perhaps she would remarry before the year was done. Society ladies like Ramola Devi needed a shoulder to lean on…a rich somebody. She was herself a rich woman. Perhaps she would sell off the studio and go to live abroad, wherever she fancied, London or America, he thought bitterly.

What if she wasn't in that afternoon? He hadn't called to say he was coming. How simple it would be to arrive and not find her in the studio. He could leave a note, with Anil perhaps, conveying his sympathies… or perhaps, if she had another visitor…she must have a dozen every day now. He could leave right away, pleading that he did not wish to be a bother, that he could always return when she was better disposed.

He had almost dreaded seeing her, as if she would read his mind. His demons had plagued him incessantly. Was it karma…that he had…thought of her…wanted her…when all the time Shankar had been like a brother to him. He had wanted to hide after he heard, like he had hidden away when his only sister had died giving birth. She was four years younger than him, only seventeen then. He had pocketed the telegram with its summon, 'Sister dead, come soon', locked his rooms, then taken a train from Howrah Station. Boarding and alighting one train after another, he had spent his nights in waiting rooms and platforms of unknown rail stations...three days, or four...until he was sure they had not waited, for him to see the body. Put her in the fire. He had cried his heart out the day she had left after getting married. She hadn't come home to have her baby, their mother and father both being dead, and no one to take care of a girl in the family way. He was glad for it, later...that she had not been with him in her dying moments. He had shut out those feelings forever, he thought. But they had come back to him, on hearing of Shankar's death. Making him want to hide away. The same inconsolable regret of an untimely passing, and anger and despair.

A half hour later, entering through the door of Shankar's office at the studio, a sense of the unreal almost overwhelmed him again, like the day that he had heard the news. Ramola was at the window, in a pale chiffon, her hair done in a simple low knot. Her sight made Avinash's heart lose a beat, his mouth suddenly feeling dry. She had had her back to him as he entered, turning with a sudden flourish, as if to deliver the opening shot of a picture...eyebrows raised, her signature style, as she beckoned him to sit.

He sat down hesitantly, having muddled his rehearsed lines and groping for a suitable opening. He was almost grateful for Anil's presence behind him. Anil lingered near the door but did not take a seat.

'Madam is in delicate health Avinash Babu, she needs me with her at all hours...advice and guidance... Shankar Da never allowed her into the studio's matters, you know...she is not made for it. Avinash Babu, only because it is you, I know how close you were with *dada*, else I would not allow it...not at this time,' Anil had confided as they had walked together from the studio's gates to the office. The *durwan* at the gate had sent word to Anil Babu when he had asked to see Madam.

'I have to keep a check. She is a lady, *na* Avinash Babu? We cannot have anyone and everyone going in to see her...Shankar Da, he could deal with all kinds, educated, illiterate, marwaris, *sahib*s,' he had gestured towards the office as they had neared, 'not her...'

Anil had seemed in command and Avinash was glad. Shankar had trusted him, he knew that. And perhaps, if Ramola Devi was not keeping well, the talk need not go towards *Mirabai* at all. Perhaps a letter to her would suffice, once he had a reply to his telegram. Though now, in her presence, he saw none of that frailty. If anything at all she looked more beautiful than ever and he struggled to speak, like always.

'Madam, I...' he started, then paused, when Ramola asked, 'Will you have tea or coffee, Mr Mukherjee?' 'Coffee,' said Avinash without thinking.

An awkward silence, then Ramola said, 'Mr Mukherjee, I understand that we will need to have some discussions...some changes...though of course we will try and make up...for...' her voice trailed off, unsteady a moment as she lifted her eyebrows, puckered her mouth and ran her eyes over the large writing table before her... trying to keep her composure, Avinash imagined. Still, she seemed to be in control, though clearly with no inkling of which way this was to go. She didn't look like a widow, and she was trying her best to fill Shankar's shoes, in a 'The show must go on' spirit.

'We will of course need to consult with Miracle,' her voice wavered again. 'Let me see, where the Miracle papers are...I did bring them in here yesterday...from the house...'

Ramola erupted in a sudden spurt of activity as she leafed through some papers on the desk, uneasy moments passing one into another. Avinash felt his heart sinking, how in heaven's name could he bring himself to tell her. Even Anil had been quiet. She's thinking though...he thought, as he stole her a glance, almost like she's trying to decide on something. No need for any papers here, she must know this is not that kind of meeting, she's deciding what to say.

The coffee arrived as a welcome distraction and they drank it in silence. Anil had stayed near the door, cup in hand.

'Tell me Mr Mukherjee, are there any ladies in the studio business in America?' Ramola looked up at Avinash from the coffee service.

'No ma'am' he said without thinking, '...I don't think...I'm not very sure ma'am...'

'Why do you think that is the case, Mr Mukherjee?' Again she had her eyebrows raised, her mouth pursed. She stirred her coffee, eyes fixed on the swirling brownness. Then looked up again.

'Do you imagine it to be a man's job?' he felt her eyes scouring him and looked away.

'I'm not sure...I mean, yes ma'am,' he felt a tinge of anger. She was rather purposefully discomforting him. That too, when his unease was only too evident. And when all he wanted was to say a few words and leave.

'Why do you think it a man's job, Mr Mukherjee? After all, the biggest stars of our industry are women, not men...' there was resoluteness to her voice.

Avinash ran his fingers over the edge of his teacup.

'Do you think stardom is an empty thing? Not real at all...only a play of light and shade? That stars are made and unmade by other people? That they have no control of their own destinies?' She was being relentless. Was it her nerves, Avinash thought worriedly as he studied the half-filled inkstand on her table, his face quiet.

'Do you imagine that the likes of us...stars I mean... that we cannot get about in this world, the real world I mean, without someone or other to hold our hand...a little bit of help, if you will, a shoulder to lean on...Anil here certainly thinks so...' Ramola cast a meaningful look over Avinash's shoulder in the direction of the door. 'I have had a difficult task, Mr Mukherjee, assuring Anil that my health is not the least bit affected...though, of course, I have...suffered a great loss...' Ramola paused, as if spent by the edge of her own words.

'But surely Madam...' Anil's indignation was sharp, 'surely, I have only your interest to mind, only what Shankar Da had asked of me. He had wanted to keep you away from studio matters, a highly educated lady as yourself...you know this line Madam...'

'Do you know Anil, why Shankar and I had agreed that he run Bharat Talkies and not me? Did he ever tell you that?' Ramola didn't seem angered. Avinash eluded her eyes but turned just enough to snatch a glance of Anil's flushed face.

Ramola spoke quietly, almost kindly, 'He didn't, did

he, Anil? But then, he wasn't supposed to. Because that was between him and me. He believed that I needed to free myself from the studio, to be able to reach the heights of my art. He gave me that luxury…that freedom. Not because he thought the studio business was his calling and not mine but because one of us had to step back…from the lights…to build Bharat Talkies. He had stepped behind. But he was getting back, you know… Anil…Mr Mukherjee…to the lights again. And he had asked of me…' she paused, almost choking and Avinash feared she would not hold herself back very much longer. But Ramola bit her lip, sat back in her chair, and went on, 'To…to stand by him, to now share with him the duties of which he had relieved me. That is why I was not going to America with him, to carry on with the studio… when he was away…'

She examined her manicured fingers closely, now almost speaking to herself.

'This picture, it was different. Shankar was…dreaming again. Like when I first met him, when he would talk of having his own studio. And I…I wasn't worried about my image, you know…if people would accept the glamorous Ramola Devi as a *jogan*…No romance, no big hero, only Devdutt, to support me, even the dialogues were so very different. I never had such lines ever, you know, Mr Mukherjee, they would make me think, every time I spoke them. So much of it was poetry, and the songs…so deep, with so much meaning…about love and forgiveness and devotion. One or two people here at Bharat Talkies felt it would be risky, you know, that people might not understand it, here at least. That we should make different versions, one for here and another for America. Shankar said no. He had wanted us to take that chance, try something brave, even if it did not give us a big hit. He had wanted it to be his best work. He said people would remember us by it…after we were dead.' She shook her head despairingly, 'Now, he's really dead…'

Avinash spoke almost startling her. 'For us all, ma'am…it was going to be a chance…to reach high, to show the world. *Dada* would say, it's not just a film, it's a fight, for us to be recognized and be reckoned with. If Hollywood can set standards for us, we too can show them a few things. What we lack in money we will make up with our dedication and hard work…our talents. You know it, how he had insisted on those big sets, he had wanted to stop at nothing. It was going to be difficult, to match Miracle's standards…scale, technique, everything. Shankar Da would say to me, there has to be a first and the first time is always the most difficult…but that should not stop us. He would say, let us not be content with what we have attained, for then we have nothing left to achieve. But now, without Shankar Da…? He stopped, suddenly awkward. He hadn't ever spoken at such length with her. Anyhow, she knew it all…surely so much better than him.

'Tell me Mr Mukherjee, will the sun not rise now that he is no more?' Ramola's eyes were fixed on the far wall behind him, so intently that for a fleeting moment Avinash thought she had seen something there. He opened his mouth then closed it again and looked out of the window at the green of the gardens outside.

'Life doesn't stop, you know, it goes on, in much the

same way, only now we must learn to carry on without... Shankar...do the things as we ourselves can.' Her eyes were on him again.

'Certainly Madam,' Anil broke in eagerly. 'We must carry on. We must follow in *dada*'s steps. You need not worry, I will see to it all. Just as Shankar Da wanted it. Be assured Madam.'

Ramola left her chair, and walked back to the window where she had earlier stood. She looked out for some brief seconds, then turned back again, with her flourish, eyebrows raised, this time a small smile on her face.

'No Anil. Now it is no more about how he had wanted or would have done it. Does that shock you?' She looked from Anil to Avinash, 'And you too, Mr Mukherjee... does that sound rather awful? For a 'widow' to say? But the truth is I am now the chief of Bharat Talkies and my decisions might not be like Shankar's decisions. They might be different. Because we are different...he was a different person, and I am not him. I could not be honest if I tried to do everything like how he would. Now this picture, would it be quite the same with me directing? Though, we...Shankar and I...we did think it together... it was our dream...but our thoughts were not always matched...not every time. Yet, I would try and read his thoughts, and be his Mira. Because after all, it *was* his picture. But now I will be the Mira that only I know, that I have imagined and lived, in my mind...'

'But Madam, who is to be director? Who...who can match Shankar Da?' Anil had abandoned his post by the door and advanced to the desk.

'Perhaps nobody Anil. Yet we must make this picture...perhaps I wasn't clear enough...'

Ramola had walked back to her chair. She seated herself slowly, stretched back and watched the two men as she spoke again. 'I will make this picture, be director and lead actress...' Her voice was low. 'It will be a first, for our industry here...this country, for Bharat Talkies... and for me. Yet, I have led before, when I entered the movies, when respectable people would often not allow their girls and women to visit a picture hall. And I quite understand Mr Mukherjee that Miracle Pictures might not now wish to partner with us. Now that we have a lady at the helm.' She almost laughed out her last words.

'You coming here made me decide, you know, Mr Mukherjee. I had been uncertain...thinking about it...I couldn't be sure. Could I fit in his shoes? Would I be able? Was the risk worth taking? But hearing what you said...about Shankar...it helped me make up my mind. I think, Mr Mukherjee, I needed someone to remind me that it had never all been so easy for him as well. Yet he did it. And it would be discreditable on our part, would it not, if we let that spirit die with him?'

V

For a small time that evening Anil had wanted to set fire to Bharat Talkies, burn it all down, raze it to the ground...get it over and done with. She was the boss's widow, and he a nobody, the way she had scorned him that morning, like he was no better than the *chaprasi* stationed outside her door...waiting there for Madam's orders. After all that he had done, the years of everything that he had given to Shankar Da and Bharat Talkies. If Ramola and Shankar had created Bharat Talkies, hadn't he as well? Could they have done it all by themselves? Without a lieutenant like him? He who had slaved his days into the nights, forever beyond the call of duty. And the others...Kedar Da, Palash Da, Bimal Da...who had faced every test...only because Shankar Da had asked it of them. Kedar Da even stopped going to his *sasurbari*, because of the things they said about bioscope work, even refused the New Talkies offer though they had wanted to give double almost...all of them that had stayed with Shankar Da through everything because they thought Bharat Talkies was theirs also, what they had together created.

Those early days of Bharat Talkies, when nobody knew Ramola Devi, and when Shankar Da was struggling to get the studio running. He himself had one year still at college and had started work at Bharat Talkies, only for Kedar Da, his elder brother-like neighbour from his hometown in Comilla. Kedar had joined Bharat Talkies as their sound engineer. He had admired Kedar Da since he was a boy. And Kedar had been like another son to his widowed mother. Kedar had told him that bioscope was not a place of just *beshya*s and *baiji*s, women of the bazaar. 'That is just the front of it, women, all the *jhak-mak*, glitter...that is just what we see in the bioscope hall. But behind it all there are people like you and me, educated people working in the studios. People like Shankar Da. Do you know Shankar Da could have made a name in Hollywood? But he came back here, for the love of art, to create something that we, slaves of the British, can call our own. Bioscope is art *bhaya*, we have to make this thing our own. Even educated ladies are coming in...Shankarda's own wife...educated abroad. People like Shankar Da need us Anu, only the educated like us can help create something truly great, not just *naachgaana* like the Parsi companies, but something that we can very proudly show to the world.'

If he had first hesitated, thinking what his mother would say, that trip to the new Bharat Talkies studio with Kedar Da and just some hours with Shankar Da had been enough for him to make up his mind. Shankar Da was that kind of man. He could make you dream, and he had the will to make dreams come true. 'I want educated young men like you Anil,' he had said. 'The art of bioscope is based on science, inventions, many inventions...made by pioneers through the years...our studios are like laboratories. Where we experiment, with light and shade and sound, what you see on the screen is the outcome of months and years of *tapasya*.'

He had pointed to Kedar Da. 'Kedar here, a brilliant student of science, he could have become a professor, gone to Oxford or Cambridge even for further studies. But he chose a much more difficult path. To work in this denigrated field of ours.' He had placed an affectionate arm on Kedar Da's shoulder. 'Do you know what experiments Kedar has undertaken...on his own? In his sound van? He is trying to devise a way to record sound that will allow us to add the sound later...to the picture. We need more people like him. We talk so much about Swadeshi. But do people see the Swadeshi in our bioscope films? Our sacrifices? Our efforts to make something out of nothing? Do we have the wherewithal of Hollywood? But still, we are not ready to give up.'

They had spent many evenings at the Elgin Road house, talking about the future, laughing, even Ramola had joined them sometimes. They would often invite him to eat dinner with them in the mahogany dining hall and though he had first been awkward, his shyness soon left him. Ramola would eat like a *memsahib*, her roast chicken and potatoes or some soup, but Shankar Da would have his *bhat*, like a true *Bangali*. 'Anil, *khachho na*, you're eating like a bird, come on, eat up,' he would scold, sometimes heaping *kosha* mutton or pulao on his plate despite his pleas that he was quite full. They had sat together after Ramola had retired and talked late into the night and even the early hours of morning. Once when it had gone past midnight, Shankar Da had himself gotten out his brand new Chrysler and driven him home. That was him, a true leader, even those that did not wish him well had secretly admired him.

His one fault was his blind love for his wife. He would hardly ever see her faults. And in any case she always had a way of getting around him, she always had her say no matter what. Still...Shankar Da would say, sometimes, that he would leave the studio to them all... him and Kedar Da, Palash Da. Would he say it only in jest? Or did he secretly fear that if ever left to herself she would destroy his life's work? The studio built with his blood and sweat. They said a person close to death sometimes could see into the future. Had Shankar Da felt his end was near? Was he afraid? He had been restless those last days. It hadn't seemed much then, only the strain of long days at the studio, the Miracle deal, the approaching tour, the hundreds of small things that he had needed done before he left. He would send for an Aspirin, most afternoons...still, who could know that he was living his last days? But he had said some things, sometimes, which were telling, even more now...after this morning's revelation from Ramola. 'Anil, acting and directing are two things altogether. It takes talent and charisma to be a star. But to be a fine director one has to look over and above stardom...personal likes and dislikes...friendships, even one's own self. That is why it is so difficult for a director to also be an actor. There remains the struggle always, between oneself and one's responsibility, to the others...other actors. To art...not everyone can rise above himself...'

Could Ramola Devi rise above it all? Be like Shankar Da. She who treated those around her like they were nothing, those to whom she really should be grateful. Did she think she would set a milestone: 'Ramola Devi...first woman director from India'. Get the whole world singing her praises? She who had ridden on Shankar Da's back. Forever shielded by him, taking advantage of his love for her...all those roles written just for her. What would she have been, without Shankar Da? Another rich girl with a pretty face? Did she know what it was to have to earn her living? Like those other girls in the pictures...girls like his Raju, who worked like slaves and still did not get their dues. Raju, now she had made her own way. No one to hold her hand, no one to show her any kindness... the hunger and despair of being fatherless and poor, and then the hunger to make something of herself. Did Ramola know hunger? Picking on her food, complaining about this or that, nothing ever was too good for her.

And now she wanted them all...all of Bharat Talkies to dance to her tunes.

It could not happen. He would not allow it. Shankar Da would say jokingly, 'Bioscope is a level playing field, *bujhle*...even more so than your cricket. The audience can lift you from the dust and put you up there...on a throne.' Bioscope was a blessing of their times, it was opportunity for one and all, not just the privilege of a few like Ramola Devi. It was a way to progress...to be one with the rest of the forward-moving, thinking world, without injustice or unfairness. Shankar Da had taught him that. 'Do you know the power of bioscope, Anil? It can make people believe that a person in the bioscope picture is Rama or Krishna or some god. It can change a person, through his work in the bioscope... one's life can change...through a creative enterprise... become more meaningful, *unnato*...' Why, then why, should that advancement not be for those that most needed it? Anil gritted his teeth. Should Raju be stuck at Unique studio doing her Raju Darling acts? When she deserved a chance at the very least? To prove herself better. And Ramola Devi go from strength to strength? Star to director? Ramola Devi, a great director? Not so easy, madam...not so easy. Anil smirked, his eyes bright. Would it do you justice to have such a great actress like yourself to direct? No madam, you are gold, you are every director's dream, you would make the director's work ever so easy...with your understanding of art and your education and your good manners. Madam, a great lady like yourself ought to strive harder...why, you could mould from dirt a *devi* like yourself, could you not?

Something from nothing? Now...would it not be your greatest achievement Ramola Devi if you could bring about a truly matchless performance from a girl of the gutter, one that has neither your class nor such good manners? By all means, Ramola Devi, make your own *Mirabai*...but surely we cannot allow you to have it all so easy. That would take away from your greatness, would it not? No, we must not let that happen.

VI

'I'll need them...all of them with me...' Ramola had jerked awake from her uneasy slumber.

She had dozed on the chair by the window, like how she had sat on the night Menoka died, the lamp glowing. It made her uneasy to get into bed, though she had often slept by herself when Shankar was alive. Knowing that he was in the study next door, hearing him through the walls as he had walked across the creaking wood floor or called Bibhu for tea. It was so very different now, knowing that only she inhabited their bedroom. It almost put her on guard, though what she feared she really didn't know. Sailen Kaka had given her some pills to help her sleep. But they didn't agree with her. They left her feeling listless and dreary. She had never had trouble sleeping before. Unlike Shankar, who would often toss and turn through the night. But then, she had never had to carry work worries home. She had always left work behind at the studio, when she had left for the day. The worries...they had all been his. The studio's running, its troubles...ironing things out with different people. She had known it all, still, how could she have understood it, this way, until it all came on her? Why Shankar had had those sleepless nights, kept awake, gotten those headaches, eaten too much or sometimes just left the food on his plate. When all the time she had rested so peacefully. Sometimes chided him for being overworked. Ramola dragged herself out of her chair and poured herself a glass of water. It was past midnight.

Her thoughts went back to that afternoon's encounter. Avinash Mukherjee had exited in a stumbling hurry as if overcome by her announcement.

He's terribly odd, thought Ramola as she put her glass down, wondering if she should take a pill. Jumpy…

He had stared at her fixedly, on hearing she was going to make *Mirabai* herself, even after she had returned his gaze, forcing her to look away. Ramola felt a sudden tinge of anger. There had been something about his face then, a kind of indulging half smile that she just couldn't get out of her mind. Almost like he was egging her on. Though he had made a hasty exit soon afterward. Anil had stayed silent after her little speech though it had seemed he had things to say. He'd shuffled his feet, chewed his lip, looked her way but then looked away when his eyes had met hers. She had not stayed on long at the studio, almost like she had then wanted to run from it all. Should she have thought this through a little bit more…the making of this picture…? She needed to speak with Anil. She would speak with them all. She wasn't really angry with Anil, only vexed with his changed demeanour. He was not himself. But then, she wasn't either. She wondered if he too was keeping awake at night, like her. Shankar's passing had made their lives all awry. All of them at Bharat Talkies.

They would need to put their heads together now, them that had been Shankar's arms and eyes and ears. Them that had made Bharat Talkies what it was. If they were going to see this through. Tomorrow was Sunday. On Monday, she would speak with Nishith Babu. He could be tiresome but he still hadn't lost his touch. And Kedar Gupta, their sound recordist... Shankar had had great regard for Kedar Babu. He had joined Bharat Talkies even before their studio was up and running, setting up station in an old van, making it his laboratory. And, there was Bimal Pal, chief of photography and cinematographer of *Mirabai*. What if Bharat Talkies did not live on very much longer...what if *Mirabai* failed? Ramola bit her lip. The more reason then that this picture should be a fitting homage to Shankar. An endeavour from each and every one of them that had believed in him...Shankar had meant so much to those around him...unlike her, he could be one with the people around him. True, he had had to keep up appearances... the balancing act...pleasing and placating the likes of Nishith Babu, still, most of it was not a façade, really. Shankar had been one of the few real people in a world that was peopled by fakes. Once he gave his word he would stand by it. And by the people that had stood by him. Like Palash Babu, their laboratory-in-charge...when his name came up in that sedition matter and the police had arrested him...Shankar had stopped at nothing to get him back.

'I know Palash...he is a nationalist but not a

terrorist...' Shankar had not wavered no matter what anyone had said.

He had given them their due. Their names had appeared at the start of every Bharat Talkies picture, before any of the other studios had started that practice...Bimal Pal, Shankar had given him a picture to direct, about this time last year. Bimal Babu's entry into direction. He had asked to have her in the picture, but Shankar had turned that down. Though Bimal Babu had seemed to think it was she that had refused to work with a new director. The picture hadn't done too well, but it didn't matter. 'We are not a one film concern...' Shankar had said to a crestfallen Bimal. 'We have a standing built over many pictures. I believed that you had a good script and that was why I gave you this picture to direct. I still think you made a fine picture...and who knows, in another ten years from now when many more people will have seen it, that the verdict will not change? We must find satisfaction in our work Bimal...and in what we believe...not only be guided by hits and flops...'

An overwhelmed Bimal Babu had tried to touch his boss's feet.

'*Arrrre, na*...never.' Shankar had drawn Bimal close, thumping his back. 'You keep up the good work *bhaya*. When I started Bharat Talkies it was not to make a lot of money. But to create and experiment...how can we serve the cause of art if we do not try out young men like you...you are our future...'

Often he would sit with them talking and laughing. 'I'm going to run this studio for another few years...' he would say fondly. 'Then...I will give it all up.'

'*Tora chalabi...*' he would tell Anil. 'All of you will run the show...you, Palash, Kedar, Bimal...you do it your way then. But mind it, no disagreements in your midst! I'm only going to watch from the wings. *Ki?* What do you say, Ramola?'

Shankar's voice was in her ears again. Ramola shook it out of her head. Shankar was gone. And she had his last film to make. She and those others who owed him so much.

VII

Kedar Gupta glared. Opened his mouth, then closed it again as his wife Minati made an entry with a plateful of fresh fried *singara*s.

'Anil Thakurpo, your favourite *singara*s. You'll live many years, I was thinking of you while making them this morning. Even Khoka was remembering you, you used to come every Sunday...and today, after two...no three Sundays. Last Thursday...you could come with your *dada* till the main road, but not inside the house? Your *dada* said to me, Anil went from the door. You've forgotten us, *bolo*? *Achha*, now eat.'

She put down the plate before him, then looked from her husband to Anil. '*Ki?* What's happening? What's troubling you two?'

She turned again to her husband, 'Your loud voice could be heard all the way in the kitchen, didn't I tell you Khoka was sleeping? Is anything the matter? At the studio?'

She sighed, as the men sat grimly. 'Don't tell me. What do I know of your studio matters? Bad enough, that poor girl Ramola Devi losing her husband like that...and so young. And so beautiful...like an *apsara*...was he much older than her? Your Shankar Babu?' She pushed the plate towards Anil, 'Eat, before it gets cold. Your *dada* never takes me to see the bioscope. But last time my sister was here, we went to see your Ramola Devi's *Mayajal*, what fine acting, such beautiful eyes, I couldn't hold back my tears. They say she's very educated also, foreign educated? Your *dada* will never answer anything I ask. They say she speaks English like a *memsahib*? *Tai*, Anil? You can tell, I always say, from a person's looks...face and features. Like a princess, your Ramola Devi, not at all like a bioscope girl...those *naachgaana walli*s.'

'Will you let us talk or not,' her husband snapped. He was furious. 'Go inside.'

'Hmmm...talk...you don't have to think about the house, it's all my headache...my rotten fate, getting cooked inside the kitchen all day. You can sit and talk...' Minati snapped back before making her exit. The *singara*s lay untouched.

'No, Anil...and that is my last word...it cannot be, you've lost your mind,' Kedar burst out as soon as his wife had left the room. 'I cannot do *gaddari* with Shankar Da. *Arre*, Ramola is his wife, his widow. What you are asking of me...take Bharat Talkies out of her hands... that too at this time when she needs us with her...all of us. *Na re*, no Anu, I cannot do this...'

He softened. 'Think it many times over Anil, this thing could finish you. Take over the studio's running *from Ramola Devi*? She's the boss now...*malkin* re...for us all.'

He picked a *singara* from the plate and handed it to Anil. '*Ne kha*, eat, and think. What you told me today sounds more unreal than a bioscope plot. Remember Anil, these bioscope girls are not like our girls. They cannot love selflessly...' he lowered his voice, '...like your Minati Bouthan. That is how they are, because of what lives they have...they only know to use men like us. I have noticed these girls Anil, for as long as I have worked in a bioscope studio. They are different...for them love is just another game, to stay alive they will play that game. The ones who get anywhere in this world of ours have a past, all of them. Except one or two, like Ramola Devi. That Rajbala of yours...do you think she has no past...?'

He shook his head. 'Anil, *bhai*, listen to me, you will not regret it. Give up this madness. These gambles are not for the simple *chaposha* like us. We are not like the rich... scandals suit them well, not us. We are *madhyabitto*, good name and goodwill are all we have. Don't throw it away *bhai*, turn back before it's too late. Can you think what *kakima*, your mother, will say? How can I show her my face, if you go and do something foolish? What will I tell her? Can she ever accept this Rajbala? Hand over her family's keeping to a bioscope girl...'

Anil put the uneaten *singara* back on the plate and looked up from the green and black of the floor.

'No, she cannot, she won't. But aren't you, Kedar Da, different from my mother? My mother who did not ever go to school, who believes in *bhoot-pret*, ghosts and evil spirits...and you, a meritorious student of science? You who told me that we must leave behind the old thinking, of good and bad, purity and pollution, when you got me into Bharat Talkies...that we must move forward. That bioscope is a thing of the future...where we would work hand in hand, rich and poor, high and low together to make this the art of the future. You are Subhas Babu's *bhakt*, *dada*, does the freedom struggle not need us all, you, me, and girls like Raju? Why should they not be a part of our society? Why should we not give them a chance? Because they have a past? Will the past always cloud our future, shut out some people forever, like the British shut us Indians out for so many years? Should some people lord over others because they have money and power, because they have always had everything in life?'

'Anil, don't mistake me', Kedar slapped his knee exasperated. 'We are not talking about the country here, this is Bharat Talkies. Shankar Da and Ramola Devi, Bharat Talkies belongs to them, *re*. Yes, we had a hand in its success, all of us, but we are the soldiers Anil, we will have to follow a leader. We cannot take that lead, ever...' He paused. 'Look *bhai*, do you think I can ever take orders from Ramola Devi the way I would bow my head before Shankar Da? Shankar Da made me feel alive, he gave me the belief...that I could be world-class, Hollywood-level...for me this was not just a *chakri* re, not just my bread and butter, it was my mission. Ramola is no Shankar Da. I don't even know if Bharat Talkies will go on for long now...'

'And still...still you will not step forward? Take things in hand? Alright, side by side with Ramola Devi, but not she alone. Shankar Da had also wanted it. Don't you remember what he used to say, that he would leave us the studio…that it belonged to us all. And don't you yourself say that workers should take control, that their fate is in their own hands…are those empty words?'

Kedar was starting to look defeated. He picked a cold *singara* from the plate and bit into it. 'Say, I agree. Anil, what about the others? What of everyone else?'

'They will listen, *dada*, if you say. You know that. If anyone came even close to Shankar Da as our leader, you did. Would I be here, at Bharat Talkies, if not for you…then Bimal Da, Potla…don't let it all go to the dogs, *dada*. Bharat Talkies is our blood and sweat, not some rich girl's plaything, to do anything she wants. You know it as well, Ramola Devi will spoil it all, in no time. Why else did Shankar Da keep her away from studio matters? I myself heard Shankar Da tell her…not once…that she had to learn…how to talk with people. She thinks we're all *chakor*s, her servants. You see, *dada*, you mark my words, how many people will be ready to do her *chakri*? They will all leave, one by one. Let her be boss, in name…but let us do what will save the studio…there is no other way, no other way.'

Kedar sighed and ran his hand through his hair. 'Let me think. This will be a big gamble. I don't know Anu. What if we fall flat on our faces?'

'You tell me, if Ramola Devi can take a gamble, why we can't? Is she Nishith Babu or Ambarish Dev Burma, that she can guarantee a hit? If she can turn director overnight, then cannot we be the masters of our fate? Think it over a little. After all, everything has changed now, after Shankar Da went. Can't we turn it all over…

into something new? Can't we try Raju? So what if she is the *char* anna *wala* heroine? So what if she is not like us? Can't we change that...for art's sake? Can we not prepare her for something different, something truly great? She has it in her, that spark...that spirit, and she has a good voice, you know that, for the songs. Shankar Da would say it, that we should keep on trying new things, or we will never rise, or know what we are truly capable of. Tell me *dada*, who knew Ramola Devi would become a great star, if Shankar Da did not give her that first picture? Give this to Raju, Kedar Da, just one chance for her...her life will change...'

'Speak about the studio Anu, I will listen. Why this madness? Don't bring up this *meyechele*, this girl business in my presence.'

'It is not madness...she is my life. I cannot stay without her. Tell me, *dada*, what do you want...should I end my life? Did you not take my mother's hand when *baba* died and tell her, that you would always look after me...all your life? You and Minati Bouthan...what happened *dada*?'

There is madness in his eyes, thought Kedar in despair, he has lost his shame, his *buddhi*, all senses. Not I, not anyone can stop him now.

VIII

'Move, *shoro toh*, don't bother me...I won't eat...' Minati pushed Kedar's hand huffily as she tidied up the utensils in the kitchen. 'Khoka, play quietly' she called out to their son as a small crash sounded in the next room.

Kedar scratched his head, mock fear on his face.

'*Aha*, why this anger...I wasn't so hungry tonight. I finished the *dal* and vegetables...will I die if I leave the fish one day...for that you won't eat, how is that possible?'

'Again...again, saying such inauspicious things in the dead of night...I will die very soon, you will see...not much longer.'

'What dead of night? It's only half past nine, the things you say...achha achha, you'll see tomorrow. Make *dal* with *macher matha*, like my mother used to, then see how much *bhat* I can eat. Now you sit, toiling away whole day in the kitchen, how will you last if you don't eat?' He pulled her arm gently.

'*Achha...*' said Minati through her first mouthful of rice, 'tell Anil Thakurpo to eat here tomorrow. The poor boy, didn't even eat the *singara*s. God alone knows what they must be feeding him, where he rents...'

Anil's name made Kedar grimace.

'Forget Anil, you eat first...here, take some *jhol*, your plate is dry,' he ladled some fish and vegetables over her rice. Minati smiled and made a face.

'*Achha*, what's wrong with Anil Thakurpo? Leaving that whole plate of *singara*s uneaten? All wasted...is he sick or what?'

Kedar sighed. 'Studio work...it's all on him now, with Shankar Da gone...he's worried, that's why...'

Minati picked a fishbone from inside her mouth. 'So then he'll give up eating? Curse on such work. What he needs is a good girl. Wait, I will speak with *kakima* when we go home next month.'

Kedar shook his head. 'That won't solve anything, Minati. You won't understand...'

'Hmmm, how will I?' Minati shoveled the last of the rice into her mouth. 'I'm not so educated like you. I stopped going to my father's place for you, you and your studio work...because of all the things they would say... and still, I won't understand...hmmm...'

'Minati...' Kedar clutched her arm as she was starting to lick her fingers, startling her. 'Tell me something. That I work in a bioscope studio...you know what things people say about the bioscope. Didn't you ever have any worries...about me...you know, if I went on the wrong path? You know what I mean, women and such things? Don't you have any doubts, ever?'

Minati lowered her eyes and raised them again, then lifted her brows and batted her lashes, lips puckered. 'Doubts? What doubts...I know everything...you think I know nothing.'

'Everything? What do you mean? Everything of what? What is there to know?'

'Why? What you just said...what you do at the studio? Women and all that?' Minati screwed her nose.

'You think I mix with those kinds of women? Minati, do you really think that of me? After all these years?' Kedar's voice trembled.

'What's in that?' Minati hid a half smile. 'Everyone does it, less or more, in your studio *para*...that's what people say. *Ei toh*...the other day, Rashu's mother was telling me, *boudidi* I know a good tantric baba. Take a *kabaj* from him, for *dada*'s protection, after all, his comings and goings are in the bioscope *para*. All those *rakshasi*s there, those fiends, they can eat men alive... *ei toh*, one poor *bhadralok* used to live near my *pishi*'s house. Bioscope actor he was. Hanged himself. Leaving wife and eight-month-old son. All for some witch that captured him and took all his money. That's why I say, *boudidi*, get a grip on *dada*...else...that's what she was saying, Rashu's mother...'

'And what did you tell her?' Kedar asked quietly.

'That...you leave it...it's women's tittle tattle...you tell me, what if I was a bioscope girl? Would you still love me?'

'The things you say Minati...you, why should you be one of them...do you even know what they are? These women?'

'I know it very well, that is why I want to know...tell me, what if I was one of them? And I loved you? Would you love me then?'

'What kind of absurd talk is this? Why should I love a bioscope girl?'

'Not even if it was me?' Minati raised her brows and fluttered her lashes again.

Kedar caught her twinkle. 'Let me think now...if it was you...then I would meet the same fate as your Rashu'r *ma*'s gentleman...rope around my neck...all for your love.'

Minati smacked his arm, 'Will you say anything? Just anything you like? Such awful things in the dead of night.'

'Really, it's the truth,' Kedar laughed. 'Even then I would marry you, and only you, whatever anyone said...'

Minati smiled. 'Then why not Anil Thakurpo?'

Kedar scowled, 'What do you mean Minati? What about Anil?'

Minati looked him in the eye. 'What if he really loves that girl, the one he was going on about? And she him? Can it not be?'

'You know nothing, Minati, nothing at all of these women...what they are. This is not a laughing matter.'

'I know...' Minati sighed. 'I heard from outside the door after I came to give the *singaras* in the afternoon, what with your voice so loud...*achha* tell me, what if a bioscope girl wants to leave everything? Wants a husband and *sansar*? What if she really wants it? Is there no way out for such girls? Even the ones that want to live an honest life? So I was thinking, what if I was one of them?'

Kedar was studying his knuckles. 'There is no place for such women in our society, Minati. Any such thing can only lead to unhappiness. I know it. And that is why I told Anil what I did today...'

'*Achha*, you remember, in Comilla, just after we were married, how you stood up in that widow marriage matter...today that girl is *sansari*, mother of two. Could it have happened if not for you? How many people will allow a widow to live a new life? You saw nothing wrong in that. Then why not a bioscope girl? If she loves Anil Thakurpo I see nothing bad in it.'

Kedar shook his head obstinately. 'This is not a play or a novel, Minati. The two are different things. Is it a girl's fault if her husband dies? But these bioscope girls...they are made from a different soil. They have no *dharma*, they have sold their souls.'

'And still, if such a girl can be lifted out of that quagmire, you will not stand for it?'

'Minati, Anil said nothing about marrying this girl. He only wants to get her into Bharat Talkies? What do I say to that?'

'So can you? Get her into your studio? There are other girls in your Bharat Talkies. What if there is one more? And what's more, you can keep an eye on her then...see for yourself, what is what...'

'And what about Ramola Devi, Minati? What do you think she will say, if I tell her I want this girl, in Bharat Talkies...Minati, there is no place for her there, she is not made for Bharat Talkies.'

Another crash from the next room was attended by a loud '*Maaa*,' and Minati rose with a start.

'Who knows, *baba*, what is good and what not. But I think Ramola Devi will understand, if you tell her...she looks like she has kindness in her heart'.

Kedar scowled, as Minati darted in the miscreant's pursuit.

IX

'Minatiii...see who's here.' called Kedar even as Minati entered the small sitting room that opened on the lane outside.

'*Omaa*, Palash Thakurpo, Bimal Thakurpo, which way did the sun rise today? You two have stopped setting foot here, forgotten your *bouthan*.'

'Not so easy *bouthan*, we won't let go of you just like that! What have you got in your kitchen today?' Palash laughed.

'*Achha, achha,* let me see...' Minati smiled and disappeared in the direction of the kitchen. 'Khoka, look who's here, your Palash Kaku and Bimal Kaku. Come fast.'

'Ki go, what happened...' Palash turned to Kedar. 'You didn't come to the studio today? Even Anil didn't know. So we thought we would come by in the evening'.

'Good thing, you did well. What to do with myself, the whole day in the house, not my habit, this. Fact is I wasn't feeling well this morning. So Minati said, it's just one day, stay at home today, don't go to the studio... that is why...anyhow, there is not much work now, until things get settled a little bit more...'

'That you did well *dada*, *bouthan* did right, I haven't seen you take even a day off, ever...'

Bimal cut in, 'Have you heard this morning's news from the studio?'

'*Na re,*' Kedar looked troubled. 'Something's happened?'

'What's to happen? Ever heard, *dada*, no *sradh-shanti* for a Brahmin Hindu? No rituals, no rites, no *puja*, nothing?' Bimal scowled.

Kedar's face fell. 'Who's do you mean? No *sradh-shanti*?'

'Shankar Da, our Shankar Da. No *sradh* for the peace of his departed soul...his *memsahib* wife does not want any *tamasha*, understand *dada*, Hindu *sradh* is now a *tamasha*...'

Kedar looked from Bimal to Palash. Palash nodded grimly.

'Be clear, Bimal, what happened exactly?'

'What is to happen? Shankar Da's elder brother came today, with his son. After they got the news. Shankar

Da has no children, they wanted to do the *sradh*, in their ancestral house, where Shankar Da used to stay, before he had gone to America. Our Ramola Devi sent them away, saying she did not want any *tamasha*, that Shankar Da's memory was good enough. Think *dada*, Hindu Brahmin, sudden demise and his wife not the least bit bothered. With what metal is she made, that lady...'

Kedar had turned ashen. '*Na na*, how is that possible, you must have heard it wrong. She is very modern, I know it, but Hindu widow she is...Shankar Da's widow...she cannot do this. Perhaps, she will do the *kaaj* herself... you know that Shankar Da had kept no relations with his own family.'

'No *dada*, you ask Anil, he was in the room then. She even insulted him. Anil was not himself today, *dada*, said he was not coming back.'

'Why...what happened to Anil?' Kedar's voice was low.

'What was to happen...he had taken Shankar Da's brother and nephew to the office, to see her. In front of them she told him to go out...ordered him to go away, just like that.' Bimal paused as the curtain parted and Minati bustled in, a sullen-faced cook in tow, both carrying bowls of *ghugni* and steaming cups of tea.

'Thakur, put the plates down here and check on the *beguni*s, they shouldn't get burnt,' Minati instructed.

'What *bouthan*...' Palash lightened the air. '*Ghugni?* So quickly? That is why you are great, *bouthan*.'

Minati made a face. 'Enough. As if it all gets done just like that, so quickly? I made it this morning, I had a feeling that I would get to see you two today! *Beguni*s and *phuluri*s coming...'

For some minutes the studio was forgotten as the visitors eagerly devoured the fare and sipped their hot tea.

'Not eating *dada*?' Palash looked up at Kedar through his mouthful.

Kedar nodded absently. 'You eat...' He was staring out at the narrow lane outside. 'But how did you two hear all of this? About Shankar Da's *dada*?'

'They told us themselves, Shankar Da's *dada* and his nephew, what treatment they got from Ramola Devi. Anil got them to our studio canteen for a cup of tea afterwards, he called us out to sit with them. In a state he was, the ageing *bhadralok*, Shankar Da's *dada*, what with getting the news and not seeing Shankar Da for so many years. Blamed himself, for not coming sooner, while Shankar Da was still there. But he had a reason... do you know brothers, he said, why I didn't come and see him all of these years. Because I knew, I would come away insulted, at this age, by that bioscope heroine, your *memsahib*. I sometimes thank god our father died early. He could never have accepted Shankar's choice of bride. *Chi chi,* what shame. So decent a boy, but waylaid by a bioscope girl. Even his son told us, there isn't a single day that *baba* didn't talk about *kakababu*, your Shankar Da. But we never came before, for this same reason, the reception that we got today, we should have known. They went saying, don't mind brothers, but people say rightly, bioscope is not a *bhadralok*'s place. How you can survive here, you alone know.'

Bimal paused, then added, 'In truth *dada*, how long? How many of us will be able to bear with this, and for how long? See Anil, he said he has had enough, she made him wait outside her door, while she spoke to them, like some orderly...'

'And what was it about Shankar Da's *kaaj*, the *sradh*?' Kedar looked grim.

'What about it *dada*? Only that she will not do it... doesn't believe in such things, she told them. Such things! Shankar Da's *dada* pleaded with her, leave us Ma, you do your bit, for your departed husband. You do the *kaaj*, we will only stand by you. She said that she has thought it over, many times...tell me *dada*, what is there to think in this, too much *memsahibi*, that's what. And thinking so much, our Madam has decided that Shankar Da himself would not like any of it, that is what she has told them. He did not believe in *achar*, rites and ritual, nor does she. Shankar would do the same, if I died, she said to them. No mourning, no *sradh* ceremony, work is our only ritual, our only *puja*...can you think it even, Kedar Da? Even talked some nonsense about some Parsi custom of feeding the dead to the vultures...supposedly much better than our own practices.'

'Do you think she's losing her mind, *dada*...' Palash asked.

Kedar did not reply at once. Thakur arrived with the fresh *beguni*s and *phuluri*s.

Kedar picked a *beguni* and absently broke off a bit of the crisp coating. 'I was wondering myself...about the *kaaj*...I was thinking perhaps she would do it on the fifteenth day, I didn't like to ask when...after all, it's a family matter. I had thought I would wait till it was done, to have our own memorial *sabha* at the studio...now, I will have to see.'

'What are you thinking *dada*, tell us.' Bimal beseeched.

Kedar smiled, 'Nothing *re*...' He sighed. 'I don't know, yet, but I will tell you...you both and Anil...who else is there? And remember, not me, not any one person, and not even Ramola Devi alone is Bharat Talkies. Bharat Talkies is us, we are in it together...us all, otherwise, not at all. That was how it was when Shankar Da was there and that is how it will be even when he is with us no more.'

He placed an affectionate hand on Bimal's shoulder, then called out to Minati, '*Ki go*...another round of tea, may we...?'

X

Shankar's voice was in Ramola's ears. And it was making her head hurt. She still couldn't sleep, and she had taken one of those pills.

'You always say it's my fault, Shankar,' she snapped at him in her mind. Then turned over under the sheets another time and pressed her throbbing temples.

'He did it again, I had to stop it somehow, some time...I had to tell him in some way. What nice way is there to tell someone to behave themselves, when they simply will not get the message?'

Shankar was quiet. She decided to get up. The darkness made her feel sick. She would turn on the lamp, its glow comforted her.

She poured herself a glass of water and stared at the chair by the window. Why ever had she sat there...that night when Menoka had died? Doomed thing. Sitting there like it wanted to swallow her. Ramola pressed the back of her head where it felt numb, then ran her hand through her messy tresses. Nothing she did seemed right. How had Shankar managed to do it all the time? To get his own way and not ruffle quite so many feathers, everyone had thought what he did was for their good. Even when he had put people in their places, which he did rather often, he would temper it with a dose of sentiment, something she never could. But it had worked, it had worked so remarkably well. Though it would anger her.

'Why do you need to sugar coat everything, always…' she would ask him.

'Because it makes people sorry they did you a wrong, and not anger them, which it most certainly will do, my dear, if you say it in the very matter-of-fact Ramola Devi kind of way.' Shankar scolded inside her head.

She had had to send Anil out that morning. How many more times could she have allowed him to do it, this taking of things into his own hand…and this wasn't even a studio matter. Coming in unannounced, bringing in those awful relatives of Shankar's. Someone should have informed her first, she never would have seen them. Who knew if it really was Shankar's *dada*, she had never met any of Shankar's family. He hadn't wanted her to.

'I would have taken you there if *baba* were still alive,' he'd said after they were married. 'My brothers are best kept away…by miles.'

They had not left in a hurry. She'd seen them, father and son, lingering outside the studio's gates later that afternoon as she herself had left the studio to go home.

'They were having tea with Anil Babu in the canteen,

that *babu* who is *saab*'s *dada*, he was crying...' her driver Kashi had said.

'Who else was there?' she'd asked.

'Palash Babu...Bimalbabu...'

Creating a scene out there, no doubt. They should be in the pictures. She wondered that Shankar had been so remarkably different from his people. And Anil...he only had to show them out through the gates. Why in the wide world had he been drinking tea with them?

'Poor Anil,' Ramola felt a pang of pity. Somehow, he had taken upon himself the task of seeing them through this impossible time. Dancing attendance on that blabbering man, Shankar's *dada*, getting him cups of tea...only for his love of Shankar, no doubting that. Silly, dutiful Anil. He simply had to learn where to stop. Perhaps he was trying to be like Shankar, how Shankar would always balance things out. She sighed.

She would call him to her. Talk to him. He simply had to stop thinking the onus was on him.

'He's diligent...too diligent for his own good,' she rubbed the back of her head another time. Should she take one more of those pills? She needed to sleep. Anil, he too had not slept in peace, since Shankar had gone. More than anyone else at the studio Anil was affected, she could see that. But somehow, she did not like it very much, it just wasn't normal, not like him at all. He was even staying the nights there, she would have to tell him it was not needed.

Perhaps because his father had died when he was still quite young, some kind of accidental, sudden death, Shankar had told her about it once. Perhaps that's why he was so very deeply affected by it all. They had all been close to Shankar...Kedar Babu, Bimal Babu, Palash Babu, all of them that had been with him from the start, but none had acted like Anil...almost as if his world had changed...like her own world. She would speak with Kedar Babu. Ask if he would speak with Anil. He was the most reasonable of them all, Anil would listen to him. They all seemed to listen to him. He was a large-hearted man. Forever loaning people money, so she had heard. Carrying home-made tiffin for everyone at the studio.

Kedar Babu had not been in that day though. She hadn't known him to take a day off, he even came in on some Sundays. Shankar would joke with him, 'Kedar, your wife will file a case against Bharat Talkies in the High Court...that we're working you too hard.' Perhaps he wasn't well. Anil might know, she simply hadn't remembered to ask him, what with all of that drama at the studio that afternoon. She had been so weary after it all.

She looked up at the clock as it started to strike the half hour...half past eleven...she must have come up to bed early...it seemed ages now that she'd been trying to sleep. She would have to take another pill.

XI

Almost that very same instant, Kedar Gupta blinked through the glow of the light bulb in the small sitting room at the timepiece that sat atop the showcase. He had dozed on the sofa. 'It's the middle of the night, Anil, whatever are you thinking...are you off your head?' His hair was disheveled and he had been roused by the tapping on his front door.

Anil was on the doorstep, standing in the deserted *galli*.

Kedar felt his pockets for his pack of cigarettes, then remembered that he had put them by the sofa. He beckoned Anil, 'Come inside...what if I had been inside the house, would you have broken down the door, at this hour?' Silently Anil stepped in, stood stiffly, then sat gingerly on the sofa's edge.

Kedar closed the door, scratched his head and sat down across from him.

'What is it? What has happened? Is...is *kakima* alright?'

Anil nodded.

Kedar rubbed his eyes then ran a hand through his hair. 'So? Then what? What are you up to so late? What if Minati wakes up? What is the matter?'

Anil didn't answer at once. He mumbled, pointing towards the earthen pitcher that stood against the wall. Kedar grunted, got up and poured a glass of water.

'Here, drink...now tell me.'

'I'm leaving Kedar Da...Calcutta...'

'Leaving...for where? Where are you going?'

'Back home to Comilla...'

'And...' Kedar blinked. 'What's for you in Comilla?' He asked again, 'Is *kakima* alright?'

Anil nodded. 'Ma's alright, nothing wrong with her.'

'Then? What are you going to Comilla for? For how long?'

Anil pursed his lips then parted them again. 'I don't know Kedar Da, but I will be back. I'm leaving Bharat Talkies...'

Kedar blinked in disbelief. 'What? Say it again. You're doing what? Have you really gone mad, Anil?'

'Na Kedar Da. I have thought this over many times. I will go home and sell what *jaega-jomi*...whatever land we still have left, after *baba*...it shouldn't be too little. It's all in my name, that much I know, the money will go some way...and I will raise loans here, on interest...'

'But for what, Anil?'

'I'll start my own bioscope company Kedar Da. When I first went to Raju, I had told her that I would have my own company, and make her the heroine...I don't know if she believed me then, but I had not lied to her. I had thought that someday, perhaps, Shankar Da would help me start my own company...small perhaps, but my very own. Had he lived, I know that he would have stood behind me. Shankar Da loved me *dada*, like a son. But now that he is gone, I'm no more than a *chakor*...a *chaprasi*, a paid servant. Why should I stay *dada*? What's here for me? If even we could do something for Raju, I would take it all...stay on. But without her, I cannot live Kedar Da, it will be her and me together or nothing at all.'

Kedar was wide awake now. 'Wait...wait...surely you cannot be serious, Anu? Don't do *tamasha* with me, that too in the middle of the night...'

'It's not *tamasha*, *dada*, I mean it.'

'You mean, you goat, you will sell your everything... your mother's very last resources...to lay at her feet, that bioscope girl?'

'You can say what you like, anybody can say anything but I want to give it one try, just one try. I will pay

Unique her price, get her out of there, it's my only way now...I'm going by the first train tomorrow, how could I leave without seeing you?'

Kedar's shoulders dropped. He stood slowly then put a hand on Anil's head.

'You've not eaten, have you? You want tea? I can call *thakur* and see...'

'Na *dada*, I have to go, pack a few things before I leave...I'll telegram you once I make some headway there...'

'Na, Anil...wait...where do you think you're going?' Kedar grabbed Anil's arm as he got up.

'Sit...' he pushed him back on the sofa.

'You're not going anywhere Anil. You have to listen to me. I won't let you go...is this some kind of childish game, or what? Will you throw your life away, for this girl? What will I say to your mother?'

'Nothing Kedar Da. What can you say? What can anybody say? I have made up my mind. No one can say or do anything now. I had given Raju those dreams. Now, I will have to give it one try. If not Bharat Talkies then our own bioscope company, to make our own pictures. Hit or flop, no matter. Even if I lose everything *dada*, I will know that I had tried.'

Kedar's head was in his hands. 'You won't listen, *bhai*...'

Anil took his hands. 'Look here, *dada*...look at me. You brought me here to Calcutta. I was just a village boy, you showed me the world, taught me so many things. I will always be indebted to you and *bouthan*. If only I could, I would get Raju to you, just once...to touch your feet and *bouthan*'s. But that is not to be *dada*. I know there is no place for her in your world. But for me she's the only one...'

Anil stood, then sat down again. 'One more thing *dada*. If anytime you feel that you too cannot carry on, at Bharat Talkies, remember this brother. The world is big, there is place for us all. If you and I and Raju, if we all put our hands together? You don't know *dada*, Raju is no ordinary girl. One day she will be bigger than us all, even Ramola Devi, you will see *dada*. If anyone could be a match for her...that Ramola Devi, it is Raju.'

He knelt closer. 'Don't worry *dada*. You carry on, for now. We were together for so long, now we must go our own ways. I pray that Bharat Talkies lives on, for Shankar Da's sake, your sake...Palash Da...everyone.'

Kedar raised his face. 'It will live on Anil, not for me or Palash or Bimal or Ramola Devi, but for you as well.'

'But *dada*...I told you...'

'Be quiet, Anil. Do as I say. Come to the studio tomorrow, as you always come. I will be there. From now I will do whatever needs to be done...whatever it takes. And remember, this is not for you alone. It is for us all. Bharat Talkies needs us all...now, at this time...all five fingers of the hand together. I cannot let go of even one of you.'

'But *dada*...I cannot, without Raju...'

'I have said it Anil, I will do what is to be done.' Kedar sighed. 'It will not be easy for me. But I give you my word.'

XII

It was lunch hour. A furiously pedaled bicycle slid to a halt before the green and white gates of Unique studio.

Mishtu Modak, manager and proprietor of Unique Pictures had been in the bioscope business for over ten years. Mishtu was Modak's nickname, his family being in the confection or *mishti* business, and Mishtu himself reminded one of a rotund *rossogulla*. The studio had been one of the Modak properties, with large grounds and a *karkhana* of some sheds for the preparation of *mishti* that Mishtu's father, the senior Modak, had supplied to *annaprasan*s and weddings across the city. As a young man Mishtu had had a great love of theatre, and then bioscope pictures. Egged on by a bunch of no-good companions he had started to see himself in the line of the great impresarios, a connoisseur of talent. Upshot was the Unique film company. Modak Senior had an untimely demise and Mishtu had put his earnings from the *mishti* business into his new company, clearing off the sheds, building the studio and installing himself as a patron of 'artists'.

He had prided himself in being a dispassionate recruiter, and an avowed *brahmachari*, but when he chanced upon Lily Joseph, actress in the silent bioscope pictures, he knew that he was a lost case. He had fallen hopelessly in love, and Lily soon knew that he was '*murgi*' in her hands. Not once did Mishtu make any inappropriate gesture. He only stared longingly and smiled lovingly at her, wanting to grant her every wish. When Lily had asked for Raju to be retained by the studio, Mishtu had seen no sense in it. Why in god's name, that sulky, oily haired little nobody? He had tried to reason with Lily but it was what she had wanted, and after a weak try Mishtu had given in. Raju became artiste in the Unique Film Company, and Lily had declared she would turn out a winner. That idiot girl fit only to play *sakhi*s and *dasi*s...Mishtu had wondered if the girl or that *masi* of hers had done any *tuk-tak*, black magic, on poor Lily.

But Lily had proved him wrong and Mishtu had marveled at her instincts.

'What, Sir?' Lily had smiled at a delighted Mishtu after Raju's first hit. 'Where's my *bakshish*, my reward?'

To her utter amazement, a blushing Mishtu had reached under his table and brought out a small red box. 'For you, madam,' he had mumbled.

It was a blue turquoise ring set in gold. 'What...*yeh kya*...' a bewildered Lily had demanded, 'you gone mad or what?'

'No, no, madam,' Mishtu was red-faced. 'No bad purpose madam, only to capture your beautiful hand...I take it back, madam.'

As he had tried to grab the box from Lily's hand, she had snatched it back. 'What kind of man you are, man, giving, then taking away?'

She had slipped the ring into the middle finger of her left hand, admired it an instant then waved her hand before Mishtu's flushed face. '*Khush*, happy?'

As she had gathered up her things in a flurry, he had kissed her on the cheek, and then as he stood unsure of his next move, Lily had kissed him back. It had unfolded tenderly on the sofa, Lily perched on Mishtu's knees, his arms circling her waist, her hands cradling his head. Mishtu told Lily he would become Christian if she would marry him, but she wouldn't hear of it. 'What *bakwaas*, Sir, rubbish...' she had laughed in her usual manner.

Mishtu Modak would know real love when he saw it...like that afternoon. The young man that leaped off his bicycle in front of Unique studio was in love. And he would not take no for an answer. He might have gotten her outside the studio, as she left for the day, and somehow whispered to her the news. But for once he wanted to make a show of it. He wanted to lift her off her feet and take her from Unique studio, from right in front of the noses of her Madam and Mishtu Da.

As he strode in through the green and white gates a sleepy *darwan* jumped to his feet. 'What *babu*, what's your work?' he tried to stop the forward march.

'*Bhai*, my heroine...I'm only here to take her with me...' he laughed at the flummoxed Bihari.

He wondered where Raju would be at this hour. In the rehearsal room, with the music or dance master? But he would go find Modak first. And he hoped her Lily Madam was close at hand, to see her bolt. He was holding the papers, the contract for Rajbala Dasi, stamped and signed by none other than Ramola Devi, proprietor of Bharat Talkies. And it named the price...to be paid to Unique studio for releasing their star.

The office was up the stairs in the old bungalow built by Modak Senior, he knew that from Raju. He had not seen her in the month gone. Not since she had stormed out, that day before Shankar Da had died. He had wanted to speak to Shankar Da about her...*dada* would have understood. Still he had not done badly. He smiled as he ran up the stairs. She had vowed to never see him again. 'Come and get me out of Unique, if you want me back...' she had said. He had done better. She was going to be the heroine, of the most talked about bioscope picture.

He stood for a moment at the top of the stairs, unsure. A deserted verandah lay before him, the sunlight filtering through overhead *ghulghuli*s and an open door at its end. A perfume...of spices...he couldn't tell. The trace of a voice. He then spotted it. The door marked 'Office' on his left, so near that he could reach out his hand and push it open. He came close and put his ear to it. A woman was speaking but what he couldn't be sure. Then some moments of silence. Again the muffled voice. He pressed closer. Then pushed gently, parting the hinge a few hairs breadth...it wasn't locked on the inside.

'*Chalo, baba*...come now...' the woman's voice was cajoling. The door parted another few hairs as he leant forward eagerly. Then the woman again, a clear tinkly laugh, '...no *baba*...see, it's slipping...careful now.'

A man grunted, 'I'm trying...don't hurry me...' He sounded breathless.

The woman's smooth tones again, '*Arre baba*...you're not doing it right...didn't I tell you, *haath ko lagao*, take hold, right one, then the left one...don't let it slip, now push in...and...in your mouth...' She giggled.

Her unseen listener gulped, wasn't untrue then what Raju had said...about what things went on here in the afternoons.

'*Arreee*,' the woman's voice raised, then the clanging sound of something knocked over and falling.

The man was angry. '*Dhuur*...leave it...I don't want... leave it.'

The woman giggled again, 'Why? Why you don't want? See...so nice...for you.'

He'd heard enough. Better make an entry before things got out of hand. Anyhow, he had a job to do. He braced himself for the unimaginable, then pushed the door to enter the sanctum.

Mishtu Modak looked up annoyed, 'What's up? I'm eating, won't you people let me eat in peace even?'

The invader looked from Mishtu to Lily, then Mishtu again. Mishtu was hunched over the green top pedestal desk, red and white napkin knotted about his neck, fork dangling from his left hand. Its companion, the knife, had bounced off and now lay on the floor. A king's feast sat before Mishtu Modak...only, the monarch was yet to partake of it. The culprits, fork and knife.

'*Kaun hai tum? Kaisa andar aya?* Who are you? Who let you in?' Lily demanded.

The young man laughed aloud. A guffaw, as he picked the knife and laid it on the table. Mishtu blinked.

'Mishtu Da...' he smiled wide. Then turned to Lily where she stood, hands on her hips. 'Lily *bouthan*...'

Lily recovered sooner. 'What *bakwaas*...who are you...where from you came?'

The lively stranger took no notice. He addressed Mishtu. 'Mishtu Da, you will understand...I know it now. Whatever people say. You and I...we are the same, travelers of the same path...'

Mishtu blinked again.

The young man leaned forward and gently extracted the fork from his hand. 'Eat with your hands *dada*, and listen to me.'

He turned to Lily, '*Bouthan*...no knife-fork, for today...'

'*Tum saala*...you rascal,' Lily hissed, looked at Mishtu, and glared in disbelief.

Mishtu had started to eat, tipping more of the bowl of red brown oily mutton over the mound of rice and speedily shoveling the curry and rice into his mouth.

He smiled again. 'Can't you see *bouthan*, how hungry he was, and still carrying on with knife and fork, only for you...only to please you. That is how it happens...*tai na*, what do you say, Mishtu Da?'

Lily sat down slowly.

The intruder was at ease. 'Even I do things like that, you know...to please Raju...your Rajbala...steady... steady *dada*...' he warned, as the bowl nearly slipped from Mishtu at Raju's mention. Mishtu had stopped eating, he gaped, his mouth full.

The young man mocked. 'Eat *dada*, don't stop...hear me while you eat.'

Lily found her voice, 'Raju...you...how you know Raju?'

'She's the one *bouthan*...' he smiled shyly. 'Like you are for Mishtu Da, she is for me...'

Lily eyes blazed. 'You *pagal*...you mad or what? Bloody rascal *kidhar ka*...Raju? Raju has no time for no loafer like you.'

Her opponent grinned. 'Why not, *bouthan*? Ask Raju.

If a beautiful lady like you can love Mishtu Da so much, why not Raju me…see here, such a feast you cooked for him…mutton *kasha*, *beguni*…what's that…*rui* fish, isn't it? You have to cook for me one time, *bouthan*…what Mishtu Da?'

Mishtu had found his voice. '*Arre, na na…*' he mumbled through the rice. 'Not Lily, my *thakur* here… he cooks it all…' then chuckled '…all of this…not Lily… Lily can make stew…roast…and what else?' He grinned at her showing grains of curry caked rice against yellowed teeth.

'Quiet, *buddha kidhar ka*…keep quiet, you old fool and don't talk with your mouth full…' Lily snapped at him. 'And you…' she flew up and threw an arm to the door, 'you get out of here…or…or…I'll call the *darwan*… police *ko bulaega*…'

He was not to be daunted. 'I'll go *bouthan*…I'll go, but I'm taking Raju with me…do not worry, no loss to you, you'll get her price…' He thrust the papers at her.

Yeh kya…what's in this?' Lily snarled.

'Don't be so angry *bouthan*, it is for your benefit. Bharat Talkies…most certainly you have heard of Bharat Talkies…Bharat Talkies will pay you, to release Raju. Today…here and now…read it bouthan…the money is not less…see here.' He pointed to where the sum was inscribed.

Lily pushed it aside. 'Release Raju…you *gadha*, stupid donkey, you full mad or what. We have her contract, two more years…she's going nowhere. We're making a new picture with her…you…you get out of here…*darwaza* is behind…*jao bhago*…go on…' she flayed the air again.

The young man had stopped smiling. 'Mishtu Da... you say...do you want the money now without any hassle or *jhamela*? Or, do you want to show Raju that contract, that one which you haven't still shown her. Bharat Talkies can go court-*kutcheri*, you know...they want Raju...they have the means.'

Mishtu had forgotten the food. He was looking at Lily.

Lily squinted at her contender. 'Now I know, you're the one. You *saala* rascal. You fed her all that *bakwaas*... about doing that outside film...you been eating her head, you *badmash*...'

'Yes *bouthan*, it was me,' he looked pleased again. 'I told her that she was made for better things...true, you made her a star, but then, you made her like the frog in the well...you did not let her rise, held her back, at every step. But now she wants to be free of you...of Unique studio...take your price, let her go.'

'She's going nowhere...' Lily said again, turning to Mishtu, 'Why don't you say something, you...show him the contract, then throw him out of here...*nikhalo isko*...'

Mishtu was eating quietly again. He raised his eyes then shook his head, 'What to show...leave her... besides...' he threw the foe a glance, 'that girl now has a *pukka* contract with somebody, it seems...'

Lily sank back into her seat 'All that hard work, running after her...giving her money, behind that *masi* of hers...making her a star from nothing, so that one day she can kick my butt and run off...Lily Joseph, you *saala* donkey...'

Mishtu was looking worried, he wasn't used to seeing Lily capitulate.

The fellow paramour motioned for action, 'Go *dada*... go on...'

Mishtu hastily rose upsetting his chair, wiped his curried fingers on the napkin around his neck, then looked to the abettor, who nodded encouragingly. Lily looked up at Mishtu. '*Aap bolo*...you say...how will we *chalao* Unique now, without that girl? No Raju Darling... no Unique...what will happen, Mishtu?'

Never before had she called him that. Only Sir, or Modak Babu, even in their most intimate of moments.

Mishtu seized his chance. 'I'm taking the money...' he announced. 'And here and now I am closing Unique studio. Enough of this bioscope business. *Mishtiwala*'s son I am and *mishti* I will make...'

'And *hum*...*humara kya hoga*, what will happen to me?' Lily seemed stricken.

Mishtu pumped up to his full size. 'You too madam, enough is enough. No more of this bioscope nonsense for you...troublesome line this, full of trouble-makers... *mishti* is much better...'

He looked again at the young man. 'You know *bhai*, my mother died, early last year. She was too much strict...*tai to*, that is why...and Lily also, always doing *na nà*, else, tell me, does it look nice, she and me like this...not married...'

Mishtu looked happy. 'Now brother, all we need is a good *purohit*...*bas*, then Lily and I, off on pilgrimage... Kashi...Haridwar...enough of this bioscope...what say, madam?' He beamed at her.

For once Lily was at sea.

The young man rose. '*Dada*, should I take Raju with me...now?'

Mishtu threw up his hands. 'Take her, right away, right now. *Bajjat* girl…very mischievous, disobedient, gutter of a mouth, don't say I didn't tell you…*dekho*, perhaps you can teach her a thing or two…'

The trophy's recipient grinned as he turned to depart.

'You'll find her downstairs in the studio building on the other side, in the rehearsal room. Tell her I don't ever want to see that face again…tell her to go…' Lily said to the floor.

The interloper returned, this time with hands folded. 'Don't be angry, *bouthan*. One day she will stand higher than us all, you will see…*dada*, come to Bharat Talkies any day, for the money…it will be arranged, bring the papers I gave…ask for me…'

As he was stepping out, Mishtu remembered.

'Your name, *bhai*…what is your name?'

'Anil…just newly appointed, manager-in-chief, Bharat Talkies.'

PART 3

I

Ambarish Dev Burma sucked his finger crossly, where the needle had pricked it. Then looked up at the clock on the mantelpiece. Ma had been so fussy about winding it up every morning. Now he did it. Though it no longer shone like before, when Ma would clean it so lovingly. Its hands looked frail now, like they would fall off its face sometime soon. Still, it gave the time like before, never a minute ahead or behind...now a few minutes to four in the morning, almost dawn.

He had been up all night, working on the wig. And thinking, through them happenings at Bharat Talkies, these last days. The new heroine, she had sprung from the blue, even he had had no inkling. He had imagined that Ramola Devi would abandon that precious *Mirabai* of hers, what was to have brought undying fame to the boss. Ambarish snorted. Shankar Chattopadhyay, maker of some *chalta-hai* films, those too had had their run because he had fronted that tight-arsed, snooty wife of his that everyone wanted to die for. Why he never understood. She was way too clean, always looked like she was freshly washed. Wore that jasmine perfume that reeked every time you came close to her. Like Ma. He simply couldn't bear it. Ma used to have jasmine by her bed, and every morning the room would be heavy with the scent of the dying flowers.

Better the smell of dead hair, he smiled at the locks he had strewn around him. And dead flesh. Ma had smelt good the night she had died. He had sat with her...right there...near the carved head of the bed and watched as her breath had turned heavier, lips parched, her tongue stuck to the roof of her mouth...she'd gasped a few times. He might have poured a few drops of water in her mouth, he'd thought later. But he had been so very taken, just watching her like that...her beautiful face twisting, then her breasts heave as she had struggled for air, he hadn't wanted to miss the moment when it all stopped suddenly. It had thrilled him, when he had put a shaking hand under her nostril and not felt the warmness of exhaled air. She that had forever pushed him away had beckoned, and he had climbed atop her and hugged her close. Rested his head on her bosom like when he was a little boy, until that monster Putu had arrived and started to suck on her breasts. They used to be so beautiful, Ma's breasts, when he had watched them enter Putu's hungry toothless mouth. How he had wished that soft flesh in her mouth would choke Putu to death. That night, when he became her little boy again, he had taken Ma's breasts in his mouth. They had turned dry...shrunk and shrivelled, but they had smelled nice. And he had taken her hair. Turned her on her side and cut the locks from behind her head so they wouldn't know. And washed them and smoothed them out to dry. Perfumed and rolled them up. That night Ma was his again. They took her away...but then, there were those girls. He could have his pick, and they could never have enough of him...he smiled.

The new heroine, now, that one was something. One

look at her and he knew she was going to be the next one. He hummed to himself. Just the thought of her made him happy. Even finding Menoka had not given him such delight. He knew about her, of course. Who didn't? She had sprung out of nowhere some three, no, two years before, making all of the *chotolok* want to stuff theirs' up her. Craze she was for them, the whole bloody lot of low-class swine. Went mad after her, the vermin. Even Ramola Devi couldn't claim the same frenzy to her name, one had to give the girl that. And she had lasted...not a one-picture wonder, like some of them. Though he himself hadn't seen any of those pictures... way beneath him. But now he would have to try and see if he could sneak a show somewhere, when they had a rerun...some back-street show house, where nobody would know him. Packed with the screaming scum it would be, mad dogs baying for that whore. He needed to see just one time, how she looked...in the darkness... against light and shade.

He picked another lock and held it against the mesh on the wooden head, where he was going to weave it. He had to admit though...he too had wanted to scream in delight when he had watched her on the studio floor, day before. What a twist she was giving to that holy girl Mirabaï. Twirling her buttery waist and throwing herself at that Krishna doll like she was going to give it to the Lord himself, there and then. And that dear old boy Nishith Babu...standing there, tearing his hair, and Ramola Devi frozen like she'd seen a ghost. He chuckled. Your days are numbered, Madam. This bitch will eat you whole, and your precious picture.

What got into Ramola Devi's head though, he wondered. Why in hell's name had she gotten this Rajbala Dasi to be the new Mirabai, the role she herself was going to play? Might have had Nishith Roy direct her, once the boss went kaput. Would still have been something passable. He had heard something about Kedar and his cronies prevailing on her...to get a *chalu* face, to make this one a quick hit, but it sure smelled wrong somewhere. Kedar, always spouting some righteousness or other, leader of that pious lot that would wag their tails around the boss. Wouldn't he rather fall dead than dish up such tricks, that too this slut Rajubala? Kedar that had refused to budge when they were giving him his weight in gold...New Talkies was it, or that Marwari house? Only because he never would get sold in the market, like *aloo* and *pyaj*...blah blah blah. How then could he have pushed Ramola for a quickie? True, Bharat Talkies needed a hit now, at any cost. What with the boss popping off like that and even his own picture seven feet under, that Menoka now rotting in hell. And Rajubala was sure to get the money ringing in. Still, it was odd... very odd. Why get a girl who stuck out in this place like a rotten thumb he couldn't imagine. Wasn't like Menoka or any of the girls that he had gotten. They were little nobodies...easy enough to fit them in the Bharat Talkies set, make them into little *devi*s. So much so that they had themselves started to believe it. He snorted again. But Ramola Devi, how in the world are you going to make a *devi* out of that piece of arse? That Rajbala. How will you stop them from throwing coins and kisses at your Mirabai? You really have lost your mind Ramola Devi, he hummed again as he started to sew onto the mesh. You must really have loved that buffalo of a husband you had. It has made you stark raving mad, my lady.

Ufff, he'd pricked himself again. But he didn't really mind it, now that it was nearly done...it had taken him days...and nights...but he'd done a good job of it. Now, just that patch on top, the crown. He'd thought he would do it with Ma's, and the rest of the hair he had off Menoka, she really had been his favourite one. But now, he chewed his dry lip...that bit was going to have to wait. For *her* locks. She would need some working on, that he could tell, way too much fire in her...but he loved that in them. Menoka had that fire in her, she had wanted to be at the top, only somewhere she had lost track, then she had only wanted him...to be his. He would watch as she would comb her long hair every night, and lovingly collect what came off on the comb. Still it had not been enough. So he had made her sit before the long mirror and taken more of her tresses, from where she did her parting. She had let him, she would let him do anything that he asked. It had, of course, spoiled the thrill a little bit, towards the end. Getting it all so easily out of her. Not like at first, when she would fight him off sometimes. He had liked to play that game with her. Giving her the advantage, letting her think that she had won...that he loved her enough to step back, let her have her way. Day by day it had enslaved her to him, to the love that she thought bound them together. And then she had lost that fire...the more he had pushed her the more she had given in. It had gotten so very tiresome, Menoka and the tears that welled up in her eyes. He had wanted to see the fire there, fire that he could then play with…like the sparks that had flown from that Rajubala's eyes.

He put down his needle. It was light outside. He took the mesh off the wooden head and studied his night's work. Then looked at himself in the long mirror and placed it on his head. The hair fell nicely together…well below his shoulders…what he had taken from them, all of them. Now only that bit on the top where the mesh still gaped. And for that he would have to wait a bit. Till he could run his hand through her tresses…till she would let him slice off, from just a hair's breadth above the scalp from where it sprouted. He had spent days at that wig maker's opium smoky den in the China *para*, watching as the old man's shaky fingers threaded his sharp needle… how he had so deftly woven strands after strands after strands on his wig heads. Hair that once grew on living heads, now dead. He had imagined it so many times, sitting Ma down at her dressing table and shaving her off, like they took the hair off them widows. Ma hadn't shaved hers, it made her look even more beautiful in her widow's whites. He had looked long and hard as she had sat by the window in the sun drying her long hair. Then Putu…Ma would rub oil on her head, comb, then plait her hair tightly. Say to Putu that she would have hair like her. He'd gotten that turd-like coil, held her back by it and snipped it away…all of Ma's work gone in making it long and fat. He'd wanted tresses of his own when he was still not as high as her waist and her locks would sweep the top of his head. Only Ma wouldn't hear of it. She'd screwed up her nose and laughed at him, 'Long hair like me…*ja*, stupid boy…'

He'd gotten his tresses alright, so what if Ma hadn't let him. How nicely the dark hair set on his head. It wasn't for them worms, such beauty.

II

Ramola stared at her plate of roast chicken from the studio's canteen, then pushed it away. The chicken's legs wagged themselves at her, like they would jump out of the plate and start dancing about her. Goading and mocking her...like that girl. She shook her head. Made her head reel, even thinking of the rehearsals they had had these last four, no, five days. Poor Nishith Babu had come close to tearing out his hair. 'No, no, *ma*, no, not that way... be calm...', he even called her to him, putting a hand on her head, but that little wretch simply wouldn't take heed. Kept on with it, like it was one of those *char anna wala* action romances of hers. Mira was emotion, it was about her eyes, and the pain in them and her devotion. She was the Lord's *dasi* lost in His love...his *sevika*, not a charmer. And here was this girl, throwing herself like that, so very insolent...uncouth. She couldn't look their young assistant cameraman in the eye. Even Bimal Babu had hung his head. Those shots could not be used, of that she was certain.

She took a sip from her glass. Would she have to give up on *Mira*...close down Bharat Talkies, by and by? She still wanted to go on, but how, with this wretched girl they had thrust on her? She still found it hard to believe. Kedar Babu...Shankar had trusted him so very much. That morning, two weeks before, when she had called him to the office, only to ask his assistance for

Mira, he had come prepared. It would be foolhardy, her acting and directing, he had said. They could not risk it. Not at this most critical of times. It might cost Bharat Talkies its good name...his mind had been made. 'And the truth, Madam...' he had paused a few seconds before saying it, 'is that it might be best that you not appear in a bioscope picture just yet, given your good name...your very illustrious family, your image. The public might not see it in the right way, a widow...people have their ways of thinking, you know that. They are not so educated... and there are one or two', he'd coughed delicately, 'love scenes I understand...with Devdutt, dream sequence... and then, a little bit dancing also, all in the dream sequence, naturally. But you know some of the studios. They will pay the papers to write just about anything... about you and Shankar Da. It will not be good Madam, for you or the studio.'

A popular face, he had said. Some young girl perhaps, he hoped that Madam did not mind, him saying it. It would cut the risk, at this time, what with the studio now having only this one big picture. Dev Burma *saheb*'s picture, who knew now what would come of that one. Madam herself was in a class of her own, but she might not be accepted by the audience, not right away... not so quickly after her husband's sad demise, that too in the role of a woman lost in love, and leaving the home of her husband. Perhaps in one more year, a more mature role befitting her present position. No explaining, no argument...nothing had moved him. He had put it simply to her, 'You take up the direction Madam, but get another face...it is the general view...'

She had asked, 'Who Kedar Babu? Which of our girls could do it? You know, it will not be an easy character to play, especially in the later parts...'

'Why one of ours, Madam?' He'd fumbled an instant, '...someone...from outside.'

'From outside, who?' she'd been flummoxed. Surely he knew it that any actress worth her name would be contracted with some studio or other. 'Do you mean someone from Bombay? Or Lahore? This is not any *naachgaanawali*'s job Kedar Babu, you know we need somebody with a screen presence, someone who is an artiste in her own right...perhaps somebody like Bombay's Mrs Khote if she were not too advanced in her years...not just anybody with a pretty face will do.'

'There is Rajbala Dasi, Madam...she...had shown interest. They say she is made for the bioscope, though most certainly, she will need a little bit of direction...and guidance.'

'Rajbala who?' she had been unable to place her at first. No one in the business really called her that.

'Unique Pictures Madam...Raju...Darling.'

She'd balked. 'Kedar Babu, are you in your right mind? What are you saying? This is not some two anna, four anna picture. Do you even know what class of public goes to watch that girl...how could you even...' she'd felt her cheeks start to burn.

Kedar had replied slowly, a little bit unsure even, she had thought later.

'If you will pardon me, Madam...this is a critical time for us all...for Bharat Talkies. If we are to survive, then...for a little while we must step down...from the high values that Shankar Da had imparted to us all. I am sure you know what rumours are floating. That Bharat Talkies is finished, now that Shankar Da is no more. We need a quick hit, something keeping an eye on the market…it will keep the audience with us.'

'And you want to make Shankar's Mira that quick hit Kedar Babu, what had been his labour of love…what he…and I…what we have spent our days and months over?'

He had refused to meet her eyes. 'I understand that Madam, but it is the only way out now, without Shankar Da directing. I beg your pardon, but it cannot be that same great work now…also, if I have not heard wrong, Avinash Mukherjee is now uncertain at best, of Miracle's partnership? Then why not make it commercial, for the market…the studio has to run…'

'And Kedar Babu,' she had had to fight hard to keep her rising anger from showing, 'you say this Rajbala… this Raju Darling is the one for us?'

Kedar had not answered her directly. 'She has her market, Madam, whatever anyone says. True, she is not of high class, but how many of our studio girls are? Haven't we trained and educated them, as far as it is possible? It is the nature of our line, you know it as well as I. Rajbala is under contract with Unique studio but they have allowed her one outside picture…that is known in studio circles. They will release her twelve days a month or for good even, as I understand it, depending on how Unique can be compensated. She herself…Rajbala… is rather eager to leave that place. She could be engaged wholly as a permanent staff.'

'May I ask Kedar Babu, what is the source of this information, on this Rajbala? Has she contacted you directly? Or through someone else at Bharat Talkies?'

Kedar had pursed his lips and studied the teacup before him a few long seconds as her unease had built up, then looked in her eyes.

'Let us say Madam that she is known to me…in a… very personal way,' he had spoken strangely, making her frown.

'Personal Kedar Babu? How…do you mean? Surely…' Ramola's voice was a whisper, 'you cannot mean…' Kedar had dropped his eyes. But the sharpness of his voice stayed.

'No Madam, there is no mistake here. I stand personally for Rajbala, and I request you to engage her for this one picture at least…for my sake…in the present situation…we must see how we can keep our market…'

'I…I find this very hard to believe Kedar Babu… you…it cannot be…'

Kedar had shaken his head, 'I had found it hard to believe myself, but so it is. I have given my word…I cannot go back now. You have tried so many girls, can you not train her Madam, artiste of your calibre? Rajbala…she is not high class but she is…highly popular.'

'And if I do not agree to this Kedar Babu? You understand, of course, that the final decision will be mine and this Rajbala of yours seems to me to be rather a miserable and cheap way out, even in our present circumstances. Also, I am not sure how you or I can explain this to anyone here at the studio. This will not be like any of our other girls…we created them, here at Bharat Talkies, gave them screen names, introduced them to the world as we wanted them to be...without Bharat Talkies they were nothing. But this Rajbala... she is already rather a sensation, as you yourself say. She has her image, how in the wide world can we make her fit here at Bharat Talkies? Can we introduce her as we in the bioscope business are so used to doing...as so and so educated girl from such and such good family, who considers bioscope a form of art? It will become a laughing matter. What of our image? I will be answerable Kedar Babu...it cannot happen. I simply cannot allow it.'

Kedar had laughed. She had not known him like that before. 'Certainly Madam, you can turn me away. You are the *malik* here, I am just a worker. Yet, Madam, your studio is run by workers like me, Palash and Bimal, and Anil whom you had shown the door after all what he has given to Shankar Da...to Bharat Talkies.'

'Anil...shown him the door...what do you mean, Kedar Babu? Anil was here even this morning to speak with me on some matters...here at this office.'

'Yes Madam, he came back to the studio, only on my telling. He was leaving on Sunday, in the night. Back to his hometown. He had come to me to tell me. That he could no longer be at Bharat Talkies. I stopped him.'

'Leaving...for Comilla? Why? Whatever for?' she had been astounded.

'Because Madam, he had made the mistake of trying to guide you through some matters...feeling a responsibility, and knowing that Shankar Da had forever wished to keep you secure. But you told him his place...like you told me my place, here, just now,' his eyes had blazed at her.

Ramola had struggled to find words. Why hadn't she spoken with Anil like she had thought she would? She had just let it blow over, that day of Avinash Mukherjee's visit...then, again, the day that Shankar's *dada* had come to the studio. But then, Anil had seemed alright...

Kedar was speaking softly. 'We...us all...we are in Shankar Da's debt. There was no distance between him and us. He was one of us, and he would say that Bharat Talkies belonged to us all. You might think differently Madam, but we still believe in him, what he had given to us...and in that we are all together. That is why I did not let Anil go away. You can refuse me, but then they will refuse you Madam...this studio will come to a stop.' He had sighed, looking suddenly despondent. 'Bharat Talkies will be finished, only you do not realise it...'

'I'm not sure what you mean Kedar Babu, I have made no changes whatsoever. Everything is the same as before, as Shankar had it, as we have always had it.' Ramola was sharp.

Kedar was shaking his head. 'No Madam, you do not understand. It is how they now feel, that they have no say anymore...that Bharat Talkies is no more their own, like it used to be, when Shankar Da was there.'

'Is it Anil only? Or, the rest too?'

'Anil is not alone. I said to you Madam...there is no difference between us. We are all together, Anil, Palash, Bimal, myself...we who were with Shankar Da from the start.'

'But that is why I had asked to see you Kedar Babu, to ask your assistance. Because I wanted you...you all...to stand by me like you had stood with Shankar. You were there, *dada*, when I acted in my first picture, when I was not Ramola Devi. You had stood by Shankar, and me... why should everything change now that I have stepped into his shoes? Now that I wish to make his picture? Is it because I am a woman Kedar Babu that you do not have trust in me? That I could lead Bharat Talkies like Shankar? What is it?' Ramola's voice had risen.

She had gotten up and walked to the window where she would unfailingly position herself during her arguments with Shankar. It had allowed her to steady herself.

'Why do you think I cannot act and direct? Because I have never directed before? But that was why I wanted you all with me...? Do you not have faith in us all together?'

'Madam, it will be seen as your endeavour to benefit yourself, through and through, in the circumstances... if you act and direct. As if...do not take it otherwise Madam, you are not sufficiently affected by Shankar Da's death, that you now wish to make it your stepping stone. There has been a...a discontent...within the studio. Not to speak of all the talk outside. You must allow people's sympathy...mark my words, it will serve you well.' He had been beseeching, yet unyielding.

'But I don't want sympathy, Kedar Babu. I want the best for Bharat Talkies. And no one knows Mira more than me, or how Shankar had thought it. And certainly not your Rajbala, Kedar Babu. That class of girl cannot give shape and form to Shankar's last work.'

'This is no longer Shankar Da's work, Madam. He is gone. And if you wish, I will go as well...leave Bharat

Talkies today, here and now. I have given my word, I cannot go back on it. And if then you cannot stop some of the others, do not hold me responsible.' He had not relented.

She had given in in the end, knowing Kedar would be true to his words. And to Rajbala Dasi's entry into Bharat Talkies. She hadn't spoken with any of the others, though she had wondered first if she should. It would not have been of any use. Kedar Babu would take it as an affront. It would break Bharat Talkies. Kedar was right, it was he...and them...that were holding the studio... not her. She had thought long and hard after that day. And the truth was that all of this time she had had only Shankar by her side. She had kept formality and they too had built their walls.

Why hadn't Shankar seen it...that she was alone? So far removed from the rest of them. But then was it even possible for a lady to be one with her workers in the way that Shankar had been? She had valued her superiority, and her distance from them all, and it had come with its price. With Shankar gone they were one in their love for him...and against her. Was it also because Shankar had been so open in his love for her? Perhaps it had done her more harm than good. Pitted her against everybody else that had loved him so dearly. It was Kedar they now sought, a leader who was one of them. And Kedar had gotten his way, on her giving up Mira to that girl he wanted to bring to Bharat Talkies. He would speak to them all, he had said, about this change, the reasons for it. They would understand if he explained, Madam needn't worry. They should get a contract done, to release the girl from Unique studio guaranteeing them a suitable sum. And best to keep Nishith Babu at hand while they went about making the picture...him being a veteran in the line, and not knowing what might be said if she took it all over.

'Who has spoken with her, Kedar Babu?' she had asked as she had put her signature on the contract papers. 'Will she...come here to sign it? How is the money to be paid to Unique studio? Do you know that they will not ask for more?'

He had been like the Kedar Babu of old. 'You can leave it to me Madam, it will all be done, I can assure you that. There is somebody there...to speak with her, and Unique. Rajbala...I understand...will be at your service from the date given on these papers, which is... Monday next.'

How she had dreaded it, coming into the studio on that day. Coming face to face with Rajbala Dasi. The new Mira.

III

Nishith Babu had a red face, and quivering lips. Ramola feared an outburst. Nishith Babu used to be known for his quick temper though he had calmed with age. But he will blow his lid today, surely, this wicked wretch of a girl.

Raju's blank eyes shifted from Nishith Babu to her own finger nails. Then backwards to Anil where he was stationed by the bookcase, causing him to look away, discomforted. She had the cheek. Ramola couldn't imagine why though, why she seemed to pick on Anil.

She needed a talking to, poor Nishith Babu was at his wits end.

Listen, now Rajbala,' she started, 'you have to understand this very clearly...'

'Yes Madam, I have understood...' Raju nodded.

'What...what is it that you understood?' Ramola was grim.

'What else, that if you do *prem-pirit*...love affair with *thakur*, god...meaning, like Mirabai *didi*, then no juice. Only singing and crying. I understood.'

Nishith Babu's head disappeared in his hands.

Ramola pursed her lips. Before she could speak again, Raju asked, '*Achha*, tell me Madam, can there be love without juice? God or no god?' She bit the end of her lip and again looked back at Anil. This time he glared at her.

Ramola struggled to find words. Nishith Babu tried again.

'This is *rasa*, *ma*, *bhakti rasa*, devotion. That is what you have to understand, *ma*. Mirabai's bhakti for her Lord, God Krishna, that love is a very high love...full of *rasa* but no *bhog*, enjoyment, only *tyag*...sacrifice.'

'She told you...?' Raju snapped.

'*Ke?* Who told me? What?' Nishith Babu paused, taken aback.

'Mirabai *didi*, that *prem-pirit* is no fun? Why do it, if she got no fun?' Raju snorted. 'Eating my head for nothing. You did *prem* ever with anyone, that you will know?' Nishith Babu's outburst arrived.

'*Ma*,' he turned to Ramola. 'Spare me. I agreed only for your sake, but I cannot bear this insolence. I have not whitened my hair in this line to be insulted by such girls.

Bharat Talkies used to be something else, girls like this one would know their place. They could not ever look me in the eye. Why you made this humongous mistake I cannot say...you know best...*na, na,* leave me, *ma*. I am too old for all of this now.'

He stormed out of the office. Anil rushed after him. Ramola shook her head. Was she purposefully doing it? But why? She simply didn't seem to care. What anyone thought of her. Unlike other girls of her ilk who would bend over backwards to make a good impression, trying to appear well-bred and ladylike. Had it all gone to her head? Them whisking her away from Unique studio almost overnight. If only Kedar Babu had not been so hell bent. Oddly though, he had taken leave, from the day itself that Rajbala had made her entry. Put the assistant sound engineer on the picture, sent word that he had taken ill...asked for a few days off from work.

That was a week now gone. The first two days they had sat with the girl, she and Nishith Babu, telling her about Bharat Talkies...Shankar's dream...about *Mirabai*. Through it all she had fidgeted with her bangles and nails and the ends of her sari, and Ramola suspected she had not heard much. They had rehearsed and tried to take the first shots. She had looked beautiful in the costumes, there could be no argument about that. But she simply failed to grasp the gravity of the whole thing. It was next to impossible. She was far too ecstatic. The close-ups they had taken simply went against the whole idea of it... the seriousness, and the sacrifice of Mirabai. She looked ready for a rapture, like it was not a spiritual thing... but...a...a carnal attraction. She simply couldn't get the thing right. Not surprising though, girl of her class. No matter how much Nishith Babu tried, or she herself, for that matter.

Rajbala asked, 'Madam, can I go? It's lunchtime, I'm hungry.'

'No, not yet...wait...' Ramola snapped.

She pulled out a drawer by her side and rummaged inside. Where had she put those biscuits? 'Here, take this...' she handed the girl a packet of milk creams.

'She's not shy,' Ramola thought, as Raju tore open the packet without a word. 'She's not quite grown up, really...but she knows the ways of the world.'

'So Rajbala,' Ramola recommenced two biscuits later. 'Are you sure that you do not understand what Nishith Babu has been trying to tell you? You know that we have paid Unique studio to release you, very specially for this picture. You will have to obey the director. Or we cannot make the picture. Do you understand that?'

Raju nodded. Ramola doubted that she'd heard. She waited for the girl to finish the packet.

'You are no longer at Unique studio, Rajbala. It is your good fortune that you are here now...at Bharat Talkies. Do you know what that means?'

Raju nodded again.

Ramola was starting to grow impatient again. 'No Rajbala, I don't think that you do know. Any other girl would give anything to be in your place. You have been selected heroine of Bharat Talkies' top picture,' she paused, 'the role that I myself would have played. You will have the papers writing about you if you do it well, like Nishith Babu tells you. People will remember you.'

'That they will remember, Madam,' Raju spoke with certainty. 'I am so famous, you know, everybody knows Raju Darling. I will make your picture a hit Madam, do not worry. That old director *babu* of yours does too much *bak-bak*. You tell him Madam, Raju cannot work like this.'

'Rajbala, I will not have you talk that way about him. Didn't they teach you at Unique to obey your director? Do you know how much everybody respects him... Nishith Babu? What books he has read, what knowledge he has?'

Raju smirked. 'Hmmm books...those books told him about love also? What if Mirabai did not love Krishna *thakur*, if she loved somebody else and pretended she loved Krishna? Because she couldn't say to everyone, could she...about who she really wanted? How will your director *babu* know?'

Ramola was aghast. 'Really Rajbala, what utter nonsense, I don't know what to say. What is there to know? It is written in the books.'

'Hmmm books. Good that I cannot read so well. What use would it be? Books are also written by men, like your director babu, *na*? How will they know what we girls feel? Our hearts? As if we will say the truth to them...men? I am Mirabai, *na*...not him? Then why, all what I do is wrong, and what he says is right? When you were Mirabai, Madam, you liked everything your director *babu* said? Everything?'

No, I didn't agree with him...on everything...thought Ramola that evening, though she had sent that wayward Rajbala off with a scolding that afternoon. She sighed.

She had given in to Shankar's script for *Mira*, when and where they had differed. He had been so very eager, she hadn't had the heart to dispirit him. Though sometimes she really had felt he was overdoing some things, sometimes she had resented it just a little bit. Shankar really could be so undaunted sometimes that he failed to see his own faults. But it had been his picture. And she had tried her best to be his Mira.

In some things...in all of those years that they were married, she had relented, without him ever knowing. Like when he had pushed her away, almost in revulsion when she had tried, only that one time, to get his mouth in her mound...only in the heat of the moment. She had been a little bit ashamed later, not ever tried it again. But she had had dreams, of him bringing her to fulfilment, his head between her legs. Poor dear Shankar, he had been so very constant, she always knew what to expect from him in their moments together...ever so loving, enfolding her, wanting only to please her. She had sometimes craved to be bonded, be made captive...to be made to do things against her will. To scream. And writhe and cry for help. But Shankar had worshipped her, he couldn't have imagined it, and she had buried those longings.

Strangely enough, that awful Rajbala had reminded her. That silly, stupid girl with her 'us girls and our hearts' babble. Love for her was only a pleasure and delight... what would she know of the pain of love? Mirabai was not just any woman, not mere mortal like us...Ramola sighed again. Mira had liberated herself from desire and lust, she had embraced anguish and agony. Mightn't they aspire to be her?

IV

Avinash Mukherjee lay back on the hard wooden *takhtposh* soaked in sweat. In the anteroom where he practiced his *dand*s. He had done close to a hundred, but it had not had the desired impact, of relieving his body and mind. He was restless, he simply couldn't make sense of it. Why would she do it? Had she become completely mad? Who was guiding her? It did not sound plausible, what he had heard that afternoon.

Shankho had come home. With the news. 'Have you heard? About Bharat Talkies?'

It had stunned the full studio *para*, he said. That Ramola Devi, now proprietor of Bharat Talkies, had engaged Rajbala Dasi, known to the world as Raju Darling, to play Mirabai. Shankho was bubbling.

'I'm saved *baba*. The very thought of that Raju Darling in Bharatmata was giving me sleepless nights. The boss is furious though. She had said she would take their offer, then whew, she is at Bharat Talkies and no one the wiser...but I'm saved, *baba*, I am saved.'

Avinash had not let Shakho know his utter amazement. 'Tea?' He'd wanted something to do, to allow him to turn away from Shankho.

'Hmmmm.' Shankho had nodded. He never said no to Avinash. Especially to his home brews of his own mixing of different teas and herbs, of which Avinash was rather proud. Shankho would drink stoically, as long as it made Avinash happy. Avinash had placed a yellow brown fluid before him.

'A little milk?' Shankho had mumbled.

'No milk. Drink it.' Avinash had ordered. He wanted

Shankho to put his mind to the tea. He needed to think. 'Rajbala Dasi...Raju Darling.' He'd said to himself.

'What am I saying?' Shankho had cut in excitedly. 'They've released her from Unique. Paid them off.'

'So Ramola Devi is no longer the heroine...' his voice had trembled just a little bit when he had said her name, but Shankho never noticed such things.

'Na, not anymore. She is overseeing, meaning directing, so I heard...but there is also that Nishith Roy, that old *buro*. Potla was saying, he's my good friend...'

'Potla who?' asked Avinash absently.

'Sound assistant, to Kedar Babu, their chief sound engineer...great man, don't you know him? Everyone in Bharat Talkies swears by him.'

'Hmmm...I know...' Avinash knew Kedar Gupta well. 'What else was this Potla saying?'

'What to say? Bharat Talkies is finished now, you take my word...now with Ramola Devi the new *malik*. Though, Potla was saying this Rajbala, he just couldn't understand it. Why a man like Kedar Babu had said good things about her...that she is a very popular artiste and they had better chances of getting a hit now, with her. Didn't sound right, Potla said, just think, this Raju Darling and Bharat Talkies. Nishith Roy has already thrown his hands up. They're having to change the full script, what to do...getting in more songs, much less dialogue...this Rajbala, she's messing the serious scenes, that's why.'

He had packed off Shankho. 'Come another day. I'm a little bit preoccupied.' Shankho had downed only half his cup.

What had gotten into Ramola Devi? Whatever was she thinking? Making a *naachgana* of Shankar Da's *Mirabai*? All of those lines, penned with so much thought, the whole beauty of it...all gone?

He wouldn't have thought it of her. This backing down. Better do away with the whole thing than this *tamasha*. Raju Darling! Even some chorus girl at Bharat Talkies would be a better choice...at least, the public wouldn't want to tear off Mirabai's clothes.

The cold water felt good. He poured another two mugs on his head then dried himself slowly. His body felt taut, he wanted to feel something soft...silk...that had once held together the softness that cascaded from her head and down her shoulders. They were in the wooden box by the window, locked, where his manservant wouldn't get them...the silken scarf and that chain girdle with those little balls on it. He had stolen them from her and never felt ashamed of it. The scarf had carelessly held together her tresses, knotted just above the shoulder, showing her bare nape. She had slipped it off absently and forgotten it, he doubted that she had missed it even. There had been some searching for the waist thing though, it was part of the Mira costumes. She had designed all of that stuff herself. He'd watched furtively as she had slipped it off that day after rehearsal. 'It's pricking my waist...' she'd said softly to her maid. He had read her lips. He had picked it up when nobody was looking, scrunched and slipped it into his deep trouser pocket. He had caressed it, many nights...held it close to his heart. He loved to feel it, more even than the softness of the scarf. The jeweller had missed a sharp edge or two, where it had hurt her...on that dainty waist. He had thought of it, again and again...slipping it back on her, that chain with its baubles...making it so very tight against her white flesh that she would writhe, begging him to take it off. Then he would unshackle and kiss her, where the sharpness had cut her.

V

Raju contemplated another kick, this time on Kamala's bent head, then let it go. She was thinking hard. He was no small fry...this one. And Kamala Masi had said that he was dying to get fried by her.

'*Shona*, my lovely, listen to me...' Masi had pleaded after the first kick, 'after that, hit me, kill me, I won't say a word.' Dev Burma *saheb* had seen her in Bharat Talkies. And fallen in love with her. He wanted to make her his new heroine. But first, he would see her, alone. They had to keep it secret, for now, not knowing what Madam Ramola Devi would think. But he would speak with Madam himself...soon...if she said yes.

'See him one time, *ma*, for my sake...' Kamala squatted at Raju's feet. 'Look here, I know you take them *babu*s, I know it all. That Jhantu *saala nyaka* half-man, he and that other one...king of them all, that Natabar, both spoiling you. But I am your *masi*, re, have I ever said a word? Stopped you, ever? See, you got called from such a big studio, tell me, wasn't it this Kamala that got you in this line? Not one day did you take Kamala Masi to see the big studio. Before, I went everywhere with you...and now...people in the studio *para* think Kamala is dead. Still, I did not say anything? You going to the big studio is like Kamala's going. Not even asked for a new sari, ever...see, what rags your Kamala Masi is wearing.'

It was true. Kamala, whatever her faults, had learnt to keep her mouth shut. But today her mind was made. It was going to be *iss paar* or *us paar*, her way or nothing, enough of kowtowing to the little slut. Padma, her dear friend and confidante of many years, had sought her out after so many long months. 'What *re*,' her *soi* had scolded, 'taken *sanyas*, left this world, or what? Left the studio *para*. I went to your old *basa*, where you stayed before...Kalbhairab Lane...no one could tell your whereabouts. Then finally that *cha-wala*, Kadamba, he told me, Kamal Di, she's *memsahib* now, stays in a new *basa*, with her girl, Raju.'

Soi had made good in the line. Kept a cheap room where she had homed studio girls, the ones that had eluded their erstwhile keepers, mothers or aunts or husbands and needed a place to live and eat. Padma Masi became their eyes and ears, and took care of them. She had set up her girls with some big fish. And grown fat on them. Padma Masi could be trusted, the fish she'd hooked could swear to that. When one of the girls new in the line had choked to death because of some silly game her poor young *babu* and his two friends had decided to play in the night, *masi* had taken full charge. 'Could I let the boy hang, even his milk teeth haven't fallen, the lamb...when the fault is that girl's?' she had consoled the boy's hapless rich father. *Masi* had gotten the price for her silence and for getting done with that mess of shit, vomit and girl. Even the *dom*s that burnt the dead humoured Padma Masi.

'That Tara...' Padma had reminisced to Kamala over cups of hot tea and fried *papad*s. 'With Dev Burma *saheb* she was, full six months...more. I set all up with *Saheb*, but these girls, no gratefulness, thinking they can put one over *masi*, thinking these *babu*s are little boys they can keep tied to their *aanchal*s...happens like that, *na ki*, you say? Drinking finished her, what to do. But *Saheb*, he is kind. Never returns *masi* empty handed...' Padma had devoured her tea and *papad*s as Kamala hung on goggle-eyed.

'*Saheb* sent word to me, through his *khas chakor*, I went to see him, four days now. Head has turned, seeing your Raju...' Padma had winked. 'Has his heart on her, wants to make her his heroine. Get her...*Saheb* will make you happy...what? Tell me, how long will you do *jhi-giri* here, be slave to that slut?'

Kamala was in a quandary. What did Padma know of Raju? So very easy to say, but not so easy done. This girl was not like other girls, she too had seen many years in the line. What if Raju threw her out? Who knew, with that girl? What she would do when.

Still, greed got the better of her. That fat gold chain around Padma's neck. Kamala hadn't been able to take her eyes off it. 'New one, or what? Never saw it before... let me see...' She had leaned closer and fingered the shining gold again and again. 'Wear it, take, here...' Padma had taken it off and placed it around her neck. 'How much I had wanted, gold *bala*s...my fate...that girl, *bala*s, *chur*, necklace all for herself, and not even a new sari for me...' Kamala had shed a tear or two. 'All will yours, *soi*, now, don't lose heart...only ready the girl.

Saheb will give with both hands, then say, that *soi* had not said for nothing...' Padma had consoled Kamala as she extricated the gold chain from her neck.

'What use living like this, under that girl's feet? Better I wash my *soi*'s feet and drink. *Bajjat magi*, you whore, you think you've become too big a heroine? Kamala has seen many such *magi*s, this time you don't listen, then gone is Kamala Masi. My *soi* will give me a roof on my head. I will lick my *soi*'s spittle, do her *ghulami*...better than this fate.' Kamala had murmured to herself after Padma left.

Once she had her mind made, she was the Kamala of old. Kamala gleefully hugged herself to sleep that night. She had gotten the girl to say yes, where will you run, *ma*...where will you hide, my lovely? Kamala Masi has kept quiet so long, but not anymore. This Kamala fears nobody. *Saali*, taking Kamala for a ride, you see now, what Kamala Masi can do.

Raju too had lain awake that night. She had said yes to *masi*. What harm in going? Wasn't it what she wanted? To be called by them big studios and directors, to be the biggest heroine. And she wanted to show Anil Babu a thing or two...even that doddering old *buro* of a director, eating her head, telling her she was doing everything all wrong. She could teach him a thing or two, that goat of a *buro*.

And Anil Babu, he of all people had pretended to not know her...a full month now she was at Bharat Talkies, and he rolling his eyes if she so much as looked his way. No one at the studio knew it, that Anil Babu had got her there, that day from Unique. No one knew anything.

And then, when he was with her alone, then so much love...as if she did not know what was what. But she had said nothing. She was new in Bharat Talkies and they all were after her...that old *buro* of a director, that singing master...*nahi hua, thik se karo,* Ramola Madam, everybody. Nothing she did was good enough for them. No, she would wait, she would test the waters...and, why not Dev Burma *saheb*? People said things about him. She would see for herself.

VI

'It's impossible...' Anil shook his head in exasperation. 'She just won't understand.' He felt frantic. 'How to make her understand?'

He had scolded her bitterly that evening, when they had met. It was easy these days to tell her when they were to meet again. He could run into her as and when he wished and no one the wiser, a whisper or signal and she would know if she was to reach the rooms after work. Not like her Unique days, when he had had to devote all of his ingenuity to get word to her. One time he had waited outside the studio's gates almost half the day, but she had emerged late in the afternoon with Lily by her side. At long last, he had gotten word through the shrivelled *buro* selling *chandrapuli*s and coconut *nadu*s outside the studio. At Bharat Talkies, no one knew... yet. But how long, if she kept making eyes at him in everybody's presence. People would put it down to her being a *chalu* girl, but then someone might think something...why him, why not any of the others.

Anyhow, Kedar Da knew. And he had not been the

same since. True, it was for Kedar Da that Raju was out of Unique, and the new star of Bharat Talkies but he wished he hadn't had to tell him. What Kedar Da had said to Ramola Devi he did not know, to make her get Raju to Bharat Talkies. Kedar Da had refused to say. For more than a week after Raju had arrived he had disappeared. Taken ill, was what everybody at the studio thought, but he had known. Kedar Da had gone back home, to Comilla, *bouthan* did not know why.

'Who knows *thakurpo*, what got into his head...' a worried Minati had said. 'Just told me, aren't the colleges still there in Comilla...won't they need a science master?'

Kedar Da had come back to the studio, but he had dodged all questions about the trip home. 'I just went, *re*, hadn't been for so long...that's why,' was all he had said. But something was not right. Kedar Da was not alright.

Even Kedar Da's assistant Potla had complained, 'What's up with *dada*, tell me? Anything at home? With *boudidi*? Shouted at me, for such a small thing yesterday. Then called me and held my hands, said, when I'm not there you will have to do it all by yourself, how can you make such mistakes? Not like *dada*, losing his temper like that.'

Mishtu Modak had presented himself to claim the price they had put on Raju. He looked happy. 'Making *mishti* again, understood *bhai*...sold off all that stuff from the studio, all of it rubbish *janjaal*. I would have come much before, if not for all of this *jhamela*...' he'd gurgled. 'Lily...she's getting a hang of it now, sari I mean. I said very strictly, madam no more frock business, now you be decent. And you two, how's it going?' Mishtu had winked. 'I won't say to anyone...I swear on Ma Kali,' he'd whispered.

Why did he have to do it like that, that day at Unique studio? Why all the drama, the fretfulness, he had wondered later. No one needed know, about him and Raju. He had only to present the papers to Mishtu, like it was a fait accompli, and get her out of there. Raju herself had been only too glad to take flight. They had had no way of keeping her, no contract, nothing, Mishtu had almost said it. It shouldn't have taken that much doing. Perhaps he had wanted to boast to someone...he was so very tired of living his double life. Of hiding, about himself and her...even now, at Bharat Talkies he lived every day in fear. Even more so because Raju herself was so unaffected by it all.

VII

'Masterji, one inch at the back...and half inch that side... all of the blouses will need loosening. Raju stand still and let him take the measurements,' Ramola instructed from her chair as Muqim master closed his tape around the new heroine. Raju was slender but bigger than Ramola and better endowed, and she had complained of the costumes being too tight.

'She is rather beautiful...and such perfect proportions,' Ramola thought as she watched Masterji gingerly tape Raju's chest and waist. She wished her breasts were so full, like Raju's were, straining against her sari blouse. Her own were rather small, barely giving her the fold in the middle of her chest. She had sometimes wondered what men found attractive in her. Perhaps it is the face after all. And that too she had, this girl...a mix of sugar and salt, as her old Bihari maid would affectionately say of her. She could understand why a perfectly upright man like Kedar Babu had gone astray. This girl had it in her, to make a man lose his mind. And she didn't seem to try, really, like the other girls with their laboured *rang dhangs*. She didn't seem to care very much for men, she was too full of herself. Men were almost like her playthings. There she was at it again, making eyes at old Masterji...now she's frightening the poor man, Ramola frowned.

'Raju stand still and look up...at...at the fan,' she ordered. The girl had been at Bharat Talkies for more than a month, and she had gone from Rajbala to Raju. She never would answer straight to Rajbala. Like it wasn't her name at all.

Raju made a face, stopped her wriggling and tossed her head with a sudden force, swishing Masterji's nose with her thick plait, almost knocking off his glasses. Ramola glared. She's going to hurt her neck if she turns it like that. It's the very last thing we need now, the heroine injured...and just as they had started to make some headway.

They had taken some good scenes, finally. The scenes in the royal palace, what she herself had shot before, with Shankar, and some more. The costumes suited Raju, she did look so very like a young princess, a revolutionary... fighter against injustice...more warrior than devotee. How very different this Mira was from her own. Still there was something to it, the way she had hugged the Krishna idol close to her chest, the defiance with which she sang her songs. Somehow she reminded one of the *swadeshis*, for all her mischief. Like those young boys that would throw bombs, then go smiling to be hanged, Ramola thought. It was something about those boys and about this girl, them being so young that they simply didn't care. They had had to bring in more songs, cut out some of the dialogues. Raju's extravagance suited it better and their writer Kamal Sahab had willingly obliged, being first a theatre man and himself full of flourishes. Still, it wasn't looking bad, not as dismal as she had imagined it would be.

'Sit...' Ramola said to a still sulking Raju once Masterji had taken his leave. 'You're not doing badly. I will speak with Nishith Babu, for him to join us again when you give your shots tomorrow...make sure that you...'

Raju yelped, stopping her. 'That old *buro*, again...to eat my head,' Nishith Babu had instituted his now third or fourth boycott of rehearsals and shoots for Mira three days before, declaring that enough was enough.

'Raju!' Ramola snapped. 'I have said before that I will not have you talk like that about Nishith Babu, in that language. You are now a Bharat Talkies artiste, not some two paise *ka* Unique studio *wali*. One more complain from Nishith Babu and I will stop this picture. You have things to learn, so be quiet and do as you are told.'

'Why can't I learn from you then?' Raju lowered her eyes.

'*From me*...what do you mean?' Ramola looked her up and down.

'If that old *buro* tells me I won't listen...ever...' Raju

was being stubborn. 'If you say...then...' she hinted compliance. 'You only said *na*...my work is better now? You...you...don't scold me in front of everyone. And he...always going on...*ma*, like this, not that...' she mimicked Nishith Babu.

Ramola was not amused. 'Your work is better Raju, because Nishith Babu has taught you and shown you, with great dedication and patience, even after everything. Is this how you behaved with your director, Raju, when you were at Unique studio?'

'What director? Lily Madam would show me... you know, Lily Madam, before me she was heroine of Unique. She's also beautiful, but not so beautiful...like you...' Raju smiled shyly.

Ramola bit back her own smile.

'And this Lily Madam, did she love you very much?'

'Yes...' Raju nodded.

'Then why did you want to leave? Unique studio?'

'For Lily Madam only, always eating my head...like your director *babu*...' again Raju made a face.

'Hmmm, and what makes you think I won't...eat your head...like your Lily Madam...or Nishith Babu?'

Raju giggled. 'You're not like that. Madam, any more of those cream biscuits?'

'I don't carry biscuits in my handbag Raju. Stop by my office on your way home and get them from me.' Ramola stepped out of the costumes room leaving Raju to change back into her own sari-blouse.

Perhaps I will wait a little bit more, before I ask Nishith Babu again. She really does seem to do better without him about. Pity though...he still knows a thing or two, Ramola thought as she walked back to the office.

Raju smirked to herself as she pulled off the costume and got back into her own clothes. Madam knew so little of the world, that too having worked in the pictures for so long. High-up lady like her, what would she know of anything? Scolding her, for only saying that old *buro* Nishith Babu was eating her head. Little did Madam know what other things these old *buro*s liked to eat! These babus...*saala*...something by day and something else by night. That night she would see what was Dev Burma *saheb*'s liking...

VIII

Something was not right, she could swear that on Ma Kali. Raju had fallen off her seat on the bed's edge, or almost, when he had said she was very like his mother. MOTHER...she didn't know whether she should laugh or cry. And then she had been afraid, why she didn't know. He hadn't even tried to touch her, all of the time that she had been there, in that house with him. Even Anil Babu had never talked of his mother to her. Girls like her...could they ever be like anybody's mother? Then why call for them in the dark of night? Why keep it all hidden?

The car had dropped her back in the dead of night. 'What...what happened?' Kamala Masi had bubbled as Raju had started to pull off the *benarasi* sari. 'Nothing...' she had replied. It was the truth. He had sent the sari, the day before, asking that she wear it when she came. It had been a little worn, an old one. But expensive looking. He said it was his mother's.

'Do you love anyone?' he had asked. '*Na*...' she had

shaken her head. She wasn't lying. She didn't love Anil Babu. Never had.

He had pulled out a pair of old velvet shoes with *karigari* on them. 'Try these on...' A little too small for her, but the velvet jacket had fitted right. How heavy it was. 'These were the fashion at the time of the Durbar in Delhi. She was just a girl then, still not married...' he had sighed, '...untouched.'

'I have seen your pictures, two of them...you are good, very good indeed,' he had smiled. 'Who's your guru?'

'Nobody', she had replied.

He had laughed aloud. 'Why? Ramola Devi? She got you to Bharat Talkies, didn't she?'

It had been her turn to smirk. Dev Burma *saheb* didn't know about her and Anil Babu.

'You know about Menoka, don't you? Haven't you heard? At the studio?' his eyes had widened, his mouth a thin line. She had nodded.

'And still you came to see me? What if you too...like Menoka?' there had been a glint in those eyes.

She had played with her fingers not knowing what to say.

'Weren't you afraid coming here, in the night?'

'*Na toh*...no...' Raju had shaken her head. 'I'm used...' Still, she had hidden from Natabar Da that *Saheb* had called her. This one was not like the other times. Only Kamala Masi knew, and her *soi*. He had sent the *benarasi* with Padma Masi. No jewellery, he had said. 'Who knows *baba*, god alone knows...' Padma Masi had grumbled. 'How am I to dress the girl, old *benarasi*...no jewellery...only some jasmine in her hair, no colour on her face...has *Saheb* lost his mind or what, that too at this young age?'

She had herself been flummoxed. He had not come within three hands of her. But as he had talked, he had circled her, going slowly around in that room with the bed. Making her feel like she was in a cage. At first she hadn't known it, only after a while. He had walked about...getting up from that big chair where he had sat, past the carved three-legged table and then round again past the bed where he had made her sit. She had had to turn this way and that to keep her eyes on him.

Another funny thing...he had not allowed her to drink water.

There had been a plateful of *sandesh* on the three-legged table. '*Nao*, eat...', he had held the plate to her. She had taken one, eaten looking at the plate, all the while feeling his eyes on her. 'Water' she'd reached out towards the lidded glass, but he had jumped, snatching it from her reach. He had smiled, 'Your throat is dry, *na*? But there is no water here.'

She glugged down the *gholer sharbat masi* had made. Summer had set in and *masi* always made *ghol* from her homemade curds. She'd told *masi* to put away her food. She wasn't hungry. Though she always ate no matter how late it got. But today...that *sandesh* had stuck in her throat. She'd swallowed, again and again, trying to clear her insides of it.

'You will come again?' his eyes had bored into her insides.

Should she? Go again? Will he really make me his

heroine? What did he want from her, she wondered, if not her body?

He felt it again and again...that part of the bed where she had sat...where he had made her sit. That side where Ma had lain on her last night. When she had gasped and hiccupped. For only a few drops. He sprinkled the sheet, wetting the *gaddi* underneath...no matter...he would tell one of the servants to put it in the sun. He had sprinkled Ma that night, after those very last breaths left her. Some droplets had trickled from her face inside her dead open mouth. Nobody could say he hadn't done his duty to her, put water in her mouth...it was she who all her life had wronged him.

The girl had warmed it again, Ma's cold bed. He hadn't taken his eyes off her. Not that she was so very beautiful, none of them ever could be like his Ma. But she had seemed unafraid...so very determined...one to get her way at any cost. She would come back, he knew that. Even if she did not want it. Because she would not admit, to herself even, that she had been afraid. She would drive herself to him. If only Menoka had hanged herself here in the house and not in the studio. The servants would swear him innocent, because, after all, he was their goddess-like Ma's little boy. Still swore by Ma, the swine...no mother's boy could have pinned Menoka's death on him. And then, didn't they all want to see these sluts hung by their little necks, to pay for their sins? The thought of Menoka pulled down from where she had hung that night by some *darwan* or *chaprasi* had driven him mad. What a shame, she must have been so very beautiful then...the smell of her just dead hair...her body still supple. How he would have liked to feel her over and over with his hungry fingers. He had wanted it of Ma that night as he had unbuttoned her *shemeez* and taken her breasts in his hands. But Ma was no longer so lovely, her body not so full anymore, and he had not wanted her nakedness to fail him. He would remember her from when he had first wanted her...when she would change from her *kal-ghar* soaked wet sari into her fresh crisp ones, her little boy looking on.

Menoka had put one over on him. No matter. He had fresh game. He whispered her name as he bent down and put his face on the clammy sheet where she had rested her *pachha*, that shapely round rump. Rajbala...

PART 4

I

'*Beti, hum bara papi...ab paap humara dhul jaega*... sinner that I am, my sins will wash away, don't turn me away, my child...' Makhandas Khemka was putting the finishing touches to that afternoon's performance. For good measure he let another tear roll off his cheek. But the job was done. Mukherjee Babu had promised to get him those pictures, somehow, if only he would hold poor Ramola *beti*'s hand at this sad time, though how he had known it all god alone knew. *Haramkhor kamina paji*, that rascal Dhonu, no *kadr* of his love, he never should have strayed from his very dear *sethani*, his wife of many years.

Mukherjee Babu's face told him that he had done the job to satisfaction. Avinash Mukherjee was studying his own palms with a sincere attention though his mouth hinted at a smile. Ramola herself smiled a weary smile.

'Still, Sethji, are you quite sure? You know there is nothing that you can bank on, heroine nor director...' she had cautioned Makhandas again a minute before. But Makhandas Khemka was undeterred.

'Shankar Babu's picture, then, who better to carry forward his great name than you, *beti*, his *ardhangini*, his *devi*-like wife. Your good sense has prevailed *beti*, you have heeded this Marwari. Bioscope acting, *naach gaana*, no *beti*...but *yes*, director...*shabaash beti*, bravo...only so educated a girl like you could think it, and then, will not this Makhandas Khemka be by your side, like I was there always with Shankar Babu? Money is no matter, my child. Will Shankar Babu's dream go waste? To hell with those white-skinned Americans...those Miracle people. Is Makhandas dead, or what?'

A tearful Makhandas had arrived with his offer just before the lunch hour, not willing to heed any words of caution. With him had come Avinash Mukherjee.

'Mukherjee Babu, he is my *pathpradarshak*...my guide, the driver of my chariot,' Makhandas had sobbed to an astounded Ramola. She herself had had no inkling of Sethji's profound love for Avinash Mukherjee. If anything they had first met here, in Shankar's office, and wouldn't Shankar say that Mr Mukherjee would sometimes pull poor Sethji's leg, even angering the poor man?

'My sins are beyond any measure, *beti*, I am your *doshi*, your offender, punish me *beti*, this Makhandas Khemka, he forgot his *kartavya*...his god-given duty,' had not his girth prevented it, Makhandas might have prostrated himself at Ramola's feet. 'So many days passed since Shankar Babu's sad demise and this Makhandas did not think once even of his *devi*-like Ramola *beti*... *dhikkar* hai, shame on this Marwari, I have shamed the full Marwari *samaj*.'

'But Sethji, you did come to see me...remember? Anil, you were here that day,' Ramola had turned to Anil.

'Yes Sethji...I even went to your *gaddi*, but you only had said then that, *beta*, now with Shankar Babu not there I will have to think again, my relations with Bharat

Talkies. My full faith was in him, but now...don't you remember Sethji?'

'I had lost my mind...my *buddhi, mat mari gayi thi meri*', Makhandas had let out a piercing howl silencing Anil. 'Mukherjee Babu has brought me to my senses, he is Devi Ma's messenger...'

His Devi Ma had ordained, through the medium of Avinash Mukherjee, that he resurrect Shankar Babu's dream of taking his picture to the '*phoren*' *firangi* public, bioscope lovers the world over. Show those Miracle people that they were but nothing. 'I will take this picture to the world *beti*, take it from me in writing, here, now,' Makhandas had swelled his chest fourfold.

'But Sethji...you...how is that even going to be possible? I mean, abroad is not exactly between Calcutta and Rajasthan,' Ramola had started to lose patience.

'*Na na beti, hum kuch na kare*...I have nothing to do, all will be in Mukherjee Babu's good hands, he will do all...book showings, publicity, everything...yes, money is mine, but *buddhi*, the brains will be his. So long he has worked for those Miracle people, will he not know to do this much?'

'Do you mean to say you are leaving your job with Miracle Pictures, Mr Mukherjee?' an incredulous Ramola had turned to Avinash Mukherjee.

'Err...no...not exactly, not really...no...Madam,' as always he had faltered speaking to her. 'It is an understanding between myself and Sethji...Sethji wishing to take this picture to foreign audiences, as Shankar Da had wanted it...I merely offer my...err...assistance...to this...err...noble purpose.'

'Yes *beti*, yes...Shankar Babu's last wish is my command. I will not hear no,' Makhandas had beamed at a confounded Ramola.

Avinash Mukherjee had found the words to sway her. 'It cannot hurt anyone, Madam. I know the proper channels...and the people, through my work for Miracle. Even without the big partnership it can still reach the foreign public. True...it will not have the same prestige as a Miracle co-production,' he'd faltered, 'nor could I guarantee any degree of success, still it cannot hurt, to try it...to see if we can make a mark, and now that we also have a backer for it...' he had turned to smile at Sethji.

No, it cannot hurt, thought Ramola, once a visibly calmed Makhandas Khemka had departed. But what was in it for Sethji? Or Avinash Mukherjee, for that matter? Unless Avinash Mukherjee really did still feel a certain closeness with this picture? Like she did, no matter that everything had turned on its head in these last months. Possibly...he blamed himself for the Miracle partnership falling on its face. Hardly his fault, though she had not been kind to him, when he had come to see her before, she remembered that. Shankar had thought highly of Mr Mukherjee, perhaps he had not been wrong, clearly, he had prevailed on Sethji...somehow...to undertake this enterprise. Who knew what would come of it, if anything at all. Indian pictures hardly ever showed abroad. It would be quite something really...if Makhandas Khemka did keep his word...if they could open *Mirabai* in picture houses in America, perhaps...Europe. She herself could not take that gamble, not without a backer for it, like

Sethji. She would have to speak with Mr Mukherjee though, about how the picture was shaping up now. Not really what he or Shankar had imagined it, nor she herself...but still, it was not bad...Raju had put her heart and soul in it. That girl wasn't what she had thought of her. There was something about her that made you take notice, even outside of the picture, when she spoke or looked at you. Kedar Babu had not been wrong. But why...why in the wide world would Makhandas Khemka put his money on *Mirabai*...now that they had neither Shankar, nor her playing Mira? Surely, he was not so very naïve, Seth Makhandas, even with his antics...it simply did not explain. Ramola sighed. She hoped Sethji was not being too emotional for his own good.

Emotion would be small name for the fear that Makhandas Khemka had felt in his bones when Avinash Mukherjee had said the name Dhonu. That slim lithe beautiful creature that had taken his heart and a lot more. Dhonu was the Nepali boy at his *daftar*, rosy and fresh from his village in the mountains. His *chacha*, the *darwan* who guarded the gates, had begged he be kept in the *malik*'s service and Makhandas had not said no. In the afternoons Dhonu would set out the *thali* for Sethji, a full meal of *chupra hua phulka*s, *dal*, two or three vegetables, *mithai*, *papad* and *achar* sent from home by the *sethani*. Dhonu had known the art of pleasing, coaxing his *malik* with an extra *phulka* or another helping of the *sabji*s. After clearing away the plates he would sit at Sethji's feet like a shy bride and start to knead his soles. Makhandas had sighed in contentment and leaned back in his big chair, feeling the softness of Dhonu's fingers as they had moved from his feet up to his calves and knees, parting the folds of his dhoti. In course, those fair delicate hands had reached up, to that which had lain supine, the *sethani* having forsaken all such indulgences for her Guruji's service once they had had their fifth child.

Dhonu had awakened the tiger in Makhandas. Forever subdued by the formidable *sethani* who had commanded his life from behind her *ghoonghat*, he had reveled in being lord and master to the pliant nymph. So much so that he had given in to Dhonu's pleas of getting him into a bioscope picture. Sethji had discreetly pulled a string or two, and Dhonu had arrived in the studio *para*, and in that circle of *nyaka*s where everybody knew what the next one was up to. And Avinash Mukherjee would be forever grateful to Shankho, who had so fortuitously revealed to him one of the circle's well-known little confidences.

'That Makhandas Khemka, don't you know?' Shankho had laughed his head off. 'Backer of your Shankar Da...do you know what else he backs?' There were photographs even, taken at some backstreet photo studio, of which the nymph had bragged in the circle.

Avinash had acted on hearsay, but he had not had too hard to try. Makhandas had capitulated without much ado.

'*Hum mar jaye* Mukherjee *babu*, I will kill myself. What of my good name, what face will I show my sons, my full *biradari*...my brothers, *hey bhagwan*, the *sethani*...' Makhandas had sobbed into his hairy paws.

'And that is not your only wrong-doing Sethji,' Avinash had reproached grimly.

'Why Mukherjee *babu*, except for that *saala harami beiman*, that rascal Dhonu, I am pure as Ganga *maiya*. That *jhutha kamina* miserable liar, not even shown his face to me after all of that *paisa* he took from me... all new notes, said his mother was sick, the liar. Just as well, that I was rid of him, but, Mukherjee *babu*, if anyone should know, then, what will become of my good relations...with everyone?'

'And what Sethji of your relations of so long with Shankar Chattopadhyay...and Bharat Talkies?' Avinash had worn his most menacing face.

'Yes, yes, but that was while Shankar Babu was there...now...' Makhandas had been bewildered.

'Yes Sethji, now...when she...' Avinash had bitten his lip for so inevitably faltering over her name, 'Now that Shankar Da's dream is to be lost forever, of taking his picture to the world, now, with Miracle Pictures not anymore a part of it. Do you and I have nothing to answer for...Sethji?'

'Yes *babu*, but what am I to do? I am a simple Marwari. If it was a matter of Jaipur or Jodhpur...but America? No one in my whole *biradari* ever set foot in England or America, Mukherjee *babu*.'

'And that is why you will be counted a true leader Makhandasji...a man of the future,' Avinash had kept a straight face. 'You will take this picture to the world. Can you imagine it, Sethji, *sahib*s and *memsahib*s in America watching this picture that you will bring to them, now as a distributor.'

'But why me...?' Makhandas had sounded stubborn. 'All of this will cost money, *na*, Mukherjee *babu*? And what guarantee of this picture now...now that they have got that *naachgane wala chokri*, that little slut to be their heroine. What is left now of the prestige of Bharat Talkies? Of Shankar Babu's good name...you tell me? *Na na*, Mukherjee *babu*, my money is not there to waste.'

'But you could throw enough money Sethji, on that boy of yours...' Avinash had caused Makhandas to pale again. 'Do you want to wash away your sins, or not? Or do you want the whole world to know? I will wash my hands off but then...tomorrow someone else might get wind of it, *na* Sethji?'

Makhandas had been wise. He could well be an actor in the bioscope, Avinash smirked as he set out the milk that evening for Manimala, the cat. Makhandas Khemka had wept copious tears, in the end getting the nod from Ramola Devi. Avinash hummed a tune as he picked up Mani and fondled her. Mani knew, he kept no secrets from her. She had watched, through glassy green eyes, as he had played again with her scarf that evening...lain it on his bare chest, then buried his face in it. He had made his way back into Bharat Talkies...as Sethji's advisor, Seth Makhandas Khemka...backer of Bharat Talkies. Not that he really didn't wish this picture to go far and wide. Though...it was to be seen where it was all going, what with that new heroine. But for now he had gotten what he had wanted. A reason to call on her...and sit close to her, to be able to furtively watch her again...each and every bit of her.

II

Natabar was worried. He ran his hands again through Raju's long hair, and threw another anxious glance at the girl. She had said no, even with what the party was going to pay. But it was not that. He didn't care so much for any fat party as much as he cared for this girl. It wasn't even the moods that these girls got, when it was their time of month. It was something else. Natabar just couldn't put his finger on it.

Raju pushed away his hand. Natabar smiled. 'What, *didi*? Angry with me, or what? What have I done, tell me?'

Raju turned away. She was finishing her lunch of muri-cononut and ripe bananas in her spot in the studio's back garden. Unlike the other days when he would come by, she hadn't offered Natabar any of it.

'Go now Natabar Da...I have to go for rehearsal.'

'Should I stop by, tomorrow or day after?'

'Don't come now Natabar Da, work is too much. This is not just any picture. You won't understand...this is not your *naacha-gaana* Natabar Da...this is art...'

Natabar looked away, then smiled wryly. 'Who said, *didi*, *naacha-gana* is not art? Who can say, what is art or not art? Pour money, and you get art, you think that, *didi*? That art only happens in your Bharat Talkies, in your big studios? Art is your own thing...how you will do or not do something, understood? I have seen so much art come and go, *didi*.' Natabar sighed. 'I have not been in the line for nothing...saw it all, from the time of the first silent pictures, don't teach me art, *didi*.'

Raju was feeling her temper rise. She had started to clean up the remnants of her lunch.

'You can say what you like Natabar Da. But then, tell me, who cares for you, people like you? Tomorrow, if you die, who will give any *patta*, will anyone even notice? But the big names...Ramola Devi, Barua *sahib*...' she bit back *his* name even as she had started to say it. 'People will remember them, because they are the true artists. Do you know, there are books...on acting...they have read those books, gone to America...they are up there because of what they are and not for any of your *naacha-gana*.'

Natabar was nodding to himself.

'Right...right you are *didi*, us and them,' he smirked. 'My mother was a *baiji*...singer, *naacha-gana wali*. I picked up my first steps from watching her. She sang even when she had my brother inside her...full nine months. My father put her in this line. He lived on her, all his life. Then on me. I couldn't leave him. We...those like us...can we ever be the artists? We come cheap *didi*, our lives...art...everything comes cheap.'

Raju was not going to give in. Why should she...*he* had said she had art in her.

'Na, Natabar Da. I don't come cheap...then, I would still be there, at Unique Pictures.'

'Don't forget *didi*, what you are today is for Unique... who would have known you, otherwise?'

Raju laughed. It was an angry laugh.

'Natabar Da, you've become just like Lily Madam... *hum tumko* star *banaya*, we made you a star! Natabar Da, why doesn't every other girl in the line become

Rajbala? Get called by Bharat Talkies? Become heroine of their top picture? Because...not every girl is Raju. Unique Pictures will be Unique Pictures...nothing more... so many like Unique will come and go, you will see, Natabar Da, people will remember Unique for Raju, not Raju for Unique.'

It was Natabar's turn to laugh aloud.

'Slow *didi...dhire chal*, look and see then put that foot forward, my pretty. In this line Natabar has seen so many get left by the way.'

Raju tossed her head as she walked off.

'Raju too will leave many by her way Natabar Da...if they try to pull her down.'

Natabar had understood. Raju was not turning away that new party. She was turning her back on *him*...and on what she was herself.

III

Avinash Mukherjee blushed and looked away. Ramola was smiling. He really could be so very shy, almost like a boy, it amused her. Yet, Shankar had thought him rather persuasive.

'Avinash is quiet in his ways, but he can get things done. I've seen him, he has his way with people.'

It was true, Ramola thought as they both played with their teacups. He had convinced his bosses at Miracle and pushed for the partnership, and now Seth Makhandas. Though it still baffled her, how he could have such a hold on Sethji. Seth Makhandas was no fool...yet...she looked again at him. Avinash Mukherjee was smiling at his empty teacup.

She smiled again.

'No, Mr Mukherjee, I mean it, really. It is awfully nice of you, to come by. I was quite elated yesterday, I must confess, with your endorsement of Rajbala. She has been rather a revelation. You did see her...while we took the scenes. She does have a rather singular style...her very own, don't you think? So much like how it would be in the old American pictures...speaking through her arms and hands and legs and eyes, leaving those cues for the watchers,' she laughed, 'mix of pride and pluck, I should say. She's a plucky girl, a little bit too spirited for her own good...I must say Mr Mukherjee, I have become rather fond of her over these last few days. I never thought I could ever get attached to...you know... girl of her class, but she is rather different from the rest. You did see how she transformed that song, the way she performed it...you did think she was good, didn't you?'

'Yes ma'am, quite...err...' he hadn't looked up from cup and saucer. 'She is...umm...rather quick in her uptake...as I understand...from speaking with Nishith Babu.'

Ramola giggled. 'Oh yes, Nishith Babu has warmed up to Raju now. After all of that drama between them, thank god for that. Though Raju doesn't still lose a chance to talk back to him, she can be very naughty sometimes. And of course, he firmly believes that *he* taught it all to her, dear old Nishith Babu...we don't ever change, do we?' She leaned back in her chair, 'Mr Mukherjee, do you find Bharat Talkies changed very much from how it was before...after Shankar? I do understand that there has been a lot of talk, about my suitability as a studio head...the choice of Rajbala.'

He seemed at a loss for words, suddenly a little bit uncertain. Perhaps she shouldn't have asked it. She tried to turn the conversation.

'Mr Mukherjee, is there something you would like to say to me...by way of your ideas for Mira, to enhance our efforts? We still have half the picture to shoot. I know that he...Shankar...did greatly value your views,' she smiled gently.

'Err, no...not exactly, ma'am.' He still wasn't looking up at her.

Did she say something to upset him, Ramola wondered. He seemed suddenly so overcome.

She tried again. 'Is everything alright with Seth Makhandas? He was in such a state the other day. I was quite afraid he would take ill if he went on that way, and I do hope he knows what he's doing...unless, of course, he's putting on an act, and not really serious about taking the picture abroad.'

'He is serious alright Madam, no need to doubt that, he has given me his word.' Avinash Mukherjee sounded sharp, though he had addressed the teacup.

Oh dear, thought Ramola, now he thinks I doubt his sincerity. I can be so very stupid sometimes.

'Tell me, Mr Mukherjee,' she was going to lighten the mood. 'Is this a very busy time for you, at office?'

He hesitated. 'Busy...yes...well, not greatly...just the regular.'

'In that case, would you like to have lunch, day after? At the Grand? I can pick you from your office. Should we say one-thirty? It would be nice to talk things over... over a meal?'

'Madam,' he looked definitely annoyed. 'I will have important things to attend to…that day. Should you wish for a meeting you can inform me so that I may come by…now I must take your leave.'

He glanced across at her for a brief second, through his dark rimmed glasses, almost defiant, then stood up pushing back his chair, looked again at the teacup like he had something to say to it…then turned and walked out.

'Well, I never.' Ramola muttered. Such rudeness, what a very odd man he was.

IV

Avinash Mukherjee held his head in his hands. The newspaper lay before him downside up, the weight of his resting elbows creasing it at the corners. He had come straight from Bharat Talkies to his office. To shut himself in.

He had scowled at the newspaper for over an hour. The inverted Ovaltine baby smiling up at him had now and again become the face of Ramola Devi.

Avinash gritted his teeth. As if she was giving alms to him. Offering to lunch with him. Who needed her courtesies? Did she think him to be one of her admirers? Craving her closeness, worshipping her. He had done right. To keep her at arms' length. He smirked bitterly. How many fellows could refuse you, Ramola Devi? How many of them have you got wrapped around your little finger, now that Shankar Da is gone? Were you at it even when he was there, the poor man, never looking up from his work…he wouldn't have known, whatever you did.

He felt angrier still. These bioscope women, they were

all alike. Thinking they could take anyone for a ride. Not him. She would know that now.

Thought no end of herself, she, Ramola Devi. Turning her back on all the talk around her. Didn't bat an eyelid when the Miracle deal went kaput. Going from heroine to director. Anyone could, if they had the Bharat Talkies wherewithal...why, hadn't Shankar Da once said he himself had the makings of a director. Perhaps, one day...if Shankar Da had lived. Dada had liked his ideas, thought them worthwhile. And she...asking his views on *Mirabai*, Avinash snorted angrily. Like it was a matter of some amusement. As if his thoughts were of any great import, when you Madam are more than half finished with your great picture. You might well have called on me before, knowing this picture had mattered to me, just as it did to you.

He had himself returned. Dragging with him that crafty Makhandas. How much doing it had taken, did she even understand? How difficult it was for him to say even ordinary things to her...how he always got that lump in his throat...how much she had hurt him...all alike they were, these bioscope women. Shankar Da, he was different, a true gentleman. Always to be remembered and respected. Ramola Devi, best kept away.

He had Mani...he rubbed her as she purred against him. He had gotten out of his office and driven around a good part of the afternoon. Until the throbbing inside his head had left him with a dull ache. Mani had lain in wait, stretching herself, then running up to him. Could *she* ever be like that, Ramola Devi, ever belong to anyone? Had she ever even belonged to Shankar Da? Why couldn't she run like that to him, like Mani...give in, let him look after her.

He found the anger stirring again inside him. Anyone in his place would think the same of her...that she was like any other bioscope heroine, playing her games. No matter what everyone said about her being a true lady, a class apart from the rest. And then going on about that two *paise ka* heroine of hers. Mr Mukherjee, I have become rather fond of her...wasting herself on that little nobody...you'll know Ramola Devi when she puts a knife in your back, that Rajbala of yours, that one that you're so much in love with now.

What do you know of love Ramola Devi? Of pain? To want someone so much that even her sight makes you feel sick with joy...you won't ever know. He felt the anger rise up in his eyes and swell into the tears that made Mani a black and white blur.

Why couldn't he despise her? Why did he let her come out of nowhere sometimes, to take him over...cloud his mind even when he was laughing, darken his mornings and lighten his nights? Why hadn't he simply taken her offer of that lunch, the chance to look in her eyes... perhaps hold her hand?

Because he was afraid...of her...that if he looked in her eyes for a while she would read his mind. Those fears behind his calmness, his feelings of unworthiness that crept in when she was before him, those that he would then cover up with his nonchalance...or indignation, like he had, that morning. She would see it all, he knew that, if he ever did let her come close. She would uncover him, know his faults. And that he could not let happen.

V

Anil was feeling sick inside.

Potla picked another *khasta kachori* and bit into it. 'Mmmm...*khasha*...outstanding,' he closed his eyes and munched dreamily, then opened them again. 'What Anil Da...not eating?'

Bikash, production-in-charge at Bharat Talkies, rose from his corner on the floor, dusted the crumbs off his dhoti, then yelled. '*Eii* Ganshaaa.'

Ganesh, cook's boy at the men's mess house, yelled back from the hallway's end, 'Whaaat...?'

'One, two, three...Anil...Prabal...no?' Bikash yelled again. 'Three more teas, *jaldi*...' He looked around at his guests assembled in his lodgings at the boarding house. 'What I was saying, things have changed, *dada* has changed, he's not his old self anymore...Kedar Da. Something's not right. I told Potla that day...and all after this Rajbala came, say whatever you will. Even after Shankar Da died he was not like this. Gone into a shell, he has, true or not? You say, Potla...' He looked at Potla.

Potla cleared his throat, raised his eyebrows in consideration, picked a *lyangcha* and bit into it. 'Not untrue that,' he mused through his chomps, flashing the breakdown of *lyangcha* into lumpy pieces of *kheer*.

'Close your mouth, you *rakshasa*, you'll get fired if our Madam sees you...learn to eat like a *memsahib*...I mean, *sahib*.' Shyamal slapped Potla's back.

A maddened Potla hit him back. 'Is eating also some art...or what...you *shaala* assistant cameraman? What's your work? Big artist you think you are, three and half years I've been at Bharat Talkies, so many like you came and went, understood?'

'*Ei*, stop it you two.' Bikash snapped. '*Ei* Shyamal, let him eat...and Anil, you fasting or what? *Ne*, eat a *lyangcha*.'

Slowly Anil pulled a *lyangcha* from the plate and took it to his mouth. He looked at Bikash, 'You were saying... about Kedar Da, he said something to you?'

'*Naaa*...nothing, but it's there for everyone to see. Put Potla on *Mirabai*, and himself doing sound for that first time director. Kedar Gupta, famous sound recordist of our industry not working on the big picture...why?'

'Why...am I no good, or what?' Potla scowled at Bikash.

'*Ei* quiet, eat another *lyangcha*...ne...' Bikash pushed the plate to Potla. Then pursed his lips thoughtfully. 'Remember, he didn't come to the studio some days, just after this Rajbala came. Sent word he was sick. Nothing happened, guaranteed, I know it. My *masima* is their neighbour...next door...they'd have known, had there been some illness.'

Anil felt his heart sink. Bikash knew.

'Even then I would think nothing of it. But, you say Potla...what things he said about that Rajbala...' Bikash nudged Potla.

'Why don't you? Always poking me everybody,' Potla looked uncomfortable.

'Say it, acting shy like a girl...tell them...' Bikash scolded Potla.

Potla picked another *kachori*, viewed it for a moment, then put it back. 'It was Kedar Da only who told me about the heroine being changed for *Mirabai*. I couldn't believe...from Ramola Devi to that Rajbala...said Madam had called him and said to tell everybody. Kedar Da said...that she was a good choice, and that we should all stand with Madam's decision...'

Bikash slapped his leg. 'Madam's decision my foot! He didn't even hear me out, when I had started to protest. Same thing he said to me, that it was final and Madam would hear nothing more. But...this much I can say, Madam did not want this Rajbala, her face, the way she spoke that first day we took Rajbala's shots...I was on the set. Madam did not want even to look at that girl...you say, Shyamal, weren't you at the camera, with Bimal Da that day?'

Prabal was nodding. A Shankar Chattopadhyay find, Prabal at twenty-nine was reckoned the industry's most promising music director. 'It's true, *re*, the first music sittings also...same...Madam would just sit, looking out of the window.'

'One more thing,' Shyamal cut in. 'that day when Rajbala first came to the studio, we were all waiting, remember, to see her? She came alone, in the car they had sent from the studio. Anil Da, you said to me to take her to Madam's office. First thing Madam asks me, isn't Kedar Babu with you? Where is Kedar Babu? Her face... like she thought Kedar Da would get Rajbala to her... why? I didn't think anything of it then, but now...'

'Then? Tell me then?' Bikash grimaced. 'What are we to make of all this?'

Potla interjected. 'Aren't we making too much of it? And anyhow, now Madam seems quite happy with Rajbala. Not how she was before.'

'Naturally...' Bikash cut him off. '...Rajbala has become better. Madam and Nishith Babu have been after her, night and day...even I could become some top heroine if somebody like our Madam trained me.'

'That is all fine', Shyamal chewed on his lip. 'But it still doesn't explain Kedar Da's *haab-bhab*, his demeanour... we have all noticed it, whatever we may say. This is the world of bioscope brothers, everything happens here,' he nodded meaningfully.

Anil had had enough. He got up slowly.

'I have to leave, *re*...some work, before I go home...'

'You ate nothing. You also in some trouble, or what, like our beloved Kedar Da?' Bikash laughed. 'Or being manager-in-chief doesn't agree with you?' He winked.

'Bikash, you really are too much sometimes.' Anil heard Potla as he walked away.

What if any of this talk got to Minati *bouthan*? She who had mothered him like her own son, she and Kedar Da. What had he gotten Kedar Da into? And, what had Kedar Da told Madam about Rajbala? Whatever it was it had taken his peace away...they were right. Kedar Da had not been himself. He had known it before any of them...and it was all for him.

And Raju...Raju had changed, she too was not herself. The last two times they met alone, she hadn't become angry even once...nor complained, it just wasn't like her, like she was in another world. And...last evening, she had not come...though he had signalled clearly in the studio when he had gotten her alone for a minute. And she had understood it, he knew that. Then why? Was she not well? Was anything troubling her? Madam, he knew, was pleased with her, Anil, this girl will go far, she had said to him. He had not expected it, and it had made him happy. But she...Raju, was she happy? He had to get her alone for a minute, somewhere in the studio...he simply had to know.

VI

'It's all in the mind', sighed Ambarish Dev Burma. 'All of it. If you can take over their minds you will have their bodies. Get to skin and flesh in haste and you get only a part of it...' Their living bodies could not ever be so delightful. The body had to die and be rid of its dirt, to become beautiful. If Putu had died when she was little... if...if only he had thought to take her up to the roof and fling her down, like Baba had come flying down from atop their estate house. Then perhaps she would have become beautiful, a pretty little thing. But no, she had lived, and grown into a monster, an ugly oily-headed pug-nosed good-for-naught. He might have loved her, if he had held her little bloodied body...its crushed pulpy skull and broken face, like how they had found Baba.

He had loved Ma with all his heart that night as she had lain in his arms, as he had felt her slowly stiffen. He had liked it when she was cold but still gentle...soft. When he still could part the folds of skin and the hinges and openings...enter them with his fingers, feel the last of the moistness, before it all became like wood. Like how that keeper at the studio must have found that gone-to-hell Menoka...soft and cold...the idiot, then racing to call the boss, when he could have had so much fun with her. Such waste, if only he had known what was on her mind, he never would have let go of her that night. He groaned. To have watched, as she had noosed the sari around her thin neck. She had used one of the chairs, or stools perhaps, from the dressing room. The tin roof, with its low girders, she had managed to get that sari through one of them, knotted it below then twisted the other end around her neck...and swung. She must have been in some state, that *beshya*, to be drunk and still have managed all of that. Must have needed all of her strength...to kick away the chair from under her feet. He had not understood the whole of her, he must have left just a little bit of her mind free...and she had trumped him. He might have pushed her a tiny bit too hard, he had to admit, in those last days when the picture had gone on the floor. He had gotten so very tired of her tears and clinging. He had wanted a fight from her. And the more she fought back, the more fun he had had...taming her back again. He had never thought she could free herself...just like that.

She would pay for Menoka...Rajbala would...she would make it up to him. He was flushed, he ran his fingers through his hair, then rubbed his face with his hands. Even his thoughts of Rajubala made him feel all funny these days, like he hadn't ever felt before. He'd never really...he mused...well, greatly enjoyed his physical intimacies with those other girls, not even Menoka, not as much as he had loved playing all of those games with them. Tiresome, how such intimacies always had meant looking in their eyes...how they unfailingly tried to suck you in, thinking they could make you happy. Still...it made them yield, that whole charade of love, you could take over their silly daft little heads.

Only…he had never really fancied the apogee of it, with those other girls. Menoka had stirred that in him, with her death. He hadn't slept two nights and two days in the thrill of it, after he had heard. True, he was angry, furious at himself more than her for letting her get away. But then…he had fallen truly in love…with Menoka… it all had passed so very clearly before him, her swaying limp body, her sari come undone…perhaps, she had clutched at her neck, tried to free herself in those very last moments. And then, her neck had hung forward, tongue bitten…those fists…and tiny toes still tight from clawing the air. Perhaps the keeper, when he had got her down… he must have needed a hand, called an accomplice…the two of them, perhaps they had had a bit of fun with her. He hoped that they had. He chuckled as those thoughts came back to him.

And now…how he loved Rajbala. Never had he loved living flesh and skin in this way, except Ma. Ma hadn't let him come to her even in her last days, not while she still could look upon him. Then her eyes had closed and he had crept in beside her, sent them all away… and watched, as her breaths had turned to gasps then slowly run out, like air from a white clothed balloon. Ma had wanted to die, he knew it…even Menoka…but they didn't die for Him. No, they had died to get away from him. And for that they would rot. Rajbala would die for him, in her love of him. He would see to that. All soft and cold, hung from a rope, eyes open staring at nothing…eyes that wouldn't then peer into his insides. He would lay her down ever so gently, and look in those dead eyes when he would make love to her.

VII

'That dog in that picture, he is also a star,' he'd smiled at her. 'Like you Rajbala. Do you want to be a star like him...like that little dog?'

Raju tossed in her slumber and twitched. She was in the old house with the statues and marble floors, those wooden stairs, the pictures on the walls. One of them had a man wearing nothing cutting the throat of a little girl, a girl with golden hair. Had he cut off more heads, like Ma Kali? Were they real, that man and that girl? From somewhere far off?

He had seen her looking. 'You like that painting? My father had bought it...he was like that man.' She hadn't known what he had meant.

He had shown her some photographs, from bioscope pictures made in America. In the dark library room, the pictures making blocks of brightness as he had held the oil lamp over them. He hadn't switched on any lights. Only the two big oil lamps, carried in by that man who would open the door to her. The man who never looked at her.

Raju sat up in bed, her throat dry. She ran her tongue on the roof of her mouth. The water-filled earthen pitcher was by the side of the bed. Could she get to it? Might not she get pulled into some dark underworld if she so much as put a foot out of bed? Crocodiles crawling below her in the dark...waiting...to bite off her two feet if they hazarded their way out of her bed.

When she had gotten back from the old house, it was the dead of night. She had heard the church clock strike the chime of one as she was stepping into the car, his car that would get her back every time. Now her visits were closer, more often than before. He would send for her through his man Asghar, the driver who came sometimes even as she was finishing her evening's meal, and waited as she got quickly dressed. Like the man who would open the door in the old house, Asghar never spoke to her. She knew his name because *Saheb* had called out to him one time…'Asghar…' for him to take her back.

Saheb would always be in the corner room upstairs, the room with the big bed where she had first sat. Sometimes he wouldn't speak or even look her way, as she would creep in and climb onto the bed, like on that first night. Somehow she had known it to be her place…*Saheb* had a way of telling her things without saying them. She understood from the way he looked at something, or leaned back in his chair. Like he was speaking to her through his arms and feet…and those eyes. And there were some things…a long lock of hair laid on the pillow. Who's was it? She hadn't seen any woman ever in that place, it had to be a woman's. And then, the jasmine garland laid on the bed's side. It was for her, she had known it. Though she hadn't touched it. It had lain there, awaiting her, buds half-open, like *Saheb*'s watching eyes…she would feel his eyes on her even as she would look away.

He still had not come close. Why? They…men… they all tried it, sometime or other, why not he? She'd even tried her own little things…to draw him, in the beginning. He had looked away, almost ashamed. When he had led her to the darkened library he had walked straight ahead…not behind, so he could lay his eyes on her bottom. Led her like she was that little dog in the picture.

'Fame...' his face had flickered red in the lamp's glow. 'Like sand...quicksand...like the hair that comes off your head, alive now, dead tomorrow. Do you waste hair Rajbala, when you do up your hair?'

She had felt suddenly bald, like her head of long dark hair had been shorn by the glint of his eyes.

He had smiled. 'You cannot imagine it, but for art, we must learn to lose, sacrifice, give up...we must live our lives through our art, else we will be like that little dog, a bit of something today and nothing tomorrow... forgotten...finished.'

Raju tried again to moisten her lips but her tongue was parched. She had to get to that pitcher by the bed. She stretched her toes, then her feet...faltered an instant, then dragged her feet off the bed. For a moment a black dread choked her as she felt hidden fangs grab her feet and pull her by the legs. Then the spinning in her head stopped as she felt coldness under her feet. Her feet were on the stone floor.

The water was cool, it swilled her insides. She poured herself another tumbler and glugged it half. Her head felt heavy, the water swam inside her. She was going to vomit. She needed to breathe. She walked to the open window and pulled aside the fluttering curtain. Outside was the first hint of dawn. Raju gasped. Then passed wind...a small burst from her behind, then another one, loud and lingering. Her insides eased.

Was it what she had pressed inside her, night before, for fear it would let out in front of him, the hastily eaten *luchi-aloodum*. Asghar had presented himself when she was only half way through. Kamala Masi had opened the door to him, and she had had to stuff the rest before running to wash her hands. Asghar would sit solemnly but his face would start to twitch if she did not rush. *Saheb* is waiting, he seemed to say...he cannot be kept waiting long.

She had smelled the jasmine again, in the room with the bed...and the old almirahs. But last night there was no garland. That was another day...before...when they had had jasmine flowers on the set also, for her Krishna puja song. She rubbed her eyes. Was it then...or last night? Raju blinked. Her head ached. She hadn't felt like this ever, even when she would be half the night at some lodge or motel, taking them...one...or by twos. She sighed.

She hadn't seen Natabar Da in so many days. He had come again, another day, to the studio. She had sent him away. 'Go Natabar Da. I have to eat, then rest...I have work to do...my days don't pass roaming about in the studio para.' Natabar had looked away. 'I know, didi, I am a worthless no-good.' He hadn't come back. His shrill voice was in her ears, the ring of his steps as he put up one of those impromptu acts that would have her in splits. She now loathed his sight. What would he know...of art...the likes of Natabar Da, with their cheap *naachgana*. But that was all behind her. *Saheb* had said she had art in her...a hundred like Natabar Da couldn't keep her down.

Again she rubbed her eyes. She wanted to stay in that day, not go to the studio. Could she send word, to Madam, when the car came? Madam would not be angry, she would understand. But no, how was that to be, they were going to go outdoor that morning...the forest scenes. It was all arranged. The whole unit would leave from the studio. The car from the studio would come at eight, to pick her.

VIII

The man sitting across the table from her smiled, showing half of a row of very white teeth. Ramola saw red. He spoke again.

'Madam, you are misunderstanding me, it is only a social visit. If you will ask her, she will not say no...'

Dey Babu was secretary to one of their Board members. He had arrived with the customary *Nobobarsha* offerings. And a proposition, for Ramola Devi's new heroine. The said Board member would like to meet with Rajbala in private, in his country house, one evening. He had been told about Madam's remarkable new find...if Madam could persuade the girl, and knowing how much the said gentleman had benefitted Bharat Talkies and Shankar Babu, and how much he could be of assistance to Madam herself, now that she had at hand the very difficult task of running a top studio like Bharat Talkies...a burden, truly, for a lady so gentle.

'You swine...' escaped Ramola's lips and she said it again, 'you swine.' She watched his face change. Her voice trembled. 'You think I am sitting in this chair to put a price on the girls that work here, in my studio?'

He opened his mouth then shut it.

'What do you think Bharat Talkies is, Dey Babu...a marketplace...a bazaar?'

She stood up, picked one of the large boxes of sweetmeats that Dey Babu had brought with him, and hurled it over his head. The box landed with a thud, scattering its contents along the floor behind him. She banged the bell on her desk.

'Send Anil Babu, at once...' she shouted to the startled orderly.

She looked again at Dey Babu. He was frozen in his chair, eyes blazing, jaw hard.

'Would you...or your malik, our revered board member, have dared to make this suggestion to Shankar, if he was there? Do you dare say this to me because you think I am helpless now, without Shankar? That I am now ready to hear anything?'

Dey Babu stayed silent. Ramola gritted her teeth. She wasn't going to let him off, so easy.

'Your *malik*, Dey Babu, he had lost his family estate, no? Taken over by the government I heard, for mismanagement. Now, the zamindari *ruab*, that princely temper, has it come down to this?' she squinted savagely. 'Do you know how old this girl is, Rajbala? Nineteen or twenty...younger even than his charming daughter, who I happen to know well.'

A knock sounded. Anil opened the door, walked in and slipped on a pink *chamcham* before he saw the mess on the floor.

'What...*e ki*...all this...Madam, you wanted me?'

'Yes Anil, I called for you. Step over that mess, will you, we'll have it cleaned later'. She felt like her insides were burning. They thought they could push her, in the name of Bharat Talkies...and in here, inside the Bharat Talkies studio. They would know better.

Dey Babu made a move, to extricate himself.

'Madam...I see that you are busy...' he smiled weakly as he half stood. 'I must take your leave. My apologies for the mess...my feet slipped, and the box from my hands...' he waved at the floored *chamchams*.

'Sit...sit down, Mr Dey...' Ramola ordered, causing Dey Babu to sink back in his chair. She raised her eyebrows, her signature style, like how it would be in a critical scene.

'Anil...' she turned to him. 'Do you want to know what Mr Dey has proposed to me, on behalf of our honoured board member?'

'Madam, I beg you...for your own sake...' Dey Babu face had reddened.

'Are you trying to warn me off...Mr Dey?' Ramola leaned forward with a flourish. 'For my sake, is it? Or for the sake of covering up what you really make of us? How you look upon these young girls, who work in the studios, to earn their living...how you attempt to push them down, no matter all your talk of freedom...and progress. And how you imagined you could make me a party to it.'

She turned again to Anil.

'Mr Dey here suggested we send Rajbala...to... entertain his *malik*, our famous educator and leader, *desh neta*, who is such a voice in our nationalist politics.'

Dey Babu had had enough. 'I warn you Madam, say no more, or you will see the consequences...' He pushed back his chair angrily and stood up. 'Do you think that Shankar Babu never made any concessions? That he could run this studio without keeping all parties...

happy? You think you can, Madam, give a certificate of character to such a class of girls that you keep on pay in your famous studio...surely their truth is not hidden from you?'

'You say Shankar's name in this one more time, Mr Dey, and I will see that the whole world hears of this. The truth of these girls is hidden from nobody, and not least such honourable and respectable persons as claim to uplift their kind. And yet...you come to me here seeking such a favour. Kindly, Mr Dey, take your belongings and leave my office...forthwith...' She gestured to the boxes and packets that he had arrived bearing.

'Anil, I want a certain name taken off our Board of Directors, here and now...despatch him a letter, with my regards. I will take the full responsibility for my decision. We would be better off...and more respectable, without such names to grace us.' She watched Dey Babu as he tiptoed out past the *chamchams*. She was feeling calmer.

'Sit, Anil.' She gestured to the empty chair across from her. Anil hung his head as he gingerly took his seat.

'Anil, look at me...' Ramola sensed his thoughts. 'What makes you so ashamed?' She paused to catch her breath. Anil still did not look up.

'Should I not have called you in, do you think? So great should have been my discomfort, being approached thus, a lady of my place in society?'

'Should...I...Madam, ask someone to clear it...' Anil gestured behind him, seeing possible escape.

'No Anil, not just now. I want you to hear what I have to say,' Ramola pursed her lips before she spoke again. She was thinking clearly now.

'Listen Anil, I was horrified...at the impudence. That he dared to even say such a thing in my presence. I might have pretended, that I did not quite understand, as it is so easy to do in such things, changed the talk...and who might have prevailed on me to send Raju anywhere. I was not forced in any way, to face up to him. After all it was not really about me...Ramola Devi, was it... but one of these girls, and don't we all know the truth about them? And still...it angered me...so much that I could not help myself...' she regarded the mess on the floor.

'Rather unlike me...' she murmured running her hand over her hair. She laughed, 'And so very like Raju... wouldn't you say, Anil?' Anil smiled weakly.

'That man...that awful loathsome man...' she felt the anger rise again, '...and he that sent him, they felt no shame broaching it to me. I never would have faced such a thing, had he...Shankar...been there. All this while, I was so far removed from these girls...like Menoka... and whatever happened to them. Because he had stood between me and everything else...everything that really is real, in our world,' she sighed. 'But now, not any more, not if I choose to still be a part of this our world of bioscope pictures. Whether I appear in the pictures or not is no matter...'

Anil's voice shook. 'Madam, no one should have dared it...an insult to you is an insult to us all.'

Ramola smiled. 'And Raju? What of her? How they thought of her? What about such other girls, Anil?' Anil looked away. How was Madam to know how he felt about Raju? What if someone else had been in her place?

If they had forced Raju...if Raju had given in, for the sake of a big name like Bharat Talkies...what if...

He looked up at Ramola. Should he tell Madam, about him and Raju? Would she understand? She spoke softly.

'You had better ask someone to clean that mess...'

IX

To
Mme. Ramola Devi Chattopadhyay
Proprietor, Bharat Talkies
Tollygunge
Calcutta

Dear Madam,

I trust this letter finds you in good health and spirits. Kindly inform me at my office address as noted below, as and when you would wish further consultations regarding your under-production motion picture *Mirabai*, as being undertaken at the Bharat Talkies studio in Tollygunge under your own direction and supervision.

Thanking you

Faithfully yours
Avinash Mukherjee
8 Royal Exchange Place, Calcutta.

Her pursed lips opened out in a smile, as she read the brief missive another time. The letter had been hand delivered to the studio that afternoon, and somehow it had lightened the day for her. What a remarkably odd man he is, she thought again, an air of mock exasperation about her as she held the fountain pen to her lips before starting to write her reply.

Dear Mr Mukherjee,

Thank you for your letter. May I suggest Saturday, the 3rd of May as a suitable date for a consultation?

I understand that you are not kindly disposed towards the Grand. Might it be the Ritz then? 1 o'clock on the given day.

Thanking you

Most sincerely
Ramola.

She beamed mischievously, as she folded the notepaper and pushed in inside an envelope with her name printed on it. She would get it delivered by someone at the studio, in the morning. She'd smiled to herself on her way back home in the car as she had imagined a mortified Avinash Mukherjee, in all his stiff formality really trying to make amends for his very queer abruptness of that last day. Flinching like that at the idea of lunching with her! She couldn't resist the temptation to tease. He would still cringe, of that she was sure, Grand or the Ritz...he really was so peculiar in his ways, unlike anyone else that she knew. So very sincere, and yet charming in all his unease...not a bit the overly ambitious attention seeker, or those annoyingly over-interested fawners that she so frequently encountered. Anyhow, Saturday was still three days, he could well write back and refuse if he really did not wish to come. But then, why write to her at all? Surely, he was well aware that *Mirabai* was close to being finished...two more songs to take and the last scenes, for which she had told Raju to take a bit of time, to ready herself...the end would need some serious attention. She was thinking of releasing it in July, or possibly August...

What in the wide world then could he, Mr Mukherjee, now hope to offer her, by way of a consultation! Her lips quivered as she stopped a smile. It had been more than a fortnight since he had last stopped by...soon after that most curious visit from Seth Makhandas.

She hadn't heard from Sethji since, she had started to imagine it was some kind of intimate jest between Avinash Mukherjee and Seth Makhandas that somehow got played out in her presence...what for though she couldn't imagine, for all the world. She knew now what she hoped of *Mirabai*...the new *Mirabai*. Not anything outstanding or very highly cultured as she and Shankar had imagined it, what with the original script changed and so many of the dialogues cut. She had also cut down on the scale of it, she would have to watch her steps going forward. Their books were in order...for now, but backers like Seth Makhandas had their doubts, she knew, and then, there had been so much talk on Raju being the new heroine. They had put their trust in Shankar, they would look out now for what she would make of Bharat Talkies.

In a way, Ramola mused, perhaps, it had not been such a bad thing, getting another heroine for Mira. It had allowed her to take charge of the studio...to understand and act...rather than having to worry about her own performance. She could get so absorbed in her characters she was inclined to become withdrawn, and that simply would not have done. She had only shot for a few sequences, though of course Mira was a part of her now, it always would be. She smiled. Raju had written herself all over Mira now, with her vigour...a force and energy that somehow made this Mira more human, a living and breathing thing, rather different from her own. Somehow more lovable, more close to this world. She smiled again in recollection...poor Devdutt Chowdhury...Raju had fairly decimated him in the few scenes that they had together. She had decided to keep the shot of Raju's impromptu snatching of a sword off one of the palace guards to encounter Devdutt's Bhojraj as he had ordered a removal of her Krishna idol. Devdutt's face had been a picture to behold. 'Messing with the script like that, confronting me, am I a villain, *naki*?' he had moaned later in his decorous fashion. True, it had gone a bit against the grain of the picture, that scene. Bhojraj had been an accommodating husband to Mira, her confidant. Though occasionally aggrieved by her actions, she imagined, like Shankar had been, by her. But it had been such a rare moment of unscripted exuberance, unrehearsed and so very artless...like any other moment of conflict, between any loving wife and husband.

What would happen after *Mirabai* was finished? Would she release Raju? Or keep her? She had not thought through it. Their contract with her was for this one picture. She would have to take stock...but in truth, she didn't want to let Raju go, that girl was one in a hundred. Ramola rubbed her eyes. She would have to see how audiences took to Raju before she made up her mind. Funnily enough, Kedar Babu, having pushed her so into getting Rajbala, and then to promoting Anil to his new position of manager-in-chief, had simply gone into the shadows these last months when they had remade *Mirabai* with Raju. His assistant Pankaj...Potla as they all called him, was capable enough, and she had had no reason to complain. And Kedar Babu did visit the sets occasionally...like that last day when they were taking the outdoor shots of the horses, and then another day, when they had canned the durbar sequence, and both days Raju had not had her scenes, she remembered that. He had come in to see her privately in the office, on several occasions, to apprise and reassure her. That he had had Pankaj report to him every day after work, and would instruct him for the next day's shoot.

'How long will I stay on Madam,' he had said wistfully. 'You and Shankar Babu have always given me so much respect...I am not deserving of it...now I have to prepare someone to take over from me.'

She had protested, but hadn't liked to press him. She hadn't brought up Rajbala either, and for that he had seemed grateful. He had been the Kedar Babu she had known all of these years, kind and affable...not one bit how he had been with her over those few days, when he had prevailed on her in the Raju matter. She still couldn't imagine it, him and Rajbala...perhaps she had misunderstood something, those days were like a blur in her mind now. She had watched out for Kedar Babu's encounter with Raju, but it had not happened. And she had been far too engrossed with everything to give it more thought, more so now, that Raju had turned into such a surprise, after the first trouble she gave, the little rascal. She had been like an astonishment to them all, not least old Nishith Babu, who had gone so far as to declare she was his best pupil after herself...dear old Nishith Babu...even Bimal Babu had praised her shots, and he was known to be a little bit mean, with the girls especially.

Though surely nothing next to Ambarish...how he had pushed Menoka to the very edge, somehow she couldn't get Menoka out of her mind. It kept coming back to her, more after Raju had come. Had it been Raju in place of Menoka, would she have kept her silence? How were they different, Menoka and Raju, both studio girls...both so beneath her station in life that they did not merit to be in her thoughts even. Yet, she would go back to the night of the New Year...sometimes in her sleep, waking troubled, and then angry. Angry with herself, and most of all Shankar. That night she had not held it against him...but later...perhaps it was Raju that had changed her mind. And that loathsome Dey Babu, he had hinted that Shankar had given in, to keep the big people happy...at the cost of girls like Raju and Menoka. Daring to make that kind of proposition to her. Like there was no distance really between herself and Raju... or any studio girl, for that matter. How it had infuriated her, his insinuation about Shankar...but Shankar, you did let Menoka's death pass, like it was nothing. And all of those poor wretches, those other girls, and all of it happening under our very noses...only because we did not wish to irk one of our own. We kept quiet, us all... only whispers. If she, they all, had broken that wall of silence...in some way...perhaps it might have warned off the likes of Dey Babu. Well, he did get a taste of it, and better late than never, she thought grimly.

But Ambarish...he worried her, more than she liked to admit. He had come to see her, after Shankar died, his courtesies had not seemed regular...somehow rather odd, why she still could not fathom. Not once had he uttered any commiserations. Though of course Ambarish had always been a little bit odd. So brilliant in his work, but he mingled with none of the studio lot. No family that she knew of...his mother had died some years ago. He had turned more reticent after they had had to stop work on *Pativrata*, after Menoka. It was to be his next big picture, though he had directed those two educational shorts in the meantime, the stuff that the big studios had to keep turning out these days. He had himself offered it...given he was out of work, he had joked. And, of course, that comedy short, which had done quite well, really...who knew Ambarish could have a flair for comedy. He really was rather brilliant. He had said he would find a new heroine for *Pativrata*, and she had left it at that...only Mira had been on her mind. But she had seen less and less of him at the studio. The last time was soon after Raju had arrived, when he had come on the set one morning and watched as Raju had rehearsed. Two months in a row he had not taken his pay from the studio. Was he severing his ties then...with Bharat Talkies? She would need to find him, and speak with him, sooner now than later, though she hardly relished that prospect. What was he up to...Ambarish?

X

The pork curry had tasted good, with the hot chillies. She always made it special for him, how he liked it. He had chanced upon Fan on one of his visits to the China para. Fan kept pigs, and cooked them for the nearby leather workers. It was hard to tell from seeing her how strong she was. He had watched her one afternoon as she had dragged a squealing swine into the open yard and struck it with her axe. The screams kept coming as it had slowly bled, while Fan had busied herself tossing up some lunch. They had eaten silently in her kitchen, by the yard, hearing the cries and the tossing. Fan liked him, he could tell that. He liked her too, though they only spoke in signs. He could see it in her eyes. That she liked being close with them, once the life had ebbed out of them, while she cleaned the bloody mess and skinned them.

Fan's husband adored her. Why she had to do it all herself, he had said to Ambarish in his broken pidgin. She could get a man for the dirty work, they could afford it. What did he know, that Cheena opium *khor*? She likes it, she just doesn't tell him that. That old fool was lucky to have her. He might himself have gotten Ma a *bouma*, a very dear daughter-in-law, had he found someone like Fan...he giggled at the thought.

He might have taken a rickshaw back to the end of Cheena *para*, after dinner at Fan's, but he had chosen to walk. Through the dark allies he knew so well. The darkness that hid him from the world. What a pity, he thought, that one couldn't axe one of them *beshya*s and stand by and hear the squeals. Were those *beshya* houses any different from Fan's pig sty? What was different... between those pigs and the flesh on a whore? But these English and their darned laws...they'd still call it murder if someone did it to a rotten *beshya*.

Though he hadn't gone to one, since he had found Rajbala. She was different from those others. She captivated him. So eager to be at the very top...be seen and counted. He smiled. To put her past behind her, at whatever cost. She had made it easy for him, after a bit. To get inside her head. Build the castles and prisons there. Prisons that she wanted to escape and castles where she wished to ensconce herself. Just as he had wanted it. Rajbala, the prisoner princess.

Menoka...he had made and then unmade her. The little nobody had started to think no end of herself. So he had had to put her in her place. It hadn't taken him much doing. He had known her...inside and outside... he would, wouldn't he, picking her from the gutter, that cage stuffed with pigs. Rajbala now, she was another thing. He had to give that to her, bitch in the midst of them dogs, girl that could give the men in their line a run for their money. No matter what *raddi* junk pictures she was queen of. She'd had the cheek to try her juice on him...those first days, slipping her sari from her chest, making eyes at him...he snorted. Had she imagined him to be one of her Raju Darling public? She had made him think a little bit though, how to get inside that smug head of hers...muddle it up a little bit, and hadn't he enjoyed it. He was so tired of the likes of Menoka, clutching and clinging, their surrender at his feet...he needed more...a game, like those pigs Fan hunted, petting and pushing them out of their dens to where she had her axe ready. Making them think she would feed them, humming and calling out to them by their names.

He had pictured it...Ma in a cage with Putu when Putu would feed at her breast, then Putu pulled away from Ma, like Fan's fattened piglets. Putu streaming blood at the neck, while Ma looked on. Still, he sighed, one had to be sensible about these things. Not get carried away. And Rajbala was no Putu. Putu had pulp in place of brains...Ma's little piglet, but Rajbala, she was sharp alright. How clever are you Rajbala? Clever enough to force back a dream? Because, after all, it is only a dream, is it not? You never could get there, could you? One of your kind be one of *us*? No matter what the great and good Ramola Devi says to you.

Ramola Devi...our big director of tomorrow, so sure, are you, that this picture of yours will see light of day? He grinned, keep a hold on your heroine, Madam... keep her very close to you. For who knows, what might happen?

PART 5

I

Natabar had known something was wrong. But what could he do about it. The girl did not want to see his face even. Still, he had not lost sight of her...no, not he... *nyaka* Natabar knew when he had to keep his eyes and ears open. He had put Kajol on the job.

Kajol was fifteen or sixteen. Birthed and left to die beside one of the *nulla*s in the studio *para*, he had found a nest with Natabar, though these days after he got the high from his *nesha*, he would swear and beat Natabar, sometimes causing Natabar to run out onto the street to escape the blows. Still, Kajol had his uses. Dark and shrunken with two or three bald patches on his head, he could melt into the shadows of the night. Nobody ever noticed Kajol, or if they did, they never remembered him. Kajol had kept watch outside of where Raju lived, in the evenings and until the early hours of morning when the car from the old house would bring her back.

'Big car, black one...' he said to Natabar. 'Dent in the side.'

'Whereabouts does she go? You made anything of it?' Natabar asked eagerly.

'You *saala nyaaka*, what can I make out,' Kajol spat at Natabar, '...middle of the night...what, will I go flying after the car, to see where it goes? Picks the girl and off it goes, then back again, how do I know where that *saali* slut goes in the night?'

'Who drives?' Natabar tried again.

Kajol pondered. 'Man's a *musalman*, one day he stepped on something dead, something in the dark...rat or cat or something...then said, *ya* Allah.'

'Hmmm...' Natabar mused, that was precious little to go by, so many of these rich people had *musalman* drivers.

'But it's the same car every time...now, give me the money...' Kajol was getting thirsty. He wanted to get to his *adda*.

So, she's got a fixed *babu* now. But that was the funny thing, Natabar pondered. Raju had hardly ever wanted to see again the face of anybody she took once...how could it be that she had changed, just like that. Why... so many of them had pleaded with him, but she had refused. Else, Natabar sighed, they would be sitting on a mountain of notes. That girl always had too many likes and dislikes. It wasn't like her, to settle with a *babu*, like some of these other girls.

Who put her to it? That *magi* Kamala? Surely not. Wouldn't she shrink in fear in front of Raju? No, Raju had kept her under her feet. But then, who else? If only this boy Kajol wouldn't be so stoned.

And her man? Who was he? Someone of the studio *para*? But whoever it was had to be somebody important. Natabar knew Raju well enough.

'*Ei buro*, you old fool, you give my money or I'll find that stick.' Kajol was lounging in the corner of their dingy room. Suddenly, he perked up.

'*Arre*, see I forgot...*saala*, without drink in my stomach I can't even think.'

Natabar was fumbling in his pocket for some change.

'What now...' he was fed up of this boy. Showing his face after so many days, and with what?

'...*Arre*...I forgot, that old *magi*, that one that keeps them whores, feeds on them...*ufff* I can't remember my own name sometimes these days...' Kajol cackled. 'Some flower, that's her name...*jui*...*golap*...hmmm yes, yes, I remembered, *padma*, Padma masi of the studio *para*. That *magi* came to that girl's house one day, before the car came, stayed a half hour...or maybe one...I fell asleep on the footpath, woke up when the car came. That *buri*, that hag went in the car, with your *pyaari*, your precious slut.'

Natabar had frozen. Kajol grabbed the money from his hands, and ran out. Natabar sank to the floor.

Padma, that whoring bitch. She would sell the skin off the back of these girls, eat their flesh. How she hated them, him and his kind, and he for one had turned half the studio *para* against her. Everybody knew it was him against her, in their side of the line. Only, he could fight tooth and nail for his girls, so what that he put them in the line...and that Padma, Natabar smirked...in her hands, those girls were as good as dead. Raju had never said anything about Padma. Not even her name. How did Padma get her hands on Raju? Kamala...must be that. Kamala, that rotten old *magi*, she'd left the studio *para* a long time but she had her friends. Padma...that was it, Padma had gotten Raju to where she would go in the night. That Padma could kill...for money. He had to know, somehow, where Raju went. Kajol wouldn't do. Who could he tell? Should he tell Jhantu? Perhaps, but first he would have to know more.

II

He's going to run, Ramola thought. He's not going to be able to go through with it.

The tall man in the grey trousers was hovering near the door of the main dining hall of the newly opened private hotel, the Ritz. It was twenty minutes past one in the afternoon, and she had come in sharp on time. He was late, and he was looking like someone had dragged him there.

Avinash Mukherjee bowed slightly not looking at her, then walked across stiffly and gingerly seated himself across from her. Ramola puckered her lips.

'How are you Mr Mukherjee, I thought you weren't coming after all,' she raised her eyebrows in mock displeasure.

'I...I am late...I...' he fumbled before looking up at her. She was smiling. He looked away.

'You're really making me feel rather ashamed Mr Mukherjee,' she said. He had ordered only soup, she the chicken and gravy, her favourite. 'Are you not hungry?'

'Yes...no, not exactly Madam, late breakfast I took, in the office,' he took another swig from his glass. She wondered what might be a suitable subject of talk.

'Tell me Mr Mukherjee, you have been...err...involved with the pictures for some years now, the business side of it, I mean? Did you ever think of getting in them, I mean as an actor...you do have that kind of face you know.'

It wasn't something she'd thought before, why, he really was rather good-looking, now that she had looked at him more carefully. In truth, he might have been in the pictures.

Avinash Mukherjee choked on his glass, coughed, then unexpectedly broke into a smile.

'Well in fact, Madam…I did try my luck, in the very early days of my career. Silent picture it was…but not quite my thing, as it turned out.'

'Now that's a little secret you've hidden from us all,' Ramola beamed. 'But even my first picture…it was a success of course, but I was still so, so raw, I still had so much to learn, then. You might have given yourself another chance, don't you think?'

A bashful Avinash Mukherjee ran his hand through his hair.

'But then, it is direction…that side of it that draws you now, is it not? Shankar did tell me a little bit, about your conversations,' Ramola leaned forward eagerly.

'It's nothing really, just some thoughts in my head. Nothing very serious.' He shook his head deprecatingly.

'But why?' Ramola had not seen the front of her sari starting to dip into the sauce boat.

Avinash Mukherjee's arm shot forward even before she knew it, and had gently pushed her back by the shoulder. The very next moment he was up on his feet looking fairly stricken.

'I am most awfully sorry Madam…I did not mean, I…' He looked again like he might bolt forthwith.

'Do sit down Mr Mukherjee,' Ramola laughed, 'and thank you…tomato gravy sauce does rather ruin clothes, white especially.' She gestured to her white chiffon.

Avinash Mukherjee glanced around uncertainly, lowered his head in what looked like a small bow then sat down again. Ramola turned the topic.

'Tell me, did you have occasion to watch any of Rajbala's pictures, the ones she made earlier? I must admit I haven't myself, though of course I did know of her, and, of course, the pictures of her, in the magazines...'

'Well, yes Madam, one or two with a friend...he is himself in the pictures, character artiste...' he paused, 'though...they are not exactly to my taste.'

Ramola nodded, 'I quite understand that Mr Mukherjee. I worry...how the audience will take Rajbala in *Mirabai*.'

'In that case, Madam, if I may ask, what had prevailed on you...to engage her?'

Ramola mused for a moment. How could she tell him?

'Well, you see, it was thought best, in all quarters, that I not appear in a picture quite so soon after...you know, Shankar...that the public would not accept it,' she sighed. 'Also there was the studio, so many things that I needed to put my mind to, I possibly would not have given my full to this picture.'

Avinash Mukherjee appeared a little bit agitated.

'But Madam, whoever told you that...that the public will not accept you, in the present circumstances? As if you were in some way responsible? Surely, it is just a passing thought? You do mean to appear in future pictures...soon enough?' He seemed about to scold her.

Ramola puckered her lips, 'I don't know yet, I really don't have something in mind, for myself,' she laughed.

'I'm suddenly a little bit uncertain, like you yourself... about those thoughts you have in your head.'

Avinash grinned and looked away, scooping up a spoon of his lemon soufflé.

Ramola smiled as she skimmed off the top of her own caramel custard.

'Quite unlike my heroine, Rajbala, you know. Never a doubt in her mind, ever, about her own capabilities. She is quite convinced that she is the very best and no less.' She rolled her eyes in mock disapproval. 'Really rather impetuous, but rather a remarkable young woman.'

'I noticed, she has her own mark, over and above how she is directed...' Avinash Mukherjee nodded thoughtfully to his half-eaten soufflé.

'You did see it, didn't you?' She was pleased. 'And that I do think is the mark of a star. When you can write yourself into the picture, hand in hand with the director... whatever his views. Nisith Babu is rather opposed to that, he is rather fixed in his ways. With me too he did do his very best to...smooth over my own peculiarities... on the screen.' She laughed.

Avinash looked up at her, 'Those very same peculiarities are what so many ladies model themselves on, Madam'. Ramola reddened, then gathered herself.

'But in truth, Mr Mukherjee, we have such thoughts, about good pictures and bad pictures...which is art and which not. Yet, somehow, this girl has rather opened my eyes. About how superfluous they are sometimes, these markers of high and low...how Raju could move on from such a very different class of pictures to the Bharat Talkies kind, bringing to us her very own way of doing things...rather remarkable, really.'

'Do you plan to retain her further, after this picture is finished?'

'Truly, I couldn't say yet, Mr Mukherjee. Though I would like to. I hope to, if we do get a favourable response to her…you know what the business is like, we must not go too far away from the audience'.

Avinash Mukherjee nodded his understanding.

'Though I must say…' for an instant, lines creased Ramola's forehead. 'Raju has been a little bit…different, of late. More serious…you know. She is almost a child, coming into my office to ask for biscuits, throwing fits for nothing at all…why…those things are rarer now.' She seemed suddenly struck by the fact of it.

'Perhaps it is the role…' Avinash Mukherjee proffered. 'If the last part is still how it was first written, rather demanding in its terms…was it not?'

'Quite…you are right, Mr Mukherjee, it must be just that. She has not been used to such deep immersion in a character, possibly it has made her think. Some things change you so much, don't they?' Ramola was pensive, not seeing Avinash Mukherjee's eyes as they came to rest on her face.

'Though…' she sighed. 'I am a little bit worried. Of course, her work is not to be reproached, rather she makes every last effort. But she has looked…well, fatigued. The make-up hides it of course…but her eyes are…sunken. I do hope she's not unwell…'

III

Raju shook off Anil's hand, glared at him and walked off.

He had been lurking around the girls' dressing room, cigarette and matchbox in hand. In case someone came by he could always feign that he was there in that quiet corner of the building for a quick smoke...not wanting to go all the way to the back garden. None of the other girls were in sight. She would step out any minute, he knew. She would always eat her lunch in the back garden by the *peara* tree, he only had to wait.

She had emerged clutching her *jhola* in which she carried her victuals, spotted Anil, made a face and turned the other way, when he had run up and held her arm, 'Raju...'

She'd shrugged him off and tried to walk away. But he was having none of it.

'What has happened? Have I done something? Tell me.'

Her face had hardened as she had looked down at the floor, 'No...nothing...'

'Then...?' he'd pleaded.

'Then what?' had come her retort.

'Why didn't you come, last day? You don't even look at me anymore.'

'Why, didn't you only say, don't look at me...no one should know? Then, what now? Move aside, let me go.' She had tried to dodge again past the corner, but he'd put out his arm stopping her.

'Raju!' Anil had fondly placed a hand on her head.

'Don't you even understand why I said that, what I had to do to get you here to Bharat Talkies? I can never forgive myself for all of that, still, I did it for you.'

'I don't need it, your pity, I could have done it myself too.' She had tossed her head stubbornly.

'Raju, don't be angry, see, your picture is almost finished. After this we will tell everyone, I have decided. Enough of this, no more hide-and-seek. We will take Madam's blessings, she praised you Raju, I had misunderstood her…I will touch her feet and ask you from her.'

'Don't pull Madam into this.' Raju had looked even more determined. 'What if Madam wants me for another picture? Will she take me if she hears all this?'

'But Raju…' Anil had felt the anger rise in him. 'Hadn't I said, after you came to Bharat Talkies, that after this we will go to Kalighat, get married? You wanted to show Unique Pictures, your Lily Madam and Mishtu Da…now what else?'

She had snapped, 'You said…so what? Do I have to do all you say? Am I your bought slave or what? You feed me? Keep me? I earn my own keep…'

He had felt the blood boil inside him, 'Who got you to Bharat Talkies, Raju…that today you can talk back to me? You would still be there, at your Unique studio, if not for my doing. Not another word from you after this picture is done or else…'

It was the wrong way, he had known even as the words had escaped his mouth.

Raju had spoken with poison in her eyes. 'Is that so, Anil Babu? You think that Rajbala would be nothing, if not for you? Like Lily Madam would say, like they all like to say...' She had twisted her face, 'What will you say Anil Babu, if a very big director makes me his heroine, for his best picture?'

'Big director...who?'

'You find out, Anil Babu, if you think that you made Rajbala. Do what you want.'

He had taken her hand. 'Raju listen to me, is this all that there is...these bioscope pictures and you being a star, am I nothing to you?'

'No...nothing. You tried to keep me under your feet, you never would have got me to Bharat Talkies had I not gone away from you. You only wanted to keep me, like a *dasi*...but Rajbala is nobody's bonded servant. You stop me Anil Babu, if you can. I have art in me. I will be the biggest star, bigger...than...than even Ramola Madam, if even I have to hang from the roof.'

As Anil stood agape, Raju had stridden away her plait swishing behind her.

IV

'Menoka had not understood. She could not take her art to its highest.' He had told her. 'She put a rope around her neck and hung. And the others, before her, haven't they told you, at the studio, tongues wagging, all about me...and those girls?'

Raju had not replied.

Saheb had laughed. 'They had wanted me, Rajbala, not my art. That is why they failed.'

Tonight, again, he was speaking of Menoka, how she had wasted her art, not done his bidding. 'It ate her inside...got her...in the end.'

'She became mad, I heard?' Raju whispered.

'Mad? No, why mad. She became disobedient, in her mind.' *Saheb* shook his head. 'She thought too much, about everything, it became her sickness. She would think too much of herself. I turned her out. I will get a new heroine, I told her...she could not bear it. It was her fault...all of it her fault. Will you do as I say, Rajbala? Will you be my heroine?' His eyes made her look away.

'It will not be easy, being my heroine. You must never say no to me...never question...if you are to reach the highest step...the very top. If you think too much, it will become a cause for worry, for you and me.'

'But...Madam...' Raju hesitated.

'Madam...yes...and what about your Madam?' His eyes twinkled.

'Madam says, listen to your own voice in your mind. Hear the director carefully, then do it in your way... think...and then...'

'Think, think what Rajbala! It is not your part to think.' He pushed back his chair, stood for a moment then walked to the open window. They were in the room with the bed and the big almirahs. *Saheb* had sat in his chair with the long arms, she on her side of the bed.

For a while he stared out at the darkness. Then turned back.

'Your Madam...Ramola Devi, do you know why I never cast her in any of my pictures, in all of my years at Bharat Talkies? Because she thinks too much...way too much. Only a third grade director will tolerate such impudence...when the heroine tries to think, when her task is to act, and act only at his behest. That husband of hers, he would lick her feet, that was why he lost his touch…not that he ever was much of a director.' *Saheb* grinned.

Raju sat still.

'Have you ever eaten pig meat, Rajbala?' His eyes were somewhere else, he wasn't seeing her anymore. But something made him smile, before he looked back again at her.

She wasn't sure what he meant, she shook her head.

His mouth twisted in mock surprise. '*Shey ki*, you don't mean it, such a forward thinking girl like you. Do you know, in some places they eat human meat, humans like you and me, cooked alive sometimes.' He laughed. 'You must try everything, you know, once at least in your life. It is a must for an artiste…to feel, taste, smell, if you are to bring life to your work, you must live life to its fullest, do you understand, Rajbala?'

He let his voice trail as he leaned back to study her face. Raju turned her eyes away. She never could look him in the eye, not when he looked like that. But it would make her heart run, like she had not ever known before. Sometimes it would make her want to fall at his feet.

'Menoka, now…' he was speaking again. 'Far too finicky, too much *manamani*, too many observances. I am a Brahmin father's girl, she would tell me, not willing to let go of her obstinacies. At the end, marriage and home was all she could think.' The scorn poured from his lips. His voice turned a pitch higher, 'An artist cannot say no, if it is demanded of her. Menoka refused my commands, to play the role that I…I myself had written for her.' His face curled into a smile, 'She paid for it, with her own life.'

'Why...' Raju's voice shook. 'Why didn't she want... that role?'

He shrugged. 'Perhaps she had her reasons, but that is no matter, Rajbala. Your own wishes...your mind...they must all turn to dust if you are to become one with your art.' He thought for a moment, his eyes on her. 'Perhaps she imagined that I would give in, to her whims, what she had asked of me. She imagined...that I loved her.' He stopped, again making her heart jump.

'I might have given in, you know, just a little bit, even at the cost of art...if it had been now. If I too had loved... like I do now...'

V

'How nice you look, it suits you', Ramola smiled her affection. 'Not a colour that I should wear anymore. It was a present from my father, when I was like you. It hasn't aged a bit, still looks new, doesn't it?' She ran her eyes over the pink silk that Raju had worn to the tea-room. The pink of the sari matched the famous pink chandelier that hung in the room's middle.

Raju blushed. She looks happy but somehow not herself, like she's got something going on in that head of hers, Ramola thought. She'd been so very odd, so quiet when they were shooting outdoors, even when they had had a picnic. Then again her old self, that last row with Nishith Babu, but, after that, all funny again. Starts at nothing at all, not even looking you in the eye sometimes. Just not our Rajbala. What indeed is up with her, she thought again, as she studied the girl seated across from her.

First time probably, that she's at a place like this, she must feel a little bit strange, though she's trying to live up to it...English and all, Ramola mused, as she reached out for the plate of scones. 'Try one of these, have it with some of that jam...here, let me.' She placed a warm scone on Raju's plate, leant over to cut it open and spread it over with some of the home-made jam.

'Is it nice?' she asked, trying to not notice the two *memsahib*s at the next table as Raju licked the jam off her scone and then bit into it. As it was, Raju had fairly distressed the young waiter with her solemn 'How do you do, sir...I am fine, thank you,' all in one breath. Not used to patrons greeting him thus, the poor boy, he must think she was making a fool of him. Must have picked it from some Hollywood picture, Ramola thought.

She poured herself another cup of tea. 'I've been coming to this place since I was little, you know, it used to be a favourite of my father's. He would always get me the pink sugar cakes they used to have, to match that *jhar* you see up there,' she pointed upwards to the pink chandelier. 'See, it matches with your sari...'

'Can I keep it, the sari, just a few days?' Raju gingerly picked some crumbs off her sari, then tossed her curls and announced. 'If you please, kindly...'

'It's for you Raju. I won't wear it anymore, you can keep it,' Ramola smiled. There she goes again! Trying to be Rajbala from Hollywood.

'Your father, won't he be angry?'

'No. He's no more.' She eyed Raju. 'Where are your parents, Raju?'

'Ma...going up.' Raju tried her English, then pointed

to the roof through her mouthful. 'And your father?' Raju made a face, 'Never heard his name even.'

Ramola stirred her tea. Why had she asked? Wasn't it all the same, for these girls? Why else would they be in the pictures? Cast into the world, a world that sucked the life away from them.

'And how did you get into the pictures, Raju?'

'Kamala Masi, she was in the theatre, she got me into this line, or we would have starved, ma and me. I would go where *masi* said, before. And now...Kamala Masi... she is Rajbala's *dasi*...' Raju smiled mischievously.

Ramola laughed, 'I can quite imagine that, Raju, who could ever tie you down?'

She pondered a moment, then asked, 'Raju, is everything alright? I mean, you have been a little bit... different.' She lightened it, 'Very...*memsahib*-like, all *chupchap*...quiet, like you've been thinking about something. If there is anything, you can tell me, you know.'

Raju gulped, looked like she'd been caught taking something that didn't belong to her, bit her lip, and shook her head at the half scone on her plate.

Ramola frowned, 'Raju, look at me...look here.'

Raju pouted, looked up a second, pulled a face and looked away again.

'What is it Raju? Whatever is the matter?' Ramola's heart sank. 'You're not...not...in any kind of trouble are you?'

Raju smiled and shook her head again, more deliberately this time. The little donkey, Ramola glared, whatever is she smiling about? Surely, the little idiot... good god...surely she hasn't...

'Raju, have you…err…have you…been somewhere… with someone?'

Raju blinked. How in Ma Kali's name did Madam know? She pressed her lips together, she wasn't going to tell, not till she was full ready. She picked up her fork and started to butter the rest of the scone with it.

Ramola's patience left her, 'Raju, will you say something, for heaven's sake? Have you…have you… lost your shame? When was the last time you had your monthlies?'

Raju blinked again, then hid her face to stop the burst of giggles, startling the two ladies at the next table and causing Ramola to go red.

'This is not a laughing matter Raju,' she hissed angrily. 'You must tell me if it is something of the kind.'

'What Madam?' Raju was trying hard to stop laughing. Had some *bhoot*, some spirit or *jin* gotten inside Madam…or what?

'Look here, Raju, if there is someone that I could speak to…if he will hold your hand, if his family will allow it? Does he have a family, Raju?'

'Who Madam?' Raju asked, making Ramola more cross still.

'Don't pretend with me. How could you Raju, I never could have thought it of you. Though I should have known, really, after how peculiar you've been. You girls…your kind…do you even understand the kind of trouble…you foolish girl…'

She sucked her breath in then let it slowly out, it wouldn't do to lose her calm, 'We could find a way still. It's early days, it seems. Is he in the pictures…actor?'

'No Madam?'

Ramola raised her eyebrows. 'Then what?'

'What Madam?'

Ramola clutched her head.

'Does this *masi* of yours know?'

'No Madam?'

Ramola thought for a moment. 'Well, then you had better not tell her, not just yet. It's bound to get to the whole world. Women like her are so inevitably without tact.'

'Yes Madam'

'How long has this been going on Raju?'

Raju made a face. 'You won't say to anyone…until…'

'No, I won't say it to anyone, for your sake. Now tell me, how long have you been at it?'

Raju considered, 'Five…no…four days Madam. Three days in the last week, and one day this week, then no more. No time Madam. What to do? So much work in the studio. Even this last Sunday was rehearsal, you know it, Madam.'

'Wait…' Ramola snapped, 'whatever do you mean Raju…four or five days…'

'Hmmm…' Raju was smug. 'She's a *memsahib*…' She pointed to the mems who were preparing to leave. 'Like those two there.'

'A *memsahib*…what *memsahib*, Raju?'

'That one I went to, for learning English. How do you do…I am fine thank you. Sunday…Munday…Thusday… Wed-nesday…good morning. Memdidi said *socho phir bolo*, think before you talk, think in your head in English, then say. So Madam, I was little bit *chupchap*, quiet like, thinking, then talking...in this English place...' Raju nodded smilingly.

'Well reaaaly...Raju...' Ramola was shaking her head in disbelief. 'Do you mean you've been taking English lessons on the sly from some *memsahib*! Anyhow I wasn't meaning just today, really, but how you have been, for a while now. You really will be my death someday Raju... English, from a *memsahib*! So that's why your "how do you do", and "I am fine, thank you"...whatever got in your head, Raju?'

Raju pouted. 'Why, won't everybody say, such a big star and no English! After our picture becomes a hit...'

Ramola shook her head exasperated, 'Really Raju, how in the wide world do you know the picture is going to be a hit? We never can say such thing...beforehand...'

Raju grinned, 'With Rajbala Madam, your picture will be hit, that everybody knows. Only, now I have to become like a *memsahib*...like you Madam,' her face glowed. 'If I have to be a true artist I have to be cultured...you will see Madam, one day they will write in the papers, Rajbala was born with art inside her. She gave her life to her art.'

Ramola stared at Raju. Wherever had she learnt all of this?

VI

Shankho was crying. 'I will hang myself. Put a rope around my neck and hang from the roof. I have said to him, after I die, put me in the fire.'

Dhonu winked at Kusumkumar as he poured more of the golden liquid in Shankho's glass. 'And...he said what?'

Shankho wiped his eyes and took a swig. 'Nothing. I wrote a letter, three letters I wrote, not one reply'. More tears welled up in his eyes.

'*Tum saala*, you fool. What are your hands and legs for? Put them to use. Remember my Sethji?' Dhonu grinned.

'He's not like that. What will you know...you Nepali...' Shankho pouted through his tears.

'Not like that!' Dhonu mimicked him. 'They're all like that, you just have to get them in the right way, you *saala nyaka* good-for-nothing drunkard. *Kya*, Jhantu Da? You say...'

Jhantu was dressed as King Pandu of the great epic, his tin helmet of silver and gold lay despondently beside him. His heroine Miss Duniyabala had taken flight, also in full costume, with her lover, the director himself, leaving behind the missive that she was very close at hand and would return if her full pay was given in advance to one *bhai* she had left waiting outside of the studio.

When he became Kusumkumar, Jhantu liked to think of himself as a messenger of love, what with the amorous roles he was so adept at playing. Love that was shot through arrows from the eyes, and with that the dancing of the eyebrows, the puckered lips and heaving bosom. Though in real life love was not something he kept much faith in. What was it, except the same old pattern? You just had to change it around a little bit every other time. He nodded quietly. The Nepali was right.

All this talk of love was starting to get to him. What with having to sit through the afternoon, awaiting the return of Miss Duniyabala in this den where the studio lot came for liquor.

Still, he didn't like to openly disparage love. It went against how people looked upon him, in their studio *para*. Though, love made him afraid sometimes. The way it could rob people of their senses. He looked again at Shankho. And the rascal Nepali. Shankho was on his third or fourth glass, eyes bleary. He really will give his life someday, for that prince of his, if this *nesha* doesn't get him before that. Love is not for the likes of us *baba*, he thought. Who loves people like us? We were not born to be loved, not this kind of love. But who was to tell that to the mad ones...the love-struck.

He had wanted to say it to Raju. After Natabar Da told him everything. And after he had watched her for some days. The girl had changed. Become all stuck-up, *naak unchu*, after she went to the big studio. Like she's some *memsahib*, not the same angry, funny, fun-loving Raju. Spoke with him like he was some untouchable *achhut* or something, not how she would be with him before, like she had owned him...cussing half of the time.

One thing he had gathered. She had fallen in love, and a mad kind of love at that, like this *ghater mora*, this near-dead Shankho. A love that taken her over, gone to her head. Only she was keeping it tight against her chest. At first he had not understood, it had seemed so impossible, really. Raju, the fierce and fiery Rajbala... bound...and burning in love! But that was what it was, he had realised, when he thought back to how she had been that evening, when he had stopped her outside of Bharat Talkies.

'*Ki re didi*, don't you know me? You forgotten us, or what?' He had smirked. She had been about to step into the waiting studio car.

She had faltered a moment, as if not knowing what she should do. Then turned back with her smile, 'Why, no…but I have to go, someone will be waiting.'

'Who someone *didi*? Some *borolok*, somebody important? Rich?'

'What's it to you?' Raju's eyes had flashed anger.

'*Na didi*, just asking. Why, even we have some *borolok*s in hand…me and Natabar Da…if you say. All waiting to fall at those feet of yours,' Jhantu had grinned back.

Raju had opened her mouth, for some *gaali-galaj* it seemed, but had then thought otherwise. She had gritted her teeth and smiled mirthlessly.

'Those *borolok*s of yours, they would lick my feet… they were nothing. I would hold their reins, in these hands.' She had glowered at her open palms. Then sneered and looked up at him, 'What now, if someone holds my reins in his hands? Jhantu Da…then what good am I anymore…for such things?' Like she was herself no more, like this stupid *pagal* in front of him.

Jhantu sighed as he glanced back at Shankho. The Nepali would bleed him dry. Of his last *char* anna, what to do. Still, somewhere Shankho knew, that his love could not ever become a real thing. Wasn't it why he drank like that? But Raju? Did she know it? And would she stop at nothing for it?

VII

Raju felt a shiver in her spine. Her body throbbed like she had a fever. Her hand moved slowly upward from her chest to where the knot rested, against the hollow of her neck. The knot of the rope. He had said to slide it over her head...and around her neck. His eyes had devoured her, neck and face...her lips...then slid back again to where the knot was.

He still hadn't touched her. But his eyes, they told her everything. That he had chosen her. For that which they could not give, none of them. They had not had it in them, to know him...his heart...what he said with his eyes. *Saheb* never spoke much but if you could read his eyes, you knew everything. What he wanted.

He wanted her to be his. He was only testing her, to see if she was afraid. If she would say no...if her heart pounded so hard inside her that it made her heave. His eyes were on her breasts, she held her breath, so stop the gasps, so he wouldn't know how her insides were turning, ready to burst. If only, if he would come close... hold her once.

'Menoka did not trust...that I had wanted the best for her. She lost her faith...she lost me.' *Saheb* had told her as he had played with the rope. 'Rajbala, do you know it? That I want the very best...for you.'

The jasmine was laid on the bed when she had come in, its perfume lingering beside her. He had laid the rope beside it. Coiled and knotted. She had looked at his eyes...and known his wish. Like he had said it aloud. But he hadn't. Still, she had known.

The rope had ever so many tiny bristly ends springing from it. Prickly and coarse against the smoothness of her fingers. When she had slid it down, over her head and across her face, it had gently scraped her forehead and the bridge of her nose. Then rested, where her neck joined with the rest of her body...from where it could squeeze the life out of her.

Saheb was playing a game, to only see...if...if she could. Wouldn't he stop her, if it started to squeeze the breath out of her? Making her gasp. If only she could wet her throat once...just a mouthful of cold water. But how could she ask him? Wouldn't it make her small, in his eyes, if she was not able to match him, step for step? For after all, it was only a game. He could not ever bear to see her in pain. It was only his test of her.

Menoka had done him wrong. Was her life only her own, to take if she wished? It was only her way, to hurt him, when he had wanted only the best for her. She had left him like this, with a heavy heart. Only someone...if they loved him...could make him well again. She would do it for him. She knew that he would stop her, take her, and then love her.

Raju pulled the end of the rope, and felt the little prickly threads close in. Her eyes were on *Saheb*, he did not meet them. His own were on the rope, red at the ends against the edges of his eyebrows, like someone had shot arrows into each of them. His eyeballs were big, like they were about to seep all into the whites. *Saheb* was telling her to do what she had to do. Her eyebrows cringed and lips wavered as she clutched harder at the length of coarseness between her fingers. Like in those Raju Darling acts, when she had to clutch a dagger to her chest, only to fool the bad men...make them believe that she was about to end her life. But it was never for real, always it was like a game. In the end she would save herself.

The balls of *Saheb*'s eyes had started to spread, their blackness was making the room darker. The electric lamp flickered...like it was a *mombatti*, a candle. Raju wheezed but did not allow her clenched fist to lessen its grip on the noose. *Saheb* was watching. His eyes were on hers now. He leant his head forward, a signal...now she should not stop.

Hadn't Madam said to her, so many times, Raju do not overact, keep calm, let the scene lead you...let it take you over. *Saheb* had set this scene for her...he would take over, from her, when time came. She only had to do her part.

He watched, like he had counted Ma's every breath. Like how he had thought of Menoka...as the girl opened her eyes ever so wide over that gasping, gaping mouth of hers. Those eyes were not on him anymore...then as they started to swim, she came down, on the jasmine...just as he had wanted it. A perfect shot, he thought, as he sat watching her. Should he wait another few minutes, then see if she really had done herself in? They never could pin it on him, not a finger had he laid on her. Or...should he rouse the sleeping beauty, while she still had some breaths left in her? To give her yet another little game to play...and then another. To see how long she could keep on playing?

For, in truth...Rajbala, it has been fun. More fun to play with you than I ever would have thought. You will be lovely when these breaths do leave you for good, more beautiful than you ever have been...only I think now that I will take my own time with this...this, my new heroine.

VIII

Avinash Mukherjee grinned. He was thinking of Ramola and her precious Rajbala. What an odd pair they made. Like him and Manimala, he grinned again. Ramola had taken the girl under her wing. Like he had taken in Mani. He wouldn't have thought it of her, the high up Ramola Devi, now head of Bharat Talkies.

How alike they were in this, their befriending of these unlikely creatures. Ramola would look out for that Rajbala, if even the girl left Bharat Talkies. Like he looked out for Manimala.

He had seen Ramola again, that afternoon. She had called the office, asking if he would like to lunch again. He had said no, that he had a prior engagement, then called back to say it had sadly been called off, and that he had a free afternoon after all. Had she known? And smiled at his childishness? He wished he could be like her in her directness, it was something he admired in her. He never could be like that. To simply go with his heart and not think too much about it. Always, it was between his heart and his mind, a tug-of-war that sometimes left him rather spent.

They had gone to Gay's by the river. Not exactly the Grand, but she had not minded. He had proposed it, on the spur of the moment. They had found a table easily, it was a weekday afternoon, and past lunch time. The whole place had been on its toes. It wasn't every day that a big star like her came there!

She had laughed a lot. Telling him about Rajbala, how the girl had taken English lessons from some *memsahib*, and all because she wanted to be like her, like Ramola Devi. It had seemed to amuse her greatly, though it must be no surprise to her that girls everywhere wanted to be Ramola Devi. Even the commonest of things about this Rajbala seemed to strike her as rather remarkable. He sighed in resignation. He couldn't very well hold it against her. Not with his own immersion in Mani's antics.

'She has seen the worst of life, you know, Mr Mukherjee, but she didn't let it get her down,' she had mused. 'Mother died of pneumonia, I gathered, a weak sort...no father...as it is with these girls. Though of course...' Ramola had hastened to add, 'Raju is not one bit like other such girls. No pretence whatsoever. She's rather straightforward really...and quite alone in the world...all on her own.'

All on her own and near dead, curled under his steps... that was how he had found Manimala. Nengti's mother, who came in to do the floors and the washing had said she'd seen the cook from next-door bundling the kittens in a gunny sack. To drown them in the Ganga, the pests, she had said. The mother had died birthing them, but somehow Manimala had escaped the fate of her brothers and sisters. He had almost crushed her under his feet on those stairs where she had lain rolled up, so little that she could make her home in the hollow of his palm...trying to hide from the world.

He smiled down at those beautiful green eyes now. Mani was purring on his knees, rubbing him with her tail. She wasn't always so good. He pretended to cuff her ear, taking up with some *hulo* or other. Still, she always came back. Once he had thought she had gone for good...but she had returned, a mother, carrying her two kittens, one by one, in her mouth. Had there been more, he had wondered. The kittens had gone, once they had learnt to find their own way, but Manimala had stayed. He would look out for Mani, it made him smile, how she would appear through the window calling out to him. Could he say he owned her? Would she allow it, Manimala?

That girl Rajbala, she reminded him of his Mani. For how Ramola had spoken of her. 'It's not so easy to love her, you know Mr Mukherjee, she seems to not allow it...so often, with her imprudence...and yet she is lovely, our Raju.'

Was it in them both, him and Ramola Devi...to find love in the most impossible of things? Love that could not ever be so fully known or fulfilled, like everybody always wanted love to be. Like Shankho did. That was why he had had to shut him out, the pleading...declarations... and surrender, it had started to disconcert him. What was love that left you with nothing to fight for? Nothing more to desire? When it became all so certain that it didn't hurt you enough?

Like how he loved Ramola, and how he had grown to treasure the pain of it. The belief and the doubt, the charms and wiles...the riddles and shadows that would cloud him over, thrust him to unreasonableness, within his outward calmness. And then the wavering and diffidence...the feeling of a void. He was flushed. Rarely did he admit such things, even to himself. But today he had let go of himself, as he had laughed with her. Forgotten that he should not let her close, lest she knew. He had looked in her eyes as she had laughed, and neglected to hide himself from her. Because, in truth, she seemed to have desired it...to be there and then...with him.

PART 6

I

Natabar had had a bad dream. His nose and eyes were running. Like when his father would hit his mother for not wanting to sit with patrons, and then turn upon him. He had seen Raju in his sleep, Raju all bloated and red, eyes puffy, vomiting, and doing *paekhana* in her sari... foul, watery shit, like that Radha. He had seen her two or three days before she had disappeared...Radha. Gone to die somewhere, in some *galli* or *nulla*, everybody had said. They had found her in the morning...curled up like a dead dog, lying in her own *paekhana*, rotting.

Natabar hadn't known her, that last time that he had seen her alive...Radha...when he had spotted her, tin can in her hand, haranguing passers-by. Saheb had kicked her out, kept her younger sister instead, her very own flesh and blood. He turned her against me, my own sister... that *saali* bloodsucking little *beiman*, after everything I did for her, she had spewed poison. Then that poison had got her.

Natabar had been sick like he would be as a child, eyes and nose running in his sleep, since that boy Kajol had told him what he had heard. Could it be true? Raju... of all the girls? Raju had seen the world, she could keep ten men under her feet, all at the same time. How in Ma Kali's name could she be taken in? It didn't ring true. Yet,

Kajol had not lied, of that he was sure. Only thing was, that boy hadn't been in his senses. Hardly ever seemed to be, these days. Had he heard right? '*Saheb*.' Was that what the man had said, at some old house where they had taken Raju? But, anybody...any *saala borolok*, rich man, could be *saheb*. Why then had that name frightened him? Why had he thought of Radha? How she had first been, *chulbule*...so full of life, never able to sit still, and so very determined to make a better life for herself and her two sisters. And then Radha, after he was done with her. Her body, like it was ridden with such a great sickness. Her mouth foaming as she had rasped, clutching the two or three annas that people had thrown at her. '*Saheb*' was what everyone in the studio para called him, the man that had kept her, and then her sister. And then...that girl that hanged herself...Menoka. In the studio para, '*Saheb*' was not just any *borolok*. '*Saheb*' was Him, if that stoned *nesha-khor*, that *bakhate* gone-to-the-dogs Kajol had heard what he said he had heard.

Kajol had not given up. That was something about that son-of-a-pig, when something got into his head, it really got into his head...*nesha* or no *nesha*. Natabar had tried to find out, too, about Raju's comings and goings, but nothing. And at that time of night, didn't he have his own little shop to run? As it was, Raju had left him high and dry, his prized little *didi*, but no matter, he hadn't cursed her for it. And then there were those two other girls he had just put in the line. Though with Raju it hadn't been only the business. They had loved each other, or so he had thought. She was like a goddess, to him and Jhantu, and the others like them...the *nyaka*s of this world, them that were not proper men. They who never could have a fair chance, and forever taunted because they did not know how to fit…anywhere, except in a paradise of their own making where they could turn the tables on the world as it was. Like Raju had done… in real life. He or Jhantu…they had never made her sit in the *bazaar*, like a *beshya*…no…even the very thought made him red with anger. If anything, he had showed the world, and them that went by the name *purush manush*… and *borolok*, rich men…that they were nothing, really, in front of his little *didi*. It had made him jump inside sometimes with joy, when some *borolok* or other, instead of showing this Natabar his temper, had begged him, for his *didi*. And little Raju, she knew how to make them beg alright. Natabar grinned in the dark…what moans and groans he had heard from outside of those doors.

He sighed. How they had sat sometimes together, him, Jhantu and their little *didi*, gossiping…swearing and laughing at those sons-of-bitches *borolok*s that came with their begging bowls in the dead of night. And now, that same *didi* of his, every other day whisked away in a car to what place who knew. It somehow did not sound right to him, his queen of a *didi*, her head always held high, that she had become like some kept girl. Sent for… commanded…ruled. She that was born to herself rule.

Kajol had been *fultu*, up to his neck, as usual, but that night when the driver had left the car to go upstairs to fetch Raju, he had tried the lid of the back bonnet, and found it unlocked.

'Got in there…and waited,' Kajol had grinned through his rotting front teeth.

When the car had jerked forward he had lain down to escape the bumps, and stoned son-of-a- pig that he was, had gone to sleep, again half-waking as the car had jerked to a halt. Kajol had heard the doors open, then slam shut. Then, silence.

He had peeked out from below the lid.

'Old crumbling house it was...your girl went inside, car stayed out,' Kajol had proudly declared.

'And then?' Natabar had asked.

'Then what...nothing...did I go inside, or what? To see, where the girl was giving it. I went back to sleep, in the car. Got up when it started again. Dropped me back,...to where your darling stays.' Kajol was irritated.

'*Byas*...nothing more?' Natabar's heart had sunk. If only this Kajol had been in his senses. To have gone all that way and found out nothing, the drunken son-of-a-pig.

'*Naaa*...what else?' Kajol had knitted his brows. 'Only, that driver *gupping* with some fellow there, another man...'

'Saying what?' he had prodded.

'What was it...wait, let me think?' Kajol had scratched his grimy head. 'Oh...*haaa*...wait...oh, yes, that other man, he was saying, what *re*, how you manage to get the girl, every time?'

'And...what did he say, the driver?'

'Said...what will I manage, I'm just a servant. In the studio *para*, these girls, they hear the name...*Saheb*, and they fall at his feet. You understood, you fool?'

Saheb...that's what the driver had said. Not just any saheb, but *Saheb* of the studio *para*. There was only one

Saheb there...the one that everyone in the studios knew so well by that name. And everyone knew also what he could do to these girls. Was that why he had dreamt of Radha?

Could it be? Was *Saheb* the one? Whose name she had not said to Jhantu? He that now owned her...the one that she was ready to give her everything to. *Didi re...* what have you got yourself into.

II

Was it a bad dream, or a good one? Raju couldn't decide, not at once. Her throat hurt...a dull pain, and she stopped herself trying to swallow and clear the heaviness in her chest. Each gulp felt like she had a stone stuck inside her neck. She slipped her hand slowly upwards, towards her throat, did it feel different to touch? Then stopped. His smile was teasing her. Her heart jumped. He was there, his face right over her own, smiling in a way she had never before seen. Not known even that he could ever look like that, so very delighted...like he had just gotten his prize, like he had won some battle. She smiled back, and started to cough. A lump of hardened spittle was stuck inside her neck choking her. She had to cough it out, somehow, and then she would be alright.

Raju pulled her head off the pillow and took her hand to her mouth. To stick her two fingers in her throat to make the spittle rise, like when she would rinse her mouth in the mornings.

His hands were on hers. '*Naaa...*' he ordered.

'I can't breathe', she gasped. Her voice was broken, like when she had got that pneumonia fever.

'It will be alright, it's not anything,' his thin fingers held onto hers. He was so close. She noticed a *badami* nut-coloured mark on the side of his lip...she hadn't seen it before. Had it been there? Why had she not seen it? Had it come to him just now, like how she felt, that she was changed? Like she was in someone else's body. His mouth was moving. *Saheb* was saying something to her.

'Rajbala...do you remember, anything?'

She remembered. How she had felt her body float in the air before everything went dark. The rope...it wasn't there anymore.

Her heart leaped. She had been right. *Saheb* had only tested her. He had saved her, pulled off the rope and laid her on the bed. Sat beside her until she was awake again. Again, *Saheb* was speaking...he was smiling.

'I am pleased, Rajbala, you have done well,' his smile froze. 'But how far can you go from here? I had told you. It will not be easy, if you are to be mine.'

He had not said, my heroine...only 'mine'...What did *Saheb* mean? What did he want of her?

She tried to sit up. 'Water...' she whispered.

He held the glass to her eager lips. 'Drink, but not too much.'

He pulled the glass from her even as she felt the first seep wet her parched throat.

'*Atma sambaran*, Rajbala...self-control,' he instructed. 'Remember, you are not just any studio girl. If you are to be a true artiste, you must rise above your own needs... see beyond the pain, and hunger and thirst,' his voice trailed off.

She had understood.

Nishith Babu had said to her, '*Ma*, work is *sadhona*... devotion, like a puja, and for that you must be ready to give up anything, accept pain and sorrow. It will get you closer to your end, your *lakshya*.'

She had not understood then, what he had meant. But today, she knew it. It was for a purpose, for true art, and not just any other song and dance. And for that *Saheb* wanted her to be ready. To make her able to bear the pain and the sorrow like Nishith Babu had said. How she must have troubled him, the poor old man. If only she had understood his words then.

Her *lakshya*, she knew it. *Saheb*...she and him together, to show the world where they could take their art. How much they could bear, and give up for it.

In the studio *para* they would say he could teach even a dead tree or a log of wood to act. Those girls that he had made into stars, what hand did they ever have in it? It was all his doing, *Saheb's*. Only, they had to obey him, carry out his every wish. And even in that they failed, the likes of that Menoka.

But she, she would obey him, his every command... his every wish. Give all of herself to him. Because in the end, he would be there always, always close by her. She had nothing to fear, she knew that.

She smiled up at him again. A smile that lit up her face and doused the heaviness in her chest.

He reached out and wiped the tear that rolled down her face.

III

'I'm at a loss, Mr Mukherjee, I really am.' Ramola had not touched her plate of fish and vegetables. Only sipped her lemonade. Avinash was eating quietly. And listening.

'It's almost like she's become a different girl, and it's happened over the last two days or three, when she sent that awful *masi* of hers to the studio, to say that she had taken ill. But this morning…in my office…' Ramola stopped to take another sip from her glass.

'I realised Mr Mukherjee that there was not anything the matter with her, bodily I mean…but more, in the mind, if you know what I mean. She just wasn't herself.'

Avinash looked up from his roast chicken. 'You should eat a little bit, before it gets cold.' Ramola seemed not to hear.

'You will not believe it, she said that she wanted to touch Nishith Babu's feet, ask his pardon, for her misdemeanours. Almost like she was speaking the lines from a picture, taught to her, not her own. Like she's trying to be somebody else. She even tried to touch my feet, when I very firmly told her to pull herself together.'

They were lunching again at the Ritz.

'I'll still reserve that table, just in case, you know,' Ramola had said. She had seemed to know that he would telephone her back to say that he could come after all, after first telling her he couldn't. She didn't seem to mind it, his vacillations. Never seemed to notice them even. And for that he was grateful. All she ever seemed to notice these days was the ups and downs of that Rajbala girl!

He looked again at her plate. She had picked up a piece of cucumber and was nibbling on it.

'I feel rather awful saying this you know, Mr Mukherjee, but, could she…you know how they say it, could she be under some…well, influence, you know, spells and such things, the kind of things that these classes tend to practice sometimes?'

Avinash looked up, not hiding his amusement. '*Tuk-tak*, you mean ma'am? Black magic…tantric *vidya*?' his eyes twinkled.

Ramola looked away.

'You may laugh, Mr Mukherjee, perhaps I might have done so myself, if someone else had said it to me. But she has been so very odd, it's hard to not notice.'

'Perhaps she really has changed, for the good, I mean,' Avinash hazarded. 'Girl of her class, possibly never had anyone telling her the right things, before you, that is,' he smiled.

Ramola shook her head doubtfully.

'Well, you know, it just seemed so false…like…like she was trying too hard, to be somebody she really isn't. Very unlike her.' She sighed. 'I would much rather she be her old self, all blunt and direct, insolent often…'

'How is the last bit coming along?' Avinash was getting a little bit tired of this going on and on about Rajbala.

'Oh yes…that too. We were not able to shoot the last song…her throat…she kept swallowing, like she had something stuck in there, couldn't keep her breath. Said she'd gotten a fishbone stuck in the night. As I was saying, I really couldn't tell what she's been up to. What,

Mr Mukherjee, if...if she was given something...you know, something that could make her weak? Who could know anything? I did not one bit like the looks of that aunt of hers, not her real aunt of course...one does hear about some odd goings-on sometimes.'

'Why do you think of her so much...this Rajbala?' His eyes made her look away.

She broke off a piece of the fried fish and put it in her mouth. Then looked up again.

'She is so young, I could have had a girl like that, you know...if...if it had been given to me, perhaps if I had wished for it. But I never did. I always imagined it to be burdensome. Even Shankar. Bharat Talkies was our life. And I had him, but now...' She smiled, 'it does not seem quite so very burdensome, to have such things to think of...in one's life...'

'No, it does not...not anymore', Avinash thought as he cuddled Manimala in the dark. He was smiling. He had bought *puti maach* for Mani, on his way home.

'You would make a good father, I think...I hope that you do not mind me saying so,' she had said. He had wanted to tell her, about Manimala. How she would know his mind, like the back of her tiny paws, his sadness and joys. Run over to him when he needed somebody. And how he would worry about her, and fret and fume when she played truant. Did Mani know that he worried? He wished he could know what she really said to him sometimes, when she purred against him. But then, did it really matter all that much? To know and be certain, to fathom it all entirely? Would Rajbala ever know that Ramola cared, in the way that she did care?

Ramola herself did not care to show it too much, not to the girl, anyway. Was it a powerlessness...a fault... like a failing, to love like that? A love that could not be shown or returned in any measure of certainty, not even so well understood, always. Or did that very same love sometimes become a joy and a force...a gift...a kind of rapture and agony that paled away the certainties.

IV

Kamala's eyeballs jumped about uneasily against their redness. It never did agree with her...spirits, even in her theatre days. She had not drunk in years. But today, at her *soi*'s den, where her *soi* Padma was queen, she had not said no.

'Want to vomit?' Padma asked from where she was lounging, beside the oil lantern. Kamala shook her head. Not yet, today she was going to drink till she could take it no more, she didn't want to be in her senses.

'*Soi* re, do something. I don't like it...' Kamala said again. Her own voice sounded so far away, did *soi* hear her even? Kamala blinked and looked again at Padma. Padma was smearing the lime on a fresh leaf of pan.

'Want one?' Padma asked. Kamala shook her head. Padma smeared more lime, settled the supari pieces and *dokta* leaves, then carefully folded and stuffed the pellet in her mouth.

'You seeing these *meye-chele*s, these girls first time today or what? That you've got shivers up your back. Or, has my *soi* forgotten our theatre days, what goings-on we saw before our own eyes?' Padma smirked through a mouthful of red spittle. 'Only that day I gave more money, *na*? Then what?' She lowered her voice, 'He will give more...*Saheb*.'

Kamala rubbed her eyes. Padma's face looked like a *thala* in the lamp's glow, the big one in which she would serve Raju her meals. She liked it, cooking for that girl, even though she had grumbled about it so many times. Even though that ungrateful little *beiman* treated her like a *jhi*, a servant. When she ate her face would glow, and Kamala would watch proudly from behind the door as Raju would devour her *luchi*s or *singara-kachuri*s. She still needed looking after, that girl.

'Na *didi*, it's not the money. Seen the girl from when she was so big...' Kamala showed two hands high. 'Been with her since that mother of hers died, from seven days of fever. She never took to me, that one, never trusted this Kamala. But I grew her up, like she was my own. Now if some evil comes on her, you say, how will I show my face?' Kamala pointed skyward, 'What *jawab* will I give...what will I say, when I go up there?'

'*Thaam saali*, shut your mouth you slut.' Padma was still resting her back on her pillow, but her eyes flamed like two balls of fire. 'Up there, who said, you and I are going up there? Up there is for the rich, those blood-sucking *babu*s, not us, old *magi*s. And what if she was your own? Wouldn't you still put her in the line, feed off her? Didn't I put my own one in the line? Ran away with that pimp of a *musalman* sarangi player, rubbed this Padma's nose in the dirt. Came back with that *paap*, that sin growing inside her stomach, six months it was. And that *saala hature* quack, bled her to death. But I said to myself, better this than that sin seeing the light of day. Tell me, did this Padma give it all up for that and go to the jungle? Then what, *saali*? In this line of ours no one is your own, even the fruit of your own womb will sell you and eat your flesh...and you *saali* slut, eating my head over that girl of yours.'

Tears were streaming down Kamala's face. 'Pig meat, *didi*...he makes her eat it,' she spluttered.

'What?' Padma wrinkled her brows in disbelief. 'Pig meat? Just now you said, she's not eating, *didi*.'

Kamala wiped her face with the end of her sari. 'Not what I make. She used to order me, *kachuri* today, *singara* tomorrow...and now...nothing. Picks at what I give her, half of it left on the *thala*.' She lowered her voice. 'Eats what he sends now, then sometimes vomits in the *kal-ghar*...I know it.'

'He who?' Padma's gentle buzz from the *dokta* was fast clearing.

'Your *Saheb re*...sends her boiled meat, back with her in his car, every two or three days. Makes her eat it...*ma go*, one glance of it made my vomit come.'

'How do you know, that it's...pig meat?' Padma demanded.

'How will I know? She told me herself, the girl...said it's from the Cheena *para*. Said, artiste like me cannot have so much *baach-bichar*, be so finicky. Am I some Brahmin's girl or what?' Kamala rubbed her eyes. 'Saw so many artistes in my stage days, *soi re*, never heard such things in my whole life. She's changed now, that girl. Before she would hide such things from me, now she openly talks, like it is some great *punya* or something, some blessing from somewhere.'

Padma had slipped back into her languor. 'What's to you...pig meat or dog meat, tell me that?'

Kamala shook her head. '*Na re*, I heard they mix things in the meat, those Cheena *afeem-khor*s, makes people lose their heads. Before, anything I asked she would shout the house down, raise her hands even, and now, she tells without me asking even. Like...like she wants to tell the whole world...' Kamala's voice was a whisper, '...about *him*. Sings to herself...and her eyes shining, but all sunk, *didi*, her eyes sunk inside her head. I am afraid. Say *didi*, nothing will happen to her?'

'Listen, look at me', Padma leaned forward, her eyes bright. 'Those girls that *Saheb* takes, they go...fast.' She flipped her fingers skyward. 'What? Heads go all funny first, then the girls, they go. One or two went where, God himself knows, but they give golden eggs, *Saheb's* girls.' Padma chuckled in delight. 'Better if the girl goes, for good! *Saheb* knows how then to keep this Padma quiet. *Arre*, then we two *soi*s, we will loot with our two hands. And, say, will it stop with this one slut? Doesn't this Padma have more of them in hand? Think of it...one girl, and then another and another, faster they go to hell, the better. *Amra duti soi, khai dai ar gai*, we the two *soi*s, we eat, drink and sing.' Padma rolled in glee against her pan-stained pillow as she sang her impromptu song.

Kamala knew it, then and there. That she had to go... to them.

V

Raju raised her tear-streaked face. To look into his eyes. She looked again at the old pink *Benarasi* that he had laid out before her. And the camera, settled on three legs, and gaping...set and ready like in the studio, all ready to take her pictures. She shook her head again. No, she would not to do it, not for him, not for all the world.

She had left it all so far behind. She didn't think anyone knew anymore. Kamala Masi had herself said, gone to rot all of them. Those companies had gone *hawa*, disappeared, after the talkies came, so little of what was before had stayed. As it was, those bioscope pictures, they would run for only a few minutes, and so little light in them...half-light and half-darkness, taken anyhow, just any way at all. Once, they had put a red sari like a *ghomta* on her head, to hide her face only till below her neck, like the veil on a bride, and then, nothing...all *khali*, naked, her chest down...the sari trailing behind her, all the way down from her hidden face as she had walked, turned and twirled, feeling as if snakes were crawling on her bare body. Even as they had made a bioscope picture of her. 'That face, best not seen,' the man at the camera had smirked. She did not even look like this Rajbala then. Skin and bones...skeleton-like, no breasts, her head crawling with lice. There had been other girls, girls like her. Who was to know it was her, this Rajbala of today, if ever they saw those pictures?

But she had been wrong. Someone had known something of them, those her first bioscope pictures. They had stayed somewhere, all of this time, and now, he knew, *Saheb* knew...and he was testing her, again... another test...but why this? She bit her lip. She would give herself to him, give him her everything, but not like this. Not how it was with her, then. Why ever did he press her so? What was in them...those naked bioscope pictures of hers that he wanted it of her, now again?

'Rajbala,' his hand was on her head.

She bit her lip harder. She would not look at him.

He was running his hand through her hair, gently loosening the top of her plait.

'Rajbala,' again he called her name. This time closer, his face was by hers.

'Will you disobey me, my wish…like Menoka did… Rajbala?'

She shook her head, tears welling up again in her eyes.

'What then?' His voice was so gentle, it made her want to throw herself on his chest. Would he understand, if she did tell him? How they had been, those days of nakedness and hunger. Her mother's eyes when she had told her about her 'acto', what they would make her do in front of the camera. Still, Ma had danced to Kamala Masi's tunes, she and Ma, giving up her shame… forever…and not even knowing it for what is was, then.

'What shame before me?' She started. Could he see the inside of her heart, know her fears? 'Will you not give me your all, Rajbala? Or is it too much for me to ask of you?' His breath came heavy against her neck. Like he had run up all of those stairs, from the stone-laid hallway below, to this room with the bed and the big almirahs. 'Only for my eyes, Rajbala…I give you my word. No person shall set their eyes on them, ever…these pictures.'

'But why…why?' Her tears choked her words.

'Why what, Rajbala?' Sharply he drew back his hand. 'Are you to be just any studio girl? Are you not fated for greatness, Rajbala? And for that, you must give up the shell that holds you, that *morok* of ordinariness. You must shed your old skin. What is your shame if not your chain? You must let go of it...be free, like in your first days when you would go before the bioscope camera. I know it all. You must go back to her, Rajbala, that girl who did not know shame. Let yourself become one with the skies and the winds, so that the real skin that covers your blood and flesh may show itself. You must free yourself of these worldly chains like the heavenly beings, *apsara*s and *yakshini*s, that lived a thousand lives, beyond life and death.'

'You...you saw those pictures?' For one brief instant her anger blazed in her eyes. 'Or, is it somebody else? Who is it? Who told you?'

'I know Rajbala. What is told to me...and also what is hidden.'

'And others also? Madam?' Her heart jumped. Madam, she never would understand, how could she? Madam would not ever see her face again, if she knew.

Saheb laughed, a quick small laugh.

'Your Ramola Madam, Rajbala, has lived her life in her own *morok*, a shell...her shell of privilege and arrogance, and ordinariness. What is she? What would she be, if not for Bharat Talkies? If not Shankar Chattopadhyay? But you, you are not ordinary Rajbala. I knew it, that very day when I saw you first, at the studio. I knew you to be the one. The one that could break out of that *morok*... of *samaj* and *sansar*, society and its bindings.' His voice trailed as he ran his hands again over the old Benarasi.

'You know, Rajbala, my mother,' he paused. 'She was no ordinary woman. She lived a very ordinary life, doing her ordinary chores, surrounded by small people with their little mean heads. But in her mind...in her mind, she proved to be...' he paused again, then laughed. 'Much more than that *morok* of hers, the skin that she showed to the world. She was a true artiste, my mother. Teasing and toying with this, her only son, sometimes telling him things that were not real, and not ever tied down by anyone. Not my father, nor he that married her, nor her son, the only one that ever loved her so truly. Rajbala, my mother, she was naked, free of bonding. You too, must relinquish your bonds...your false shame. Your spirit that is now tied, give it *mukti*...make it free. You are my *kamana*...my desire. Will you Rajbala...will you give me your all?'

She was crying again, now fallen at his feet. Head on his knees, her arms clutching his legs, his hand gentle on her head again.

'Go now, drape it on yourself, my mother's Benarasi. Like how you would wrap yourself, as a girl, when you first stood there...before a bioscope camera. And do as they would tell you then. Let it fall...when you walk before me...remember, as you would, for those, your first bioscope pictures. Remember them, for that was the real Rajbala, not this made-up one with her false pretences, who is now heroine at Ramola Devi's Bharat Talkies. You must return...to the real Rajbala, the one that I desire.'

The real Rajbala. After all of this time, and so many hit pictures to her name, and still...still...that was the real Rajbala? She, of those naked pictures. Her face stung, 'And, these photographs?'

'Ah yes, the photographs, they will be true art. For so many months I did not lay finger on it...this very dear camera of mine. I did not feel the urge. It was my first one. My first ever instrument...for my art, I had ordered it from London. I had wanted to take a photograph of my mother. She was beautiful, still bountiful then...her wet hair about her waist. But she denied me, her only son.' He sighed and smoothed her dishevelled head. 'But no matter, it is ready now, see...for you Rajbala. Will you not make me happy?'

VI

Ramola shook Raju hard.

'What have you been up to, Raju? Speak up, or... or...' She clenched her teeth behind pursed lips, her eyes narrowing as they searched Raju's face. Her heart sounded like a drum in her own ears and she gasped as she gave the girl another thrust.

'Raju, if you do not tell me I will stop this picture here and now. And I do not care if I do not make another picture, ever again.' She heard her own voice tremble and blinked back the tears. This girl would be her death, few things ever moved her to such a state. And Raju, she seemed to have turned to stone. Not a word had she been able to draw from her, since they had discovered... it first bewildering, and then frightening her, she did not know why.

Manna, their hairdresser, had appeared on the set in a state of disquiet. Raju had still not emerged from the dressing room.

'Madam, one minute, this way,' he had signalled.

'What is it? What is taking her so long, Manna?' Ramola had crossly followed him to where Raju sat.

'See here Madam. How am I to do her up? Take a look here...never seen such a thing in all my years in the line.' He had pointed to the parting on her head.

'Whatever is the matter now, Raju?' She had peered impatiently. 'Why, what...*e ki*! Raju, what have you done to your hair?'

Manna had his hands on his hips. 'Think my state then, Madam, my state when I first saw! And this girl, she tells me, it's nothing *dada*, don't tell Madam...cover it up, take the hair from the side.'

Manna had puckered his face. 'No *baba*, not me, not Nemai Manna's job this. Will not the camera catch it? Then, what answer will I give? Not me, *baba*, I will call Madam, I said straight to her...so I went to call you, Madam.'

Raju hadn't dropped an eye-lid, she might not have been there, like she wasn't even hearing.

Ramola had felt disbelief turn to anger. How indeed were they to take the last song, the climax, what everybody outside was waiting to record? With Raju's hair gone in those clumps. They might have to get a wig now. But it was what she had not wanted with this picture, from the start. Not for Mira. It was to be all natural, no wigs, very little make-up, a spirit of plainness and simplicity. That was Mira...If even they did manage to cover it up, how in heaven's name could it have happened? Had Raju taken complete leave of her senses?

Ramola shook herself, Manna's harangue in her ears. 'What kind of girl this is! Chopping off her own hair. That too heroine of such a big picture. Whole head's a mess Madam! All up and down, how will it look, in close-up? It's a trick Madam, ask her, some other studio must have paid her...to spoil the picture. This Manna has seen enough trouble in this line.'

'Manna, go tell Bimal Babu to break for lunch.' She had tried to sound calm. It wouldn't be any use telling him to not speak about the whole thing. If she knew it, Manna would spread it to the whole studio *para* by the end of that afternoon. She had waited for Manna to depart before turning on Raju, fire in her eyes.

'Is that what it is Raju, what Manna was saying? Are you really trying to spoil this picture, now that we are at the end of it...now...with this, your half-bald head! Good god, Raju, what have you done?'

She had run her eyes again over the shorn patches in the midst of the long locks, her blood rising inside her. What the girl needed was a walloping, and if she had been her mother...Ramola had quite forgotten that she so hated the corporeal punishment of girls.

The shaking had done her no good, Raju hadn't opened her mouth. She just isn't herself, thought Ramola, a cold sweat beading her brow. What has she been up to? No girl in her right mind would do this to herself. And still less Raju. Why, she was always so full of her own self...why ever would she spoil her own looks, her beautiful long hair? Avinash Babu had laughed at her, but perhaps...perhaps, she had not been wrong, not that she had ever had any faith in such things herself. But people did say things...and one couldn't help but wonder. Could the girl be under some kind of spell, some malice that was eating her? Or was someone making her do things... things that she herself had no power to battle? She had not worried about the girl for nothing these last few days. She had heard of girls in the villages chopping off their long locks when taken by evil spirits. Maiming their own bodies, giving up food and drink...even shedding their shame and wandering naked at the behest of *petni*s and *nishi*s, those that called out those girls in the dead of night, in the voices of people that they knew. Calling out to take them to where they wanted them to go...to be how they wanted them to be.

Ramola felt her legs tremble and sat down slowly. Raju had not moved. She put a hand on the girl's head, feeling the unevenness of the cropped hair against the smoothness of the open tresses.

'Raju, look at me, *lakhiti*...look this way, my dear...' A tear rolled down her face. She hadn't cried in the studio even on the day that Shankar had died. Raju sat stone-faced, her eyes on the wall in front, like those words had fallen on dead ears...though...Ramola peered and blinked. All of a sudden...all at once...her lips twitched on one side and nostrils opened just a little bit, like they would when she had something that she wanted to say.

'Raju, do you not want to be the top heroine? Tell me, do you not want this picture to see the light of day?' Still not a word.

Ramola leant forward and pulled the girl into her arms.

'Raju, tell me, should it all be wasted? Getting you here, to Bharat Talkies. Holding your hand, moulding... making you anew, for something that people will remember you by. And poor Nishith Babu, will you not think of him, the hours and days that he has given to you, to turn you from what you were into what you are now? Possibly, he will not direct another picture, you know that he has not been well. He had come to me, to ask that he be released by the studio. I told him to stay, until this picture is made, for you...because Raju, you will not have another teacher like him, even though he is old-fashioned and often out of sorts. You know, don't you, how much some people want this picture to fail?' She bit her lip.

'Even some of them here, inside of Bharat Talkies, so they can say I made a big mistake. That I had lost my head, getting a two penny heroine to appear in a high-class picture. That I played with the name of Bharat Talkies, what Shankar had taken all of these years to build...that a girl like you is good only to get the shouts, and the coins thrown at her. Is that what you want them to say? After everything that you have given to this picture...and I...letting you do Mira your way, so different from how I had thought it. How I myself would do it...but still, I let you, Raju. I must say, I had felt a very deep mistrust of you and your kind, studio girls like you. But I grew to understand, how you and I were of two worlds, and yet, perhaps not so very different...in some ways. How our world puts up these walls between us, of good and bad picture, high-class heroine versus studio girl. But it is really about making your own mark, isn't it Raju? Your very own mark, something that nobody else can match, no matter what. That is what makes you a star, and that Raju, I saw that in you, like how they would write and say about me...what Shankar would tell me, you have it in you or you don't, Ramola, nobody can put it inside you.'

'Madam, you and I...' Raju laughed. Her eyes still fixed on the wall in front.

'What do you mean Raju, you and I?' Ramola frowned.

Raju raised her eyes and forced a smile, a bitter smile.

'What *tulana*, Madam, what match, between you and me? You are Ramola Devi...and I, Rajbala Dasi, not fit even to stand by you, or speak two words with you. You and me are alike...no Madam.'

'Don't talk like that, Raju. Whatever is the matter with you?' Ramola glared at Raju.

'Na Madam, it's the truth.' Raju stood up and smoothed her sari, then bundled her hair in a loose knot at the nape of her neck. She spoke, not looking up.

'You Madam, your kind, the big people, you are the stars. It is like your zamindari...your right. And we, girls like me that have to earn their own keep, for them...' Raju smirked, 'to be a star is like a joke Madam.'

Ramola was shaking her head in disbelief. 'How you have changed, Raju, over the last few days! You hardly know what you are saying. Wherever did you learn to speak this way? This me and you, high-low, *boro-choto*. When you would come knocking at the office for the cream biscuits, when you so gladly wore my pink silk, you did not think then that I was Ramola Devi and you Rajbala Dasi? That you Raju, and you here now, speaking like this with me...I could not have believed it.'

Raju smiled. 'Those things, then Madam...I was like a little girl still. I had not started to think.'

'Started to think what, Raju?' Ramola felt the anger return.

Raju waited for some moments before she spoke. Like she was thinking her words through rather carefully.

'That, this Rajbala is no star, Madam. Because that Rajbala, of the hit pictures is not the real Rajbala. That is all false, pretence...only her *morok*, like this skin.' She touched her bare arm. 'The real Rajbala, she is an artiste, and for the sake of art she can give her all.' She ran her hand over her head. 'What are some locks, Madam, Raju can give the hair off her head, the skin on her body...*laj-lajja*, her shame, her everything.' Raju's voice softened, to almost a whimper. 'If he asks it of me, if that is his wish.'

'And who, may I ask, Raju, is this he? To whom do you wish to give your all?' Ramola's eyes narrowed under knit brows.

Raju smiled again.

'He...his name is not becoming on my lips. He is high up, and I, not even worth the dust of his feet. I am *atma-samarpit*, surrendered at his feet.'

'That is enough Raju, I have heard enough, of your balderdash. This talk...this, what you have so newly learnt. These words are not yours, Raju. *Atma-samarpit*, indeed, like in the pictures...' Ramola had snapped out of her stillness. Brusquely, she gathered her sari and pushed back her chair. 'And from now on, remember Raju that you are a contracted artiste of Bharat Talkies and I will not, simply not have you, under any circumstance, spoiling this picture. We will think of something, to tackle this,' she pointed to Raju's head. 'Manna will cover it up if I tell him, and I will speak with Bimal Babu about the shots, so it doesn't show.' She turned to leave, then spun back.

'And you Raju, are coming to live with me, today, to the house, and there you will stay, until this picture is finished. Raju, I cannot any longer put my faith in you, that you will not foolishly harm this picture and the studio's name. I should have known, before, with how you have been...but not again, not anymore. No more of your foolhardiness while we finish this picture...and of that let me warn you.'

VII

He had made up his mind. He would have to tell Madam, then and there, he had realised, when he had heard. They had all heard. That the heroine had lost her mind, gone full mad that girl, he had heard Manna say. Started to cut the hair off her head...next she'll try to cut her own head, you mark my words, sirs, he had said to those that had gathered around him on the set. Some tantric or *pishach sadhak*, worshipper of evil has got her, Manna had nodded knowingly.

Anil had stood at a little distance, not joining that audience, his heart pounding inside him like a dynamo. Raju hadn't spoken to him all of these days, though he had tried to accost her several times. He had been afraid she would make a scene, if he got in her way too much... there was no knowing Raju, she might just let the cat out of the bag. And that he simply could not have had.

Yet, that was just what he had done, right there, in the moments that had passed him by ever so tardily, when he had said everything to Madam. Her face had not changed, but her eyes...he had had to look away, so fierce was the anger in them. Still, he had to tell her, the rest of it, all of it, there and then.

'We met…alone, even after she came here, to Bharat Talkies. She was not so different, at first, but then she changed, like she became another girl. Not her anger, that was there before, but how she started to talk. No cursing…and she became proud, Madam. She would talk about being a bigger star than anyone…even you. And then, she stopped seeing me, or even speaking. I thought…that…that it was something that I had done. I had scolded her for making *ishara*, signs to me in front of everybody. But no, it was not that, not really, it was something else, something more…but what it was I could not fathom. I still do not know.'

'Anil, why do you choose to tell me this now, today, at this time?' Ramola spoke so quietly that Anil had to lean forward to catch the words.

'Because Madam, I am afraid, now, after what I have heard today. That she has been spoiling herself. Raju… how can I ever believe it of her? Raju…who used to love herself more than anything, or anyone in this world. Something is not right Madam. Something has happened to her. She's been up to something, that girl. Something behind our backs.' He paused to catch his breath. His voice had risen.

Ramola's face was like a thundercloud. 'Others too, Anil, even others have been up to things behind my back, wouldn't you agree with that, Kedar Babu?' Her eyes came back to rest on him.

Kedar Gupta had sat stone still through Anil's confession. Though his lips had twitched a few times. Anger, was it, Ramola had thought, anger at being waylaid, and not being able to say no. Or shame? For what he had done to her, after everything that Shankar had done for him, and for them all. He had put Bharat Talkies on the path of ruin. And then hidden away, like a coward. They were cowards, both of them. How different from Shankar, who had always faced up to things, no matter what they were, no matter how difficult. No wonder then that they had all sucked up to him.

'Madam, Kedar Da had no fault, he...he tried to tell me, but I wouldn't listen. Even today, I pleaded with him to come here with me, to speak to you...so you would not disbelieve me.' Anil ran his hand through his hair, then shook his head.

'I know what you are thinking Madam, of me, about my *charitra*, my character. But I wanted to marry Raju. Yes, Madam, a bioscope girl who does not even know the name of her father. I wanted her to leave it all... this...this world of bioscope pictures. But she did not want it. Not yet. Yes, she had wanted to leave Modak's Unique Films...the Raju Darling pictures, she was fed up of them. Her Lily Madam would tell her she was nothing, that Unique Pictures had made her a star. She had wanted to show them, she wanted to show the whole world what she could do. I could not bear it, that pain in her heart. I wanted her to have one chance, just one chance. And Madam, you yourself had said it, that Raju has *pratibha*...talent in her. You changed your mind, after the first few days, you told me so, that you would not have thought it possible for a girl like her...that she had astonished you.'

'Anil...you are right.' Ramola sighed, her crumpled brows easing as she looked away, out of the open window of that office at the flowerbeds outside. Like how she would always look away in her moments of discontent with Shankar. They seemed so slight now, so unimportant, her tiffs with him, when at the end of it all he had been there to shoulder the worries and keep her happy. And removed from the callousness of it all. Perhaps, she wasn't so very angry after all, just dismayed at how things had turned out. How they had hidden things from her...Anil...Kedar Babu. How Raju had turned out, not so very different from the others, the other girls of her ilk. How could she ever have expected it? That a girl of that class would return her kindness with gratitude or love. She was starting to feel again the way she had those very first days after Shankar had died. Like she wanted to give it all up, there and then. How she had mistaken Raju! She looked Anil in the eyes. 'Yes...I was rather surprised, taken aback almost by her qualities, that so few have in them, and those that have them are fated for great things. But...' she turned again to Kedar Gupta.

'...who had any way of knowing that...before, when you cast her my way? Forced me to take her, make her my top heroine. Did you, any of you, give a thought to Bharat Talkies? To me or to Shankar?'

Kedar Gupta spoke, the first time since he had sat himself down before her that afternoon. 'I am your culprit Madam, and for that god will not forgive me. I have lost all, my self-respect, peace of mind, love for my work, everything. I have betrayed Shankar Da and you. I wanted to go Madam, but you, you did not let me. You held my hand, you stopped me. But today, I must take your leave...forever. I will leave this city, go back to Comilla. I will not ever work in a bioscope picture again. How can I, after all of this?'

Ramola slowly bobbed her head, starting to feel the anger rise again, hot against her insides. 'But of course, Kedar Babu, that will be your *nistar*, won't it? Your release from it all. And what more could I expect of you, now...at this time, when I have come close to losing my all, even the good name of this studio. And when, after having made this picture with this heroine not of my choice...but at your insistence, it seems, we might now not finish it. When all I have is a standing set...and no heroine.'

'But why Madam?' Anil interrupted eagerly. 'Manna's habit is always to paint the gloomy picture, but he did admit that he could cover it up. I spoke with him Madam, and it is only three or four more days of work now.'

Ramola felt her head would burst. She struggled to keep composure. 'Cover what Anil? Hide what? When we have no heroine here. Raju has gone. Disappeared. And I have a feeling that it is for good, that she will not come back.'

'But...but...she was here, in the studio, in the dressing room. Manna had gone in again, after you had left, after you spoke with her.' Anil balked.

'Then Anil, Manna must have been the last person to see her, for she has not been seen since.' Ramola bit her lip. 'I did wrong, to tell her that I was taking her to stay with me, till our work on the picture was finished. Possibly she thought she would be like a prisoner. And I do not imagine that she will be found in her home. She has run away Anil, and nobody knows where. She must have slipped out through the gates without anybody seeing. Where were you Anil, all of this while? They have searched the whole studio...she has gone.'

PART 7

I

Fan hadn't been ready for it, when he first told her that he wanted it. He had seen them, just some days old, and then returned to watch them. Pink rats with their puckered lips. He had kept count...ten days old... then thirteen...twenty...thirty-three. Suckling under that monster sow. He didn't dare go near her. That beast only trusted Fan. And she had given them up to him, after all of that *na na*. He grinned. Fan loved him. He wished he could love her back...how delicious she must smell when she got naked to wash herself, after she had skinned and cleaned one of them. He sighed.

Fan had shaken her head fiercely when he had signalled his plan to her. 'It's going to be a game Fan, be a sport. Only three...' He had held up three fingers of his right hand. 'Give me three of those...' She had motioned back angrily, 'Can't you see they're little...' and then broken into that smile, and motioned again. 'Let them grow up...' He had known then that she would give in.

She had left them for him in the other yard, the one that was further from the kitchen and the sties. From where the muffled cries would not reach the sow...or perhaps they did. It had startled him at first, how loudly the first of those piglets had squealed, as he had landed the stick on it. Fan had watched from the kitchen window, he had seen her watch. Later she had smiled shyly, like a woman smiles at her man when he has proven his worth. He had handed her some notes, the price for three pigs. She had taken them smilingly. Business was business after all. And then he had gone about his own little business, the business of giving a taste of things to that *malkin* of Bharat Talkies, the high and mighty Ramola Devi. She had dared to think she could snatch his game from him. Gave you the slip, didn't she now, your little Rajubala.

Ramola Devi. How that rosy mouth of yours must have drawn a startled breath. Your face twisted, your guts churned. When you chanced upon them, lain in your path, this very same morning. He had come in early to the studio, not wanting to take any chances. The *durwan* had greeted him as he had opened the gates wide for the car to pass, '*Saheb*, after many days...'

He had stationed Asghar by the gate. To slip in and tell him the minute madam's car arrived outside. His old faithful Asghar, ready to do anything for his *Saheb*. Only he had not told him about the dead piglets in the small trunk in the backseat. Haram for him, Asghar could be rather stubborn about some things. The car had smelled of course, of the bloody mash inside, though Fan had lined the trunk with some herbs from her kitchen. He had been afraid Asghar would ask but dear old Asghar, his lips were sealed. After all, what were some dead piglets next to that woman he had taken, the time of that *danga* in his village...cut her up after he was done with her. Not a Hindu woman, he had confessed, but the young wife of the old *miyan* from the *madrasa*. She had smirked away his endearments so many times, and still teased him with her walk and her smile. And if not for his *Saheb*, Asghar would have had the *sipahi*s on his back. He had told the police that Asghar had been in the city on that day, driving him to the studio and back. And Asghar had not gone back since, to his village or his wife. His son had come to visit, a boy of eleven or twelve, and Asghar had extracted a promise from *Saheb* to put the boy in some line in another two or three years.

No. Asghar would not talk, he thought, as he ran his hand over his chin and lips again, sucking in the scent left from so quickly laying out the garnish in Madam's path. But he hadn't minded getting the gore on his fingers, her face had been enough reward. When she had leaned out to catch the air, throwing open her window right across from where he had stationed himself, hoping and praying he could see her. How he had wanted to see, how she looked, after taking in that sight. He had laid them in the little niche by her office where the orderly wouldn't so easily see, but where *she* would find them when she turned the corner. All of it done inside a minute or two even as she had left her car and walked inside.

She had stood there quietly, her face empty, but shaken, he could tell that. Later he had heard the rushing about in the corridor and grinned. Madam had deployed her troops to clear the mess. But what of your mind's eye Madam? When you see them in your dreams...and then that darling girl of yours, when you see her, after she hangs from the roof? Rope around her neck. Not that long a wait Madam. It would have to be soon now. While that girl was in his hands still. Before somebody from outside got to know.

All because of you Madam...all for your own mistakes. Sorry Madam, but your little heroine dances to my tunes.

II

The *nyaka*s knew when trouble was at hand. Natabar... Jhantu...Dhonu...even the *fultu*, drunk to his neck Shankho. With them was Kamala Masi.

Kamala was shouting. 'That Padma...this Kamala will chew up her insides, that *rakhshasi*, that monster, too long she has feasted on the blood of these girls...but not anymore, this Kamala will cut her and fry her...and eat her alive.'

'*Chup*, be quiet *masi*...cut her and fry her and eat her alive...' Dhonu mimicked Kamala. '*Kon saala jinda rahega*, who stays alive after cutting and frying?'

Kamala snapped back. 'What else? Took the girl from under my nose. If only I had known, never would I have let her go. When she came back so early that day from the studio I should have known...so close to finishing they are too, that big picture. Only three days before she threw the *thala* at me. Would have broken my knee, and all that uneaten food all over the place. For what? Only because I asked why she took so long at the studio. Will your *baap* finish this picture...whitened your hair in this line, don't you know how it is when they are finishing a picture? But then, how will you know...this is Bharat Talkies, not some teen *paise* theatre, she said.'

Kamala paused to catch her breath. 'And then that last day, she comes back in the afternoon just when I am finishing my *bhat*. Face is white, like all the blood went from it. I said, what *re*, so soon, I didn't hear the studio car, who brought you? She said, I walked...covered my face, nobody saw, then I got a carriage on the main road. Didn't let me sit for even one minute. Said get Padma Masi, I have to speak with her. Hundred times I asked her, what work, tell me. *Na*...that same thing, get Padma Masi. Anyhow I got to Padma's *dera*...had to wait, that *magi* was gone somewhere. Then, when she returns I get her straight back home with me. God alone knows what *phish-phash* whispering they did...then off goes Padma. Comes back after dark...in that car...*byas* what else? Then off goes Padma...with the girl in the car. Last that I saw of that girl. Whole night I waited, but *na*, that bird had flown. Still, I counted my breaths...waited another night, then only I went, to this here Natabar. By then everyone in the studio *para* knew, that Raju had gone *hawa*, with whom nobody knew...no one, only this Kamala.' Kamala squared her shoulders.

'Why you didn't go another time, to that your *soi*'s place?' Dhonu demanded.

'*Tham*, be quiet, Nepali *minshe*, stupid bumpkin.' Kamala pulled a face. 'Go again...there? Didn't I say what she did when I went, that morning after...spat on me...she spat on this Kamala. After so many years of sharing her joys and sorrows, that *magi* she spits on me, says whose thing has gone to him, *tor ki*...what's it to you, you whore. But I said to myself, she is no man's jamidari, not Raju. That girl cannot be any man's slave... *achha*, put your hand on your heart, Natabar, don't I know how many she ate alive? That same Raju will now be some sati, all washed, clean...then keep a dog in my name.'

Jhantu spoke up. 'You only said she went on her own, with that *haramzadi* rascal Padma. Then what can you do, or we?'

'There is poison in love. I know it all...she has gone there to die.' The drunk had stirred from his slumber.

'*Chuup*, quiet you drunk.' Jhantu scolded.

Natabar spoke quietly. 'True it is. If she went there on her own, then who can do what? Why will she listen to us, and how can we get there even? To her...inside of that house?'

'She's still there?' Dhonu demanded. 'It's been what... three...four days, *na*?'

'Four days, today.' Natabar bit his lip. 'She's there alright. I sent Kajol, after I heard where she had gone. He got it from the *durwan* there, Kajol. She's there, but for how long? Those girls before...one day they were there, then just *hawa*, gone, the last one went and hanged herself inside that studio.'

'Saw *him*, three four times, when I was at Sethji's. Put my ear in the door and heard...he wanted paisa, to make his own picture leaving Bharat Talkies, after that *malik* of theirs went *phuss*.' Dhonu signalled skyward. 'But Sethji, he said no. Our Sethji, he knows, from seeing the face...who is what.'

Jhantu slapped his knee. 'We...*saala bekar* people, we good for nothings. If we were some *borolok*... some *keuketa*, a big somebody, then still we could do something. But us. Who will hear us, believe us even?'

'Why, there is a big somebody...high up...who can do something.' The drunk looked out of bleary eyes.

'Someone big will do something, hearing from

us, about him...hear this drunk! That man, he is a *bhagwan*...a god, of this our world of bioscope pictures, understood, you drunk?' Dhonu spat his words.

'One person...might make that high up, that big somebody listen.' Shankho smiled bitterly. 'I know who.'

III

Ambarish Dev Burma was feeling pleased with himself. And his *kapal*...fate. For how it had all turned out in the last few days. Really, it couldn't have been any better. *Pativrata* would be his masterpiece, his slap to the face of the *meki* false hollowness of their make-believe world. He would show them how it looked, a real work of art, no pretence and no *meki* beauty. And what a truly great director could get from his actress...unquestioning obedience and full surrender, to his every wish. Though that producer of his would need some persuasion, after he laid his eyes on Rajbala. Her appearance. He smiled, picturing that poor man's face. But, of course, he would come around. After all, this was no ordinary picture, and she was no ordinary heroine. And how he had made her now, why, wasn't that the key to it all? He already knew how he would turn the script around, to suit Rajbala's new appearance. It was to be an experiment, like in the great laboratories of the world, where they transformed living things, sometimes with remarkable outcomes. She would play the part that he had given to Menoka, what Menoka had run away from...to her death. Now Rajbala would give it her all. For art, he had said to her, beauty had to be sacrificed in the service of art. It had delighted him, beyond any measure, when he had sat her down before Ma's mirror and taken them off her, the last of those tresses. He had made her how Ma ought to have been, bereft...shorn.

It always got a tad tiresome with these girls at the end...always. Like how the *bolir pantha*, sacrificial goats knew when they were going to get loaded on the *harikaat*...the wooden racks, blood-caked from previous sacrifices. Could they smell the blood that had run there before, like Fan's pigs could when she dragged them screaming into the yard from their pens? And, the girls... they knew alright, when their time was nearing. Menoka had known, and before her Jumna, that fair girl with the big eyes. He had taken her from the Benaras *kotha*... and before that, Renu...or...was she Radha? They had all known their end. And then, the *pae dhora* pleadings, the smiles edged by tears, *maan abhimaan*...sentiments. It would only spur him on, make him push them harder, till it was finally over and done with.

And now Rajbala...she knew it too. And how every part of her writhed and racked in the hell of it. That which she now knew inside in her bones. Though still, she was holding her own, through clenched teeth, that doggedness...*zid*, not giving up. Rajbala, she was different from those other whimpering wretches. He had not wanted her for nothing. He had pulled her in little by little, and still some part of her had held back. Made his blood rush, it did, the delight of it. To see her slowly break, and then, still, sometimes, stand strong and stare him in the face. Yes, she had held out, this Rajbala. But then, for how long?

Such lengths he had gone to. To know those things

about her...little bit by bit. Some of it from that yakking whore Padma. But Padma herself had not known it all. Where she had been, and what she had done, before she had become Raju Darling. But still, he had found her out...hunted...back again in those fuzzy muddled years between the silent pictures and the talkies. And then he had known, what she had thought was forever hidden... gone...with the tide of the talkies, when everything had changed in their world, the world of bioscope pictures. Gone were they, the fly-by-night companies that had fed on starving girls like her, girls that had sold themselves naked to a dark room full of louts for four annas, worse even than the *beshya*s. Whatever did you think Rajbala? That nobody would know any more the naked girl of those two minute silent pictures? Nodu Babu...Nodu Gopal Ghosh, cameraman from one of them companies, he had known. He remembered...the girl who even then had been different from them all, her face...those eyes. And then, Nodu Babu had told about the photographs... of unclad beauties like her, hidden inside the handbills for those companies, sold in the evenings outside Hogg Sahib's market. He had himself taken them. Nodu Babu was a true artist. He had won medals, as a student of art. He could sketch on his old drawing board those photographs he had taken then, he had said, that girl he remembered so well...if *Saheb* would say the price for it.

How very stark and beautiful she was in them. Black chalk on white paper, those pictures that Nodu Babu had drawn for him. He had gotten her alright, his little heroine, dug up her old skeletons. Rajbala, she would go any lengths now, to show him she was not afraid, that she was worthy of him. He grinned. Perhaps... even a naked shot or two in the new picture, taken in half-darkness half-light. Surely, he could talk her into it. He would have to be careful though, too many of them pious prigs around these days. He could already see the hand-outs for the picture...'Sensational! Heroine sheds her shame, for art's sake!' He smiled again. Art it would be like they had never seen before. And wouldn't it make their hair stand.

He still could not believe how it had all landed in his lap. The invitation to leave Bharat Talkies and make his picture, all costs taken care of, and all in the matter of one week. All of it so sudden...just like that, out of the blue. Why now, he wondered again, and not before. He frowned, then shook his head. His doubts were for nothing. It was karma...fate...his reward at long last for all of those wrongs they had done to him. Ma, and then Ramola Devi, putting him down with her 'I am *malkin* now' airs. Who could have thought it, he making off with her little heroine? He smirked. Whatever would she do, that *malkin* of Bharat Talkies, when she heard of his new picture, with her very own Rajbala? Would she take the girl away? He ran his hand through his hair. No... he did not think so. He might tell, might he not, what Madam's saintly Mirabai had been up to in those her first bioscope pictures? What if he let it all out now, all in the papers, and a little something on the side? Interview of Nodu Gopal Ghosh, cameraman from the silent pictures! Nodu Babu would fairly jump, given one chance...and Rajbala, she would give her everything to stop it. No, she never would, never could anymore go too far away from him. Only he had to be careful. So that he did not get carried away again in the night, not right now, before the new picture. Night before last, she near did herself in again...naked...neck in that noose. He had coaxed her to it, then watched...feeling the fun of every little second of it, as the water had run from her eyes and nose...and between her legs. No...he would have to wait a while now it seemed, till *Pativrata* was made, much as it irked him. He could not lose his chance to make this picture, not this time. He would take his time with her. Perhaps as the picture would finish...then Rajbala's time too would come.

He looked up at the car's sound. Was he here already? But it was still early, wasn't it? Still not even the half hour after ten. Makhandas had said he would call in after half eleven that morning at *Saheb*'s house, to present his *jaan*, his own girl...the other heroine, so there could be a little *alaap parichay*, an acquaintance with *Saheb* before they started work on the picture. He had said yes, he had been so very eager, Makhandas Khemka. Rajbala was out of the way, for the time. He had commanded her to not move out of Ma's chamber, upstairs. Not until he called for her to appear before Sethji.

He lifted his voice. 'Who's here?'

Ma's old faithful Dinu stuck in a grey head at the library door. 'Two people *babu*...a lady and gentleman... in a car. I saw them from the downstairs window.'

Really, these Marwaris, sometimes too late, and now way too early. No matter, it was a fine morning. He pulled his silk dressing gown around him.

'Hmm, get them inside.'

IV

'It might be a house that nobody lived in, for a little while.' Ramola thought as she slowly walked in from the porch, and through the wood-carved main door, its pale glass front cracked down the middle. She blinked as she stepped inside.

So dark, and it was the middle of the morning.

The front had looked clean though, like it was broomed and wiped every day, white marble stairs leading into a pillared porch. But the hedges were overgrown, around the driveway where their car had stopped, the garden unkempt. She had looked up, shading her eyes against the sun…three floors, the upstairs windows all closed. She never could bear closed panes in the daytime.

She peered down the hallway, her eyes now used to the dimness, but the man who had led them in had disappeared into one of the doors. She wasn't sure which one.

She felt Avinash Mukherjee's hand brush against her arm. He hadn't ever come this close before. She could feel him behind, almost against her. As if he was on guard…his long arms ready to enfold her.

'That one, with the black glass,' his voice came softly. Then as the man appeared again, he hurriedly stepped past, beckoning to her to follow him inside.

Not you ahead, not here, he seemed to say.

She couldn't say whose entrance had surprised the room's occupant more, his or hers.

Ambarish Dev Burma did not rise from his seat on the faded chesterfield sofa. Nor ask them to sit. The room had dusty book cases lining its walls. A dusty chandelier.

Two open windows without curtains let in the light. On the table with clawed feet and a stained top were some old movie magazines.

Ramola spoke first. 'I'm sure you know him, Ambarish...Mr Mukherjee?'

Most certainly he did, that hopeless nobody that would trail the boss around the studio. He raised his eyebrows and slowly nodded. Why, was he now the *malkin*'s favourite? And...why had she come, Ramola Devi?

Avinash Mukherjee shifted from one foot to the other, then abruptly lowered himself on the old chesterfield next to Ambarish Dev Burma. Slowly he stretched out his long legs, as though he wished to fence her off from the man next to him. Ramola's eyes were on Ambarish as she took the high-back chair across from him. 'You've come for her, haven't you?' His eyes were turned away from her.

'Yes Ambarish...Raju, I've come to take her back with me, to Bharat Talkies from where you took her.'

He laughed.

'Me? I took her? But Ramola Devi...Madam, where was I, when she escaped your clutches? She came on her own to me. She is here of her own will, and of that you can be quite sure.'

'I wish to see Raju, Ambarish, right away...this very moment.'

He ran his hand through his thin hair. 'I am not sure Madam that she is in a state fit to be seen. She has been in a state of sorts. You know what these girls can be like.'

'Your doing, of that I am sure Ambarish. Menoka

took her own life...it was because of you. And those other girls...and we let you, Shankar...and me, us all. But not Raju, not her Ambarish.'

'Those girls, all of those girls...Madam...they got what was their fate.' His voice was like a bird's. Shrill, sharp. Again he ran his hand through his hair. 'They were like *keet-patanga*, worms. I only tried to better their lot, but they are such a rotten lot, you know...you know that only too well, don't you? Passed from one hand to the next, playing their little games over and over again, day after day...day in and day out. It eats into their own insides, hollows them out, even the gutter's black water is cleaner.' He nodded knowingly. 'Is that not why you have always shunned girls like Menoka? Loathed them, grand lady that you are. Why one time, Menoka had greeted you in the studio...*namaskar* Madam, with folded hands. You had turned away your face, walked away! It had brought tears to her eyes. Don't you remember?' He was smiling.

Ramola bit her lip. It was true. Menoka had run up to her. It was after her big hit and she was Bharat Talkies' new star. Yet, she, Ramola Devi, had walked away, her head held high, even as the girl had cowered in shame. Raju had never thought to please her, unlike Menoka and the other studio girls. Raju, always so full of herself, like the world did not even exist apart from her. Like...she was no less than Ramola Devi herself. Raju had made her see her own failings. Raju, how did you not see what was coming your way?

'I want to see Raju, Ambarish', she said again. 'Take me to her.'

He wet his lips, slowly and carefully.

'I am not sure that you are anymore in that position, to order me about. You know, I have decided to leave Bharat Talkies. I have not taken your pay, now for three months. You may ask your people. I am not any more your servant, Madam.'

'But Rajbala is still my contracted artiste, Ambarish. And she is here, in your custody. She fled the studio, left my picture unfinished. It is reason enough for me to order you to bring her to me...here and now, in my presence.' Ramola's breaths came faster as her eyes flashed and mouth twisted.

She caught Avinash Mukherjee's eyes, watchful and wary behind the dark rimmed spectacles. No...it is what he wants, do not show your anger, he seemed to say. He looked away again as her eyes rested on him.

Ramola drew in her breath, then spoke quietly. 'Will you take me to her, Ambarish? Because if you do not, I will find her myself.' She stood up.

His eyebrows lifted and lips parted as the end of his tongue slid again on his lips, his head rolling back on the sofa's edge, and shoulders falling as he sat back, like he was about to see a bioscope show.

'Then, go ahead, find her. You are free to search her out, she is in this house. But let me say this to you Madam, you might not like what you find.' He sighed. 'You might find her no longer in your thrall and truly free of your *meki*, make-believe studio world. Not anymore willing to lean on your shoulders. Now prepared for a greater purpose in life.'

'That I will decide Ambarish, after I lay my eyes

on her. I am rather afraid for her at this moment. I do very much hope, for your own sake, that you have not harmed Rajbala in any way, or else…' Ramola gritted her teeth, at a loss for words.

'I will come…with you.' Avinash Mukherjee stood up, then sat again. 'Errm…no…I think rather that…I will keep Dev Burma *Saheb* company, here. How many servants do you have, Dev Burma *Saheb*?' It was the first that he had spoken.

'Two, man that brought you in and there's one more, they are not allowed to go to her. And, of course, the *durwan*, the donkey that let you in…and my driver Asghar.'

'Would you be so kind as to order the servants outside, when she…' he gestured towards Ramola.

'Most certainly.' Ambarish Dev Burma smiled. 'I must make sure her ladyship is unencumbered. Dinu…' he raised his voice.

The grey-haired man that had opened the door to them appeared.

'Where is Bibhuti?'

'In the kitchen…preparing the food.'

'Tell him to cut the grass outside, don't you see how overgrown it is? Whatever do you people do the whole day?'

'Now *babu*…or after lunch, in the afternoon?'

'Right now. My esteemed guests here have been complaining about the state of the garden…tell him to get to it right away. And you too, go with him, so he doesn't take till evening.'

He watched Dinu creep away, then turned back to Ramola. 'There Madam, now the house will be cleared in just a few minutes…for your excursion. Though I still would advise you against it. Your heroine, you might no longer know her. You never did know Ramola Devi, what you had on your hands with this girl, this Rajbala. Perhaps you will hear it from me, what this your Raju had been, before…what she is really, and what she has kept so carefully hidden from you, and from the world… and what is known to me.'

Ramola tossed her head impatiently. 'I know her well Ambarish, well enough. And if I know her at all, she will not be defeated.'

V

She was wrong, Ambarish was right. Raju was taken… possessed…a captive without chains. Free to go where she wished, only she herself did not know it anymore.

Tears ran down Ramola's face as she laid a hand on that head. He had broken her. When she looked at herself in the mirror she would see only her lack. Her rutted head, shorn of its locks…and those streaks on her neck, what were they? And Raju, she had shrunk.

'Don't you eat, Raju?' she whispered. The girl nodded…yes.

Why was she in this heavy old Benarasi in the middle of the morning?

'Where are your clothes Raju? Whose sari is this?'

She was quiet, then replied. 'Mine.'

'Yours? But why are you wearing it now, at this time, this Benarasi?'

'For the new picture…I have to sing. In front of everybody.'

'Sing, where?'

'Here...' her brow furrowed. 'They will call for me, downstairs. When Sethji comes.'

'What picture is this Raju?'

'*Pativrata*...'

Ramola's eyes narrowed. 'Where Menoka was the heroine?'

Raju did not look up.

'Raju...do you know what happened to Menoka? Raju...Raju...' Ramola nudged the girl. 'I am speaking to you, Raju, look at me. Do you know how she died, Menoka...for whom? And those girls before her...Radha and Tara. They came with him to Bharat Talkies. He kept them, like he has kept you. Do you know that you are just another of them, and after you there will be someone else, and then another, and another. Do you understand, Raju?'

'I know it all.' Raju's head jerked back and her eyes glowered. 'It is what others say, because they are jealous, of him...but you Madam...' She turned her face away bitterly.

'Raju, can you not see for yourself, what he has done to you? What picture...who will make you a heroine, like this? Look at yourself Raju.'

She had heard whispers in the studio about one of the girls...Radha was it? How she had looked when they had found her dead on the side of the *nulla*. Her hair cropped, like a boy's...shrunk, skin and bones. He had kept her with him, in his house. Was it this very same room, where she had found Raju?

The house had been so very dark as she had climbed

up the stairs. Her hand trailing against the black coldness of the stone staircase. No pictures anywhere. Why, their own house, the walls were so full, of her own photographs...from all the pictures. Shankar had mounted new ones all over the house, after every picture. The downstairs walls outside the dining room, and in the drawing room and all the way up, along the walls of the staircase. He had been so eager, so very proud of their every picture, and she too had not failed to admire the beauty of those photographs every time that she had come down the stairs. But this house, its walls were so bare. Why, there wasn't a single photograph, anywhere, from Ambarish's pictures, famous director that he was. Like he did not even belong here, in this place. Like somebody else owned this house...and he...Ambarish, had simply let it wear away.

The house needed repairs, those cracks on the walls along the staircase. She had tripped on a loose marble on the first floor as she had looked about, calling Raju's name. A door with a lock on it, other rooms left in darkness, with windows fastened. Mirrors, crusted and spotted, but still clean. They were doing their work, the servants, she had thought as she had climbed slowly. Her fingers trailing on the banister had picked dust as she had neared the last of the steps.

They...the servants are not allowed to go to her, he had said. Then she must be here somewhere, she had told herself, one of these rooms here, upstairs, where they do not come to do their chores. And then, all at once...that picture had startled her. Of the bejewelled lady wearing a Benarasi, in a gold flowered frame that had blackened over time. Mistress of the house, surely, her eyes watchful and piercing, the proud lift of her face, an almost audacious half smile at once summoning and dismissing. Ambarish would smile like that sometimes.

And almost at once, she had seen the other photograph at the corridor's end. She had turned suddenly, thinking there was someone behind her. And there…almost hidden away, he was so very good looking in the dusty frame on the wall. She had come close, to get a good look at him. Such delicate features and fair, the high forehead and straight nose, the thick lock that fell on his face. She was taken aback…could it be Ambarish, when he was much younger? But no, his coat, with jewelled buttons and the embroidered cap he wore on his head, they were of an older time, like her father had worn as a young boy, and her grandfather.

Raju was crying. 'I gave my hair, it is for art…my *sadhana*, dedication. And this…this Benarasi, it was his mother's. She wore it when she was going to have him. He gave it to me…not anyone else.'

So that's who she was then, the lady in the Benarasi… Ambarish's mother. And the man?

'Art is beauty Raju, not this, not what he has made you. And what are these marks here, on your neck? Will the camera not pick it up? Raju, what have you done to yourself…you left Bharat Talkies, you left the biggest picture of your life…for what Raju?'

Raju tossed her head.

'Madam, why did you leave it all, you had everything, all the riches of the world. You could marry a prince if you wanted. Everybody knows it, how they talked about you, rich people like you, when you came into the pictures. Why did you, Madam? For what? It is not a line for you, it is for girls like us. Still you came. Why did you want to give your all...for art, Madam, for Shankar Babu, *tai na*? Then, why not me? Why can I not give my all to him...and his art? Because I am not so high up like you? Because...how can a girl like me love somebody high up, like him...is that not what you think?'

Ramola was shaking her head.

'It is not the same, Raju, you foolish, foolish girl. Shankar, I was his wife. He cared for me, with his life. Ambarish, why has he kept you here, hidden from everybody? Why has he spoilt you, your beauty...like this? Why does he not hold your hand then, tell the world...why Raju?'

'Because, the world will not understand...like you, you did not understand Madam. My beauty, it is not spoilt, whatever anybody says, Madam. This picture will show them all, that Rajbala is a true artiste. That...that for a role, she can give her all, why, her life even.'

Raju smirked bitterly. 'Tell me Madam...I have heard that in one picture you had to kiss your hero. Nishith Babu told me. How Shankar Babu, he told you to do it. How you first did not want to, but then you did it...is that not true? Nishith Babu, he said to me, a lot of people said a lot of things, but Ramola Ma, her beauty and purity, they were untouched. Because, it was for a reason, it was for art, was it not Madam? Then what if I gave my hair? Why can I not be like you? It is for the picture.'

She tilted her head, eyes bright.

'And it will not be long now. He will take me to the new studio soon. He will say everything to everyone.'

Ramola ran her hand over her hair. She must get Raju downstairs somehow. Before Ambarish came up the stairs and tried to stop her. Though Avinash Babu had seemed rather determined to not allow him that. The tinge of a smile softened her face. She had seen, how Avinash Mukherjee's eyes had followed her out of that room downstairs, the room with the books. But it would all go to waste, if she was not able to get Raju out of this room, and down the stairs and face to face with Ambarish Dev Burma.

She laid a hand on Raju's arm. 'Raju, you left *Mira*, but you are still a contracted artiste of Bharat Talkies... did you not think of the picture when you came away... not once?'

She watched as the girl paled, her eyes falling.

'No matter Raju, do you know that I have loved you...like a sister...why you are so young, you could be my daughter even,' she laughed tearfully. 'I have decided to let you go...your contract with Bharat Talkies, make you free...so you can be what you want. You want to be his heroine, don't you...isn't that what you want, Raju?'

Raju looked up disbelievingly.

She smiled back. 'Yes Raju, it was the last sequence, we...we will manage it another way, somehow.' She shook her head, 'You would not be any good now, not any more...like this...for *Mira*.'

Raju nodded tears welling up again in her eyes. 'Yes Madam, you are right. *Mira*...that was in my past life, and this life, I have given to him...and his art.'

Ramola gritted her teeth silently. 'Very well then Raju, you must come with me downstairs now. We must put pen to paper in everybody's presence...so that we may release you, and use somebody else to finish the picture. We will have to make it up with your close-ups... like they do in the action pictures.'

She stole a glance at her wrist. Past half eleven. Would he have arrived downstairs, in that room with the bookcases? She wouldn't have heard the car come, all the way up...anyhow, she could not linger very much longer.

Raju looked afraid. 'But, he said to stay here...and not go anywhere. I always stay here. He will call me down...when Sethji comes.'

Ramola frowned. 'Raju, do you know that I could take steps against you...and Ambarish...after knowing your whereabouts of these last days, for harming my picture, and causing loss to the studio. I could stop you, you know, from working in another picture, when you still are a contracted artiste of Bharat Talkies. Do you want that Raju, do you want me to do what I would rather not?'

She softened. 'I do not wish to do any of that, Raju.' She placed her hand on the girl's arm. 'Raju, from now you are free. And I too wish to be free...of the hopes that I had built on you, my expectations and my unhappiness for how you have pained me. Do you understand that, or don't you?'

The girl nodded.

Ramola took Raju's face in her hands.

'Come down with me, Raju. So that I can go from here knowing I myself gave you away. Of my own. Sethji is coming, I know it. I will myself take you to him. My Mira will be heroine of his picture.'

Smilingly Raju stretched her arm to take Ramola's hand.

VI

Seth Makhandas Khemka's eyes very nearly popped. As Raju crept into the library after Ramola, '*Hey bhagwan*... good god!'

What was this bald thing that Ramola Beti was leading by the hand? They had said it was their heroine, Bharat Talkies' *Mirabai*, and that Dev Burma *Saheb* had made off with her. And that he and only he, Makhandas Khemka, could trick that devil, *woh shaitan*...Ambarish Dev Burma. Still, Ramola Beti, she was *devi*-like, but this Mukherjee *babu*, what lies he had had to tell at his behest...Ram Ram. And now this *chudail*, this ghoul with only some clumps on her head! Would they now tell him to make a picture with her? Was he a *gadha*, a donkey, or what? He threw an angry glance at Avinash Mukherjee.

Makhandas cursed himself another time. For still not getting over Dhonu. That nimble nymph that could make his heart heave, and his old bones feel young again as he touched him ever so gently. And his tongue had gotten all jumbled every time that he had tried to say, *na na, nahi*. To this *pagal jaisa* mad plot of theirs.

God alone knew how Mukherjee *babu* got his hands on Dhonu, both arriving one fine afternoon at his *gaddi*. Dhonu after so many months, after he made off with all of that *paisa*. Still, he had not had the heart to scold him, so beautiful had he looked, in his fashionable pant-shirt. Even now, as he stole a look sideways his heart jumped.

Who could tell it was Dhonu...so sweet in the red sari-blouse, and that long plait on his head. Pretending he was that other heroine for this picture...Devaki...that *bakwas*, all of those lies he had had to tell Dev Burma *Saheb*. All for Dhonu and Mukherjee *babu*. Dhonu had known surely that Dev Burma *Saheb* had come asking for *paisa* to make his own picture. That too, saying he would leave Bharat Talkies, and all so soon after Shankar Babu's sad passing. He had turned him away...how could he not, after he had held Shankar Babu's hand all those years, and with poor Ramola Beti a *widhwa*. Na, he had said to him.

Only to have to go back rubbing his hands. What with Dhonu and Mukherjee Babu on his back. Even Ramola Beti had pleaded with him, that evening when Mukherjee Babu had driven him to see her in the Bharat Talkies studio.

'Sethji...' she had said, 'will you not do something for my sake. You have heard Sethji, the whole story, how I have been betrayed. Ambarish, he will not hear us, but you, he will not turn you down.'

He had not been able to raise his head before her eyes. He had taken her wish to be Devi Ma's command. But, what was this? Why, wasn't he only to present Dhonu as Devaki, and *baas*, that was to be that. End of this little *natak*, Mukherjee Babu had promised. How was he to know they would both be here, Mukherjee Babu and Ramola Beti, in the house, at this time, with *Saheb*? Ramola Beti entering just now with this *bhootni*, this ghost of a girl...*chi chi chi, beti* seeing him with Dhonu like this, and that too the boy dressed like a girl.

He had wanted to hide his face inside his dhoti. The anxious moments he had passed in that room had seemed to Makhandas Khemka like the fourteen years of Ramji's *vanvaas*.

Ambarish Dev Burma spoke first. His voice was cold.

'Rajbala what are you doing here, downstairs? Go back to your room.'

The girl trembled slightly as her eyeballs shifted and she took a step back, towards the door. 'No wait, Raju. Sit down.' Ramola held her hand. 'Ambarish, I have told Raju...Rajbala, that Bharat Talkies will release her, let her go...that we will not be able to use her in her present state.' She coughed delicately. 'We will have to make do without her, in the last bit...alas.'

She turned again to the girl. 'There Rajbala, was that not what you had wanted, why you ran away from Bharat Talkies? Now you can be Ambarish's heroine. Sethji...here is your heroine, for your new picture. Alas, Sethji, such a big thing and you nor Ambarish thought to tell me. And after all these years of our knowing each other.' Ramola smiled wistfully.

Seth Makhandas was starting to feel afraid. Did they really think he was going to put his *baap-dada ka paisa*, his hard earned money into some picture with this *adhmari*, this half-dead half-bald little urchin?

He started to speak. 'But *beti*, you only had said... and Mukherjee Babu...'

'Sethji...we only heard from Devaki here...of your partnership with Dev Burma Saheb, when she came to show us her...errm, photographs', Avinash Mukherjee cut him short. Devaki was playing with the end of his sari. His lips speaking the unsaid as he fluttered his lashes at Seth Makhandas.

Makhandas Khemka shrank into his seat. This *kamina badmash* Mukherjee Babu, forever saying 'photographs' 'photographs' to him. Making him dance to his tunes. And his very own Dhonu, stabbing his back...*hey bhagwan*, why had he taken those photographs with Dhonu: And Ramola Beti, surely, she did not know, about him and Dhonu? She was speaking to him again.

'Sethji, Rajbala here tells me she is to be heroine in *Pativrata*. The part that ill-fated girl Menoka was to play...you know, don't you Sethji, how Menoka hanged herself inside Bharat Talkies, took her own life. That too within days of us starting work on that picture. Such a tragedy it was...'

Seth Makhandas swallowed. *Atmahatya*...self-annihilation, *Hey* Ram. Was it that picture then? People said she had brought bad luck to Bharat Talkies, that girl...Shankar Babu, so young and passing just like that, so soon afterwards. He had heard all the talk then, when the girl did herself in...but...who was to know it was that very same picture. A trickle of sweat ran down the side of his face.

Ambarish Dev Burma was looking hard at Ramola.

Seth Makhandas was trying to stop the trembling in his knees. He rose and slowly walked to where Raju now sat, on the low stool by the door, Ramola by her side.

'*Beti*...' his voice shook. 'What happened...to that long hair. I saw you before one time, in Bharat Talkies... how did you change...so much?'

Raju lowered her eyes.

Tell me, *beti*', Makhandas Khemka's words came in gasps. 'It's her, *na*? That *atma*...it is her, is it not, that other girl? That is why you ran away from Bharat Talkies...because she gave you *aadesh*, commanded you...she does not want you *beti* to take her place...'

Ambarish Dev Burma laughed aloud.

'What other girl Makhandasji, how very ridiculous!'

Makhandas Khemka's eyes bulged.

'That spirit...*woh atma*, it has gotten in her...made her sick. Can you not see it Dev Burma *Saheb*, how this girl looks...so pale, her eyes red...her beauty all gone, like the hair on her head.'

Makhandas was himself like a man possessed. Even the stony-faced Avinash Mukherjee shifted uneasily in his corner on the sofa. Only Ambarish Dev Burma was laughing.

'Sethji, girls like Menoka have no *atma*, only *sharir*... only their bodies.'

'But what of Raju, Ambarish?' Ramola broke in. 'Is she not different, from Menoka and those other girls that you kept before, in this house? Is she not fit to hold your hand? Surely, you will not find another girl so ready to give her all for a picture?'

'Madam...' Ambarish spoke quietly. 'It is no secret that girls like Rajbala have been many in my life. And they have all obeyed my wishes. Given their all, as you say, when I have so commanded it. It is Rajbala's good fortune that she caught my eye, that I chose her, over the many other such girls that cross my path every day, and who would gladly give their lives if I so much as glanced their way.'

'But Ambarish, surely, Raju has proven her worth. She is herself a star, and second to none.'

Ambarish was looking at the clawed feet of the marble top table. He chewed his words before spitting them out.

'Star indeed! Like you yourself.' He grinned. 'Why, in America they have made stars of dogs and cats that have appeared in the motion pictures. Like you, Madam, such little animals have scores of admirers, who cut their photographs from the pages of magazines and paste them in their little notebooks. It is nothing...take my word Madam, you yourself are nothing. I have myself made and unmade many such stars...they are nothing but puppets, little playthings...'

He nodded his head, his eyes bright.

'Cats and dogs can be made stars. But not artistes. Madam is not just any star. She is a great artiste. She is the sky, and we others...we are not even the little toe of her left foot.' Raju spoke without looking up.

'An artiste is she, your Madam?' He glowered at Raju, his voice thin. 'Is that why she left her own picture, her very precious *Mirabai* and got a *char anna wala* heroine, like you? What happened Madam, did you get afraid, after the boss died? But of course, however could you move a finger even, without his hand to hold, or his shoulder to lean on, still less direct that picture. Isn't that why you needed that old fogey Nishith Roy at your side? Because Madam, you simply are not good enough...and you know that as well as I.'

'*Beti*...' Makhandas Khemka nodded tearfully to Ramola. 'I always knew it, no good would come of this, getting this...this *bazari* girl. Now see what happened.

That *atma*...it has got inside her...*Hey Ram.*' His eyeballs darted to the glass door and back. 'Is she here then...in this house...*woh atma*?'

Ambarish flicked his head impatiently.

'Enough of this talk, Makhandasji. There is only one spirit in this house, she who has always commanded everything here. And that is my mother.'

His mouth pursed as he ran his hand over it. He shouldn't have said it, he knows that. Ramola's eyes narrowed as Ambarish smiled again, his half smile. He's not really smiling, she thought. He's angry.

'That's her isn't it Ambarish, in the picture upstairs, where you had kept Raju? Did you also keep Menoka there, Ambarish?' That same smile, Ramola was thinking...but still, not the same really, not all of it.

'Yes, that is her...my mother. And such girls,' he glanced towards Raju. 'They are not fit even to look upon her face.'

Ramola felt Raju stiffen beside her.

'But...but...you had said that I was...like your mother.'

'My mother, Rajbala, was educated...and high born, a princess...a queen, with a curse on her head.' He sighed. 'That curse still lives on...here, in this house.'

Makhandas Khemka let out a sob. 'Did I not say it? There is a *saya*, a curse...a spirit...it has got inside her, eaten her from inside...taken her hair.'

'I gave my hair of my own.' Raju had fire in her eyes. 'I gave it for art...for him.' She pointed at Ambarish Dev Burma. 'Why...did you not say to me, I want a girl as my heroine who is brave enough to show the world that art is not only beauty...art is *tyag*, sacrifice...that, only a true artiste can sacrifice beauty for art.' Her voice lowered as she ran her hand over her head. 'A girl like my mother, did you not say? My mother did not care for the world, that was why she had me. But then she did not care, for me even. And then Menoka, you said, she was afraid of the world, that was why she ran away. You said, Rajbala, I want you to give your all, for me...did you not say it?' Again, her eyes burnt.

Ambarish Dev Burma smirked. His eyes fixed on the grey and white of the stone floor. 'You think, Rajbala, that you are any different from Menoka, or any of those other girls? That you can be like my mother, only because I chose you? For what, Rajbala? Only to be heroine in my picture?' He laughed.

'What picture, *Saheb*?' Makhandas Khemka was shaking his head, mopping the beads of sweat on his face. '*Sab bakwas*, bogus all of it. This Makhandas Khemka is not making any picture, *Saheb*. That too with this hairless *bhootni*, this wretch.'

Ambarish Dev Burma held up a hand.

'Patience, Makhandasji, we will make this girl your heroine.' He pointed carelessly to the sari-clad Dhonu. 'That was your wish, was it not?'

'*Haan*, but...' Seth Makhandas gulped.

'And me? What of me?' Raju cried.

'You Rajbala, will do as I say. And do not dare to question what I will do in my picture. Heroine or not, you will do my bidding. For that is what you are made for, to bow to my wishes. You...and Menoka and Radha...and Jumna, you all.'

'And this sari, your mother's sari, what you gave to me, only me?' Tears rolled down Raju's face as she clutched the Benarasi.

Ambarish Dev Burma let out his breath through clenched teeth, and rubbed his face with his hand. 'My mother...she was different. She never gave in to me. Not once.'

'And your father, Ambarish...what about your father?' Ramola was thinking how alike they were, that high forehead and the hair that fell across their faces.

'Only person that ever made her give in, that was my father. But that too not forever.' Again, he ran his hand over his face.

'That is him, isn't it, Ambarish, on the wall upstairs... where she is, your mother?'

He forced a smile through his gritted teeth. 'You are sharp aren't you, Madam Ramola Devi?' He sighed. 'I couldn't hide my good looks if even I tried, could I? Yet the man that I was forced to call father, by the world and by my mother, he was little and ugly, like a rat, his daughter like him...my sister Putu. But me, I am like my real *baba*. I made them all give in, all of those girls...like he had done to my mother. His sister...his very own little sister.'

He turned to Raju, his eyes filled with loathing. 'I was high...high born, no mix in my blood. My father and mother were of a line of kings...and then, she lay with that man, Putu's father, spoilt herself. She became like one of them.' He pointed at Raju. 'Like a *beshya*...low... lowest of the low.'

Ramola held Raju close as the girl wept inconsolably.

Ambarish was laughing. 'She would cry like that every night. I think, it was after he knew it...Putu's father. He would punish her for it. Then...when Putu was inside her he jumped from the roof. And she...she said afterwards, that I was her *paap*, her sin, she said to me. That she should have killed herself and me, before I could see light of day. For what? For only wanting Putu out of the way? Putu never should have come into this world. She was Ma's *paap*, not me...rotten little worm, like Menoka and Radha and her sister, and her...' He pointed again to Raju. 'I had wanted...so very much, to see Putu like her father, bloodied and broken. But Ma, she stopped me, every time.' He shook his head. 'She couldn't stop me forever, though, could she? Those girls, all of those girls in this house...then...upstairs. I put them there, in her room.'

'And this picture Ambarish, *Pativrata*...why did you push Menoka to it? And Raju, why did you make this of Raju?'

'Because...' his head rolled as he again smiled that half smile. 'They thought that they were above their rotten lot, that they were different from the rest. And good enough for me. Why? Because they had become heroines of the bioscope? I showed them their place. Like how he, my father had done it with Ma. Ma...she would try to better him always...in everything, when they were children. He showed her her place. I would call him Mama...my mother's brother, not ever Baba. Ma did not let me take any photographs with him ever, she was afraid that somebody would know something. She always tried to keep me away, from my own father. But how could she? He would take me to his chest. He took me hunting once, in the forests. He used to be a wonder with the rifle. He shot dead my mother's pet parrot the night she got married to Putu's father. She had me inside her then. He had planted his seed in her, after her match had been fixed, to punish her...held her down with those strong arms, not heeded her silly crying...he told me. And that parrot, he had plucked its feathers before he had killed it. He gave them to me...I was three then, or four. He would come and see me, here, in this house, even after Ma told him never to come...after Putu's father had died.' Ambarish got up and walked to the open windows and looked out at the garden, where the servants were cutting the grass.

'What happened to him, Dev Burma *Saheb*...your father?' Avinash Mukherjee broke the silence.

'He is alive, my father, old now, but still strong. He lives on his estate in the hills. There is a shrine, and a *gurukul* for little boys there, from the nearby villages. They are...in his care. Boys like how I was...when he would take me close...and tell me, about him and Ma.'

'You are not well Ambarish, you never were...' Ramola had a knot inside her stomach. Was it all make-believe? Was Ambarish only being uncouth...or...?

'I am perfectly well, thank you Madam. My only regret is that I could not take this picture *Pativrata* to its finish. It was not just a picture, you know. It was my experiment...a test...after I saw how Menoka was getting out of hand. Flying high she was, thinking she was somebody, or something. And all because your Bharat Talkies turned her head. Sacrifice on the altar of art, that was to be her redemption...their only redemption, all of them. But first Menoka, she spoilt it all...and now, you...you come to take away this...this *beshya*.' His eyes grazed Raju. 'To again let loose this rot in our society, our *samaj*. This rot that thrives in our midst for the comfort of society ladies like yourself. You who think you can uplift them and change their lot...make them like one of us. You do our society a great disservice, Madam.'

Dhonu was pulling off the long plait covering his head. His eyes on the floor, voice soft.

'Rot we are, those like us...hum *saala janjal log*, spoilt and rotten, *beshya*s...and *nyaka*s. We, we have no place anywhere. We do bioscope pictures...*naachgaana* with all our heart, but still, this world of bioscope pictures does not call us its own. We are lowest of the low...and we, we live on, thinking it is our fate, *kismet hamara*! But sometimes...we can even turn things our way. Where there is no way, we make a way. From under the very feet of such big people like you...we...those like us, *beshya*s and *nyaka*s.'

He looked up at Ambarish Dev Burma, smiling. 'What will you...you and your kind do, if our lot is washed clean, like *gangajal*? You, who are so high up, only because we are so low.'

Two and half months later

I

'That last part...she looks like one of us, whatever any of you tells me'. Nyaka Natabar gushed, rubbing his hands in glee. 'That Ramola Madam, what spleen she has! Ending the picture with the heroine looking like that. And see the public also, lapped her up, hair or no hair. Yesterday's *naachgaanawali* Raju darling, today's Mira rani...fate...fate! My *didi*...my rani, my queen,' smilingly Natabar wiped a tear off his face.

Jhantu made a face. 'As if she will remember you, or me? They're saying she's getting calls from everywhere now, Lahore, Bombay. God alone knows what she will do.'

'She will leave Bharat Talkies...*naaa*, never.' Dhonu was cleaning his ear with a peacock feather. 'Ramola Madam, she kept her with herself, all those days, then, after they got her back. And now, they say she will adopt her, Raju...like her own daughter, give her Bharat Talkies. What *kismet*...and see us, same old *janjal*!'

Jhantu snapped at him. '*Tham*, quiet! You have that one, your big Sethji, *na*? As if we don't know? What's your worry, *rani bankar raaj kar*...rule over him.'

Dhonu hid a smile as he switched the feather to his other ear.

Natabar was looking pensive. 'Remember what he had said, that drunk? That someone high up would hear, and do something, about the girl. God rest him, why he did what he did who knows?'

'For love, what else?' Dhonu nodded dejectedly. 'For that *babu* of his.'

Natabar was scratching his head. 'Always crying for him, but he never told us his name, any of us. Got *fultu* and went and drowned himself...*kapal*, his rotten fate. These rotten *pukri*s, these ponds, how many more of us will they take? Remember that girl that was in the family way, Naseem? Same place they had found her, bobbing up and down in the black water...*saaala*.'

'What he went and did God knows,' Jhantu puzzled. 'Else...how did Ramola Devi get into all of this? Tell me, who told her? And why she even believed it was him...that *rakshasa*, that devil? After all, he was the top director of her own studio. Only we knew, but who believes people like us? But still she went and got the girl from his clutches.'

Dhonu was quiet. He had known more, put two and two together, even what Shankho had not ever said to him.

Jhantu turned on Dhonu. '*Ei* Dhonu, you *saala* you never told us the full story, tight-lipped Nepali *saala*! You only came and gave the news that Madam has got her out of that house, and then for two months nobody saw your face in the studio *para*. Where were you, *haan*? Warming that your Sethji's bed, or what?'

Dhonu turned away his face. It wasn't Seth Makhandas. Though Sethji had not forgotten him. No, Avinash Babu had paid him. Go away for some days, he had said, till this trouble is settled. He had gone away to his village in the hills, the money had been good. When he had come back, everyone had forgotten everything.

He had gone to see *Mirabai* in the picture hall. What a picture! And in the last scenes...he had almost become stuck to his seat when he saw that girl Rajbala, same like he had seen her in that house, her cropped head, and eyes still sunk inside her face. But singing like she was possessed, like she had had the *darshan* of god himself. Like she had lost her all, and then become one with *bhagwan*. Something had changed in her, since when he had seen her, skeleton-like in that house. Like she was now neither man nor woman anymore, but something above them all. Tears had come streaming down his face, he had wanted to lie down and put his head on her feet... that girl had become like a *devi*.

Shankho had taken him to Avinash Babu. Shankho had known somehow that Avinash Babu would do his all to get Rajbala from Dev Burma *Saheb*. It was Avinash Babu's plan, to use Seth Makhandas to bait that *rakshasa*. So he keeps the girl safe, for some days, in the hope of the new picture...until we can get her from there, Avinash Babu had said. Dhonu had himself let Shankho in on it, that Dev Burma *Saheb* had come to Sethji for money. Shankho had put it in Avinash Babu's ear, but that whole doing was his, Avinash Babu's. He had snatched the calf from the tiger's mouth. He and Ramola Devi.

He had puzzled over it all of those lazy afternoons that he had spent in his home in the hills. What indeed was Avinash Babu's relation with Ramola Devi...that goddess of the world of bioscope pictures? She so high up that nobody could touch her even. Yet, she had listened to him...saved the girl...and if not for her then who knew what would have become of that Rajbala?

How had Shankho known that Ramola Devi would hear Avinash Babu? Had he, in his heart, known something that had eaten him inside...and in the end driven him to that *pukri*?

Dhonu blinked as Jhantu shouted in his ear. '*Eiii saala* Nepali, daydreaming...you *fultu* or what?'

II

'*Jai ho, beti, apki jai jaikar*...glory to you!'

Ramola hid a smile. Really, Sethji could be such a clown sometimes. But Seth Makhandas was elated, his Ramola Beti had proved herself to the world. And why not, she had Shankar Babu's blessings on her.

He nodded gleefully. 'We will become *maalamal beti*, full loaded, this picture is gold *beti*, solid gold. Everybody, everywhere is talking...only *Mirabai Mirabai Mirabai*. More than one month now, and still full house everywhere. And your heroine, she has shown the world, *shabaash ladki*, bravo, that girl. *Jai ho Mirabai ki*, *Jai Ramola Beti ki*.'

He thought a moment.

'You are like my own child, *beti*, I will not hide the truth from you. I had thought that this picture will not run, after people saw that ending. When you said that you will finish the picture with her only...Rajbala, like that only, how we found her in that house, her long hair gone and all ghost-like. In seven or eight days you got her back to the studio, everybody said Madam has become *pagal*...full mad. The girl too, she was not ready I heard, to stand before the camera...crying...shaking like anything, I heard in the studio. But you *beti*, you made her do it, you took care of her like she was your own child. I had thought then, *zid hai beti ka*, Ramola Beti, she is adamant. She will drown my *paisa* that I had put in Shankar Babu's hands, and also her husband's good name. But I was wrong *beti*, we all were wrong.'

Ramola smiled, not looking at him. 'I really had no way of knowing, Sethji, how it would all be in the end. But I did not want to finish this picture without Raju, nor put a wig on her head...no...that would not be my Mira. And how could I not hold Raju's hand, after everything that happened, what she suffered, and when there is so little that we can do to stop what they go through in this world, girls like her.'

She looked up, 'Tell me Sethji, you are a *bhakt*, a believer. Does not the sacrifice and the pain and love of Mirabai show up the most beautifully in the end...where Raju sings like that, like she has given up her everything? Somehow...you cannot take your eyes off her, can you Sethji?'

'*Theek beti*, you are right.' Seth Makhandas rubbed his face thoughtfully. 'I heard that people are lying down in the picture halls, folded hands to their heads...when she comes like that in the end, like she is some *devi ma*.'

'Hmmm...I did hear it.' Ramola nodded. 'And there was a report in *Picture Weekly*. I told Anil to keep a copy for me. They were shouting "Mira Bai *ki Jai*"... "Bharat Mata *ki Jai*", in that last part, like she was some *swadhinata sangrami*...freedom fighter or something.'

She shook her head disbelievingly, 'Really, what the public makes of us bioscope actors and actresses sometimes, they alone know. Raju herself is rather taken aback, I can tell you that. I showed her that report, and she simply cannot fathom it, how yesterday's Raju Darling can become like a *devi*...overnight. She's not sure at all if she likes being worshipped like that!' Ramola laughed. 'She's her old self again, thank goodness for that...and rearing to go.'

Seth Makhandas grinned happily. 'And now *beti*, we must take this picture to the world, like Shankar Babu had wanted it. It is my Devi Ma's command to me... America...England.'

Ramola raised her eyebrows. 'You really wish to? It will not be so easy Sethji, like in the home market, I can assure you that.'

'*Kuch parwa nahi beti*, Makhandas Khemka is afraid of nothing.' Seth Makhandas appeared wounded 'My mind is made up, and when this Makhandas makes up his mind then nobody can stop him.' He grinned again. 'Like you *beti, shabaash beti*, how you showed what you could do with that *adhmari* half-dead heroine of yours.'

Ramola lowered her eyes shyly. 'I too was not sure Sethji...I...I had somebody with me, he said to me that I should hear my own voice and not give in, whatever happened.'

'Shankar Babu, na beti? It was him, his blessings, was it not?'

Ramola stopped, taken aback, then spoke again. 'Sethji, Shankar was there, like a part of my own self, and he will be there, always a part of me. What I am today is for him, because of his dreams for me and for Bharat Talkies...and yet, perhaps,' she drew in her breath, '... perhaps he would not have made this picture like I have done it. Perhaps he would not have let me do it in this very same way. Perhaps, this time around it was me alone, and perhaps...there is...somebody else, someone who is able to see things differently from Shankar.'

'*Kaun*, who?' Makhandas Khemka puckered his face, not understanding.

Ramola smiled. 'More tea, Sethji?'

III

Raju twirled her hip as she pertly landed her bottom on the chair across from Ramola. Her hair done in fashionable finger waves and grown back till just below her neck.

'How does it look, this sari Madam? From Cawasji Sahib, of Bombay Pictures. He came all the way here, only to see me.'

'Nice, very nice.' Ramola smiled. She did look rather sweet in that pink and orange organza. 'So...are you doing the picture with them then?'

Raju raised an eyebrow like she was thinking, but Ramola knew her mind was made up. 'Hmmm...yes Madam. I always wanted to go to Bombay, Madam, and the money...you will not believe Madam, how much they are giving.'

Ramola felt her heart sink. 'Will you be alone there, all by yourself? Nobody to take care of you...'

'Kamala Masi is coming with me Madam.'

Ramola rolled her eyes. 'Good god Raju, you'd be better off without that dreadful *masi* of yours. I really had had enough of her fits while you were recuperating.'

Raju giggled. 'I know Madam. Yesterday only, I hit her again, with my new sandals, what to do Madam, she wants to take the whole house with her to Bombay, even the *ghoti* she uses to wash her backside. But what will come of her Madam, if I leave her and go away? She has nobody, only me.'

'And Anil, Raju? What of him?' Anil had stopped by at the house every day, asking after her.

Raju bit her lip. 'I saw him...three...no, four days ago, Madam, here in the studio. I told him, Anil Babu, I am going. He put his hand on my head, but said nothing. Is he going away too Madam? I had heard something, before.'

'No Raju, he is going nowhere. I couldn't do without him...nor Kedar Babu...or Bimal Babu, or any of them. I need them all with me. And Anil, I think, has made peace with himself, and I think he has forgiven you, Raju.'

For once she repents what she has done, Ramola thought, as the girl's face clouded.

'And Ambarish? Have you forgiven him?' she asked gently. Raju did not look up. 'You still love him, don't you? After everything? Even now that you know the truth.'

Her lips trembled. 'I knew Madam, much before. But what to do Madam? Some things are not in my fate...'

Ramola smiled wryly. 'Do you know Raju, what they are all saying, here in the studio *para*? That I am about to adopt you as my own daughter and that Bharat Talkies will then be yours.'

Raju giggled again.

'It could be true, you know Raju, after all anything

could happen, couldn't it?' Ramola bit her lip to stop the tears from welling up in her eyes.

Raju pouted, 'And what will happen to Cawasji Sahib, Madam? I gave him my word.'

'But Raju, have you thought of your image? Now that the papers are writing such marvellous things about you. Why only last week, *The Statesman*...no less, wrote of you, that, a true artiste has been born. Do you now wish to spoil it all by doing the Cawasji type action and adventure pictures...do you not want to be counted an artiste, a proper artiste?'

Raju pondered. 'Will that make me a *devi*, like you Madam? Will the world allow it? Or will I always be Rajbala Dasi, all of my life, whatever pictures I do? Do you know Madam...I...I did some bad pictures, before... when I first came in this line. What to do Madam, we had nothing, nobody, Ma and me...I had thought nobody will know, after all this time, and now I am a star. But he knew. He would say to me, that is the real Rajbala...' Tears misted her eyes. 'Perhaps...perhaps he was right Madam, and it may be that others also know. One day they will say to me, we know Raju, what you did. Whatever the papers write, Madam, I am that same Rajbala, of those pictures. I thought that I can be like you, I can change. I even thought that...that I could change him. I went after art Madam...and look what happened.'

She smiled, 'Raju Darling I was Madam...Rajubala I will be.'

IV

29th August, Tuesday
Dear Mr Mukherjee,

I trust that this letter finds you well. Seth Makhandas Khemka came to the studio last week, and he has resolved to take *Mirabai* for its showings around the world. Without doubt, the poor dear has taken in right earnest a proposition that I understand now was possibly the matter of a little convenience. Yet, I must thank you for it. And also for Seth Mahkandas being rather an important cog in the wheel of several matters that have passed in our lives.

I never could have imagined so outrageous a plot (though I have spent a good part of my life now in a picture studio and appeared in many bioscope films!) for getting back Rajbala. Nor indeed that we might be able to get that fiend to desist from further harming her, should he think it to be inimical to his own prospects. You were right, Rajbala says the *Pativrata* trap did make him stop a certain very dangerous game that he had forced her to play, and to which I am rather certain Menoka fell prey. Though, sadly, we have nothing to name and he will live a free man despite the misery and harm he has caused.

It is not in my power to stop Ambarish. Nor can I tell the world what I in my heart know and what you too witnessed inside that house. For he is well-known, and of high class and a social position, unlike the girls that he had drawn to himself. My comfort remains that I was able to bring away this one girl from harm's way, a girl that is very dear to me, and I do not hesitate to say it to you, that she is like the daughter that I never had. And I imagine that she too cares for me in her own rather odd manner, for I doubt it very much that Rajbala is able to love in ways that are common. She took the train to Bombay yesterday, leaving Bharat Talkies. Also, finally, after much trepidation, and after your own counsel, have I written to Amy, inviting her to visit with her daughter, who should now be a young lady. I do very much hope that she will write back.

In the matter of *Mirabai*, I have given my consent to Seth Mahkandas. Sethji is determined to initiate his own bioscope company for the purpose. And as I understand it, he looks to you to instruct him in this matter, for which I am most certainly grateful. Dear Sethji has truly been of the greatest assistance and service, and evidently in one certain matter, of which he himself is rather oblivious.

That certain matter should proceed as it is fated. I hear that the strawberry gateau at the Tearoom is rather a rage. Should I book a table for two people, Saturday, for tea-time? Of course, should you not be unavailable.

Yours truly,
Ramola

31st August, Thursday
Dear Madam,

Thank you for your kind invitation to have tea with you. Sadly I am rather occupied at the present moment and must decline.

As for Seth Makhandas, he has been a true well-wisher and friend to you in your times of need. My presence in the Rajbala matter was only rather partial, and it was you yourself that led her away from the fiend's web and nursed her to good health again. You end by mentioning one certain other matter. Of that I am sadly unaware.

I remain at your assistance in the future.

Yours sincerely,
AM

Ramola read the last lines another time, then looked up at the bedroom clock. Her blue chiffon was laid out on the bed. A line of pearls would go best, she had decided. It was half past three and her hair was done. Still, she would need a half hour to get dressed and a little over a quarter of an hour to get to the Tearoom. She had asked for a table for half past four. They would hold it, if even she got a little bit late, though they did get so very crowded on Saturday afternoons. She was Ramola Devi, after all.

The phone rang and she reached over hurriedly, the sudden blush of her cheeks colouring her face.

The voice at the other end stuttered, '...errm...good afternoon...I...as it happened, I did have a bit of time, only about an hour or two...at most...'

V

He had giggled as he had watched it. All through the night...the stripes and swirls of black and grey and ginger, sometimes stretching out his hand to feel how it felt, fur on dead flesh. Its green eyes popped from their sockets, their death stare piercing the wall in front in the dread of its very last moments. She had given it *afeem*, so it would be easy. She had known what made him happy, what he had wanted, like a good wife...what Ma never could be to his real father. Fan, she was his, he knew it now. She always had been, only he had not known it soon enough.

He had spent the night at Fan's. In the kitchen where she had served him fresh meat and rice. The old tabby had sat winking by her, gulping the scraps of meat she had dropped for it on the floor. He had started to envy it. Fan had giggled when it had looked up at her and winked its wink.

'Cat eat pig...' she had said to him. She was a clever girl. With a little more English he could take her with him when he left...England, and Europe...nobody could tell she was a butcher's wife. He was her teacher.

'...I eat cat...' He had gestured to himself and the cat between his mouthfuls, making her break into more giggles.

'...I no make cat...no...' She had shaken her head mischievously, motioning to the charcoal stove where she did her cooking.

He had laughed, making her blush. But her eyes had glinted. She had understood. Dear Fan, always up for a game.

She had mixed the drug in the milk, calling to it like she would the pigs. The old Tom had started to lose himself, swaying a little bit. He had pointed out the length of rope that hung by her stove. The one she would sometimes tie the chickens with, as they flapped and clucked fearfully. She had held the legs eagerly with her strong hands as he had slipped the rope gently over its neck, suddenly afraid it would wake from its stupor. It had awakened with a start, its eyes gaping, a funny shriek in its throat as he had pulled, Fan's laugh in his ears.

She had wanted to cut it up in small pieces, throw it to the pigs. She had found it rather pleasing, '...pig eat cat...' she had whispered. But he had sent her away. To be alone with it for that night. Doing it in had filled him with a delight that he had not known before. Like he was god himself. He had fondled it, wanting to dress it up in Ma's Benarasi, like Ma had done when she was a little girl, dressing up her little kittens and marrying them to the neighbour's cats. Like how they would dress the dead, dead women in vermillion and *alta* and garlands.

Rajbala had left it behind, that Benarasi. When Ramola Devi had taken her away. Like Ma she was, Ramola Devi, taking the girl away from in front of his eyes...like Ma always would take Putu from him. That was it...he blinked as the first rays of the sun stung him in the eyes. Ma had gotten hold of her, Ramola Devi! It was Ma that had gotten the girl, from him. How could he not have known it? Hadn't he always felt it, how alike they were, that very same pride, that mocking in their eyes...like they were everything and he, nothing. He could have fed her to the dogs, Rajbala, any of the movie papers would lap up her story, how she would shed her shame for just a few annas. But she had threatened him, Ramola Devi, before she had left holding the girl.

'And Ambarish, should you try to hurt Rajbala in any way, in the future, I will have each and every copy of those pictures you made for Bharat Talkies thrown in the fire, I promise you that Ambarish.' He hadn't dared go to the papers. They were masterpieces, those pictures, and they were in her hands. How would she know their worth? But she had meant what she had said, and he had not dared it.

But, it wasn't over. No, Ramola Devi. Quite far from it. You might have got one over on me this time, but you think I didn't know what you had going with that poker-face with the spectacles? I knew the very minute you two stepped in my library that morning! I hear you have a big hit...you got the girl back in the picture. I didn't think you would, though. A masterpiece, they say, those rags. And now...wait for my *Pativrata*, Madam. My picture, it is only on hold...for just a bit...and you, you will see, and you will be sorry, for sending that nitwit Marwari my way, telling me those lies I never should have believed.

That Rajbala would have hung by her neck, if not for you, Ramola Devi. If not for your meddling. He ran his hand through his hair.

He would go away to see Baba, his real Baba, in the hills...where the shrine was. With its bells and the flag fluttering on its roof. Like when he was a little boy, and Baba had taken him alone to the shrine. Where he would take those boys from the village. Baba had always told him everything...about Ma...and that parrot...and the horse in grandfather's stable, the one that had died of the poison...and then, those little boys that he loved with all his heart. Baba had never pushed him away, though fate had set them so far apart. He was like Baba, his father's son...

ABOUT THE AUTHOR

Sharmistha Gooptu is a film historian, and author of *Bengali Cinema, An Other Nation* (Routledge, 2010). She is Editor of the journal *South Asian History and Culture* and the *South Asian History and Culture* Books Series.